THE
WAYWARD GENTLEMAN

John Theophilus Potter
&
The Town of Haverfordwest

Patricia Watkins

Patricia Watkins (signature)

A biographical historical saga

First published as a Kindle e-book April, 2012 by
Down Design Publications
Fishguard, Pembrokeshire SA65 9AE, UK
First print edition published
June, 2012
ISBN 978-0-9572104-4-8

www.downdesignpublications.com

Cover illustration by Elizabeth Lake

Spinster ———————— 25

were married in this Parish

Church of St. Martin on June 27th

1779 (by Licence)

— by me Wm. Tasker Curate.

This Marriage was solemnized

between us John The. Potter

—————— Elizabeth Edward

in Presence of Mary Stanbury Elizth

of this Parish Thos Martin ? of the

Parish of Step— ? ? of the

Griffith ? ? ?shire

PART I

CHAPTER 1

"Ruined! Completely ruined! I'm soaked to the skin, and look at my new outfit! The latest fashion too! All splattered with mud! And my shoes -- look at my shoes! Ruined! They weren't meant for trudging down a muddy road, and my feet are covered with blisters. I do declare I'm ready to go right back home to Dublin already! I don't care if we were specially chosen for this trip. So far it doesn't seem like any sort of honour at all."

"Oh stop fussing! If anything ever goes wrong, if your costume for the play isn't exactly right, you're always the first one to complain. Anyway, we should get to Wexford soon. We were only five miles away when the coach-horse lost its shoe."

"I can't believe the inn didn't have another horse to replace it, making us walk all this way."

"All right ladies, can we please make the best of this. This is no one's fault." Theo, manager of the troupe of actors from the Smock Alley Theatre in Dublin was himself worried, and conveyed his thoughts to his manservant. "I wish we could hurry everyone up, James. There's no guarantee at all that the boat to Haverfordwest will wait for us."

"It's not far now, Sir, although I have to agree with you, we *are* very late, and Wexford harbour being the way it is, I do know that timing is essential for ships entering and leaving."

Theo pointed. "Oh there we are!" He ran down the road onto the quay only to find the boat had indeed already left; it was even out of sight.

"Now what?" he said to himself. He turned to James. "Keep everyone in order while I see if I can find another boat, will you James, although maybe you can scout around too to see if there's anywhere we can stay if I can't find anything suitable." And he started running down the quay, looking for another ship that might be going to anywhere in Pembrokeshire. It was gone midnight, and the only light was from lanterns on some of the crafts unloading their cargoes, and from the braziers set along the quayside.

He came to a stop and hailed the captain of a medium-sized sloop, busy untying the reefs on the mainsail. "I see you're about to leave. You're not going to Haverfordwest by any chance, are you?"

The captain shook his head. "No, Fishguard."

"Is that anywhere near Haverfordwest?"

"About fifteen miles. Why?"

"I've a troupe of twenty actors due to perform in Haverfordwest the day after tomorrow, and we need to get there as soon as possible. Could you possibly fit us all on board?"

"Aye, but how much are you willing to pay?"

A price was agreed upon, and Theo was obliged to pay for the crossing out of his own pocket, his manager not having given him enough to take care of such an unexpected expenditure.

"I want everyone sitting down... now!" The captain, glancing across the dark expanse of water, knew Wexford's treacherous sandbanks would already be showing signs of emerging, and he was anxious to be underway. "Now!" he ordered, but the group, now all on board, was still milling around, full of excitement, chattering, and paying him no attention.

After watching the captain make several unsuccessful attempts to bring his vessel to order, and annoyed at the lack of manners displayed by the troupe, Theo stood up, climbed onto a nearby box, put his fingers in his mouth and whistled. "Everyone!" he shouted. "Find a place to sit... now!"And he stood on the box, waiting until everyone appeared to be seated, and the ship was cast off.

"I'm going to let the boom go now," the captain warned them, "so if any of you are still standing, sit now, or risk being knocked overboard when it swings."

Theo jumped off the box and sat down, only to find himself wedged between a muddy, wet and smelly sheep on the one side, and what he took at first to be a large and equally smelly woollen sack on the other. This, however, turned out to be an old woman enveloped in a voluminous dark cloak and hood made of closely knit, unwashed, sheep's wool. She was slumped down, her cloak hauled around her, almost enveloping him in it as well, her body sunk round-shouldered into its depths, the odour of rancid lanolin wafting past him. He breathed in the foul air and sighed.

The sloop was underway now though, navigation lanterns swaying and lighting everyone with a sulphurous eerie glow, and the boom was still swinging, so he could not remove himself; besides, he noticed, there was nowhere else to sit. He clasped his hands between his knees in an attempt to appear indifferent to his situation, and as the boat sailed out of Wexford harbour and headed out into the Irish sea, did his best to pretend that having his thighs pressed up against a smelly sheep was of no concern. He glanced across at James, but James, an Irishman who had been with Theo for many years and knew him better than anyone, just grinned; it was funny to see his gentlemanly master looking so discomforted. Theo was not amused.

Once out in the Irish Sea dawn began to break, and Theo looked up at the sky, hoping to find a distraction in the clouds, which had thinned out to become fair-weather mounds billowing in from the southwest. He then studied the captain, whose concentration seemed to be divided between watching the wind direction and the leading edge of the mainsail, and as they headed further out into the open water, his appreciation of the man's skill in keeping the boat on course -- afloat even -- increased. He had never been on a craft as small as this in the open sea before, and was not at all sure it was an experience with which he was comfortable.

Now out of sight of land, he turned his attention to their fragile-looking boat, the only visible thing afloat on the heaving dark rollers stretching to infinity around them. It did little to give him confidence as even to his untrained eye it seemed dangerously overloaded.

He counted everything on board. There was a large horse that had been lifted by sling onto the deck, half a dozen sheep, tethered to iron rings set along one end of the bulwarks, some crates of Irish whiskey, several seaweed-covered boxes of foul-smelling lobster bait, the troupe of actors, and the old woman.

Theo was not a fastidious man -- he was used to animals -- but with the smell assaulting him from all sides, combined with the constant heaving of the sloop, he was feeling nauseous. He looked around again to see if there might be somewhere else to sit, but there wasn't, and there was nothing he could do about it. He sat there, already feeling cramped, and wondered how much longer he was going to have endure this unpleasant, uncomfortable and stinking craft in which he could not even stretch out his legs.

"When will we arrive in Fishguard?" he shouted to the captain.

"You ask such a question! *You* don't know much about

the sea, do you young man?" The captain found his passenger's innocence amusing. "We'll get to Fishguard when God wills it."

"Oh."

"If this wind stays with us, and it bodes well to do that, then we'll be there in about ten hours or so... if not," the Captain shrugged, "well, I've been out here three days and more, tacking back and forth and getting nowhere... so you'd better pray the good Lord looks favourably upon us. Don't be so concerned young man." He laughed again, this time at the look on Theo's face. "We shan't want for food or drink. I've a good supply of excellent Irish whiskey with me, and..." He pointed to the sheep. "Why do you think we have them on board?" he teased.

Theo sank back into his seat; the prospect of three days spent cruising up and down the Irish Sea under any circumstances was more than he could bear to contemplate.

Instead, he closed his eyes, and with the constant rocking of the boat having a soporific effect on his already weary body and spirits, let his mind recall the reasons why he, John Theophilus Potter, came to be making this trip across the sea to the town of Haverfordwest, in the county of Pembrokeshire, in Wales.

It was because he was one of the Smock Alley Theatre's foremost young actors that when the most unusual decision had been taken by the manager and actor, Mr. Thomas Ryder, to accept an invitation for members of his famous theatre company to perform in Haverfordwest, he had chosen Theo to take the lead role in the selected play, which was to be Shakespeare's *Romeo and Juliet*.

Mr. Ryder had explained to him briefly how the gentry of Pembrokeshire had made frequent trips to the Smock Alley theatre in Dublin ever since the famous actor, Mr. David Garrick, had come to perform and direct there back in the

1740s. It had been at the invitation of one of these gentlemen that they were now making their way to Haverfordwest.

The foremost actors employed by the theatre, including Theo, had already spent the summer season at the Theatre Royal in Cork, and had been back at home with the winter season already started, but the gentleman from Haverfordwest had made such a case for a visit to his town, Mr. Ryder had decided, on reflection -- there being enough young actors available and in need of experience -- perhaps a visit to the south Wales town would be a good opportunity for them to exhibit their talent.

As the gentleman had explained, what was considered as respectable theatre was rarely available to anyone in Pembrokeshire, the citizens having to make do with travelling troupes who had no home theatre to call their own, and it was only on the rare occasion a high standard of acting was offered, when some Drury Lane or Covent Garden actors, past their prime, joined them, or were reduced to travelling around performing on their own.

Mr. Ryder had hurried to draw up the plans in preparation for an early departure, and Theo, as one of their best and more experienced actors, had been asked to head the troupe for this engagement and to act as their manager. It was a heavy responsibility for him, but Mr. Ryder had expressed full confidence in Theo's ability to maintain the high standards and reputation of his theatre on this occasion.

They were to hold just two performances: one privately for the gentry, to be held on one of their country estates, the other to be held in another venue which he was told would have to be in the largest room of an inn called the Blue Boar, as the town hall was undergoing repairs, and would be unavailable. The proceeds from the latter performance -- which would also contain some singing and dancing acts -- would be donated to a charity selected by the local council, and they were to return to Dublin at the earliest opportunity as Theo was already on the publicly-announced playlists for upcoming performances.

When he next opened his eyes it was daylight, and at this moment a large wave caused the boat to roll, making the horse stagger. The groom hung onto the halter rope, helping it regain its balance.

"That's a fine horse," Theo shouted to him.

The young animal had been restless all along, nervous at having the deck shifting under its feet, but the groom had done an excellent job of keeping it calm, and as Theo had at times watched him handle the horse with such expertise, so had his respect grown for someone so young.

"A good hunter, no doubt," he added. It was a superb Irish horse with typical Roman nose, great heart space between its forelegs, and a compact, powerful body. "That horse," he continued with admiration, "could jump almost anything in his path, I'd wager."

The groom nodded. "Yes indeed, Sir! He's a fine horse, and I'm sorry this is the last time I'll be looking after him."

"Indeed?"

"Yes. A gentleman of Haverfordwest was visiting my master in Dublin, and took a liking to him -- made his lordship a fine offer I understand."

"He's a lucky man to…" Theo began, but was interrupted by an exclamation from one of the ladies.

"Look! Look!" She was pointing to the sea ahead. A pod of dolphins had surfaced nearby, and were leaping in front of the bow-wave, enjoying the ride. Everyone watched in amusement as they rose almost in unison out of the water, showing their dorsal fins, then plunging back down again, playing, and slapping the water with their tails.

All on board had been amused by their antics for several

7

minutes, when one of them, deciding to make a solo appearance, appeared right alongside the boat, rising up and almost touching the side, its snout appearing over the gunwales. It was as though it was greeting everyone on board, and its actions caused great amusement. It was, however, too much for the horse. He reared up, wrenching the rope halter from the groom's hand, then plunged forward, driving one of his forelegs straight into one of the bait boxes and knocking the groom to the deck.

Theo leapt up and rushed over to grab the terrified animal, which was struggling, but prevented from moving in any direction, being clamped by its foreleg to the splintered box. The groom started to clamber to his feet.

"Stay right where you are. Don't move!... Nobody move!" Theo commanded.

The laughing stopped and, dolphins forgotten, everyone watched the horse in silence, well aware of the danger posed by such a powerful and frightened animal on an overloaded sloop in the middle of the Irish Sea. From somewhere near the stern a sheep bleated. The horse was tossing its head, whinnying, nostrils flared, the whites of its eyes showing its fear. Theo stood to its side and reaching up, took a gentle, but firm hold of its ear, gradually pulling its head down. His touch light, and his voice low, he massaged the horse, soothing him. The horse became calmer, but only slightly -- still tense, stepping from one hind leg to the other, tail and haunches tucked under, ready to leap at the slightest movement or noise.

The captain meanwhile had turned the boat some way off the wind so the deck was lying at not so great an angle, and everyone sat as still as possible, afraid to take their eyes off Theo, who, head down close to the horse's nose, was breathing into its nostrils, still talking in soothing tones, stroking it. And still nobody dared move, and the only sound was that of the sea rolling past and the constant fluttering of the jib.

After a while, continuing to caress the horse, his voice still calm and soothing, he instructed the groom. "Now, you're going to have to pull back those splintered slats -- no sudden movements though."

While Theo continued to calm the horse, the groom began to work away with both hands at the slimy green, seaweed-covered wood, wiggling the slats back and forth to loosen them from the frame, taking care not to injure the horse any further; and as the bait box had suffered sufficient wear and tear he was able, after what seemed to everyone as an eternity, to make a hole big enough to free the horse's leg.

During the crisis, Theo had been relieved to find another of this horse's fine qualities was that it was of good nature, and under different circumstances would be calm and sensible. If it had been otherwise the outcome could have been disastrous for all on board, but being as it was, and freed at last from the terrifying bait box, it allowed him and the groom to take a look at its leg to see what damage had been caused.

A small trickle of blood was oozing out of a sizeable gash between its knee and fetlock, and the groom cried out in shock. "My horse, Sir, Oh my horse! This is terrible! What will the gentleman say? He won't want him, and he'll blame me..."

"Here, hold him." Theo handed the horse back to him, grabbed hold of its fetlock and lifted its leg to take a look for himself. The gash was quite long, but looked worse than it really was, because although the skin had been scraped off revealing the pink flesh beneath, it had not penetrated any deeper, and did not appear to have caused any real damage. Despite that, Theo suspected the hair might grow back white, which would be sure to affect its value. He did not want to worry the poor groom any further by saying so, however, so lowered the horse's leg back down to the deck and looked around.

"Is there a bucket on board?" he called out to the

captain.

The captain nodded in the direction of the stern, and a pail with a rope attached to the handle was retrieved and handed down from one to another, until it reached Theo. He leaned over the side, and holding onto the rope, dropped the pail into the sea, filled it, then began washing the wound, scooping handfuls of the salty water over it until the bleeding stopped. Someone, trying to be helpful, held out his neckerchief with which to wrap the gash, but Theo, thanking him for the offer, refused it. "Better to let the seawater and the air work on it," he said.

By the time he had finished, the horse calmed, and the tension eased, everyone set up a nervous chatter and, emitting big sighs, each felt the need to express his or her own opinion, fears and thoughts about the real drama in which they had just played a role.

One of the women held her hand on her chest, taking a deep breath. "Well! Well! I've known that young man ever since he joined the theatre five years ago," she exclaimed, speaking of Theo, "and if you'd have asked me, I'd have said he didn't know one end of a horse from another!... But then," she added after a few moments of reflection, "I know very little about him at all if I think about it. He's never been one to be open about himself... not like the rest of us."

"I think he was magnificent!" One of the young ladies in the troupe gazed across at him, and sighed. "He's so tall and well favoured too... I'm sure he's an aristocrat."

"Nonsense," retorted another. "I'm sure no aristocrat would ever see fit to become an actor... although," she added, "there's certainly something different about him... he's always amiable and friendly, but..." She paused, trying to think what it was about Theo that set him apart from the rest of them. "If I were to meet him anywhere else, I would indeed take him for a gentleman... He definitely has the manners and that air of good breeding about him." She waved her hand around, unable to express what made Theo different. "And unlike the rest of us," she added, "he never seems to be short of money... even has a manservant." She looked across at James. Maybe his manservant would be willing to enlighten them.

James who, unlike Theo, was within earshot of all being said, pretended he had heard nothing. He alone knew his master had endured more in his young life than most would expect to experience in a lifetime, and even though the attention had turned on him, and there were attempts to get him to reveal any secrets about his master, James would say only that he had known him for many years, and with that they had to be content.

By this time they were nearing the headland of Pen Caer on the north Pembrokeshire coast and would, the captain told them, soon be arriving in Fishguard.

The horse taken care of, and an atmosphere of normality returned to the sloop, Theo folded his arms, allowed his chin to rest on his chest, stretched out his long legs as far as the cramped space would allow, and returned to his thoughts about why he was here on this trip at all.

It had all started on the night, five years ago, when the actor who had been playing the part of Hotspur in Shakespeare's 'Henry IV, Pt I' at Theo's Smock Alley Theatre, had taken ill, and Theo, a still inexperienced understudy at that time, had replaced him. He smiled to himself, remembering how his own performance had been so successful the Dublin audience had given him a standing ovation, and the ailing actor had not been too happy when he had heard about it.

This time he was awoken by the sound of people around him exclaiming about an armed cutter approaching at high speed. They looked at the captain for an explanation, but he was busy turning the ship into the wind, having been hailed by the other captain, and ordered to heave to. Theo counted the guns: there were fourteen of them.

Even the captain looked worried until he could see the name of the cutter, at which he relaxed, smiling with relief. He had had reason to be concerned as the vessel was one of two excise ships patrolling the Pembrokeshire coast in search of smugglers, whose favourite items of contraband were spirits, tobacco and salt -- and he was carrying far more Irish whiskey than was legal.

As the cutter loomed over the much smaller sloop, its captain shouted down. "I didn't recognize you, Captain, with your colourful new sails." An exchange of pleasantries followed, accompanied by a case of Irish whiskey, after which the two vessels continued on their way, and all on board relaxed once more.

After some further delay getting into Fishguard harbour, they finally found themselves on this, a chilly day in October 1778, standing for the first time on Welsh soil, surrounded by all their luggage, no transportation in sight, and with an exceptionally steep hill to climb.

Theo sent the rest of the group up into the town to find some refreshments, while he waited with their luggage in the hope a passing wagon might be able to help. The groom, feeling he owed Theo his support, kept him company. It was yet another half hour before the hoped-for wagon appeared, and its driver persuaded to carry the luggage up the hill, and even then, the road being so steep and unsafe, there were fears the horse would not be able to manage it. In the end, two trips were necessary, with Theo accompanying the wagon each time, and it was well after noon before all were once again assembled -- this time in the town square.

"They don't have any coaches here. We'll have to wait until the day after tomorrow for the stage from Aberystwyth, and even that won't have room. What are we going to do?"

They clamoured around Theo.

"Yes, and we look such a mess all of us -- like a bunch of itinerant actors even -- nobody will give us overnight lodging either."

"The town is horrible too," complained one of the men. "It stinks. It's all those midden heaps we passed on the way here…"

"Yes," said another, "and clouds of the dried-out manure have blown all over us. It's all in my hair and everywhere. Now I stink too. What are we going to do, Theo?"

"Walk to Haverfordwest."

"Walk!"

"We'll have to. Anyway, it's only fifteen miles. If we start right away, we should be there before nightfall, and before you say anything else, I'll arrange for our baggage to be carted into Haverfordwest early tomorrow."

Amid groans and moans, the now disreputable-looking group made their way to their destination, stopping off at The Harp Inn in Letterston just long enough to take some refreshment, and coming into sight of Haverfordwest not long before sunset.

"My goodness!" Theo remarked to James as they came over the brow of Prendergast hill. "What a beautiful town! I've never seen a whole town whitewashed like that before. Look! Even the castle and the churches and their steeples are white! And the roofs of the houses too!" He stood, looking over Haverfordwest, clinging to the side of its steep hill. "With the setting sun behind it like that, it looks more like a stage backdrop to a fairytale play than a real town."

By the time they arrived, weary and dirty, at their lodgings down on the quay it was almost dark.

"Ah! Mr. Potter," the innkeeper greeted him, "Mr. William Edwardes, your host, came in earlier. He was expecting you to arrive on the 'Venture', but when you weren't on board, he asked me if you would send him a message when you did arrive."

"Yes, of course. Thank you. Where does he live then?"

"At Dunstable Hall, a couple of miles out of town."

Theo groaned. "I don't think any of us are up to walking there and back tonight, so I'll pay your errand boy to go if he's available." On finding that he was, he then asked that the boy should also let Mr. Edwardes know they would be arriving at his home the day after tomorrow, as scheduled.

This taken care of, they all ate a good supper, washed down with some good Welsh ale, after which, exhausted from their long journey, they retired to their respective apartments, and were not seen until late the following morning.

CHAPTER 2

"Did cook manage to find Mr. Evans, our butcher from Crymych? It's so aggravating that they stopped the market people using St. Mary's churchyard to set up their stalls; cook never knows where to find them anymore. The sooner they build somewhere permanent for them, the better." The lady of the house bustled around, straightening this, arranging that. "I don't know what we'll do if cook can't find him, as I'm sure she has everything that goes with mutton, and it's too late to slaughter any of our own animals now."

Mrs. Eleanor Edwardes, accompanied by her housekeeper, Mrs. Davies, was inspecting the final arrangements for the dinner she would be hosting prior to the production of Shakespeare's *Romeo and Juliet*, which was to be performed in her ballroom the following night. It was to be a private performance for the benefit of the local gentry, but she worried about the actor people who would have to be allowed into her home. Widowed while still a young woman, she had never had the opportunity to go to London to see high quality actors perform in their fine theatres, and had only witnessed, on rare occasions, entertainments provided by people of what she considered questionable integrity and honesty. "Do you think we'd better arrange for staff to supervise them?" she wondered aloud. "You never know with actors. I've never met any personally of course, but from what I've heard and seen, they're not what one could consider gentlefolk or even honest common folk... more the sort likely to be arrested by the constable for picking pockets." She straightened a chair that was out of line. "I don't know what I should do if they went around stealing little treasures from around the house. Then there's the silver, Mrs. Davies, what do you think we'd better do about that?" She stopped and thought about it. "This whole undertaking is becoming quite tiresome."

Mrs. Davies, the housekeeper, straight-backed, immaculate, hands clasped in front of her, followed her mistress as she made her way round the huge dining salon, touching a piece of furniture here, inspecting the candles there. Polite as always, she suggested they remove any possible attractions from sight until after the actors had been ushered away as soon as their performance was over.

"Yes, yes, Mrs. Davies, an excellent idea. Please see Jemima hides such treasures in the closets, and all rooms are locked. I think, moreover, we'll have to make sure they're not allowed to enter the house until right before the performance and, as you suggest, hustled out again as soon as it's over." She leaned over and straightened a flower. "I do hope we haven't picked these flowers too soon. It would be most aggravating if they had all wilted by the time everyone arrives tomorrow."

Assured that cook had been able to find the butcher, that the haunches of best Welsh mutton were secure in her pantry, and the flowers were sure to be still fresh by the morrow, Mrs. Edwardes turned her attention to the windows from which Preseli top could be seen. "Get Jemima to go over these sills again, Mrs. Davies. That girl needs to learn to be more thorough."

"Yes Ma'am. Indeed, she's still only fifteen, and has a lot to learn. She doesn't appreciate how fortunate she is to have the position of under-housemaid in such a grand home at her age."

But Mrs. Edwardes had moved on, and did not hear. "Do we know how the stage is coming along? Mr. Griffiths is such a talented carpenter; I'm sure he'll do an excellent job... We can't have it collapsing under these actor people, can we?"

Mrs. Davies smiled. "No indeed, Ma'am!"

"Just think," Mrs. Edwardes continued, "what *would* we do if one of them were injured while here at Dunstable Hall? What would we do with him... or her? Where would we accommodate them?" The thought of some scruffy actor beneath the fine linen sheets on one of her beds designed and made by Mr. Thomas Chippendale himself appalled her.

Their tour had brought them to the western end of the room, and again Mrs. Edwardes advanced towards the tall windows. She looked out towards the orangery. "Do you know, Mrs. Davies, my orangery is the only one within the county?"

"Indeed Ma'am!" Mrs. Davies expressed surprise even though her mistress had already told her this on many previous occasions.

Mrs. Edwardes looked beyond the orangery down towards the town of Haverfordwest in the distance. Constant hints on her part had resulted in her home being chosen amongst all the homes of the gentry as the most suitable in which to host the performance, not only because of the spaciousness of her accommodations, but also because it was beyond the steep and narrow streets of Haverfordwest, yet convenient for neighbouring gentry, many of whom would be occupying their townhouses at this time of year. "Well I think that's it. Thank you, Mrs. Davies. Everything seems satisfactory."

Mrs. Davies curtsied, and took her leave.

Mrs. Edwardes was still gazing out of the window, trying to think if there was anything she had forgotten, when her second eldest daughter, Elizabeth, came in. Her cheeks were flushed and she was out of breath, having been playing hide-and-seek in the shrubbery with the younger children. "Mama, I'm worried about little Maria. I'm sure she's caught cold; she's sniffling dreadfully, and I think you should send for Mr. Nash to see to her."

At two-and-twenty years old Elizabeth was considered an accomplished young woman. She played the spinet well, had an acceptable singing voice, and the likenesses she drew and painted were always thought to reveal much more about the sitter than just the physical attributes, a talent considered to be higher than normal. She also loved to read, especially poetry, and as the library of Dunstable Hall was known to be one of the finest in the area, she had a plentiful supply of books from which to choose. She loved children too, especially babies, and was never more happy than when cuddling them, or playing with them. If she had any fault, it was in her tendency to worry, and to worry in particular about the welfare and safety of those around her, a trait her family believed had developed after her much-loved father, Joseph Edwardes, had died in an accident when she was only six. It was an event that had left the small child with the everlasting fear that someone she loved would, like her father, be snatched away from her, leaving her bereft. When people went away, she worried until they returned, and if they were ill or hurt, she worried and tended over them until they were out of danger and fully recovered. Elizabeth's concern was something the family was used to, and over the years had come to accept it. "That's Elizabeth," they would say. "She always worries."

Mrs. Edwardes had other things on her own mind to worry about at this moment, but knew that as long as her daughter was concerned, there would be no end to her fussing until she had been assured all was well. "Very well then, my dear, send nurse to fetch her, and we'll see what, if anything, needs to be done."

The problem was seen to -- the conclusion being that young Maria had probably just been smelling some flowers that had given her her sniffles. Thus satisfied, mother and daughter went to inspect the newly-created theatre.

They left the salon and entered the grand entrance hall into which the late afternoon sun was shining, lighting up with a pale golden glow the two dazzling-white stairways which, starting at either side of the hallway, joined at the mezzanine, giving the whole staircase an elegant heart shape.

Elizabeth held a dramatic hand before her eyes. "But soft! What light through yonder window breaks?"

Laughing, the two ladies entered the grand ballroom, said to be built of a size intended to hold everyone who was anyone in the county. "Just think," Elizabeth said, "actors coming especially to perform for us, all the way from Dublin!"

"I could wish they were people somewhat more elevated in society than a troupe of travelling actors. They're not the sort one would ordinarily invite into one's home." Mrs. Edwardes raised her chin in scorn. "But how could I refuse? It was expected of us."

"Oh Mother. You know you contrived it so they had no choice but to ask you to act as the hostess," Elizabeth teased her. "You know you couldn't have borne it if Mrs. Carswell had been chosen."

"Mrs. Carswell! Mrs. Carswell! Insufferable woman! Airs way above her station! Sir John Campbell would never, ever invite her to his Stackpole estate! Her manners are deplorable. Besides, her voice isn't well modulated... and she talks way too much."

Elizabeth smiled. It was usually hard, when in company, to decide which of the two ladies, her mother or Mrs. Carswell, talked more, although she had to admit there was a certain coarseness about Mrs. Carswell that her mother, the daughter of a gentleman, would never have been guilty of displaying.

19

She took her mother's arm. "Come. Let's inspect the stage... It really does look like a theatre," she said, looking around her. "And look at the backdrop and the curtains. It all looks so authentic."

The staff had stopped what they were doing, and were standing, facing the mistress of the house.

"Mr. Griffiths, Mrs. Glover, you appear to have done excellently."

Mr. Griffiths, farmer of the Dunstable home farm, and temporary carpenter, bowed, and Mrs. Glover, the seamstress, curtsied. "Thank you, Ma'am," they said in unison.

"It seems there's nothing else to do," Mrs. Edwardes added, looking at what appeared to be a complete setting for the upcoming performance, and preparing to leave.

"Wait!" Elizabeth put up her hands. "Wait! Where's the balcony?"

The staff looked puzzled.

"There has to be a balcony. You can't perform *Romeo and Juliet* without a balcony!"

"Balcony, Miss Elizabeth? What sort of balcony?" Mr. Griffiths had already lost valuable time at the farm. His wife had not only had to make the butter and cheese as usual for the big house during his absence, but to milk the cows as well, something he normally did himself. His young son and daughter too had had to perform other tasks he considered to be beyond their young age, and out in the cold and damp as well, but no-one had thought of the inconvenience to him. Now it looked as though yet another day was to be lost.

"Oh yes, of course," said Mrs. Edwardes, "we have to have a balcony."

Elizabeth showed Mr. Griffiths how it should look.

"Don't worry, Mr. Griffiths. There's still plenty of time for you to get it completed," Mrs. Edwardes assured him, "and you may take whom you please -- except for any of the household staff -- to help you collect whatever you need in the way of extra lumber from the mill. I'm sure everything will be fine. I'll let Mr. Edwardes know about the extra requirements."

Elizabeth left her mother to the rest of her arranging, and went to the orangery, where she planned to do a watercolour painting of some of her mother's favourite flowers -- a painting she intended to give her for her next birthday present. Happy, she was now devoid of any worries. Everyone was at home, safe, and all in the best of health, and she was content. In the silence of the sunlit orangery, she began a meticulous outline of the sweet-smelling orange blossoms, and thought about the upcoming performance of *Romeo and Juliet*.

At the other side of the town, the troupe had already been established in the inn beside the river since the previous day, and when not rehearsing, had been amusing themselves making the most of whatever the town had to offer in the way of entertainment, confident that all necessary arrangements would have been carried out for them in the same way they would have been back in Dublin -- and if not, then their manager, Mr. Potter, would take care of the situation. They and their clothes looking acceptable once more, they could walk around town without being taken for penniless strollers, ready to pick pockets and steal whatever else they could find.

Theo had been warned to expect that Haverfordwest was not Dublin, and so took it upon himself to see what, if anything, had been done to prepare for the performance they were to mount for the ordinary citizens this night -- the night before the private performance. Of the latter he had no doubt all would be acceptable, so his concern was for tonight.

It did not take him long to find out that, other than a hand-written, drab and uninviting announcement on each of the gates of the town's three churches, and one other already covered over by other bulletins, there was nothing at all to advertise their presence. Suspecting this might be the case, Mr. Ryder had put Theo also in charge of a small portable printing machine capable of producing a few professional-looking playbills that they could post around the town. There was not much time left for achieving this however, and his instruction regarding the machine's use had been only cursory. Nevertheless, he returned to the inn where it lay in a corner of his small room, and set about producing the required posters.

After about an hour, his hands were black with ink, and a scattering of discarded efforts lay around the floor. James, returning from a trip to the haberdasher's for some items for his master, came in just as Theo's patience had run out, and was met by a flurry of ink-covered sheets floating back to the floor, after having been tossed into the air by the frustrated printer.

"This won't do," Theo fumed. "I can't waste any more time on these... these..." He failed to think of a suitable word with which to describe them. "And I'm going out to check on this Blue Boar Inn place to see if they, at least, have managed to prepare something properly, namely some sort of area in which we can act!" He marched over the carpet of crumpled, ink-stained sheets, and headed for the door, avoiding looking at the mess he had created, and annoyed that he had failed to complete what should have been an easy task. He seized hold of the latch, and began to stride out.

"Sir?"

Theo stopped, but did not turn round. "Yes?"

"Sir, perhaps it would be wise to remove the ink from your face before you go." James knew not to allow a smile to show at such moments.

"Humph." Theo wiped his face with his clean kerchief, and turned to look for James's approval. James nodded, and Theo left.

Intending to stride up High Street to The Blue Boar Inn,

he had taken but a few steps when he tripped and almost lost his balance, much to the amusement of some local young women coming towards him. As they passed, he heard them giggling, and one said, "a visitor". Then they all laughed, and went on their way. They had known what Theo -- a newcomer to Haverfordwest -- did not, and that was that a combination of steep hills and rounded cobblestones made negotiating the town's streets dangerous for anyone except the young and sure-footed who lived there and were used it.

Even more disgruntled, Theo nevertheless began to take more note of his surroundings and where he was stepping as he climbed High Street. The young people, he noticed, skipped down the street sideways at quite a pace, while the older people kept one hand on the walls to help them keep their balance. The more affluent were being carried about town in sedan chairs, and then there were others who used horses or donkeys on which to get around.

Glad he was wearing stout boots and not his best buckled shoes, Theo made his way up to the Blue Boar as carefully as he could without falling prey to any more treacherous cobblestones that seemed determined on having him fall flat on his back. Thus, by the time he reached his destination, he was in no mood to appreciate the sign that hung over the door stating:

"Our Landlord here,
and sign, I swear,
Are very near the skin;
An ill-shaped Boar
Hangs at the Door,
And a grumpish Hog's within!"

Inside, he met the landlord, Stephen George, a young and amiable man about the same age as himself, and decided the sign must refer to some earlier landlord, as Mr. George was delighted to show him the improvised theatre which, although makeshift, was at least adequate.

"Good morning, Sir." Theo turned to find a man of short stature speaking to him. He had an accent he had never heard before, and soon found himself in a lively and stimulating discussion with him over several recently published literary works. The man, a Mr. William Sutton, lived in town, was in his fifties, a writer, a lover of reading, and a master printer. He was, Theo decided, one of the most literate and knowledgeable men he had ever met. "If you're a printer," he asked him, "why haven't you set up a printing business here? As I've just discovered, the town could certainly do with such a service."

"Oh! Mr. Potter, Sir. it's too expensive for a man like me to set up in such a business, what with the cost of all the necessary equipment and renting a suitable property in which to house it. I'm not a wealthy man. I couldn't afford it... I make my living as a scribe."

"That's a pity, having all your knowledge and expertise go to waste like that." The conversation moved on, and Theo discovered that Mr. Sutton had, like himself, come to check on the improvised theatre, and was looking forward to the evening's performance.

His mood improved, and his spirits raised by the encounter, Theo accepted that all that could be done in preparation for tonight had been done, and all being well, there would be an audience before whom they could perform. All he had to do now was to face the descent of High Street, something he was correct in fearing would be even more difficult than the ascent, so it was with relief that he arrived back at his lodgings without having further embarrassed himself.

Word of mouth is a powerful transmitter of news and information, and despite Theo's concerns, the improvised theatre was filled, people even standing along the sides, at the back, and in every other available space. The enthusiasm with which the drama was received was beyond the troupe's highest hopes, and the whole cast, buoyed by the response they received throughout the play, delivered a performance of which they and their home theatre could be proud; and everyone returned to their respective lodgings satisfied -- except James.

James had not been happy at all with his master's accommodations since they had been in town, considering them to be well below the standard to which he was used. Passably clean he supposed they were, but they were cramped, not giving a tall man such as Theo much room in which to move around, and the bed was way too short to allow him to sleep in comfort. In addition to these inconveniences, the noise at night was considerable. The accommodations being on the quay, boats were being unloaded just yards away at all hours, and the crashing and banging of crates, and the swearing of those manipulating them had encouraged James to beg his master to move to a more elegant inn nearer to the Blue Boar, but Theo had refused. To begin with, he was already setting himself above the other actors by being the only one in the troupe to employ a personal servant. He did not want to make himself look even more superior, or risk alienating them by leaving them so as to move into more expensive accommodations he knew they could not afford.

On this night, however, James had left The Blue Boar before the end of the play so as to make sure everything was ready and as comfortable as possible for his master's return. On arriving outside Theo's room he was surprised to hear loud snores coming from within. He marched in and found a member of some vessel's crew sprawled on Theo's bed. The man was filthy and stank of fish and stale tobacco. It was too much for James. He grabbed his master's belongings, all of which had been left untouched by the intruder, packed them into his travelling bag, then went up the road to another inn, "The Traveller's Rest," which had a room available -- no doubt because its accommodations were the most expensive in town. James knew his master's situation well enough to know he could well afford it, so booked the room, then waited outside until he saw Theo walking down High Street from The Blue Boar along with the other actors -- several local young ladies in pursuit.

Theo was tired, and did not want to argue with his servant in front everyone, so without comment, he allowed James to escort him to his new chamber with its four-poster bed and clean white sheets, after which James left to spend his own night back at the inn alongside the quay.

CHAPTER 3

Mrs. Edwardes's lavish dinner had been eaten, enjoyed and praised for its excellence. Nobody had ever tasted finer mutton, and the vintages of Mr. Edwardes's cellar had impressed even the most sophisticated palates. The accolades drawing to a close, the ladies retired to the drawing room to discuss the latest London and Paris fashions, to flatter one another on the style of their hair, dress and other accoutrements, and to indulge, within the limits of what was considered good manners, in the latest gossip.

Instead, they found themselves captive audience to Mrs. Carswell who, strident as ever and determined to impress, was treating all who would listen to a detailed report of the trials she had endured trying to find footmen with legs of a suitable shape with which to show off the magnificent green and gold livery she had designed for them. "Ladies, I must tell you..." Her shrill tones would have done more than simply raise the eyebrows of less well-mannered company. "I just *had* to tell Mr. Carswell. 'My dear Mr. Carswell,' I told him, 'do *please* impress on William the importance of finding footmen of decent stature and with fine calves!' You just can't *imagine* how difficult it is to find men with shapely calves! The height isn't usually a difficulty, but the *legs* ladies!" She raised her arms in seeming despair. "It's the *legs* that are the problem -- either skinny sticks like bean poles, or beef to heel, as my grandmother used to say." Her voice rose and descended as she emphasised the relevant words.

She then went on to relate how, when she and her daughter had, a couple of days previously, been out shopping for a new pelisse for herself to wear this evening, they had encountered the scurviest looking troupe of strollers making their way into town, and prayed they may not be the ones who would have the audacity to present themselves at Dunstable Hall this evening. "My dear Mrs. Edwardes," she almost screamed, "I said to my daughter, 'Martha!' I said, 'I do declare I pity the poor folks who would have to spend time in the same room with them! I've never seen such an unkempt and dirty lot! Thank goodness we can rely on the good people of Dunstable Hall to make sure we're not exposed to such wastrels,' I said." She swished her fan in front of her face. "'It would be insupportable.'"

There was not much the other ladies could say to this, so after a few murmurs of what they considered appropriate to the occasion, they were able to change the subject to something more to their tastes.

In the dining room, time was passing with greater enjoyment for the men, enhanced as it was by Mr. Edwardes's fine cigars from the West Indies, along with a succession of bottles of his finest port which -- as most of them already knew, as they also owned some port of similar origins -- had lately been retrieved from an unfortunate vessel that had foundered off Pembrokeshire's treacherous coast. The subjects of discussion were horses, hounds, and hunting.

It was on the subject of horses that Mr. Edwardes had a special story to tell. "Gentlemen, if time permits after the play, I should like you to come down to the stables to see my new gelding. It arrived from Ireland only a few days ago, and is a horse I set my eyes on while over in Ireland to discuss the agreement I came to with the theatre in Dublin -- and why we're here tonight of course." He took a deep breath. "I just had to have him, but must tell you, I paid a pretty price for it. His owner just didn't want to part with him." He sighed.

The gentlemen, knowing Mr. Edwardes had sufficient fortune to buy a whole stable full of exceptional horses, nevertheless sighed in sympathy.

"No, no. it's not simply the price," he assured them. "Everything is going to be all right, but on the way over there was an accident."

The gentlemen tutted and shook their heads over this, and listened as Mr. Edwardes went on to describe how the horse ended up with a gash on its foreleg. "The groom told me everything. The poor boy was scared I was going to blame him and send the horse packing back to Ireland. Fortunately it wasn't too serious, though I'm concerned the hair will grow back white, as it does sometimes you know."

The gentlemen nodded. Many had a hunter with a spot on its back where the saddle had rubbed the horse raw, and the hair had grown back white.

"According to the groom," Mr. Edwardes continued, "who is, I should add, an excellent fellow whom I've persuaded to stay on for a week or so to get the horse settled, a complete disaster was averted by a gentleman who was also on the passage from Ireland. Without his intervention, the horse could easily have ended up killing people as well as itself! He was also no doubt responsible for the wound not getting infected."

The gentlemen were impressed, and tapped their wine glasses with their forks to show their approval, and Lord Tavernspite even proposed a toast to this gentleman. They raised their glasses. "To a true gentleman," they said in unison, and Mr. Edwardes found it necessary to pay for his story with a few more bottles of his special port.

More tales of mishaps were prompted by this telling, but at last Mr. Edwardes took out his pocket watch. "Gentlemen," he announced, "it's time now for us to add the final touch to our evening by attending the much-awaited performance of Mr. Shakespeare's *Romeo and Juliet*. I'm sure we shan't be disappointed. I was assured by my friend, Mr. Thomas Ryder, the manager of the Smock Alley Theatre, that he would be sending some of his finest young actors to entertain us. So... shall we go?" He stood up, but some of the party were not ready.

"I'm sure these actor people won't mind being kept waiting a few minutes more, my dear Edwardes." Lord Tavernspite leaned back against his chair and smiled around. "They're only actors, and I'm sure they're used to being kept waiting." He took another swallow from his glass. "Besides this port is too damned good to be wasted."

They all nodded in agreement with Lord Tavernspite, but Mr. Edwardes was adamant. "In my house," he said, "we don't keep people waiting, even actors." He had already rung the bell, and two footmen had come to open the wide double doors, and were standing to attention, one on either side. "Gentlemen, if you please." Mr. Edwardes pointed to the open doorway, and stood back as each, including Lord Tavernspite, whose generous helpings of port had rendered benevolent, filed out through the doors to the grand entrance hall and on into the ballroom theatre, where the ladies were already assembled.

After a few minutes of muted conversation among the guests, as though all were in church, servants began to go around the room extinguishing sufficient candles to reduce to darkness the area occupied by the audience. A row of candles still remained along the edge of the stage and above it. Conversation dwindled, the double curtain -- put together by

Mrs. Glover -- rose, and the play began.

It was not long before the young ladies in the audience -- and even some of the older ones -- began to concentrate their attention on the hero of the play, and to point out to one another, in hushed voices, his attractions. "Mama," Elizabeth whispered to her mother. "Mama, Romeo, he's *such* a handsome man, I think... He has such excellent stature and presence too, don't you agree?"

"My dear Elizabeth," said Mrs. Edwardes, "he's just an actor, and we're here to watch him act, not to be moved by his own personal charms... But yes," she conceded, "my eyes aren't what they used to be, but from what I *can* see you're probably right, my dear."

Behind them was Mrs. Carswell, whose ability to appreciate the greatness of the bard's words was limited, whose voice carried well beyond the ears of her husband for whom her own words were intended, and who was not in any way troubled that she was competing with the actors, or spoiling anyone else's enjoyment. "That one." She nudged Mr. Carswell and pointed towards the stage. "Romeo. The one who's playing Romeo."

"What about him, my dear?" her husband whispered back.

"Well..." While the drama continued to be played out before them, Mrs. Carswell related to her husband something she had heard about the actor earlier. "My personal maid, Mary-Jane, was told by her sister, Jemima, who is an under-housemaid here, that when the actors arrived earlier this evening -- and were ushered directly in here, without giving them the opportunity to pry into areas where they don't belong -- one of them had brought with him a manservant, who was quite rightly sent down to the stables to wait, and he had told the coachman his master was the one playing Romeo." She paused to catch her breath. "A *manservant* indeed! Can you believe it?" she exclaimed. "A strolling actor with a manservant!"

"Indeed!" remarked her husband.

"Yes! What *does* he think he is? A gentleman?"

Mrs. Edwardes, seated in front of her, agitated her plume-of-feathers fan. How did such a woman ever manage to enter genteel society? She acknowledged to herself she already knew the answer to that, but that made her even more annoyed. It seemed the mansion and the estate on which it sat in nearby Camrose -- and which belonged now to the Carswells -- had been entailed to the nearest surviving male heir. However, the owner had died without leaving a male heir, or someone even close, and after a succession of London solicitors had traced, at great expense to the estate, the nearest male relative, this turned out to be Mr. Robert Carswell, a small Herefordshire banker of modest means, who had the misfortune to be married to this woman of no known connections whatsoever. Their position as owners of the Camrose estate, however, decreed that their entrance into Haverfordwest society was assured.

Elizabeth, oblivious to the pillorying of Romeo taking place behind her, and unaware that the object of her interest had learned his natural and appealing style of acting from the great Mr. David Garrick in London, and his fine diction from Mr. Thomas Sheridan in Dublin, continued to watch him, fascinated, and listened with increasing admiration to every word he uttered -- admiration both for his rich voice and the way he delivered it, not to mention for the man himself.

There was something special about his manner and his presence which she suspected went beyond the role, and she found herself content to wonder more about the man behind the act than about the part he was playing. Would that she could meet him! She sighed. As her mother had said, he was only an actor, and from Ireland at that, and so it was unlikely they would indeed ever meet, let alone ever be introduced.

The play continued for a while uninterrupted before Mrs. Carswell remembered something else she had discovered about Romeo. "And do you know what else?" she demanded of her husband. "Last night he had the impudence to leave the accommodations for which the town has so generously paid, and instead installed himself at the Traveller's Rest! The Traveller's Rest, I declare! Well! If he thinks the town is going to foot the bill for that...!" Her indignation required a moment in which to catch her breath.

"Maybe he's already paid for it himself," her husband whispered back.

"Never!" her voice made several people turn round in annoyance. "Never!" she repeated in a whisper. "On *his* wages? I tell you he'll end up with not a penny in his pocket if he's not careful, and then the sheriff will be quite within his rights to throw him in gaol!"

Mrs. Carswell's only previous experience with actors was when she had observed players, dressed in rags and of insalubrious aspect and questionable honesty, ranting away at the fairs and racetracks in Herefordshire, and was convinced, therefore, that all actors were nothing but vagabonds and thieves. Triumphant at her verdict on what she was sure would befall this upstart actor-fellow with pretensions beyond his status in society, and having nothing more to add to her report on his latest scandalous behaviour, Mrs. Carswell sat back contented, and the audience watched the performance, uninterrupted except for the gentle snoring of Lord Tavernspite.

Mr. Edwardes, glad his obligations of the previous evening were over, and everyone had seemed to have enjoyed themselves, was anxious to turn his attentions to his new horse, and his first need was to get it shod. He had specific instructions on how this was to be done, so feeling the need to talk to the blacksmith himself, he accompanied the groom to the smithy a little way down the road towards Merlin's Bridge, where the man had his forge.

They set out later that morning, Mr. Edwardes riding one of his other horses, the groom walking by his side, holding the new gelding. They said little, Mr. Edwardes on his horse being too far above the level of the groom's ear for any conversation to be carried on. As he rode Mr. Edwardes was thinking how one aspect of last evening's entertainment had not gone the way he would have wished. After the play was over, and he had taken care of his guests, he had gone to find the actors, intending to congratulate them on their performance and to meet their manager, only to find they had already left, having been encouraged by the staff to make their exit as soon as possible. Earlier this morning he had gone back down to the inn, hoping again to meet their manager, but he was not there, so had to content himself with asking one of the other actors to let his manager know how much their performance had been appreciated.

"Sir!" They were making their way down High Street when the groom called out. "Sir! There he is!" He nodded his head towards a tall, smart young man, walking among the many people crowding the street.

"Where? Who?" said Mr. Edwardes.

"The man on the boat, Sir. The gentleman who saved your horse!"

Mr. Edwardes raised himself up in the saddle, and looked around. "Where?"

"Over there, just passing the entrance to…" The groom looked puzzled. "Oh, he's disappeared."

"How extremely annoying!" Mr. Edwardes tutted with frustration. "I should liked to have offered him my thanks, and to have invited him to dine at Dunstable Hall." He looked around again, but the man was nowhere to be seen. "Well, I hope he's in town for a while, so I have the opportunity to see him and to thank him." They continued in silence for a few more minutes, then Mr. Edwardes leaned down over his horse's withers. "Should you see this gentleman again, please express my desire to make his acquaintance, and ask him if he'd be so kind as to let you know where he's staying, as I'd like to call on him to pay my respects."

The groom agreed, and they continued on to the blacksmith's forge.

There were two other horses ahead of them, and the groom knew it would be at least three hours of standing around waiting, before his horse would have its turn. Leaving him outside, Mr. Edwardes walked into the dim stone forge to talk to the blacksmith. The latter was a man past middle age who a few years previously had received a bad kick. Since then he had become nervous, making his behaviour towards the horses severe, and leading him to use a cruel twitch to keep them under control. Mr. Edwardes would have none of it, and wanted to impress on him that he would tolerate no illtreatment of his horse.

The blacksmith's clothing, except for his tough leather apron, was as black as the old walls and the rafters above him, where many generations of spider webs, encased in soot, hung in festoons. The heat of the fire made the room hot despite the autumn chill, and every now and then the blacksmith would pump on the huge leather bellows that hung over it, whipping the embers into an incandescent whiteness, and sending a rush of hot air throughout the shop.

Mr. Edwardes waited while the surly blacksmith continued with what he was doing. Resting on the man's knee was the rear hoof of a huge carthorse, against whose belly his head was pressed. He had removed the old shoes, and was busy paring down the animal's hooves in preparation for the new ones he was about to make.

Mr. Edwardes continued to wait. This was the only blacksmith in town, and he knew that, gentleman or no gentleman, he would have to await the farrier's pleasure, and the man was in no hurry to oblige.

After a long wait, the blacksmith lowered the enormous hoof to the ground and stood up, and while Mr. Edwardes explained what he wanted -- as well as what he did not want -- he continued with his task of first selecting one of the long iron rods propped up against the wall, then lopping off four equal lengths from it from which he would construct the new shoes. A selection of different tools lay on the side of the big iron anvil, all ready for the task, and next to it was a large pail of cold water, into which the new, red-hot shoes, bent to shape, with a raised clip in the front and four square holes on either side, would be plunged to cool. The air smelled of soot, horse dung and burning hoof, and Mr. Edwardes was glad to make his exit, leaving the groom to his long wait.

When the groom had seen Theo, the latter had been making his way to the Cock House, a gloomy, filthy place where prisoners awaiting trial, or being incarcerated, were held. He was going to the help of one of his fellow actors who had had the misfortune, not only to have been robbed of all his money, but then to have been picked up by a constable and charged with violating the Licensing Act, a law that allowed penniless strolling actors to be charged with being vagabonds and thieves. His friends had turned to Theo for help.

At the Cock House the gaoler told him he would need to go to the magistrate, as it would be his decision regarding the fate of the actor. Having at last found the magistrate, Theo gave him an account of their presence in town, and of what had happened. The discussion was cordial, and ended with satisfaction on both sides, Theo agreeing to make sure the actor would have a minimum of one silver penny in his pocket as long as he remained in town, while Theo himself would contribute a generous amount which would be donated to a charity of the magistrate's choice.

While Theo was involved with securing the freedom of his fellow actor, Miss Elizabeth Edwardes was reading the play for herself... again. She had already read it several times, having been so impressed by the actor who had played Romeo, that by rereading his lines she thought to retain his image in her mind that much longer. It was an image to which she had become so attached, she regretted it was one she was never likely to encounter again. "Don't be ridiculous!" she had scolded herself. "You're not some lovelorn little girl; you're a grown woman. How can you feel this way about some actor whom you haven't even seen up close, and whom you saw on a stage for just a couple of hours at most?" But she could not erase his image from her mind, and it continued to monopolise her attention, even keeping her awake at night, thinking about him.

Many hungry hours later the groom was on his way up Market Street towards Dunstable Hall when he saw the gentleman again. This time the gentleman saw him also -- at least he saw and recognized the horse. Theo hailed the groom, then walked over to see how it was doing. The groom then explained with great excitement how he and the horse's new owner had seen him earlier in the day while on their way to the farrier, and that the gentleman was anxious to make his acquaintance, and to visit him.

"Indeed! Then I should be delighted to meet him." Theo pointed back down the hill to the Traveller's Rest. "I'm staying there." He then bent down and lifted the horse's foreleg. "It's coming along well," he commented. "No sign of infection."

"No, indeed. And we're indebted to you for that, Sir."

Theo smiled and patted the horse's neck. "I'll be expecting a visit from your master then," he said, and turned to go on his way.

"Yes, Sir." They parted, but then Theo heard the groom calling back. "Oh! Sir! Whom should my master be asking for at the inn?"

"Tell him my name is John Theophilus Potter." It was not until he was back at the Traveller's Rest he remembered he had not asked the young groom the name of the man who was to visit him.

Mr. Edwardes held out his hand. "Ah! Mr. Potter, if I'm correct. My name is William Edwardes... of Dunstable Hall." They shook hands, and an astonished Theo invited into his apartments the guest who, to his great relief, failed to recognize him as being one of the troupe of actors who had performed in his home just two nights before.

After thanks had been offered for the rescue of his horse, and Theo had acknowledged them with a modest bow, Mr. Edwardes told him he would like to show his appreciation, but first asked him if he would be in town for at least the following day. "Well, well," he said on finding he would. "This is capital! And I have an idea." He then described to Theo what he had in mind. "Now," he continued, "it happens that my brother has an estate farther out in the country," and went on to explain. "The countryside there being ideally suited, my grandfather opened up a park for red deer there many years ago, and every year at this time -- it being as you might know, hunting season -- he opens up the park for a couple of hours, one day only, for the gentry of the area, *and*..." He slapped his hands on his knees with pleasure at the prospect. "We have a deer hunt!"

"Indeed!"

"Yes, and I should be delighted if you would be my

guest, and join me -- it takes place tomorrow." He looked at Theo. "Oh! I do hope that doesn't conflict with your other plans."

"No, no... Not at all." Theo became an actor, convincing Mr. Edwardes of his enthusiasm for the hunt. The truth was he disliked killing anything, and having once heard the dying cry of a wounded deer, he liked killing them even less than other species. To reject the offer, however, would be most impolite, so he was quick to add, "Of course, I'd be delighted. Tomorrow you say?" For a moment he hoped his lack of a mount and a weapon would put an end to the plan, but Mr. Edwardes had already taken care of that.

"Of course, I'll provide you with a mount and musket." He stood up, as did Theo. "We do have to start rather early, I'm afraid. It's necessary to be at the park just after sunrise, and it's about an hour's ride to get there. What say we'll meet you outside your inn at about six o'clock?"

Theo agreed, and Mr. Edwardes was going out through the door when he had yet another idea. "It's just occurred to me; after our return from the hunt, Mrs. Edwardes and I should be delighted if you would share a family dinner with us at four o'clock. I can show you round the estate, and... Oh yes! And you'll be able to see how your horse is faring."

Theo thanked him, and Mr. Edwardes left the inn happy he had found a fine way in which to thank the gentleman for saving his horse.

After Mr. Edwardes's departure, and while James was still holding the door, Theo asked him to wait. "James," he began, "I'd no idea the owner of that horse and the person who invited us to perform here were one and the same person. I'm grateful he didn't recognize me..." He stopped, remembering something. "Something has just occurred to me, James: because he didn't recognize me, it seemed foolish at the time to complicate matters by trying to explain how I was one of those who had acted at his home. I assumed that as we'll be leaving the day after tomorrow, that would have been the end of it, but now he's asked me to meet his wife and family, and that changes everything!" He shook his head in consternation. "James, this could be most embarrassing! What if a family member recognizes me?" He began pacing about the room, thinking out loud. "I wish now I hadn't even seen the groom with the horse yesterday! It's too bad as well, that Mr. Edwardes thought to invite me to dinner just as he was leaving. I couldn't very well call after him then, and say, 'By the way, I'm the actor who played Romeo at your house'. This isn't good at all. It could cause quite a problem for me." He thought for a minute. "I think I'll have to find some excuse tomorrow morning for declining his dinner invitation. That way, at least I won't have to go near Dunstable Hall at all...The less involved I get with the family, the better."

Still imagining with some distress what might have happened had he been introduced to some member of the family who recognized him, even perhaps exclaiming, "Romeo!" he asked James to stay a while, to talk. Now he was worried about everything to do with tomorrow, and needed James's company to help him think through and sort out what was troubling him.

"I know you spent time with Mr. Edwardes's household staff on the night of the play," he said after some thought. "Tell me what you know about them... that's if you discussed them at all."

"Well, Sir, the only person I talked to was the coachman. I didn't go into the house, so didn't meet any of the household staff... They wouldn't let me in through the door... Didn't even offer me a mug of ale..."

"And?"

"He did tell me quite a bit about them. Mrs. Edwardes's name is Eleanor, and her eldest daughter is named Mary

Hanbury, and her second eldest daughter is called Elizabeth, and Miss Elizabeth, according to the coachman is a pretty lady of twenty-two, and she's intelligent, well-educated, accomplished, loves flowers, draws and paints and..."

Theo held up his hand, smiling. "I won't be meeting any of them now James, remember? So you needn't try to marry me off. All right, I now know about Miss Elizabeth, what about Mr. Edwardes?"

"According to the coachman, when Mr. Joseph Edwardes, Mrs. Edwardes's husband, died back in '62, he had no male heirs, and the estate was entailed, so it went to Mr. Edwardes's nearest male relative, who was his cousin Mr. William Edwardes."

" Oh! So he's not Mrs. Edwardes's husband then? Is he a bachelor?"

"No, he's a widower. He and his young wife moved onto the estate, but Mrs. Eleanor Edwardes and her three children remained in the house as Mr. William had promised Mr. Joseph they would until Mrs. Eleanor either remarried or died. Mr. Joseph also made Mr. William his children's guardian until they should come of age. You see, Miss Elizabeth was only six when her father died."

"My goodness, James! You heard all this from the coachman? How much ale had *he* been drinking? So... And what happened to Mr. William Edwardes's wife then?"

"She died in childbirth just two years ago, and Mrs. Eleanor has taken over the role of mother to their three children."

"Sad, but Mr. William seems to have kept his promise to his cousin."

"Oh yes, Sir. The coachman says he's the kindest, most thoughtful man, and generous too."

"Well, just in case something *does* arise while I'm with Mr. Edwardes and his gentry friends tomorrow, is there

41

anything else you can think of that I should be aware of, James?"

"Like what, Sir?"

Theo did not know. All he wanted now was to leave Haverfordwest before his life became complicated with people beginning to ask questions as to who or what he was, and now he had become involved with the local gentry as a 'gentleman', there was a possibility this could happen.

His problem was that acting was much like trade, which covered the whole range of affairs, from the wealthy businessman who employed many people -- and therefore considered respectable -- right down to the barrow boy hawking his wares on the city streets, and therefore, not respectable at all.

In the career of acting, there was a similar range, from the competent actors performing at theatres such as Drury Lane, Covent Garden and Dublin, right down to the near-starving itinerant actors driven by the severe Licensing Act to perform illegally, or with the permission of the local magistrate, at fairs and racetracks, and who were often pick-pockets, thieves and rogues. The public's attitude to actors then, often depended on what type of actor they had seen perform, if indeed they had seen a play at all, although with the gentry there was the added snobbery towards anyone who worked for a living, which of course included actors at the high end of the scale, such as Theo.

Theo, as a gentleman of independent means, would, in the opinion of his social peers, be expected to conduct his life as a gentleman, and not degrade himself by becoming an actor. Theo himself knew some gentlemen *did* become actors, just as the gentleman, Thomas Sheridan, had done back in 1740 when he joined the prestigious Smock Alley Theatre Royal. Mr. Sheridan, indeed, had spent his whole acting life attempting to have the career of acting accepted as being both respectable and as a profession. However, outside the big cities, it nevertheless continued to be the opinion, even amongst the gentry, that gentlemen did not become actors on the public stage, and the title, 'gentleman player' -- as such gentlemen actors liked to be known -- was an oxymoron. As far as acting being considered a profession, there was still a long way to go: physicians and attorneys were 'professionals'; actors, not.

By coming here to a provincial area such as Haverfordwest, therefore -- something he had done as a favour to his manager -- Theo had no way of knowing what his reception might be. He assumed Mr. Edwardes himself would consider him respectable, but how would others react towards him? He knew he ran the risk of being labelled by the degrading title of 'itinerant actor', and treated as such if they discovered he was the player they had seen performing on the Edwardes's stage, and he had reason to be bothered by this. It would not be the first time he had found himself in such a situation, and had no wish to repeat the experience.

To lessen the chances of being so labelled he, like other gentlemen players, even took the precaution of not accepting any payment for his performances, and lived by his own means -- 'gentlemen' did not work for a living. With the situation that had now arisen, Theo was running the risk of exposing himself to his worst fears. Even so, he wished he had at least explained his dual role to Mr. Edwardes, because Mr. Edwardes would know that actors from Dublin's Smock Alley Theatre, whom he himself had invited, were actors respected in both Dublin and London. He, at least, would have been sure to have understood Theo's status, and been comfortable in accepting him as a gentleman player. Now, although it had seemed the right thing at the time not to say anything, he was feeling as though he had even deceived Mr. Edwardes somehow.

"Well..." He hesitated. "And were there any confidences exchanged in the opposite direction?"

James was shocked. "Sir! I've known you since you were five years old, and although I don't know *everything* about you, I know as much as anyone else, including you yourself Sir." Then added, "except perhaps those who could well be still alive, and who are well aware of everything... And I'd never dream of revealing..."

Theo put up his hand. "No, James. You're right. It was wrong of me to ask."

What James had referred to was a subject he did not want to discuss.

Mr. Edwardes meanwhile arrived back at Dunstable Hall with news of his invitation to a handsome and well-bred young gentleman -- an unmarried young gentleman too, he had made a point of telling the assembled family at dinner. "*And* he's staying at the Traveller's Rest," he added.

"There you are," Mrs. Edwardes said to her two elder daughters. "An attractive, young and unmarried gentleman! What more could you want?"

"That he has a handsome income to go with his other attractions," answered Mary.

Elizabeth said nothing; *her* mind still dwelt on the actor who had played Romeo.

CHAPTER 4

It was still dark when James came to wake his master and to bring him a good breakfast, specially ordered the night before. "Heavy dew in the night, Sir, and the sky clear as a bell. If it does end up being a wet day, it won't be until after you're finished with the hunt."

Theo groaned, and rolled out of bed. "Well, at least it'll be over quickly." And he was not obliged to succeed in killing anything, just to look as though he were trying.

James had laid out the appropriate clothing, and Theo -- still half asleep -- dressed, and at six o'clock they were met outside the inn, James mounted on a horse Theo had rented for him from the inn's hostelry, and Theo on a mount supplied by Mr. Edwardes.

The ride to the park was pleasant. It was not too cold, and Theo watched the moon fade as the sky brightened, the stars vanishing into the gunmetal blue of the departing night. Daylight revealed small patches of sulphur-yellow where the gorse remained in bloom, and there were sudden loud clatters above their heads when wood pigeons fled from the leafless trees as they passed beneath, and flocks of jackdaws rose up in huge clouds, their raucous chatter greeting the day.

It took them about an hour to arrive at the estate, and

once at the park they left the horses near the entrance, rather than go up to the mansion a half mile away. A couple of stable boys from the house were there to meet them. Mr. Edwardes was happy to introduce the man who had saved his horse, and over a welcoming stirrup-cup of claret Theo met with all the others who were in attendance. He met Mr. Robert Prust and Mr. John Jenkins, current mayor and sheriff of Haverfordwest. Lord Kensington, another of the Edwardes family, was there, as were Lord Milford, the former Richard Philipps of Picton Castle, and Sir John Campbell, who had just inherited the estate and baronetcy of the Stackpole estate in the south of the county.

Campbell was just a year younger than Theo, and the two men felt a rapport with each other almost immediately, falling at once into easy conversation. The other members of the party consisted of Mr. Carswell of Camrose, a Sir Thomas Sinclair of Haverfordwest, Lord Tavernspite and a Sir Hugh Marchant whom Theo found the least friendly, and to be a rather morose character.

After the introductions, and having left the horses with the stable boys, the group spread out in a line and set off in silence across the huge, tree-dotted meadow, their footsteps leaving dark-green tracks in the dew-covered grass. Theo did not enjoy hunting, but had received instruction in the correct etiquette from an early age, and knowing all the rules to be followed, had no difficulty in taking his place along with the county's elite.

They had advanced about a quarter of a mile towards a folly set in a small valley, when Sir Hugh Marchant stopped to take off his boot to remove a piece of stone lodged in it, and causing him discomfort. By the time he had found and removed it, and put his boot back on, he had fallen some way behind the others, so grabbing his musket from where he had lain it on the ground, he trotted after them as fast as his squat, over-indulged body would allow. Still at some distance behind the line of hunters, he tripped on a large mole hill, and fell face forward into the wet grass. He had no trouble getting up, but as he did so, the cumbersome weapon discharged itself.

To Theo it seemed at first as though he had been kicked in the back by a horse, the force of the blow dropping him onto his knees. For a moment, he felt surprise more than anything, but then a tearing, nerve-screaming fire exploded in his right shoulder, racing and spreading across his back and all the way down through his arm to his fingers. He knelt there, aware the hunters were starting to crowd round him, but the only voice he heard was James's, crying out to him. He looked up. Despite the pain he was in, the last thing he wanted was to be the cause of a fuss, especially among strangers. Being the cause of attention such as this was something he envisaged experiencing only while playing a part acting on a stage, not in real life.

There had been occasions in the past when his reluctance to be at the centre of a commotion had led him to downplay any discomfort or hurt, to put on a brave face and pretend he was fine. He hoped in this case also to make light of the situation, so he squeezed his eyes shut, and tensed every muscle, willing himself to stand up so he could laugh as though nothing serious had happened. It did not work. The pain was too shocking, and his body would not respond; he could not get up. He opened his eyes again. James was sitting on the grass behind him, supporting him. Theo, a sickening inertia creeping over him, gave up the effort and sank back into his servant's lap.

Mr. Edwardes sent his manservant racing back to Haverfordwest with an urgent request that Mr. Nash, the physician, be waiting for them on their arrival back at Dunstable Hall. There was not much the other gentlemen could do other than get in the way, and there was not one among them who knew what to do to help alleviate Theo's pain, but before leaving the park and returning home, they went over to talk to the owner of the lead ball lodged in the visitor's body.

The man, Sir Hugh Marchant, was a man of considerable wealth by way of property and income, but also agreed by all to be a man of limited means where intelligence and common sense were concerned. He made light of what he had done. "My dear gentlemen. It was nothing more than an accident. It could have happened to any one of us. It's not as though I killed the fellow," he protested.

"I'm not at all sure that that may not be the case," argued Lord Tavernspite.

"Nonsense!" snapped Sir Hugh. "A mere flesh wound."

"You don't know that. And even if he survives, I shouldn't be surprised if he prosecutes you."

"Oh? And who's going to believe him, a stranger? And which of you would dare to testify against me? Anyway, I'm off. There's nothing I can do, and there's no point in all of us standing around, getting in the way. I'll send a servant round to the Hall later to check on the man." Sir Hugh shrugged and started to walk back to his horse.

The other gentlemen, men who treated weapons with great respect and the utmost care, and were horrified at Sir Hugh's attitude and arrogance, nevertheless knew he was right in one regard. None of them would be likely to testify against one of their own. Even so, they all left him to walk back to his horse alone, while Campbell, showing real concern, stayed to ask Edwardes if there was any way he could be of service. He had been sincere in his like of Mr. Potter, and was in no way satisfied that no real harm had been done. Mr. Edwardes thanked him, but pointed out the best thing they could do was to get Mr. Potter back to Dunstable Hall as soon as possible. Campbell agreed, and stayed just long enough to help Edwardes and James put Theo back on his horse, something they accomplished only after Theo had fainted twice during the process.

By now it was full daylight. The dew had dried away, and the grass was green and dry. The one hour they had taken to arrive at the park dragged out into over two hours for their return, and when they were about three miles from home, Theo slid off his horse. As they happened to be near a farm at that moment, Mr. Edwardes was able to get the farmer to lend them his own horse and wagon, and so, after almost another hour, they arrived back at Dunstable Hall.

Ever since her husband's manservant had returned with the news, Mrs. Edwardes had been trying to arrange for the arrival of the young accident victim. Under normal circumstances this would have proved to be no great problem for her, and everything would have been done and organized in an orderly fashion. This time, however, she was faced not only with the logistics of her task, but with her own emotional state, which was leading her to fluster, as she could not set her mind to concentrate on what she was doing.

Her problem was that it was almost sixteen years ago to the day that her dear husband Joseph had, at the age of two-and-thirty years, been brought back to this same house after a freak fox-hunting accident, and one month later had died. The memory was all too vivid. It was October, 1762.

"Mrs. Davies! I need you to prepare a room at once for a gentleman who has been wounded. Yes, yes..." she answered Mrs. Davies's request regarding which room. "It should be in a convenient place where he can be taken care of with the least trouble. Yes, the Blue Room I think. Yes, the Blue Room."

She started to leave the breakfast parlour where she had been sitting earlier with the children, then turned back. "Children! I want you to go upstairs with Miss Clifford. Your governess will see to you." She ushered the children and the governess out of the breakfast room, then hurried out into the entrance hall. "Dawkins, where's Dawkins?"

"I'm here Madam."

"Dawkins, we need to prepare an area where Mr. Nash can see to the gentleman's injury. Where do you think we can put him?"

"May I suggest the kitchen table, Madam?"

"The kitchen table! Where cook prepares our food? Oh Dawkins!"

"Madam, other than the potting shed or the dining salon table, I can't think of a more suitable place."

Mrs. Edwardes waved him away. "Yes, yes, the kitchen table it is then. Mr. Nash can see to him on the kitchen table. Now where is Mrs. Davies? I need her to... Oh yes, she's taking care of the preparation of the Blue Room."

She hurried back towards the breakfast room, waving her arms in agitation, then remembered something else, and hurried back into the entrance hall.

"We must delegate someone to nurse him. I understand he's young and handsome, so it can't be any of the housemaids."

Mrs. Davies reappeared having given instructions to a maid to prepare the Blue Room.

"Mrs. Davies, we need to select someone to nurse this young gentleman. Whom should it be? Have you any ideas?"

Mrs. Davies suggested Mrs. Glover. She was in her fifties, and a competent woman. Mrs. Glover was sent for, and despite her protestations regarding her nursing ability, was delegated to attend to the patient.

"Elizabeth! Where's Elizabeth?"

Mrs. Davies reminded her that this was the day of the week on which Elizabeth paid her visits to some of the poor and sick in the area, including staff who had grown too old to work for the family, but still retained their cottages on the estate. It would be several hours before she returned home.

"I do wish she were here. She'd be of such great help to me now." Mrs. Edwardes sighed, and tried to think of anything that should have been arranged but had not, and even to worry about some things that had. At that moment the butler appeared and announced that the young gentleman had been taken through the servants' entrance, and was now lying on cook's kitchen table.

James helped Mr. Nash remove Theo's heavy woollen jacket, his leather waistcoat and his white linen shirt. Bowls of hot water were then brought, and Mr. Nash prepared to take care of the wound, during the course of which he noticed a scar on Theo's right side. He adjusted his spectacles so as to take a closer look. "This young gentleman has been wounded before!" he announced. "Some time ago..." He looked again at the scar. "At least five years I should judge... Looks as though he was stabbed...Not by a rapier either... more like a heavy cavalry sabre." Puzzled, he looked across at Theo's manservant standing nearby, but James said nothing.

It took Mr. Nash a long time to complete his task, most of it being carried out without his patient being aware of it. As he worked, he pointed out to Mr. Edwardes and James the damage done. "See here." He pointed to where the ball had entered. "Because the musket was firing upwards from the ground, it went in here, but then went upwards at this angle." He drew a line up Theo's upper arm with his finger. "It's lodged near his collarbone." He straightened his back and looked at Mr. Edwardes over the top of his spectacles. "Your Mr. Potter is a lucky man. If that musket had fired any closer to him, he'd have suffered massive damage, at least shattering his bones beyond repair. As it is, he was far enough away, but even so the force of it has broken both his arm and his

51

collarbone quite badly." He prodded around the area. "Yes, definitely broken bones here... Clean breaks though, surprisingly... Considerable blood loss too, I should add." He looked up. "But it should all heal well as long as no infection sets in."

At last he was finished, and Theo, his right arm strapped to his chest -- where Mr. Nash said it would have to remain for at least eight weeks -- was carried on a door by four servants to a large chamber overlooking the Preseli hills. He was then laid down between Mrs. Edwardes's finest linen bed-sheets on the large bed designed and made by Mr. Chippendale himself.

CHAPTER 5

Mrs. Carswell was a woman of unwholesome aspect, her face encased in layers of lead-based powder to hide it, curdled as it was with childhood smallpox, and further soured by a lifetime of negative thoughts. Now, she was attending to her husband's recounting of the unfortunate accident, and wished she could be the one to be looking after the young gentleman, instead of Mrs. Edwardes, of whom she was jealous. A source of particular envy was the Edwardes family's proud lineage, something she herself could not boast of, and it irked her.

"Was he introduced to you?"

Yes, Mr. Carswell *had* been introduced to him.

"And did you have the chance to talk to him at all?"

Yes, Mr. Carswell did get to converse with him on the way to the deer park.

"Well, what sort of young gentleman is he? Is he a good-looking and well-mannered young man? About how old would you say he is?"

Yes, he did think that indeed he was a handsome young man with excellent manners, and as to age, he would guess him to be in his mid twenties.

"And he was the same young gentleman who rescued Mr. Edwardes's horse on the way over from Ireland?"

Yes, he was that same young gentleman.

It seemed that Mr. Carswell had no more information to give.

"But my dear!" Mrs. Carswell was not prepared to give up. "You said you had a conversation with him. What did you talk about?"

Mr. Carswell could not remember.

"Did he say from *where* in Ireland he came?"

Mr. Carswell could not recall that he had.

"What about his family? Is he married?"

As to the first, Mr. Carswell did not know, and as to the second, he believed he was not, but could not be sure, although he thought it unlikely.

Mrs. Carswell could not wait to impart all her exciting news to her friend, Mrs. Pollard, whose husband had not been privileged to be on the hunt. That there was not much news in the way of details to impart did not matter, and at the earliest opportunity she ordered her carriage, and set off to pay her respects to her friend, and by that evening everyone in Haverfordwest who was anyone, knew all the facts, including a few that were not -- the young gentleman was gravely ill, and on the point of expiring; he had been paralysed; the gentleman who had shot him had been so overwrought he had died of a heart attack. Thus the rumours had spread, and the ladies of Haverfordwest, shocked.

At Dunstable Hall, Mrs. Glover sat near the window. It looked out towards the Preseli Hills in the distance. She was mending a lace bonnet belonging to Mrs. Edwardes, but the sun had set, and although the eastern sky itself was still aglow with shades of pink and purple, it was getting too dark for her see her work. She looked across at her patient. He had been either asleep or unconscious for the last hour or so, and had not moved, so she decided it would be safe for her to leave him while she went to fetch a candle. When she returned she found Theo thrashing around and muttering, although she could not understand what he was saying, except for the odd word or two here and there. At first she was sure he was laughing, and she heard the word, Malvolio... she thought she missed the end of that word, but did catch, "act well... cousin..." and "Walter", but soon afterwards his mood changed, and he thrust his elbow up as though to defend himself.

"No! No!" His voice was clear and loud. This was followed by other anxious words that she could not understand, then, "jealous", followed some moments later by what sounded like "inheritance". He was quiet for a few minutes, during which he lowered his arm and seemed to be having a conversation, none of which Mrs. Glover could hear. Then he raised his arm again, shouting, "unarmed!" and his hand thrust forward, warding off some imaginary attacker. Mrs. Glover became so nervous with this outburst she sent a maid to fetch his manservant, who was eating a good dinner after not having had anything since his early breakfast.

James ran upstairs and went straight over to Theo, who was still trying to defend himself from his assailant. "Walter! Walter! What has...?"

James turned to Mrs. Glover. "It's all right, Mrs. Glover. I'll take over now. You may go. Thank you for your help. I'll let you know when I need you, if that's all right?"

Mrs. Glover, however, was inquisitive enough to want to hear more of what this young gentleman had to say. "Are you sure, Mr. O'Neil? Maybe I should stay in case you need me for anything." She went to sit down, but James opened the chamber door, and held it for the seamstress to leave. He was concerned about his master's rambling, and wondered what he had already said that Mrs. Glover had understood.

"Thank you, Mrs. Glover. There's no need." And he held his hand towards the door, inviting her to leave.

After she had gone, he went straight back to where Theo was still flailing his arm in the air. James sat down on the side of the bed, took hold of his master's hand and held it as tightly as he could. It was difficult as Theo was a strong man, and was resisting him with all of his strength.

"No! No!" Theo screamed at him, trying to push him away.

"Sir!" James leaned over him. "Sir! Mr. Potter Sir! Listen to me, Sir!"

He called to Theo for several minutes, but getting no response, let go of his hand and sat back, looking down at him. To James, Theo was more like a son -- always had been -- and he could not bear the thought of his own life should anything happen to him. He sighed and shook his head. "Oh Theo, my boy!" Anxious, he sat there waiting, and after a while Theo stopped his fight, his muscles relaxed, and he opened his eyes. His mind cleared, and he blinked and looked up at his servant.

"It's all right, Sir!" James took hold of Theo's hand again, and patted it in the same way he had done when Theo was a child and had fallen and hurt himself. "It's all over, Sir!" he comforted him. "You're safe." He put his hand on Theo's forehead. It was hot, and beads of warm sweat were dripping down onto the white linen pillow. Theo had developed a fever.

As soon as she had left the chamber, Mrs. Glover had gone straight to Mr. Edwardes to express her concern over her patient's condition. She felt the situation grave enough to disturb him at his dinner.

"He's developed a fever I'm sure, Sir," she told him.

Mr. Edwardes excused himself from the table, and rushed upstairs. Seeing Theo, he raced back down, and sent for Mr. Nash again.

Mrs. Glover, meanwhile, had joined the staff in the servants' parlour, where they were discussing the day's events over a mug of ale.

"Well?" they asked Mrs. Glover as soon as she appeared. They knew so little about the gentleman, having seen him only briefly, when he was being carried into the kitchen hours earlier. They were sorry for him, of course, and concerned he might die, but such excitement was rare, and the drama unfolding around them filled them with the desire to know every titillating detail. They sat around the table therefore, looking at the seamstress, and awaiting with eager anticipation whatever she could add to their scanty knowledge.

It was rare too for Mrs. Glover to be the centre of attention, so she was determined to benefit as much as possible from these few moments of expectation on the part of the rest of the staff. "Well," she began, having seated herself where all could see her. "Well, I was sitting there, and it was starting to get dark, and there's no moon yet tonight, so it wouldn't have been bright enough for me to see my work, and so I needed..."

"Yes, yes, Mrs. Glover," Dawkins interrupted. "Do please tell us about the man. Who is he? Is he likely to live?...There was a lot of blood when we carried him in."

"Yes, Mrs. Glover, do go on," echoed the others around the table.

"Well," Mrs. Glover began again. "His name is Mr. Potter. For those of you who have not seen him, he's in his mid-twenties I should say, and..." She looked at the housemaids seated before her. "You can tell he's well-favoured too... Well, I was sitting there, doing my sewing, and he was very quiet. To tell the truth, I wondered if he was still alive. I even put down my sewing, and went over to look at him, and he was still breathing, although I don't know whether he was sleeping or unconscious. That's when I went to get a candle. Then, by the time I came back with it he was moving around and mumbling. I declare he was even laughing! I couldn't understand a word he was saying, except the occasional one here or there. I did hear one word which sounded like Malvolios, or something like it."

"Malvolio?" The children were in bed, and their governess had come down from her own apartments to visit the staff in their parlour, being like everyone else, interested in knowing more about the day's events.

"Malvolio. Yes, that was it. Yes, I do declare! You're right Miss Clifford. It was Malvolio."

"What's a malvolio?" asked Dawkins.

"It's rather, '*who* is Malvolio?'" Miss Clifford explained. "He's a character in Mr. William Shakespeare's comedy, *Twelfth Night*."

"Oh, a comedy? Maybe that explains why he was laughing then," said Mrs. Glover, then remembered other words she had heard. "I heard him say something about someone I think he called, 'Walter', and he also said the word 'act'."

"He was probably referring to some play he'd seen then," Miss Clifford suggested.

"But then he began to get violent," Mrs. Glover told them.

"Violent? In what way, violent?" Dawkins wanted to know.

"He started raising his arm as though to protect himself from someone, and he was shouting: 'No! No!' Then I heard the words, 'inheritance', and something about jealousy. Then he was crying out that he was unarmed! Well, I have to tell you..." She looked around at everyone. "I was really becoming quite afraid as to what he'd do next, so that's when I came down to fetch his servant, Mr. O'Neil... I'm sure he has a fever," she added. "And Mr. Edwardes has sent for Mr. Nash again. Mr. O'Neil is looking after him now."

Now she had told all she knew, the staff all turned to one another to discuss everything they now knew about Mr. Potter, and Mrs. Glover's moment of undivided attention was over.

Elizabeth meanwhile, having heard the whole story of the accident, felt she was old enough and capable enough to be able to look after the young gentleman herself, and did her best to persuade her mother to allow her to replace Mrs. Glover.

"No, no, no, my dear Elizabeth," her mother insisted, "I can't allow it. I know you only too well. You'll worry so much about him, you'll do him no good at all, and will only make yourself ill with anxiety and be in constant fear of his dying... No. I can't allow it." And so Elizabeth was barred from even entering his room, and had to rely on Mrs. Glover and his servant for news as to his welfare.

It was over three days before the fever was brought under control, during which time the first piece of rumoured misinformation that had passed around the town almost became a truth. Theo had been very ill, and by the end of it, though on the way to recovery, he was left debilitated, requiring another week in bed before he had sufficient strength to walk even as far as the window. After that he improved daily until he was deemed fit enough to go downstairs to meet the family, something he had been dreading ever since he had discovered where he was, and had realized there would now be no escaping meeting them all.

This occurred while Mrs. Edwardes and the younger children were occupied in the drawing room, and a servant was sent to fetch Elizabeth, who was in the orangery, still working on painting the orange blossoms for her mother's birthday present.

Theo, pale and unsteady, accompanied Mr. Edwardes into the drawing room, where he was introduced to Mrs. Edwardes, whom he thanked for all her hospitality, care and attention.

"Oh Mr. Potter! You've no idea how relieved we all are to see you regaining your health! Such a terrible accident! We have been *so* worried about you."

She prattled on until Theo began to feel light-headed from standing, and Mr. Edwardes brought a chair, inviting him to be seated. He was still seated when Elizabeth was ushered into the room. She was carrying some flowers she had picked on her way.

Theo stood up, and Elizabeth came to where her cousin, Mr. Edwardes, was waiting to introduce him to her. She looked up at him, ready to smile and curtsy, and the flowers fell to the floor.

"Romeo!"

CHAPTER 6

It had been nearly two weeks since the embarrassing revelation, but Theo was still at Dunstable Hall, and still sleeping between Mrs. Edwardes's finest linen sheets in the bed made by Mr. Chippendale himself. Elizabeth, a sensible young lady, not given to hysterics, had not fainted at the discovery that Mr. Potter, the gentleman, and Romeo, the actor, were one and the same person, but her mother, the former Miss Eleanor Morris of Steynton, had; and during the ensuing confusion, no one had noticed that the fifteen-year-old under-housemaid, Jemima, who had been adding culm to the fire at the time, had left the room without being noticed. She did, however, run to Mrs. Davies, the housekeeper, to divulge the latest news.

On hearing this, Mrs. Davies, a long-employed and trusted servant of the Edwardes family, ordered the young girl, on pain of being dismissed, not to tell anyone anything of what she had heard, instructing her on the importance of loyalty to one's employers. The young housemaid, convinced she understood, therefore told everything only to her sister, Mrs. Carswell's personal maid, in strictest confidence.

The news that reached Mrs. Carswell later the next day washed away all trace of the envy from which she had been suffering ever since the accident, and she was more than relieved to discover that she herself had not been the unfortunate hostess to have been caring for some disreputable actor posing as a gentleman all this time. Within the hour she was in her carriage, and once again on the road to visit her friend and confidante, Mrs. Pollard.

"You'll never, ever believe what I have to tell you!" She had dashed into her friend's house, her hand shaking with excitement as she handed her pelisse and parasol to the waiting servant.

"And so he's just some despicable actor after all!" she concluded some time later. "Can you imagine it, having someone like that in your house, caring for him, having him sleep in your beds all this time, and all the while believing him to be a gentleman? The indignity of it! It's no wonder Mrs. Edwardes was overcome..." She paused to take a breath. "How *could* the Edwardes family be so deluded?" she added with a patronizing sniff. "In Herefordshire, where I come from, at least the gentry can tell the difference between the upper and lower classes of society!"

Mrs. Pollard was equally appalled, and was delighted to let Mrs. Carswell know she and her husband would be visiting friends in Dublin in the near future, and would undertake to find out more about this impostor.

"We'll get to the bottom of this," she promised, "and we'll expose the scoundrel."

But Mrs. Carswell had not yet finished. She wagged her finger at her friend. "And you know something else, my dear Mrs. Pollard? I'd wager that so-called manservant of his is nothing more than his accomplice. He probably goes out at nights after dark, and picks the pockets of innocent folks, just so the two of them can maintain their lavish lifestyle!"

Mrs. Pollard agreed it could well be the case.

"All those airs and graces! Who *did* he think he was?"

"Well he's no Mr. David Garrick of Drury Lane!" said Mrs. Pollard.

Mrs. Carswell had never heard of either. "Exactly!"

Having further exchanged predictions as to the way in which society's attitude, or their own at least, might be towards the deluded Edwardes family now, given their obvious lack of propriety and judgment in all this; and having discussed the deplorable and degrading occupation of acting in general, the ladies parted, but not before Mrs. Carswell had received a promise to be enlightened on Mrs. Pollard's return from Ireland. Mrs. Carswell then returned home, confident in her new-found superiority over the unfortunate Mrs. Edwardes.

While Mrs. Edwardes had indeed been hysterical at first over the prospect of enduring the embarrassing disapproval of those in her circle, but especially that of Mrs. Carswell, whom she despised more than anyone, she allowed herself to be persuaded by her cousin that her fears were unfounded, and that Mr. Potter should not be banished from Dunstable Hall.

As Mr. Edwardes explained to her, he himself had invited the Smock Alley Theatre troupe to come to Haverfordwest, and was well aware they were respectable actors, not vagabond street players of the type to be found ranting at fairgrounds and racetracks. For this reason, if for no other, Mr. Potter was welcome to stay in his house -- although he himself had at first wondered at what he considered to be a deception on Theo's part in not revealing his dual identity. On further consideration, however, he had come to the conclusion that, had all gone according to plan, the young man he thought of as a gentleman, would have returned to Ireland the day after the hunt, and for him to have gone into details regarding his alter ego would have been unnecessary, so Theo was forgiven for not having explained himself.

Even so, Mr. Edwardes had decided to engage in some investigating of his own, and was happy and relieved to receive reassurance from his friend, Thomas Ryder, the manager of the Smock Alley Theatre, that Mr. Potter was a wealthy gentleman who, being also an actor, was what was known as a 'gentleman player', and a young man worthy of their respect.

So Theo remained at Dunstable Hall, and as his health improved, he began walking in the park surrounding the mansion, at first accompanied by James, then later by Elizabeth and her elder sister. Sometimes he would go down to the stables on his own, lingering there for a half hour or more, talking to, and stroking the big Irish gelding which, in turn, became so used to his visits that he came to recognize Theo's footsteps, and would start snickering at the sound of them. As the groom remarked to Mr. Edwardes, the two seemed to share a special bond. It was something that did not surprise James at all.

As he grew stronger, he would walk into Haverfordwest whenever Mr. Nash deemed it necessary to check on his progress, and while there, liked to take the opportunity to call in at The Blue Boar Inn, where he became friends with Stephen George, the innkeeper. Stephen George, like many others, had heard about Theo's accident, so was delighted to see again the actor who had performed at his establishment a month earlier, and they would sit in George's private parlour chatting over a tankard of ale.

As for Elizabeth, the great warmth and attraction she had felt towards the actor when she had seen him in *Romeo and Juliet*, had in no way diminished over the intervening period. She had even come to think of him with affection, and had continued to dream about him much of the time after. To discover that the young man who had been occupying the blue room all that time, was the one towards whom she had held all these feelings, was almost impossible to believe, and it was with the greatest of pleasure that she looked forward to their taking walks together.

Now too, in the time since she had first met him, and had dropped flowers at his feet, and he had started to share their home with them in other ways -- sharing their meals, and spending evenings in their company -- Elizabeth's innate need to fuss over, and care for others had arisen, especially when she saw him struggling with his one hand to achieve what normally required two; but with James ever at his master's side, she had had to be content to watch his servant attend to him. This was probably just as well, as the word had spread about the house that some not infrequent explosive outbursts had been overheard when Theo's frustration had got the better of him, and her mother had been right; she did worry about him.

While Elizabeth looked forward to their walks, Theo himself was also delighted to have the company of such a well-educated and agreeable young lady and, as their walks grew longer, he found himself engaging in long and interesting conversations with her. Intelligent and well-read, she was able to discuss matters of interest to them both. He even sat for her while she painted his likeness.

"Have you ever sat before?" she asked him.

"Yes, once."

"Oh? Was it a full-length portrait?"

"No. A miniature."

"That requires a special talent. Was it on ivory?"

"Yes."

Was the painter well known?"

"Yes."

Seeing Theo seemed unwilling to discuss it further, she changed the subject. "You have an excellent profile," she commented. "You have a high forehead which bespeaks intelligence, and a fine nose." She did not tell him she admired everything about it, and him.

Theo grinned. "I didn't know noses could be fine." He ran his finger down his own. "It has a bump in it. Doesn't that ruin it?"

"No. It just adds character. Now sit still, or you're going to look very odd indeed -- and don't look at me; it's your profile I'm trying to paint."

"I'd draw your likeness too, but I'm afraid you'd find yourself insulted. I'm no artist... although I'm told I have an elegant hand at writing."

"In that case, when you return to Ireland, you can write to me... that's if you wish to."

"Nothing would give me greater pleasure; I'm a good correspondent."

The thought of his leaving soured Elizabeth's mood, and sitting there painting him, but knowing he was going to disappear from her life soon, ended her enthusiasm for the project, and she put down her brush.

"Let's go for a walk. I'm tired of painting."

Theo stood up. "As you wish, but before we go, do you think you could do something for me please? I need to let Mr. Ryder know when to expect me back in Dublin... And I do need to let him know as soon as possible, as he was expecting me to perform right after my return... At the moment all the information he has -- unless Mr. Edwardes has written to him in the meantime -- is from the message James gave to one of the members of my troupe before they returned to Ireland... and that was quite a while ago now." He smiled. "So, if I dictate, would you write the letter for me please?"

Elizabeth looked at him. She had noticed also that he had a crooked smile, which she found to be an even further attraction. Now, only too glad to be of help, she smiled back, sat down at the desk, and Theo sat next to her and dictated a letter in which he apologised for not writing sooner, and told his manager to expect him back in Dublin just before Christmas. He concluded with the hope that his troupe had arrived home safely, and was sorry for any problems he may have caused.

While happy to have been of service, the message she was obliged to write made Elizabeth even more dispirited. "There," she said, "that's done. Now can we go for our walk?"

"Of course."

It was cloudy, but warm for the time of year, and they set off in the direction of a nearby copse which, now devoid of its canopy of leaves, allowed the winter sun to warm the earth and ferns below, so ground and plants alike emitted a similar earthy smell. They walked in silence for a while, then Elizabeth asked the question she had long been waiting to put to him.

"Why is it that, when you're a man of independent means, you became an actor? Gentlemen don't become actors, or normally engage in other such common pursuits... Gentlemen manage their estates."

"Mr. Thomas Sheridan, Richard Brinsley's father, is a gentleman, and he became an actor... Anyway, I don't have an estate to manage."

Elizabeth ignored the reference to Mr. Sheridan. "That's not to say you can't afford to purchase one, I understand."

"I don't *want* to own an estate."

"Not *want* to own your own land and property?"

"I wouldn't want to care for it all, but most of all I wouldn't want the welfare and comfort of so many people to be in my hands." He did not add that living the idle life of a gentleman, such as that lived by people such as her cousin -- much as he liked and respected him otherwise -- would bore him to distraction.

Elizabeth was puzzled. "Which people?"

"Which people? Why! All the servants, the tenants, the farmers and their families who would be dependent on my wise management of the estate, and hence on their means of earning an adequate wage on which to maintain an acceptable quality of life. Wrong attitudes and decisions on my part could -- and I've seen this happen -- cause them to lead a cold, poor and miserable existence."

"But my cousin and most of his friends treat their tenants and servants with great consideration and thoughtfulness."

"I'm of the opinion that most people don't want to be *treated* in any way. We *treat* our dogs well too."

Elizabeth was silent for a minute. "You still haven't told me why you became an actor," she reminded him.

"Because I can pretend to be someone I'm not... And because I'm good at it," he answered with a grin.

"But that's still not a good enough answer. You could equally have chosen to be a respectable clergyman without anyone questioning your actions... and I think you would have been good at that too."

Theo sighed. "My! How did we manage to get so serious here? Anyway, the answer to that is that I can in no way see me spending my life piously exhorting others not to engage in sins of which I myself am guilty. A truly religious man must surely have to live comfortably with his own conscience."

"And you're not religious?"

Theo laughed, but did not reply.

"Well, what about the army then?" She stood back, estimating his qualities as a soldier. "You'd certainly look dashing in your regimentals."

Theo made an extravagant and majestic bow. "Why, thank you, Ma'am," he answered, and remained bowing.

"You may rise, Sir," Elizabeth laughed.

Theo did not move.

"Or are you rooted, Sir, in your present, uncomfortable

pose?"

Theo pretended to be an old man, and supporting his back with his hand, struggled to straighten himself. They were both laughing, looking at each other. He looked away. He had already detected Elizabeth's feelings towards him, and now, for an instant, he had also felt an emotion he was not at all ready to embrace. Having noticed while bowing that her feet were wet with dew, he suggested they return to the house. "Your feet are wet. You could catch cold."

Elizabeth threw up her hands. "Oh why is it men are always treating us women as delicate little creatures who will get ill, fall into a decline, and die just because we got our feet wet? Anyway, your own feet are just as wet as mine!"

"I suppose it's because we feel the need to protect you."

"I wish I were a man. I like to protect too."

Theo studied her. He had already decided she had a desirable figure. "I don't think you'd make a very good man." He shook his head. "No, I just can't see it at all... Not at all," he repeated, smiling.

Elizabeth looked back at him. "Nor you a good woman either if it comes to that... Much too tall." They were both laughing again. "I like the way you laugh with your eyes. A man who laughs with his eyes, laughs with his heart also. A man who laughs only with his lips, doesn't; he's just being polite."

"That's indeed a profound comment," said Theo, then added, teasing her, "for a woman."

"That's because I *am* a profound woman."

"That I believe you are," he answered, his tone serious. Then, claiming his shoulder was hurting, said he was tired and needed to go home.

CHAPTER 7

It was December, and several balls were being hosted in the town, it being the height of the season. The Edwardes family, socially active, attended whenever possible, along with Miss Edwardes and Elizabeth, who had been out in public since her eighteenth birthday.

Although Mr. Nash had declared Theo well enough now to return to Ireland, he was invited to stay on through the festive season, and as a current member of the household, was asked if he would like to accompany the family to the next grand function, which would be the Christmas ball.

Theo knew Mr. Ryder would be missing him at the theatre, and that he ought return to Dublin, but although declared fit enough to return to Ireland, it did not mean he was fit enough yet to return to the strenuous life of performing. His body was so unfit after all he had been through, and his arm still so weak and stiff, that acting out a duel on stage, for example -- something he was called upon to do on many occasions -- would be beyond him for quite a while yet. With that in mind he felt free to accept the invitation to stay on.

"I should like that very much," he said, referring to the ball, "although I myself won't be able to dance yet, unfortunately." He tried to lift his arm above his head, and winced. "The dances in vogue right now will be beyond me, I'm afraid."

Elizabeth assured him it would not matter. She would be delighted to have him escort her regardless. "You don't imagine me unable to get a partner without you surely, Mr. Potter?" she teased him.

Theo smiled and bowed. "I think that most unlikely."

This time he wrote his own letter to his manager, and let him know it would now be just after New Year before he would be back home, but he still would not be able to perform in any plays requiring taking part in duels.

The balls held in Haverfordwest were not country dances. Attended by the county's elite, including several local baronets and two of the county's lords, they were the scene of the height of fashion and of elegance, and Theo, who had not been to a ball for some time -- the last one having being held in the Rotunda, in Dublin -- looked forward to the evening with pleasure.

The evening arrived, and Mrs. Edwardes seemed to be having more difficulty than usual in preparing herself. Her dress, her pannier, her wig, her shoes, her pelisse, everything, it seemed, was creating a problem of one sort or another, and her personal maid was relieved when her mistress was seated in the carriage at last.

Elizabeth had caused her own maid no such anxieties and, elegant in a magnificent dress designed in the latest Paris fashion, was already seated with her sister for several minutes before being joined by their still agitated mother.

"I really do think Mr. Potter should have accompanied us in the carriage," Mrs. Edwardes told her daughters. "He's not well enough to be riding a horse. What if the horse...? My fan! I've forgotten my fan!" She tapped on the roof of the coach, which was already in motion. The four matching Hanoverian horses were reined to a stop, and one of the two footmen sent back to fetch her fan. A few minutes later, they were on their way again. "Where was I? Oh yes! Mr. Potter. I'm so concerned for his safety. Why the other day I saw him..."

"Mother, I'm sure you need not be worried. Cousin Edwardes says Mr. Potter is an excellent horseman, and besides, he's given him Lancer to ride, and Lancer is the most well-behaved horse in the stables. Besides," she smiled, "can you imagine a young man such as Mr. Potter, arriving at the ball in a *carriage*? I'm sure he'd never wish to be seen descending from a coach at the entrance to the ballroom. He'd consider it most unmanly."

Mrs. Edwardes tutted. "You young people. So much pride..." she complained, and determined to have the last word on the subject added, "but worrier that *you* are, Elizabeth, I'm surprised *you're* not the one to have been fussing about his safety ever since he left the house."

"With cousin Edwardes at his side, and as it's such a short ride, I've assured myself he'll arrive at the ball unharmed."

Mrs. Edwardes tossed her head, and changed the subject. "Ever since that young under-housemaid, Jemima, was dismissed for gossiping about Mr. Potter being an actor, the servants have been much more discreet -- so much so that I don't believe the word has spread yet about his being a gentleman as well." She stroked the plumes of her fan. "This will be a good opportunity to clarify his position. Cousin Edwardes must introduce him, and..." She prattled on until their carriage, after waiting in line to draw up to the entrance, came to a standstill, and the footman opened the door and prepared the step so the ladies could alight. It was one of the few coaches being used to transport guests to the ball, and that only because they lived some way out of town.

Those who lived within the precincts of Haverfordwest

arrived in a much simpler manner, in their sedan chairs, each supported by two liveried bearers, one in the front and one at the rear, and the chairs of the more wealthy were most elaborate. They had velvet cushions inside, carved figures on their roofs, their sides adorned with colourful family crests or other intricate designs, while their bearers wore matching livery.

Mr. Edwardes and Theo, who had not fallen off his horse, were waiting at the entrance, ready to escort the ladies into the ballroom. Mrs. Edwardes took her husband's arm, and Theo offered his to Elizabeth. It was the closest she had come to him, and her heartbeat increased to the extent it left her breathless and almost light-headed.

As a result of Mrs. Edwardes's failure to prepare herself for the ball without keeping the coach and horses waiting for a considerable period, they had arrived at the same time as almost everyone else, so had to stand in line, waiting to be announced on their entry into the ballroom. As they waited they could hear above the general hum of voices around them the cries of the approaching sedan bearers calling out to any pedestrians in their path to move out of their way. "Have care, Sir!" or "By your leave, Sir!"

Elizabeth was clutching Theo's arm, rather than just resting her hand on it in ladylike fashion, and he looked down at her. She was more beautiful tonight than he had ever seen her, and he was proud to have such a partner to escort into the ball. He was pleased as well that she was following the new fashion of younger women, set by the beautiful singer and actress, Miss Anne Catley, who spurned wigs -- as did Theo himself -- and wore her hair au naturel, or "Catleyfied," as it was known. He sighed; an excellent dancer himself, he regretted he would not be able to share the evening with her in this way. "Are you all right, Miss Elizabeth?" he asked.

Elizabeth, made aware of her clutching hand, released it.

"Why yes, thank you. I'm just so excited, that's all. I love these occasions: so many acquaintances to talk to, the music, the dancing. It's all so invigorating, don't you agree?"

"I do indeed."

Mrs. Carswell had arrived early. Arriving in this way gave her the opportunity to secure a seat from which she could assess all those who entered, and comment on their demeanour, fashionableness, taste -- anything that gave her the chance to pass judgment, usually critical in content. Her friend, Mrs. Pollard was still away in Dublin, and was not due to return until the New Year. This left her with only her daughter with whom to share her commentaries.

The Miss Carswell, slightly younger than Elizabeth, was a lady of medium height and passable figure, with a face that would have been pretty, had she not maintained on it a constant expression of disdain. Miss Carswell held her chin at a haughty angle, high and tucked in towards her neck, a pose that had the unfortunate effect of making it appear her chin was double -- an unattractive feature in a lady of so young an age, or of any age, for that matter.

Hers was the sort of expression and of attitude towards others -- common to those who are insecure in their own position in society -- that led her to look down on as many others as possible, while being obsequious towards those above her. The easy manners common to true gentlefolk were a quality neither Miss Carswell nor her mother had managed to achieve during their short acquaintance with the society of which they were now a part.

"Oh my!" commented Mrs. Carswell from behind her fan. "Martha! Look! Poor Lady Walters! Does she realize how excessively drab she looks? And her wig! The style is an abomination, I do declare, and..." Her attention was drawn from the poor Lady Walters to the next people in line to be introduced.

"Lord and Lady Kensington."

"My, my, poor Lord Kensington," she remarked, "he's definitely beginning to show his age... and it's obvious he's suffering from the gout. Well, at least they didn't have far to come. Their townhouse is practically next door."

"Lieutenant Thomas Foley."

"Martha! We *must* be introduced! Such a dashing gentleman in his navy uniform! So young too! And obviously not married yet!"

"Sir John Campbell."

Mrs. Carswell patted her daughter on the arm with her fan. "What a handsome man!... Poor young man. His father died only last year, you know. Still..." Mrs. Carswell's sympathy for the young Sir John was of short duration. "He did inherit his father's title, and that beautiful estate down in Stackpole." She grabbed her daughter's hand. "My dear, my life would be complete if only we could secure him for you."

Before Martha could reply, Mr. William Edwardes and Mrs. Joseph Edwardes were announced, followed by Miss Edwardes and her beau, then her sister Miss Elizabeth and... Mrs. Carswell was so concerned with drawing her daughter's attention to Miss Elizabeth's attractive young escort, she missed the announcement of his name.

"My dear Martha! Who *is* that handsome young man accompanying Miss Elizabeth? I've never seen him before, but I do declare he's the finest-looking young man we have seen enter the room this evening, don't you agree?"

Martha who had not attended the performance of Romeo and Juliet -- having been away at the time, so had not seen Theo before -- agreed, and her mother continued. "We *must* be introduced. You *must* dance with him Martha."

She chattered on, imagining her daughter securing such an attractive young man for a husband -- providing, of course, that he had an adequate fortune to go with his looks. Her fear was that Mr. Edwardes would not introduce them.

"Oh, but surely Mr. Edwardes won't hesitate to come over and introduce him. Yes, yes, of course," she assured herself. "Yes, I'm positive he'll do that."

Martha agreed again, even she considering him to be a most acceptable-looking young man, with whom it would be agreeable to dance, and on whom to make a positive impression.

Mrs. Carswell was also of the belief that the odious actor who had taken advantage of the Edwardes family's generosity with his brazen pretence of being a gentleman, would have been removed from their sight and their property as soon as he had been exposed -- banished to the care of his fellow actors, should they be still around, or if not, to whatever charity was willing to take him in, or perhaps even to gaol. She had also discovered the actor's name was Potter; a name worthy of her scorn and derision. "Potter!" she had exclaimed. "Potter! My, my! I wonder what he does when he's not carousing with his fellow strollers!" She had laughed at her own wit as she added, "making pots in his gypsy bender, I do declare."

She waited for Mr. Edwardes to introduce the fine-looking young gentleman, who had escorted Miss Elizabeth into the ball, but there were many introductions to be made, and by the time the musicians had started playing, the two men had still not made their way to where Mrs. Carswell and her daughter were sitting.

The dance started, and Theo noticed several young men, obviously of Elizabeth's acquaintance, approach, but then turn away when they discovered she was accompanied by someone else. He stood up. "I think I'd better leave you, at least for a while," he told her, "otherwise you're never going to have a partner with whom to dance this evening."

Elizabeth agreed, and Theo left the ballroom and went outside. Moments later, she was dancing.

Mrs. Carswell, determined not to lose sight of the young gentleman, was shocked. "Martha! That young man, did you see? He stood up, but instead of asking Miss Elizabeth to dance, he walked away! He even left the room! How strange! Still, he must have been called away on urgent business."

However, when before the next, and each following dance, the gentleman continued to disappear, Mrs. Carswell became even more puzzled. "I wonder why he doesn't dance," she said to her daughter. "How very odd!"

She was still wondering why the gentleman and his partner were not dancing together, and why Miss Elizabeth continued to dance with others, when she noticed Mr. Edwardes and the strange young gentleman approaching. She arranged her dress, patted it with her fan, and waited for the introduction.

"Mrs. Carswell..." Mr. Edwardes was at his most genial. "May I introduce our guest, Mr. John Theophilus Potter to you."

Theo offered a friendly smile, and bowed.

Mrs. Carswell, taken by a level of surprise she never could have imagined, moved her lips, mumbling something inaudible.

Mr. Edwardes, not previously introduced to Miss Carswell, then waited for her mother to make the introduction. There was none, and after a few moments of silence, he smiled and bowed, as did Theo, and the two men continued their round of introductions, Mr. Edwardes only vaguely surprised by Mrs. Carswell's lack of manners. Theo did not comment.

The rest of Mrs. Carswell's evening was spent in thought, divulging to her absent friend, Mrs. Pollard, all the latest scandal regarding the odious Mr. Potter: how he was not only still residing at Dunstable Hall, but had behaved with appalling manners towards Miss Elizabeth at the ball by not deigning to dance with her even though he was her escort. She was convinced now that the Edwardes family, whom she had respected hitherto, even if she had disliked them, had disgraced themselves by continuing to associate with such a low-class rogue, and Mrs. Pollard would be the first to hear her opinion.

Despite not being able to dance, Theo enjoyed the ball. Being sociable and of an amiable temperament, he was happy in the company of others, and willing to take part in conversation, and in banter. As many discovered during the course of the evening, he was also witty, lively, and amusing -- the sort of person much in demand at society gatherings where the ladies were so often deprived of such amusement, the conversation of most gentlemen being limited to the subject of hunting.

So it was that, the art of good conversation being a valuable attribute in any cultured society, Theo soon found himself accompanying the Edwardeses to some of the county's large estates, whose owners made a point of including him in their invitations to their many parties and soirees, where he could usually be persuaded to perform one of his hilarious monologues. These he would adapt to suit his audience, and even Lord Tavernspite found it worth his while to stay awake to listen to them. Those who invited him did so, not only because of what he had to contribute to their gatherings, but because he was a most likeable and charismatic young man, with excellent manners and obvious good breeding. They were well-acquainted with his situation as both actor from Dublin's famous theatre, and as a gentleman of means, and had no reason to be troubled in the slightest by it. Many indeed, counted some of the Drury Lane actors among their most intimate friends.

Mrs. Carswell, meanwhile, was confident and feeling superior in the belief that she, and only she -- apart from the Edwardes family -- knew the shocking truth about Mr. Potter, and could not wait for her friend, Mrs. Pollard, to return from Ireland with all the sordid details, with which she would have the greatest pleasure of exposing him.

CHAPTER 8

It was well past New Year, and Theo knew it was time for him to leave Dunstable Hall. He had been the guest of the Edwardes family since mid October, and although he felt the family was as comfortable with his presence as he was with theirs, he did not wish to outstay his welcome. He wanted as well to get back to his theatre, where he could release all his pent-up energy by acting again, although he was becoming a bit worried that he had still not regained the dexterity necessary to perform the spectacular fencing displays for which he was so well known back at Smock Alley. He and James had been out in the meadow regularly, practising and performing mock duels, but he had even dropped his sword on occasion, and was worried lest some permanent damage had been done after all.

On this particular morning, he looked out of his chamber window -- as he had done so many time before -- and gazed at Preseli Mountain. A cold winter sun was just rising over the southern end of the range. A bank of bluish-grey cumulous clouds hovered over the eastern sky, and although he could not see the sun itself, its light spread out through openings in the clouds like the delicate, silk rays of a lady's fan. He had heard the local people refer to this phenomenon as 'God be here', and he watched as the rays strengthened or faded as the clouds meandered by.

Knowing the time had come for him to leave, an unexpected question had arisen during the past few weeks, and had persisted in his thoughts. The question was, "Why am I feeling ambivalent now the time has come for me to leave?" He had even spent nights pacing around his room in an anxious state of indecision because of it, and Theo did not live well with indecision.

His problem was that, while he had more or less recovered physically, the memory of his being shot had become interwoven with another event in his life -- an event that had taken place six years ago, and in which he had also nearly been killed. After that first attack he had been able to lock the memory of it away in a corner of his mind -- in a sort of little Pandora's box -- and had used his acting career to keep it locked away. The theatre had become his life, and he had been able to forget his own by entering those of the characters he played. This second attack, however, seemed to have overwhelmed him; it had shaken his self-confidence, and he felt vulnerable and even nervous. For someone with such an independent spirit, this was more than just unsettling; it invaded his consciousness at all hours, and he did not know what to do about it. He had never been a nervous man before. Even James had noticed an unaccustomed edginess in him, and it worried him too.

"Would returning to Dublin be the right thing to do?" he wondered. "Can I simply go back to my acting, and lose myself again? Am I ready?" But he felt the lid of the little Pandora's box begin to lift, and its revelations frightened him. He thought of the alternative. Maybe to stay here in the comfort of Haverfordwest for a while would help his mind to calm down.

Although Haverfordwest, like all towns, had some problems with law and order, with drunkenness and fisticuffs in some of the less affluent areas, it was nevertheless a haven

81

of calm and order compared with Dublin. Although he loved Dublin, the city was not always a safe place to walk around, and men usually carried a weapon for protection at all times. It was a city where feuds between rival areas could -- and often did -- bring the city to a standstill for days, while streets became battlegrounds and created situations from which even the sheriff found it prudent to stay away.

Two groups were known in particular, being families of tailors in one area, called the Liberty Boys, and families of butchers in another area, called the Ormond Boys. The feuds between these two groups were bloody and cruel, the tailors being known even to take their prisoners and hang them by their jaws on their own meat hooks -- this in retaliation for the butchers who used their cleavers to slice the tendons on the legs of the tailors, rendering them cripples for life. The feud had raged for years, and showed no sign of coming to an end.

Theo looked out on the peaceful landscape of Preseli and over the town of Haverfordwest. He could not imagine anything so barbarous happening here, and he never felt fear when he walked around, and never saw the necessity for carrying a weapon. Most gentlemen, of course, carried, or rather wore, a sword as a status symbol, but Theo did not do that either.

In contrast to his situation in Haverfordwest, he thought about the time in Dublin, when he had come face to face with a well-known fighter by the name of Fitzgerald, a man who delighted in making a sport of standing in the middle of a narrow road in the city, and forcing any man who came upon him to either walk in the mud, or push him out of the way. Theo, with his abhorrence of violence, had not considered himself a coward when he had chosen to walk in the mud. To have chosen the other option would have meant fighting a duel with Fitzgerald.

While he had been standing at the window, the sun's

round face had climbed from behind the clouds, and had filled his room with its golden light. Theo continued to stand there, watching as the houses of Haverfordwest turned from a dark cobalt to a mellow shade of yellow -- the start of a new day -- and by the time the sun was high in the sky, they would have become their usual dazzling white.

In Haverfordwest there were no young roving aristocrats to fear either, as there were in Dublin. When walking through that city he -- like many other young men of his class -- had needed to be wary of these young men who, known as Bucks or Bloods, and were members of the notorious Hellfire Club, enjoyed vandalising the property of tradesmen and injuring innocent citizens, and he remembered all too vividly being forced into a duel with one of them. Many had their own individual brand of harassment by which they were particularly known. There were those called the 'Sweaters', who liked to hold up individuals and make them sweat with fear before taking their valuables.

Then there were those 'Pinking-dindies'. These young members of the gentry would cut the end off the scabbards of their swords, leaving the sharp point exposed. They would then walk around the city, pricking the points of their swords into anyone they did not like the look of -- young men such as Theo often falling into that category -- and such a sword-cut could do significant damage; it could even kill.

He thought too that, even though his most recent experience of violence had come about here in Pembrokeshire, it was an unusual event, unlikely to be repeated, and to stay here would mean not having to be on his guard at all times, which his return to Dublin would require, especially as he was so well known there. What bothered him now, though, was that although he himself had suffered from violence from the notorious Hellfire Club, it had never led him to consider leaving Dublin out of fear of them, nor had the violence of

Dublin in general ever troubled him overmuch in the past. That it should now, and that he did not feel he could even face it in his present state of mind, was something he could not understand, or come to terms with.

Then there was the Dublin theatre itself, with which Theo now began to see potential problems that had not occurred to him before. Maybe, he thought, it was his recent absence from Smock Alley that allowed him to see these problems, which would have been invisible to him while he was involved with the theatre on a daily basis as he had been for the past six years.

To begin with, Mr. Sheridan, a major attraction to Dublin audiences, had left recently to join his son, Richard Brinsley, at Drury Lane, in London. Without his presence the theatre would be sure to suffer. Then, right before Theo had left on this trip, Mr. Ryder had told him he would be giving up Smock Alley in the coming year, because he had found running both it and the Crow Street theatre too stressful. He was planning, he had told Theo, to hand it over to Mr. Richard Daly, whom Theo did not know personally.

Of course he would still be expected to act for Tom Ryder at the Crow Street theatre, so would his staying here in Haverfordwest until he had recovered add even more to Mr. Ryder's woes? As one of Mr. Ryder's most talented actors, he was looked to to bring in audiences, so by staying in Haverfordwest he himself could well be contributing to the theatre's downfall.

On the other hand, the Edwardes family, he knew, was fond of him, and he felt comfort and security in their presence, something he thought would help put his mind to rest if he were to stay here long enough.

He continued to stand at the window, gazing out over the countryside and watching the greys of the night turning into the many colours of the day. One thing he was sure of at least, and that was that he could not give up his acting career permanently; it meant far too much to him, and there was no doubt in his mind at all that at some point in the near future he would return home to Dublin.

There was one last consideration, and that was the time of year. Crossing the Irish Sea could be a perilous undertaking at any time, but now, in winter, the danger was much greater. The winter storms and gales coming in off the Atlantic Ocean left many ships wrecked on the exposed and rocky shores of both Wales and Ireland, and Theo remembered being told how the famous actor, Theophilus Cibber, had died in such a wreck, back in '58, while on his way to perform at the Smock Alley Theatre. Caution could well suggest he wait until later in the season, when the weather became more settled.

For hours he talked himself through his options, coming at last to a decision. Sure in the knowledge that his manager would take him back when he was fully recovered both mentally and physically, he would find himself a place to stay here in Haverfordwest until that time.

CHAPTER 9

The Edwardes family, and Elizabeth in particular, were delighted that Theo had decided to stay in Haverfordwest at least for the time being, although Elizabeth was led to wonder how he would ever occupy himself there. Acquainted with him long enough now, she realized he would most likely never be persuaded to adjust to, or even consider adopting the lifestyle of a gentleman of independent means. Furthermore, unlike any of the gentleman with whom she was acquainted, Theo seemed to have this almost urgent need to be always *achieving* something. He displayed an extraordinary energy, requiring constant expression in creative and physical activity; and as she came to know him better, it had occurred to her he was probably one of those people, who have that unusual ability to succeed in whatever they turn their hands to, and would always be looking to learn and do something new, needing to be occupied gainfully. It was something she had noticed when, during his recovery at Dunstable Hall, she had watched him making the rounds of the estate, stopping to chat with the various employees going about their daily tasks, and had learned that, on his wanderings, he had even prevailed upon the estate's artisans to demonstrate their skills to him; and it had all led her to suspect that to be forced to lead a life of what was pleasurable idleness to others with similarly large financial assets, would bore to distraction a man such as Theo. In addition to all this, she had noticed that during those first two months of his stay with her family, his inability to do anything physical other than go for walks had often left him, in her opinion, overly frustrated and impatient. He had, she concluded, a restless spirit.

Soon Mr. Edwardes and Mrs. Edwardes themselves came to accept the reality of Theo's disposition as well, and although bemused at how a young man with so much money and gentlemanly upbringing would not wish to follow a life befitting his situation, they became reconciled to Theo's idiosyncrasies, and set about helping him settle into the town in whatever way would suit him.

Already feeling much quieter in his mind, now he had made his decision, it was Theo himself who, wasting no time, found and rented a house he had seen. It was a fairly new house on Tower Hill and, classical in design, it presented both on the interior and exterior a comfortable and simple elegance suited to his tastes. It was large and well built, and the rooms spacious. In addition, it had a small garden to the rear. He hired a housekeeper he felt he could trust, then left the rest of the hiring to her and to James. In the end, his household staff consisted of a cook, a scullery maid, and a housemaid, in addition to James and the housekeeper. He himself saw to the furnishings, and hired a cabinet maker to construct bookshelves in the largest room on the ground floor, which he designated as his library, something he was looking forward to creating as soon as possible. It was to be the most important room in the house. The probability that he would be returning to Ireland at some time in the near future did not matter; a library was something he could always take with him wherever he went. Besides, it could always be added to what he already had in his own library back home in Dublin.

These things achieved, he gave himself the task of looking for and buying a horse, something he had not done while living in Dublin city. He knew the horse he wanted, and that was the one he had saved on the boat, and which Mr. Edwardes now owned. When he first approached Mr. Edwardes about the matter, though, the gentleman was adamant he did not want to part with the animal, but Theo persisted, and finally won his case. The horse did, after all, have a defect, for as Theo had predicted, the hair on its foreleg had grown back white -- a blemish on an otherwise beautiful animal. It was obvious the horse too was particularly attached to Theo, because every time he visited the stable to see him, it nuzzled up to him in a way it did to no one else. Mr. Edwardes did make one stipulation however, which was that should Theo go home to Ireland, then the horse should be returned to him. And so Theo took possession of the big gelding, and named him Hercules.

Theo had been fully settled in his new house for several weeks. Everything had been organized and arranged to his satisfaction, and on this particular day in late spring,1779, he sat in his nascent library, leaning back on his favourite chair, his feet on the desk in front of him. He looked about him. Getting his home and his surroundings organized had been rewarding; it had improved his feeling of wellbeing, and had given him a sense of purpose as long as more remained to be done to complete the project. There had been, he conceded, frustrations along the way, and on several occasions his self-imposed deadlines had been set back by delays not of his own making. His nature being such that once he had decided upon a plan, he expected to see it completed almost before it could begin, he was often aggravated, not because the materials and the money with which to pay for them were not available for the task to go ahead, but rather because of a characteristic seemingly peculiar to the local artisans. These, he had discovered, would come to discuss a proposed plan with enthusiasm and vigour, would make a promise to start work on an appointed date at an appointed time, only to disappear, never to be heard from again. He had even lost his temper on more occasions than he felt comfortable with, and there were those who had already learned that, although he was slow to anger, Theo's temper could reach alarmingly volcanic proportions once lost.

Now, however, there was nothing left to be done, leaving him at a loss, and the prospect of having nothing to do but maintain what he had created did not appeal at all. He sat there thinking, his chin resting on the tips of his fingers. The furniture stood where it had been put; the plants and shrubs in the newly-created garden were growing and blossoming; the paintwork and elaborate plaster-mouldings and decoration were there to be admired, but there was no longer anything he could *do* with it. Even the house itself stood firm and static on its foundations, and it was silent. He had tried to chat with the servants on occasion, but they too had their little snobberies, and with the exception of James, did not approve of familiarity between themselves and their master, preferring instead to maintain a strict atmosphere of decorum and division of status.

He tapped the arms of his chair impatiently, took his feet off the desk, grabbed his coat from its allotted place in the hallway, opened the front door, and went out.

In the time during which Theo had been thus occupied, Mrs. Carswell's friend, Mrs. Pollard, had returned from her stay in Dublin, and the two ladies had arranged to meet for the first time in many weeks. Mrs. Carswell had been almost overwrought in anticipation of receiving the news her friend would surely have, particularly as, over the period of waiting, she had watched with scorn as the impostor had wheedled himself into the hearts and homes of the gullible gentry, making fools of them with his pretensions, and accepting their generosity. He had even moved into a fine house, she had discovered, and had no doubt at all that it was being rented for him by one of his new-found benefactors, so the pleasure of revealing him to all for what he was had been awaited with the greatest anticipation.

She greeted Mrs. Pollard warmly and invited her to be seated, while the maid was sent to the kitchen for a special tea to be served in the drawing room. She did not bother to ask Mrs. Pollard whether her stay in Ireland had been enjoyable, or what she had done during her sojourn there. Instead, she began, "Well, my dear Mrs. Pollard, and what did you find out about our strolling player?"

Mrs. Pollard hesitated.

"Well? Please do tell. You have no idea how I've waited to hear your news."

Mrs. Pollard then related everything she had learned, and Mrs. Carswell's initial complacency turned into extreme discomfort as the story unfolded. She sat in disbelief as she heard first how Mrs. Pollard had discovered that while Mr. Potter was indeed an actor, he was no strolling vagabond player, but an actor of high standing with Ireland's premier theatre in Dublin.

"Yes, yes." Mrs. Carswell brushed away the comparison, not knowing there was any difference between the one and the other. "But he's still just an actor…"

"Ah yes," Mrs. Pollard interrupted, "but listen to this my dear Mrs. Carswell: I've found out too that he's also a gentleman with a large fortune of £60,000, and an income of over £5,000 a year. He is, my dear Mrs. Carswell, a gentleman who just happens to enjoy acting sufficiently to have made a career of it! He's what's known as a 'gentleman player'."

"£60,000! £5,000 a year!" The realization came to Mrs. Carswell that not only had she not even introduced him to her daughter at the ball, but that she herself had barely deigned to speak to him. Her tea and cake were left untouched, and whatever Mrs. Pollard went on to say about her visit to Dublin was not heard; and when her friend departed, Mrs. Carswell was only too thankful to wish her goodbye.

While Theo had been busy setting up his new home, the Edwardes family often came over to see how he was progressing, and Theo likewise visited Dunstable Hall, recounting with enthusiasm the latest details of this progress, or bemoaning the lack of it. On these visits, weather permitting, he and Elizabeth took long walks along the many paths around the estate.

During this time Elizabeth had come to love Theo more than she had words with which to describe it; she thought of nothing but him, imagining him as her husband and herself bearing his children. Theo, however, still seemed to regard her as no more than a dear friend with whom he could hold intelligent conversations, share his thoughts and be his usual ebullient, high-spirited self. Elizabeth was forced to accept this, hoping that soon he would find more in her than just a friend, and she could not bear to think he might end their relationship by deciding to return to Ireland. Meanwhile, their time together was filled with animated discussions, banter, teasing, and exchanges of humour, laughing much of the time, and delighting in each other's company.

However, after Theo's new home was completed and he had no new project with which to occupy his still unsettled mind, to satisfy his restless spirit, or on which to expend his overabundance of energy, his mood changed, and his visits to Dunstable Hall became more sombre-toned, his customary enthusiasm deserting him.

Without the needed stimulation, he had begun to think again of Ireland and of the career he may already have jeopardised, once again questioning whether he had made the right decision in staying here. At the time it had seemed a sensible choice, but now he began to wonder if it had been a wise one. He had abandoned all his friends, his country, his home and his career, and moved to a foreign land with all its attendant strangeness and peculiarities. To visit Pembrokeshire was one thing: to abandon the world he knew, and to try to live there, was in no way the same.

Something else was troubling him as well, although he tried to pretend it did not, and that was the realization of how much he missed performing in the theatre. It was the only vehicle by which he had been able to drain his energies and use his talents, giving him at the same time that sense of achievement he needed, and this town did not even have a theatre.

In the past, when he looked at Preseli mountain, he saw a graceful and elegant backdrop to the verdant scene before it. Now though, especially in the early-morning light, it had begun to look more like a stark and solid barrier blocking his way to he knew not what. He began to feel like a starling locked in a small wooden cage. Haverfordwest was claustrophobic. He had made a dreadful mistake in staying here! What and who was he here in Haverfordwest? He was nothing and nobody. Those whose friendship he had secured during his stay here knew him only as an amiable, witty and desirable addition to their soirées; he was the Edwardes's protégé, nothing more. How different it was for him in Dublin, where he could not walk down the street without being recognized as one their great theatre's stars! There he was somebody to be looked up to, to be respected and appreciated for his special and superior talent, acting, and to be cheered and to receive standing ovations for his performances, and he began to despair of what he had done.

His renewed indecision, and all the confusion of thoughts surrounding it made him depressed, and Theo depressed was not good company, for with it came a loss of the humour, wit and all those sociable attributes that made others so desirous of that company. Aware of this himself, and not wishing to reveal this side of his character to his friends, especially Elizabeth, his visits to Dunstable Hall became less frequent, and the family, respecting his unaccustomed desire to be left to his own thoughts, but anxious for his welfare at the same time, reduced their own visits to the occasional only, hoping this would give him time to sort out whatever was troubling him.

For Elizabeth this separation was particularly upsetting in that she feared he would, after all, decide that life in Haverfordwest was not right for him, and would soon depart, leaving her with nothing more than memories of their precious time together. She too became depressed, and spent her time replaying in her mind all the details of the last months spent in each other's company. She even began writing them down, and many pages were wasted as she would remember some little, previously overlooked, detail that needed to be inserted. The number of pages grew, and still little was to be seen of Theo. Her mother and cousin Edwardes felt for her, but there was nothing they could do. Much as they had grown fond of Theo, only he could sort out his life, and all they could do was to wait in the background and hope he resolved his crisis satisfactorily.

CHAPTER 10

Theo, bored because he had no outlet for his energy, had gone to the livery stable to fetch Hercules, and was now on the road leading out of Haverfordwest on the way to St. David's. He had never been this way before, so although he knew he was heading towards the tiny cathedral city, he had no idea what lay in between.

Hercules was a good walking horse, striding out with a gait that could be maintained indefinitely. He also had a strong, broad back that allowed sitting on him for hours to be a comfortable experience, and Theo was happy with his choice. He met and greeted one or two other riders going towards Haverfordwest, and passed a wagon loaded with culm, and drawn by a pair of huge bullocks with wide-spreading and fearsome-looking horns. Otherwise, the road was deserted. It had been quite cool when he had left the stable, but by the time he came to where Roch Castle lay off to the side of the road, the dusty trail was reflecting the heat from the sun, and he had become sufficiently warm to decide to turn down the nearest path leading towards the coast.

The path wound its way between newly-ploughed patches intermixed with areas lying fallow, sometimes heading towards the sea, at other times seeming to turn back on itself.

There were so many hills and dells he found it difficult to see where he was going, only occasionally getting a glimpse of the sea glittering in the distance. He was not concerned, however. He had given himself the whole day in which to wander around the countryside and to sort out his thoughts, which were still overly confused and cluttered with unclear plans as to his future.

Flanked by bright-green areas of bracken fiddleheads and long grasses, horse and rider walked on. Colourful butterflies fluttered around them, and bees hummed over clumps of sweet-smelling primroses and violets that grew under the shelter of bent-backed hawthorns along the way. Eventually he came to a valley, beyond which he had a wide view of the coastline ahead of him. From here he could look out across the bay, beyond some rocky islets to a larger island off to the southwest. Beyond that still, across St. George's Channel, but too far away to be seen, was his home, Ireland.

He dismounted and allowed Hercules to take a drink from an old iron tub filled with water that sat beside the way, then dropped the reins and allowed him to graze while he gazed down the valley. It was hot enough, and he removed his coat and waistcoat, leaving only his white linen shirt between himself and the hot sun. The air smelt of damp undergrowth, and he watched as flocks of swallows swooped around him, snatching at insects. They were flying low, skimming the ground -- not a good sign; the insects, and hence the birds that hunted them, were staying near the earth, expecting rain. As though in confirmation of this, he noticed a row of small, dark-grey puffs of clouds forming on the western horizon.

After a while he picked up the reins, remounted Hercules, and set off again down the path, which led him to a hamlet the name of which, he was told, was Nolton. He kept going until he reached the coast where, instead of taking the road back to Haverfordwest, he followed a well-beaten path near the high, precipitous cliff-tops until he saw a long sandy beach way down below him. He stood there at the edge of the cliff for a few minutes, looking out at the vast Atlantic Ocean and the great grey and never-ending rollers gliding over it. He could never look at them without feeling an emptiness inside him. He shook his head, brushing away a sad memory, then continued along the cliff-top in the hope of finding a way down, coming at last to a worn path next to a stream that tumbled its way down a fairly steep gully all the way to the sands far below.

"Come on Hercules," he told the horse. "Let's go for a gallop."

The path was narrow and slippery in places, but Hercules was sure-footed, and soon they were standing alone on the beach, Hercules's hoof-prints showing that they were the only ones to have been there since the tide had last receded. Hercules tossed his head, and began taking playful sidesteps, chin tucked in, prancing in anticipation. Theo patted his neck. "Ah!" he said, "you understood what I said, did you? All right! Let's go!" And he turned the horse to face the far end of the beach, leaned forward in the saddle, and let Hercules have his head. The horse leapt forward, and they raced hard, the wind rushing past them, until they reached the end, where Hercules continued to shake his head up and down, snorting, nostrils flaring, but still with energy to spare. The ride had been exhilarating, and it reminded Theo of his youth, racing across the pastures of his home, with James.

He looked towards the sea where a gentle swell was spreading the dying Atlantic rollers in clear, glassy sheets over the smooth sand, then rode Hercules up above the high-water mark, where he removed the saddle, followed by his boots and stockings, which he left in a heap on the dry sand along with his jacket, shirt and waistcoat. He then performed a trick that James had taught him years ago, in Ireland. He made Hercules stand, then walked off until he was about thirty yards behind him, after which he ran at full speed, took a flying leap, and, hand-springing onto Hercules's hindquarters, vaulted onto his back. It was a trick he had taught the horse soon after acquiring him, and Hercules was now used to it. Today, and for the first time, he noticed that when he did it, his shoulder no longer hurt -- probably because of the many hours he had spent in recent weeks, going out into his garden and practising his fencing skills with James, something that had helped to dissipate at least some of his energy at the same time.

The tide was coming in, and he rode into the water, out ever further until the horse was swimming. Theo slid off his back, and, holding onto the reins, swam alongside him for a way before heading again towards the shore. Once the horse was only up to his knees again, Theo remounted, and they continued to walk back through the water to where they had started. The tide by this time was coming in fast, and having retrieved all his belongings, they were soon back again on the cliff-top.

This time Theo chose what looked to be a shorter route back towards Haverfordwest, and the two headed for home, dripping saltwater along the way. As they approached the town he passed several little cottages. Typical of the area, and quite similar to those in the Irish countryside, they sat low to the ground, only one storey high, the eves of their heavily-thatched roofs level with the top of his head as he rode by. Their brilliant-white walls were thick with successive layers of a wash made from lime produced by the local kilns that dotted the nearby coastline. The central, latched doors, were left wide open to the weather.

He rode past, and could see chickens wandering through the houses, and was, on occasion, greeted by women standing in the doorway, arms clutching the corners of their triangular, bright-red wool shawls, some of which encased a small child. Their red-flannel petticoats peeped out beneath heavy black-

and-white chequered skirts, and they wore flat-topped black-felt hats over their white lace-edged bonnets.

Most of the cottages had drovers' dogs wandering around outside, one of which came out, head, tail and body low to the ground, ready to stalk then nip at Hercules's heels, but at a sharp, whistled command from its owner the dog dropped to the ground, where it stayed, and Theo and Hercules passed by without incident.

Almost home, he noticed that the little dark grey puffs of clouds he had seen earlier, had expanded and grown darker until they filled the whole sky, and by the time he dropped Hercules back at the stable it had begun to rain. Theo did not mind. The ride had to a certain extent achieved its purpose in that a new project had emerged, not a great one, but enough to help raise his spirits out of their depressed state.

Along the way he had been thinking about one of his favourite places in Dublin, and wondering if it could be adapted in any way to suit the citizens of Haverfordwest. The object of his thoughts had been Dick Pue's, a well-known coffee shop that had been an institution in the city for almost a century. This coffee shop not only supplied the best coffee in Dublin, but people could sit there, browse through the books in a room at the back, and could read whatever newspapers they wanted while they enjoyed their coffee.

For a while the whole idea had absorbed him, and he had felt uplifted by it, until he realized he did not have the necessary residency requirements to open up such an establishment in the town. His spirits had then sunk again, until he decided that at least there was nothing to stop him from sharing his library with others. He may not be able to open a coffee shop, but as soon as his library contained enough books, he could at least share it by opening it to those of his new acquaintances whose interests matched his own. Together they could discuss the latest novels, plays and works of nonfiction, and they would share not only the pleasure of reading his books, but he would allow them to borrow them as well. In this way he could provide a service to those whose own libraries would be located out at their country seats.

Although his new idea was but a minor project, and not enough to alleviate his concerns to any significant extent, his ride had at least convinced him there was no need yet to despair about his decision to stay in Haverfordwest. It was not irrevocable, and should he want to, it was still not too late for him to return to Ireland and resume his old life as though nothing had happened. After all, he had been away from it for fewer than six months.

His spirits elevated by his plan and by his more rational reasoning concerning his situation, Theo set out the following morning for Dunstable Hall, and as he entered the gates to the estate was surprised by a sensation that made him feel almost as though he were coming home. It was a feeling he had not enjoyed for nearly seven years now, and it was enhanced by Mr. Edwardes and his cousin who were as usual delighted to see him, and happy to see his frame of mind improved, although they still would not have been able to describe his mood as being jovial.

Elizabeth, however, was not there.

Even though his idea was not that exciting, it was at least preferable to doing nothing as he had been lately, and he wanted her to be the first to hear about what he had in mind, and to be able to discuss it with her -- at least, that's what he told himself. Something else told him that if he were honest, he would admit that he also needed her company, which he had missed, so, after asking after their health, and exchanging the minimum of pleasantries, he asked where she was.

"She's out walking. She's not been gone long."

Theo jumped up. "In that case I can catch up with her. I want to see her."

And before either Mrs. Edwardes or her cousin could say anything, Theo had taken his leave, and had set off down the path at a run, anxious to find his friend and confidante. He had not gone far when, turning a bend in the path, he came across Elizabeth in the company of a young man he had never seen before. Her hand was resting on his arm, and they both turned in surprise when they heard Theo skid to a stop behind them.

"Mr. Potter!"

"Miss Elizabeth." Crestfallen, Theo bowed, and all three stood in embarrassed silence, until it was broken by Elizabeth who, having removed her hand from the young gentleman's arm, was the first to regain her composure.

"Ah... Mr. Potter." She looked at him and then at her companion, a young gentleman of medium height, with fair hair and -- as Theo convinced himself -- a haughty, ill-tempered demeanour. "Ah... Mr. Potter," she repeated, "may I present the Honourable Jeremy Stone."

The two gentlemen bowed deeply, each determined to be only as civil to the other as basic good manners required.

"Gentlemen, why don't we return to the house? I don't know about you, but I myself would welcome some refreshments." Elizabeth waved her hand across her face. "It really is quite warm out here."

The walk back to the house seemed to take a long time for all three, but especially for Elizabeth who made numerous attempts along the way to introduce light topics of conversation, all of which ended almost before they had begun, the gentlemen being disinclined to continue with anything she started, and answering or commenting only to the extent that politeness demanded.

On entering the drawing room where her mother and cousin were still seated, Elizabeth gave them a look that pleaded for their assistance, and, quick to understand a situation she had expected to arise when Theo had departed in search of her daughter, Mrs. Edwardes invited the two young men to be seated. She then continued by explaining that the Honourable Jeremy Stone was visiting his relatives' estate near Canaston Wood, where she and Elizabeth had met him ten days ago at a party. Theo thought back and remembered he himself had been invited to the party, but, to his present great regret, had not been in the mood to attend any parties, and had declined on the grounds of an imaginary illness.

After a brief visit in which what conversation there was, was awkward and attended by too many silences, he took his leave, and rode home dejected, but was once more encouraged when, later in the day, a servant from Dunstable Hall arrived with an invitation for him to join Mr. Edwardes and his cousin and their daughters at a simple family dinner that evening. Theo accepted.

He had spent the intervening hours in a state of anxiety and confusion: anxiety because he feared Elizabeth would marry the young man and he would not see her again; confusion because it had never occurred to him to imagine how he would feel if she were indeed to marry and not be a part of his own life any longer -- and also because, for the first time in his life, he had experienced jealousy, extreme jealousy. His own reaction at seeing her with her hand on another man's arm had surprised even himself. He had been inexcusably, almost explosively, angry; he had even hated someone he had never even seen before that moment!

Until now the thought of marrying anyone was not something he had considered with any seriousness after being disappointed once before. The agony -- for agony it had been -- had lingered a long time, but now it occurred to him that it was, after all, possible to love again -- that he was in love with Elizabeth, and could not allow her to marry anyone else. It was something he needed to let her know as soon as possible. As to his acting career, well, he would sort that out later. Just because he was married, should not mean he could not act as well, or that they could not both move to Dublin to live.

He arrived at Dunstable Hall with an alacrity that verged almost on the impolite, but was welcomed as their close friend with their customary kindness and affection. To his great relief the Honourable Jeremy Stone was not present, but no explanation was given as to his whereabouts, so Theo did not know whether his rival had been invited out somewhere else for the evening, or had returned to his family. Afraid to ask for fear that he might still be in the area -- that Stone and Elizabeth might be conducting an ongoing courtship -- he ate his way through dinner, took only an absent-minded part in conversation, and throughout the rest of the evening played card games to which he was so inattentive as to what he was doing, he lost every game. He gazed at Elizabeth, nervous and needing more than anything to speak to her away from all the others, to tell her how much he loved her, and to ask her to marry him. But the evening passed and the opportunity never arose, and he had to make his eventual departure as anxious as ever.

The next few days passed in torment for Theo. He was afraid to visit Dunstable Hall uninvited, lest he should find himself once more confronted by the Honourable Jeremy Stone. Moreover he had no idea how far that gentleman's relationship with Elizabeth had progressed. He agonized over the thought that she might already be betrothed to him, and that he had lost her. He could not bear to imagine her with anyone else, nor could he suffer roaming around the house agitating about it, so although it poured for several days with a fine, soaking rain out of the southeast, he nevertheless took Hercules out, and spent his time wandering around the countryside during the day, while at night he stood for hours at his chamber window, gazing out over the town. He wondered what his Elizabeth was doing, willing her to be thinking only of him, and berating himself for not having accepted the invitation to the party where she had met the other man, and for not having continued to visit the family despite his sombre mood.

After four days of misery he could stand it no longer. He was tired and irritable even with James who, knowing his master better than anyone, suspected he had fallen in love again. James was convinced the object of his love this time must be Miss Elizabeth, and he was delighted. He had been waiting for this moment since last November, and having discovered by chance that the Edwardes family had entertained a young gentleman visiting the area, James suspected that this young man was responsible for Theo's present state of mind. He had therefore taken the trouble to find out if the gentleman was still in the area, and if so, if and when he was expected to return home to his own family. The news had come back that the young gentleman had already left, and was not expected to return, so, the weather having improved, James suggested that as his master had not seen his friends for several days, this might be an excellent time to pay them a visit.

"I'm not sure this is a good time at all James. They seem to be having a lot of other visitors recently, and I don't think I should intrude. One doesn't want to be ill mannered."

"Indeed, Sir? I don't think they have any more visitors at the moment. To my knowledge they've all returned to their homes, and are not expected to return." James looked out of the window. "The sun is shining, Sir. Might I suggest a walk through the woods at Dunstable…"

But Theo had already left.

James smiled to himself and returned to his own apartments, performing an unaccustomed hop, skip and jump on the way.

CHAPTER 11

Theo, full of anticipation at being able to tell Elizabeth of his love for her, strode towards the entrance to Dunstable Hall, where he was met by a footman. "Would you like to speak to Mr. Edwardes in the library, Sir? Or would you like to join the ladies in the drawing room?"

"Oh, I don't think we need to disturb Mr. Edwardes, Martin. I'll be perfectly happy to join the ladies."

"As you will, Sir."

At the entrance to the drawing room, the doors were opened as usual by two footmen, and "Mr. John Theophilus Potter" was announced.

Theo advanced into the room, a lively grin lighting up his face, only to find himself looking straight at the upturned face of Mrs. Carswell. The temptation was to retreat and apologise for the intrusion, but his need to talk to Elizabeth overriding his dislike of Mrs. Carswell, he hesitated only briefly before bowing first to the lady of the house, then to Mrs. Carswell, then to her daughter who sat next to her, before paying his respects to the person he most wanted to see, Elizabeth. He bowed, "Miss Elizabeth."

Elizabeth rewarded him with a warm smile.

"Oh Mr. Potter!" Mrs. Carswell's shrill voice filled the

room. "How *delighted* I am to see you again, I'm sure." She fluttered her fan. "It's *such* a long time since we met at the ball, and I'm afraid prior engagements have prevented me from inviting..." Her voice trailed off, then started again as she turned towards her daughter. "You've met my daughter, of course, Miss Carswell?"

Theo bowed again. "Miss Carswell."

"I declare I'm *so* delighted you've called by *just* when we happen to be here ourselves. Such a fortunate happenstance! It's *such* a pleasure to see you again," Mrs. Carswell repeated. "As I told my good friend, Mrs. Pollard, 'such a delightful young man,' I said. 'Such charming manners'." She peeped at him from behind her fan. "And *such* an excellent actor too, I do declare."

Theo bowed again, then glanced towards Elizabeth, who gave an almost imperceptible shrug of sympathy.

Mrs. Carswell was still addressing him, so he had no option but to stand and wait until she had finished. "And I hear you've rented yourself a charming house too, my dear Mr. Potter. A new house. The houses being built these days, I tell Mr. Carswell are so *very* stylish, don't you agree, Mr. Potter?"

Theo agreed.

She prattled on while Theo remained standing in front of her, too polite to move away while she was talking.

After several more minutes, and having exhausted her fund of subjects with which to detain him, Mrs. Carswell announced, as though she herself were mistress of the house, "Now, it's *such* a beautiful afternoon, is it not? Why don't you young people take a turn along the paths in the big meadow, and let us married ladies talk together -- talk I'm sure you young people would find *way* too boring." She made a shooing motion towards the door.

Mrs. Edwardes, her own talkative tendency muted by the inability to get a word in, had been chatted into unaccustomed silence. Nobody wished more than she that the insufferable Mrs. Carswell and her haughty daughter would leave. She had been quite thankful that the woman had inexplicably vanished from her own society for the last few months, and had no idea Mrs. Carswell was now intent on re-establishing a relationship she had made a point of severing, prior to her intended grand exposé of the scoundrel, Mr. Potter, an exposé snatched from her by Mrs. Pollard's revelations. Undaunted, she was delighted that Theo had happened to arrive during her visit, and was confident that her opportunity to afford him some special attention for longer than a few minutes, as well as to offer him several well-chosen compliments, must have succeeded in restoring her to his favour.

Theo, who could not bear to stay in the same room with Mrs. Carswell any longer than he needed to, was delighted to follow her suggestion.

At last he would have the opportunity to tell Elizabeth of his love for her. "Shall we go then?" he said to her, holding out his hand.

"Why not? I'd like that very much." Elizabeth took his arm, and he led her towards the door, only to find they were being accompanied by Miss Carswell.

The trio walked in silence, Theo, trying to hide his disappointment at finding Miss Carswell at his side, Elizabeth, only too happy to have any chance to be close to the man with whom she was so much in love -- and Miss Carswell, who had decided that perhaps, after all, Mr. Potter might well be a gentleman in whom she could be interested, and that this presented a convenient opportunity in which to win him over. Seeing that Elizabeth had placed her hand on Theo's left arm, she grasped his right one, raised it, and settled her hand onto it, all in one firm, determined movement. After all, she reasoned, she had as much right to claim him as Elizabeth did. Indeed, if it were a question of money, then her own family probably had at least as much of it as the Edwardeses did, even if they did not have the pedigree to go with it.

Theo, however, seemed not even to have noticed her action, and continued to walk, his head turned towards Elizabeth.

Observing Elizabeth's light step, Miss Carswell thought to attract his attention by performing a little skip of her own, then looked up at him, intending to favour him with a coy smile. All that greeted her, however, was the back of his head, his attention still devoted to his beloved Elizabeth.

Rewarded with no success thus far, Miss Carswell addressed him directly.

"Mr. Potter," she announced, breaking the silence, and giving his arm a tug. "Mr. Potter. I feel I *must* congratulate you on your good taste. Those are remarkably fine boots you're wearing. Pray, do tell where you had them made, for I do declare they have to be none other than the work of my father's own boot-maker, Signor Carleone, of Burlington. Such an excellent craftsman! My father swears there's none other to equal him anywhere."

Theo, frustrated by the lack of opportunity to let Elizabeth know of his love for her, looked down at his feet, then at the object of his frustration. "Oh these? No, Mr. Morgan The Boot, up on Market Street, made them for me...Very comfortable they are too." His smile was benign. "I'll be sure to pass on your compliment to him. He'll be delighted... Not so sure about Signor Carleone, though," he added before redirecting his attentions once more to his love, who looked up, shaking her head at him.

"Mr. Theo Potter," she whispered, "you're wicked!"

"Why? What have I done?" he grinned.

Elizabeth merely raised her eyebrows at him, and silence descended once more, a silence with which both she and Theo were completely at ease.

Though it had taken her longer than most to grasp the situation, Miss Carswell was now aware there was something between the two of them that went far beyond the casual. Indeed, the more she observed them, the more she realized that not only were her chances of diverting Mr. Potter's attentions to herself very slim, there was no chance of it at all. It was clear, moreover, that the couple were even in love, and that she herself was playing no other role on this outing, than that of chaperone. Indignant, she pulled in her chin, raised her head, and dropped his arm without ceremony, taking a brisk step to one side.

Theo, surprised by her sudden movement, turned to look at her, and concluding that his frustration had perhaps led him to behave in a somewhat ungentlemanly manner towards her, gave a slight cough and, looking straight ahead, attempted to remedy the situation by introducing something by way of conversation.

"I've been learning something new!" he announced.

Elizabeth looked up at him and waited for him to continue.

Things had gone too far for Miss Carswell to be placated however. If she could not have Mr. Potter for herself -- and it was all too evident that this was now the case -- then there was no point in her making any effort to try to impress him. On considering their exchange regarding his boots, moreover, she decided she had no wish even to be polite to him.

"Indeed! And what has our Mr. Potter been learning?" Her chin was pulled in as far as it would go, her head locked back into its customary haughty position.

"*Our* Mr. Potter has been learning Welsh," said Theo.

"Oh! How interesting..." Elizabeth began.

"*Welsh*! Why would anyone want to waste their time learning Welsh?" Miss Carswell scoffed. "So vulgar... only the lower classes speak Welsh!"

"I'm interested in learning it for many reasons. To communicate being just one, and another..."

"When and why would you need to communicate with them? We've nothing in common with them, and I see no reason for it. It's my opinion that if they wish to communicate with us, then they should learn English... Any genteel person would be insulted were you to ask them if they spoke Welsh."

Theo ignored her last observation. "Nothing in common? On the contrary, one basic commonality is that they're all people, just like us, and..."

"Oh! Mr. Potter! Just like us? I do declare! They're nothing like us! They don't even live or conduct their lives like we do. They... they..." She paused, considering their differences. "They come from little hovels out in the countryside, and sell meat and vegetables in... " She waved her hand with distaste. "In the market."

"And I go to the market too, and I like to talk with them and to listen to them talk. It's a lyrical language that..."

Miss Carswell sniffed. "*I* would *never* go to the market. Only our servants do that... Besides, I've heard it said that those you hear around Haverfordwest, don't even speak real Welsh at all... it's a jumble of English and Welsh that only they can understand... Not that I care what it is they're speaking, and I'm sure that whatever it is they're talking about would in no way be of interest to any genteel person of higher taste and intellect."

Theo did his best to ignore Miss Carswell's diatribe against the Welsh, and ploughed on. "Another reason for me to go to the market is because I think it's good for us to understand what our servants do for us to ensure our lives run smoothly, and conversing with them in their own language would be a part of that," he said.

Miss Carswell shrugged. "I really can't see why. They

live their lives, and we live ours."

Theo nodded. "No. I can understand that you wouldn't see why."

Elizabeth, aware of the rising irritation in Theo's voice, was anxious that he not lose his temper. "Oh look! Look at that butterfly! Look at the beautiful markings on its wings." She bent down to examine it more closely. Theo bent over too.

Miss Carswell raised herself on her toes, and peered over the top of their lowered shoulders. "Humph," she snorted, then turned away, and continued walking.

Theo, regardless of the lack of decorum, could not help himself. In that brief moment of their being alone, he reached out, and taking Elizabeth's hand, raised it, and gave it a loving kiss. Elizabeth looked up at him and smiled. It was a smile that told him all he needed to know.

For a while their walk continued again in silence, neither Theo nor Elizabeth feeling the necessity to make polite conversation, both content in the knowledge that each now understood the feelings of the other.

Miss Carswell, however, was far from content. Resentful and jealous, she decided to recharge the atmosphere by rekindling her argument with Theo over the Welsh.

"And what do you intend to do with your new-found knowledge of the Welsh language then, other than use it to *communicate*?" she asked spitefully.

"The Welsh culture is very ancient, and filled with great literature." Theo was now willing to be magnanimous. "I intend to read it, and have already subscribed to several items in Welsh for my library, including a Welsh dictionary with which to help me get started."

"Have you indeed? Well, I do declare!"

"I see no point in buying books if you don't intend to read them."

Miss Carswell raised her chin even further. "I disagree

entirely. A library filled with beautifully-bound books, regardless of the content, is so elegant to look at and to sit in." She wafted her hand in the air. "It emits an atmosphere that's so dignified." She waved her hand again. "That wonderful smell of the finest leather. I know that when my father has a gentleman guest he wants to impress, he always greets him in his library."

"And which books have you enjoyed most in *your* library, Miss Carswell?"

Unfortunately for Miss Carswell, when at an age when she should have been learning the art of reading, writing and all the other accomplishments that ladies of her current acquaintance would have been taught by their governesses, her parents had not yet come into their fortune. Maintaining a governess for their daughter had been a financial impossibility, and as her mother's own level of learning had been such that she herself had been obliged to substitute her signature with an "X" in her entry in the marriage register, she was ill-equipped to teach her daughter anything. Though more attention had been paid recently to try to amend this situation, and to give her daughter some education, the latter, not being an enthusiastic learner, had appeared to have achieved little more thus far, than the ability *not* to follow in her mother's footsteps, if and when the time should come for *her* to sign the marriage register.

"I really don't have the time to immerse myself in books," she sniffed. "Anyway, since it would seem to be impossible to ever read all the books that it takes to fill a truly impressive library, you should consider doing as my father did when we took over the Hall."

"And what was that?"

"He purchased sufficient elegant tomes to fill the lower shelves to just above eye level. Then, above that, he employed a skilful artist to create the effect of books filling all the rest of the shelves to the ceiling. It's really most effective."

Theo could not bring himself to go any further with this discussion, and the walk back to the house continued in silence, he and Elizabeth -- who had withheld comment during the contretemps -- walking as close to each other as was seemly, their hands touching every now and then.

Their arrival back at the house coincided with the setting of the sun, and Theo went in to take his leave of Mrs. Edwardes. Afraid Mrs. Carswell would waylay him with more platitudes and false compliments, he strode across the room to say goodbye to his hostess, then turned to give a hasty bow to Mrs. Carswell. Without giving her any opportunity to open her mouth, he then advanced to her daughter, and bowed. "Nos da," he bade her farewell in Welsh.

"What did you...?" But Theo had already moved on.

Elizabeth had waited for him at the front door. "My dearest Miss Elizabeth," Theo bowed low. "My dearest Mr. Potter." Elizabeth smiled, and he kissed her hand once more.

CHAPTER 12

"Well, Potter, so you wish to marry my young cousin?"

This was the day to which Theo had not looked forward without great trepidation. It had been several weeks since he had been able to offer Elizabeth a proper proposal of marriage, and since she had accepted him.

Since then though, Mr. Edwardes had been out of town, and the intervening period had filled Theo with doubt as to whether Mr. Edwardes, on hearing more about the man his dear cousin wanted to marry, would agree to it. Theo had been in this situation one other time in his life, and that occasion had resulted in the loss of his first love. Since then, he had avoided putting himself again in a position in which he could be hurt so badly -- until now.

If Mr. Edwardes did not give his permission, theoretically it did not matter as Elizabeth was of age, and could marry Theo regardless of her cousin's wishes. It did matter to Theo and Elizabeth, however, as Elizabeth would not allow a rift to occur between herself and the family she loved so much, and even Theo would not want that to happen. It was important to both of them, therefore, that they had the blessing of both Mr. Edwardes and Elizabeth's mother.

Now the moment had arrived. The two men were seated

in the huge library of Dunstable Hall, and Theo had just expressed his hope that Mr. Edwardes would give his blessing to the proposed marriage. He had, of course, been in the library many times before, and had often wondered how long it would take him to build up such a collection of his own, or if it would ever even be possible in his lifetime.

Now though, he was too anxious to notice anything other than the expression on Mr. Edwardes's face, and try to decipher from it what it revealed about the answer he was about to receive. And he was indeed nervous. Although the family had befriended him, they knew nothing about who he was, or what his connections were. When faced with the question, would Mr. Edwardes be willing to allow his charge to marry an actor, even though he was a gentleman? The recollection of his last experience gave him a knot of apprehension in his stomach. Mr. Edwardes's approval was by no means a foregone conclusion, and his anxiety increased even further when Mr. Edwardes leaned back in his chair and gazed out of the window, turning his back on him.

"I'm glad you've come to ask my permission which, as you may know, you didn't have to do," he began, still looking out of the window. "Although her father put his children under my guardianship before he died, Miss Elizabeth is now of age, and can marry whom she chooses. She's also now in possession of her inheritance of £15,000, which came to her on her twenty-first birthday." Mr. Edwardes swung his chair round, and turned to look at Theo. "Were you aware of her inheritance?" He had expected this meeting, but it was not one to which he had looked forward any more than Theo. Much as he and the family had come to love Theo, they still did not know enough about him, and questions needed to be asked.

It was, therefore, exactly as Theo had suspected it would be, and he was so nervous he could feel his hands shaking. He leaned forward and clasped them between his knees. He knew what was troubling Edwardes, and knew it was time to tell him what he knew about his family and about the source of his wealth. As far as Mr. Edwardes knew, he may be a spendthrift who had already dissipated his fortune, and the annual income he had learned of could be something that could end at any time, leaving Elizabeth and Theo to rely on her inheritance alone. No wonder Mr. Edwardes had asked if he had known about it! And then there was the question about his family...

Mr. Edwardes had started to speak, but Theo put up his hand. "It's only fair and natural that you and Miss Elizabeth should know more about the person she's hoping to marry. And, no, I didn't know about her fortune, but it would have made no difference if she'd had none. I'm well able to give her the kind of life to which she's been accustomed... although I've no wish to live on an estate -- something she already knows."

Mr. Edwardes nodded, but still looked unreassuringly enigmatic. Theo's wealth, although not the source or reliability of it, he had been aware of: of his background he knew nothing.

Theo hesitated, and breathed in deeply as the memory of his last experience almost overwhelmed him. "As regards my family and the source of my fortune and continued income, I regret I know nothing."

Mr. Edwardes was startled. "Nothing!" This meeting was not turning out well at all, and he did not know what to say to continue it. He was saved from saying anything, however, because Theo, more anxious than he had been in a long time, had stood up and was pacing around the large library.

"This is all I do know," he began. "Just before her confinement, my mother, whoever she was, was taken to the country estate of Sir Edward Manderson, some miles outside Dublin. After I was born, she left, and I was brought up by Sir Edward and Lady Ann, who treated me like a son." Theo stopped, and studied without seeing it, a large leather-bound book on birds. He fingered its gold-engraved spine. "Sir Edward had a son of his own. He was two years older than I, but we played together all the time, and wherever the family went, I went as well. All I was ever told was that a most generous stipend was given monthly to Sir Edward to pay for my upkeep and for my private education, but that my parentage was never to be revealed to anyone. Sir Edward and Lady Manderson, whom I loved dearly, followed their obligations faithfully, giving me the best of everything, including the best education that money could buy, and as I said, treating me like another son.

"At my maturity, I received an endowment of £60,000, which accrues income as I've no need to spend the capital, and an annual income of £5,000 for life. This was all left to me in an irrevocable trust, so can't be altered in any way.

"I left the family estate several years ago, and embarked on a career of acting, for which I'd always shown some talent, and which had always been my ambition. My fortune made no difference to that. I'm a gentleman player, and as such accept no payment from my theatre for my services." He turned again to look at Mr. Edwardes. "And that's it. I should be happy to show you proof of my worth, should you feel that necessary... Of my parentage, I'm afraid I can't."

Mr. Edwardes shook his head. "No, that won't be necessary. I pride myself on being able to tell when a man is telling the truth. And as for your connections, while we know nothing of either of your parents, it's certain that either your mother, or your father, or both, were people of great wealth and influence. As to their heritage, I'm not one to insist on knowing that."

He got up and shook Theo's hand, smiling. "And from your stature and bearing, I think we can assume anyway that you must come from good breeding stock!... I know a good horse when I see one," he laughed. "You will, of course, tell Miss Elizabeth whatever you feel is right," he added. "However, you may be assured that no-one else will ever hear from me what you've just told me about your family, or lack of it... " He smiled at Theo. "But I don't think it would be in any way detrimental to you to let your financial situation be known hereabouts, do you?"

Theo grinned, and thanked him, and Mr. Edwardes rubbed his hands together, dismissing all that had just occurred, and walked over to the rosewood Tantalus sitting on a mahogany chest. He unlocked it, and took out the crystal decanter of Scotch whisky. "I think we should celebrate, don't you?"

The following month, on Sunday, 27th June, 1779, John Theophilus Potter married Elizabeth Edwardes in St. Martin's church, Haverfordwest. The marriage was by special license, Mrs. Edwardes being of the opinion that having banns read out was beneath the family's dignity and should, therefore, be avoided. The ancient church, described by a visitor as being 'large, old, ugly and wretched', was brightened for the good part of an hour by the elegant and colourful group of people gathered for the ceremony within its walls.

Elizabeth wore a magnificent pale-blue gown that opened at the front to reveal a white dress beneath. The gown had loose folds in the same pale blue that fell from her shoulders down her back to the hem, while the sleeves, fitted to the elbow, had a long frill that fell to her wrists. Her hat was large and decorated with orange blossoms she had picked that morning in the orangery, and with long, pale blue ribbons which flowed from it. Theo wore a suit of fine silk, an embroidered waistcoat, white stockings and black, silver-buckled shoes. Despising wigs, his dark-brown hair was tied at the nape of his neck with a wide black-velvet ribbon.

The curate, Mr. William Tasker, resembled in some respects the description of his church, and was quite formidable. Intent on impressing on the young couple the solemnity of the occasion, he read in slow, measured Welsh tones, many passages from the scriptures to emphasise his words, followed by many equally slow and ponderous prayers to reinforce them, his deep baritone voice echoing around the old stone walls.

"Your vows are taken before our Lord," he intoned. "And ye make a promise to our Lord," he continued, his Welsh voice sonorous, his jowls quivering with fervour, his index finger pointing to the heavens. "And your vows and promises to our Lord God Almighty are for as long as ye both shall live." His voice rose on the last word of the sentence, while his index finger moved downwards towards the engraved slate slabs beneath their feet.

Having reminded them of those obligations to God, he then continued by reminding them that one of the purposes of getting married was to procreate, and wished them a fulfilling future in this regard. Theo instantly brushed away the mental image of his beautiful bride being worn down by producing all the children being advocated, and instead concentrated on the more appealing contemplation of his own role in their creation.

Mr. Edwardes meanwhile, head back and not paying any attention to the powerful cadences of Mr. Tasker's continued invocations and admonitions, contemplated the state of the roof, examining as closely as he could from his seat far below, areas where dry rot or death-watch beetle appeared to have eaten away at some of the rafters; and while Mr. Tasker droned on, mused that it would not be a good start to the marriage if the roof caved in during the ceremony.

It was a hot day, and the smell of decaying wood and mildew permeated the stale air, and Mr. Tasker's voice, despite its full-bodied tones, had a soporific effect, so much so that

Mrs. Edwardes had to be awakened by her eldest daughter sitting next to her. But if others were aware it, Elizabeth and Theo were far too happy to notice anything or anyone other than each other.

After the ceremony, they signed the register with their finest handwriting, followed by the two witnesses, Elizabeth's elder sister, Mary Hanbury Edwardes, and Thomas Morris, her mother's younger brother from Steynton. The whole party then returned to Dunstable Hall where cook had prepared a wedding feast for exactly four o'clock, and at the end of this, all the servants were brought in to join in a toast for the bride and groom.

Theo was standing at the tall window looking out into the darkness. Down in the entrance hall below, the loud bell of the mahogany long-case clock had just struck four o'clock, and he watched as the orange glow of the sun slid slowly around beneath the northern horizon, getting brighter every minute as it neared the eastern sky. Soon it would break above the Preseli hills, and the first day of his married life would begin. He turned to look at Elizabeth, who after a night of pleasure and talking, had fallen asleep just minutes before. "My lovely, beautiful Bess." He went back to bed to lie close to her, to feel her smooth skin, her thick, wavy hair, to look at her in a way forbidden to him until this, their wedding night -- a night spent not only in consummating their marriage, but in telling each other of their love, their dreams, their hopes -- and he smoothed her hair.

Elizabeth opened her eyes. It was daylight now, and he could see their colour more closely than he had ever been able to see it before. They were an exciting light, but bright turquoise with a ring of deep blue around the edge. He pulled her towards him, "Oh Bess! I love you so very much."

Elizabeth smoothed his face with her fingertips. "You

can't love me more than I love you." She looked at him, and his eyes began to laugh. "No, that can never be." He drew her closer, and they kissed again.

A while later, Elizabeth sat up and hugged her knees. They had already discussed the mundane necessity of paying the customary visits to her relatives around the country, something neither was wanting to do, but it was the custom to introduce the new groom, so had to be done.

"Do you know what I should like us to do Theo?"

"Mmm? I don't know. What would you like to do?" Theo was finally getting sleepy.

"I should like to visit Ireland."

Theo propped himself up on his elbow. "Ireland! Why Ireland?"

"I should like to see where you grew up, to see the theatre where you performed, to fill in the gaps and to know what made you the man you are... Oh! Is that not something you would want to do?" she added when she saw his expression become thoughtful.

"It's not something to which I've given much thought recently, and I'm not sure... Is the Pembrokeshire me not enough?... At least for now?" The subject of Ireland, and his return there, had been nagging away at the back of his mind for quite a while, a subject he did not want to think about at the moment, as it meant he would have to face the fate of his own career and -- from what he had already learnt indirectly from his new wife -- her probable unwillingness to ever leave her beloved Pembrokeshire to go to live in Dublin.

Elizabeth smiled. "Of course it is if you don't want to revisit the past, but I sense you have some demons in you somewhere that perhaps we could exorcise together by returning to Dublin."

Theo sighed, and lay back, his hands behind his head. "I must think about it."

Elizabeth smoothed his head. Theo responded by giving her hand a long, slow and thoughtful kiss.

"I wouldn't have you do anything you wouldn't want to do, my dearest Theo," she said.

PART II

CHAPTER 13

The mid-August sun was hot; the streets of Dublin were dry and dusty, and the leaves of the trees had a spent look that already foretold the coming of Autumn, and Elizabeth and Theo, who had arrived but an hour before, were tired after their long trip from Haverfordwest. Theo hailed a Hackney carriage and asked the driver to take them to their inn, where the proprietor, Mr. Flaherty, recognizing Theo, welcomed him warmly, even calling his wife to come and see who had arrived. Theo introduced their hosts to Elizabeth, and civilities over and pleasantries exchanged, they were shown to their apartments, where Elizabeth was happy to follow Theo's suggestion that she take a rest while he went downstairs to chat with Mr. Flaherty.

"Come in! Come in, Mr. Potter, Sir." Mr. Flaherty invited Theo into his own parlour, and after wiping the table and pulling out a chair for his guest, laid a tankard of Mr. Arthur Guinness's best black porter in front of him. With Mrs. Flaherty bustling around in the background, and the aroma of baking filling the small room, Theo sat himself down and felt comfortably at home -- he had, after all, spent many hours there in the past.

"Are you come back to Dublin for good now, Mr. Potter? We have all missed you greatly at the theatre."

Theo explained all that had happened since he had last seen Mr. Flaherty, nearly a year ago. "Have things changed at all since I went away?" he wanted to know.

"I can't say they have…we had a problem here at the inn a few months ago when a group of those damnable Bucks came in here, making trouble. They were drunk as usual, and stormed in demanding everyone hand over all their firearms, other weapons and their jewellery… Indeed, it's apt that they're called 'sweaters', for I swear we were all quite in fear of our lives. No regard for anyone they had, and treated one old gentleman so roughly I thought surely he'd die of shock… I was only thankful Mrs. Flaherty and my daughters were away visiting her parents in Cork…They think nothing of taking liberties with the ladies, you know, these young men. I even recognized a few of them. One was a colonel in the army, another an aide to the Lord Lieutenant, and another was Lord FitzJohn's younger son." Mr. Flaherty shook his head. "I don't know what things are coming to when decent folks can't be left in peace for fear of these wealthy and idle young bloods… I was right there in the room as they entered, laughing raucously and swearing, and before I could do anything one of them pinked me quite deeply on the arm." Mr. Flaherty pulled up his sleeve and showed Theo the scar. "God be praised the sheriff happened to be here along with some of his volunteers, and they were driven off… Trouble is…" he sighed, "there's no point at all in prosecuting these young men; they have high connections and their exploits are invariably kept quiet, so they're never prosecuted, but wicked it is that they're allowed to terrify and maim innocent citizens the way they do."

Theo agreed. "Better not mention any of this to Mrs. Potter though, Mr. Flaherty. She's of a nervous disposition, and would have me turn around and sail back to Wales on the next boat if she thought there were any chance of them returning!"

"Of course not, Mr. Potter, Sir. We try to protect the ladies from these things as much as possible, don't we?... However, you yourself know the dangers, so I don't need to tell you how to enjoy your stay in our wonderful city without becoming a victim of violence... Anyone would think from the way some people talk, that the citizens of Dublin walk around in constant fear of their lives, but you yourself know that's not true... All it takes is some common sense."

"Yes, of course, and I plan to show Mrs. Potter the best the city has to offer... Indeed..." Theo took out his pocket watch. "I think our first trip will be to Dick's. I haven't had a good cup of coffee since I was last at that coffee house... and I assume the bookseller's is still right behind." He stood up.

"That it is, Sir, although there's talk about Dick's and the bookseller's and the printing shop closing soon. It seems there are plans to pull down Carberry House."

"Indeed? That will be a terrible shame. Dublin won't be the same without Mr. Richard Pue's old coffee house... It must be almost a hundred years since he opened up... A great shame... I suppose he'll stop publishing his 'Occurrences' too then?"

"Yes, a great shame it'll be, Sir... But another one has opened since you left. It's in the new Royal Exchange, and it has a coffee room on the first floor. I haven't been there myself, but people say that it's as magnificent as any in the whole of Great Britain!"

"Ah! Well then! We'll have to test it for ourselves." Theo began to move towards the door, anxious to fetch Elizabeth, and begin their holiday.

Mr. Flaherty held up Theo's empty tankard. "But can I be offering you another porter before you go now?"

"Mr. Flaherty, much as I enjoy Mr. Guinness's

specialty..." Theo, laughing, pretended to stagger towards the door. "I'm sure Mrs. Potter wouldn't take it kindly if I returned to our apartments unable to communicate without slurring my words... Although, as you'll recall I'm sure, it wouldn't be the first time I've left your parlour the worse for wear..." They both laughed, and Theo started again to leave, but Mr. Flaherty called after him. "Oh! Mr. Potter, Sir! Would you like me to arrange the hire of a carriage to be at your disposal for the duration of your stay?"

"An excellent idea, Mr. Flaherty. Thank you."

"What type of carriage would you be having in mind, Sir?"

"Well, the weather seems to be nicely settled, so perhaps something open would be best... Oh! And as we'll be making some excursions into the surrounding countryside, I think it would be wise to hire an extra man, along with the driver, don't you? Just in case..."

"A wise decision, Mr. Potter. And are you carrying a weapon yourself, Sir? I see you're not wearing your sword."

"No, I'm not. I think my wife would wonder where I've brought her if she found me wearing a sword, or with a gun tucked down the back of my breeches."

Mr. Flaherty went over to a shelf, and took down a small dagger in its scabbard. "I think it might be sensible to..."

Theo took the weapon with reluctance. "Hmm. I don't know how I'm going to explain this away," Mr. Flaherty heard Theo muttering to himself as he went upstairs.

Refreshed after a short nap, Elizabeth was ready to be shown the delights of the city of Dublin, and Theo took her first to Dick's, where they stayed an hour, enjoying what Elizabeth agreed was the best coffee she had ever tasted, looking over the latest newspapers, and inspecting the many books for sale in the back room. While there Elizabeth noticed patrons looking at Theo and whispering to one another -- and it was not just the women. She smiled to herself, proud that others thought her husband as handsome as she did. Some though, while passing him on the way out, even greeted him. "You know these people?" she asked.

Theo shrugged. "They probably recognize me from the theatre."

"Indeed?" Elizabeth was surprised, but said no more about it. After a while she remembered something. "I've just realized; I've not seen James since we arrived. Where is he?"

"I thought it was time James had a holiday, so I gave him enough money with which to enjoy himself during our stay... He has friends in the area, so will have the opportunity to meet up with them."

Elizabeth squeezed his hand. "You're a kind man, my Theo."

After leaving the coffee shop, Theo asked their driver to take them to the Smock Alley Theatre. On the way Elizabeth was amazed at the number and variety of shops they passed, and the imaginative names given to them by their owners. Here was 'The Hare and Rabbit', where musical instruments were sold. A bit further on was 'The Duck and Chicken', where ladies could buy stays for their corsets.

"Oh look Theo! A milliner's!" The driver was still moving ahead, and Elizabeth turned her head to look back at the 'Dainty Damsel', a prettily-designed shop that had a window display to turn the head of any woman, let alone one from Haverfordwest. "Oh please Theo! Can we stop? I saw a beautiful bonnet in that milliner's back there."

"Of course we can." Theo asked the driver to turn around, and they went back to the oddly-named shop.

Theo had never entered a milliner's before, and there were no other men inside, only groups of women out for an afternoon's shopping. Feeling out of place, he raised his hat and bowed briefly to those who turned to look at him -- which was most of them -- and Elizabeth, making her way towards some bonnets that had taken her fancy, was proud to hear the compliments being lavished on her husband. There were also nudges accompanied by whispers she could not hear, and she wondered what it was that some of them seemed to find about her husband that was so important and remarkable, other than his looks, his air of distinction and fine deportment.

Theo, feeling uncomfortable, waited near the entrance, beginning to think he was to spend the rest of the afternoon looking out on the street, and having to doff his hat and move out of the way as women came and went. Elizabeth did finally make her choice, however, and he went with her to the counter to pay for it.

The assistant took great care wrapping the new bonnet, then laid it in a pretty bandbox, finally tying it with coloured ribbon. As she did so, she glanced at Theo, and then, as she handed the purchase over to Elizabeth, said, "Excuse me Sir for being impertinent, but I'm sure I recognize you. Are you not Mr. Potter from our Smock Alley theatre?"

Theo smiled and agreed that he was.

"I didn't see you act there or at Crow Street at all this last season, Mr. Potter, and everyone has noticed your absence and missed your performances greatly... Even some of the other ladies who've just been in here and of course recognized you, remarked on it to me... Anyway, we're so glad to see you're finally back, and shall be delighted to see you again this coming season, especially now that our dear Mr. Sheridan has gone to Drury Lane... and my husband too," she went on, "he liked to go to the theatre just to see your dazzling displays of fencing, so has missed you as well, as have the other men." She turned to Elizabeth. "The men tend to get bored with all the love scenes, don't they?"

Theo smiled again, but apologetically. "I'm afraid I'll not

be back this season, Ma'am… But maybe some time." He looked at Elizabeth who was watching with amazed fascination. She had no idea her husband was so well known and regarded, and it made her begin to understand how much he had given up. The woman, she realized, was still addressing Theo.

"Oh dear!" she was exclaiming. "I do hope you're not leaving us permanently! All of us, your theatre-going public will be most distressed if that's the case… It's just not the same without you," she added. "But then, so many of our best actors leave to join Drury Lane or Covent Garden -- Mr. Barry, Mr. O'Keeffe -- and I suppose we mustn't begrudge you all any advancement in what I'm sure will be illustrious careers… And we'll have to be content with wishing you all the best."

This was no time to explain the true situation regarding his career, so Theo merely bowed, smiled, and thanked her for her good wishes.

They mounted the carriage once more, Elizabeth holding her new bonnet on her lap. She felt so proud of her illustrious husband, but now felt a concern for him as well that she had not felt before, and it tempered the happiness in which she had previously been enveloped. They continued their drive, making their way towards the theatre.

"That's a remarkably handsome-looking house." Elizabeth pointed out a large and elegant building, lavishly, but tastefully decorated on the outside, and with expensive curtains draped at its windows.

Theo gave a slight cough. "Ah yes, that's Mrs. Leeson's famous establishment."

"She must be a well-known lady for you to know who lives there. Who is she?"

"Ah, well…It's rather, 'what is she?' She's Dublin's foremost madam. Her name is Margaret, but she's known as 'Peggy'"

Elizabeth was embarrassed. "Oh, oh I see."

"And I know her quite well," said Theo, laughing.

"Do you indeed! How well, Mr. Potter?"

"She comes to the theatre all the time and brings her girls with her; makes quite a show of it too. Nothing but the best for Mrs. Leeson. It's her way of advertising her services... She's *very* exclusive," he added.

Elizabeth nodded and asked no more questions; she was not sure what answers she might receive, and Theo did not let on that it was at Peggy Leeson's that he lost his virginity with a pretty young woman by the name of Charity, "a bit of a misnomer," he reminded himself.

Finally in Smock Alley, and outside the famous theatre, they dismounted again and stood looking up at the façade of the building, which had begun to take on the glow of the late afternoon sun.

"Where is everyone now? It looks as though it's completely closed up." Elizabeth looked at the shuttered windows.

"It is, and for the next month or so. The company spends the summer season in Cork and Limerick... Ah yes! Cork!" Theo gave a sly smirk as he remembered it. "To think I was there with them this time last year... And I have to say we Dublin players are extremely popular among the ladies."

"Oh! Are you indeed?" Elizabeth was beginning to learn more about her husband every minute -- and they had only just arrived!

"Oh yes! I should like you to know, my dear Mrs. Potter, that I've had many a young lady lift her skirts for me in Cork! Sometimes it's difficult for us even to leave a theatre after a performance because there are so many women gathered around... Ah yes! Those were the days! Alas, now I'm a sedate married man."

"You don't strike me as being sedate at all, I have to say.

Married, yes, but John Theophilus Potter sedate? Never!"

Theo became serious. "Do you know there has been a theatre in Dublin for over a hundred years? And this is where I performed." He sighed. "If I'd stayed, I'd have had the chance to perform at Drury Lane and Covent Garden too, just as the woman back there in the shop said. Actors from our theatre and the two London ones are always performing in one another's theatres." He looked up at his old theatre, and Elizabeth noticed it was a wistful look. After a moment, he put his shoulders back, and smiled. "But all is not lost, is it? Who knows what the future might bring?"

"I hope you don't regret your decision to stay in Haverfordwest *that* much."

Theo squeezed Elizabeth's hand. "And not have you at my side? I think not. Still," he added after a moment, "I do wish Haverfordwest had more in the way of sophisticated theatre... Or any theatre, for that matter. However, you and I shall come to Dublin every year to watch the magnificent Mr. William Shakespeare's plays being performed by the best actors... and some excellent modern comedies too, of course, not to mention concerts. And when we come to Dublin, then you can have the pleasure of watching me act too, because I know Mr. Ryder would be happy to have me back... as would the lady at the milliner's and her husband, it would appear!" He laughed.

"That's something I should look forward to very much," said Elizabeth.

"Then we'll enjoy Shakespeare together. Indeed, let's have a preview," and to Elizabeth's embarrassment, Theo stood back and opened his arms wide. "*Friends, Romans and countrymen...*" For a few minutes, oblivious to the rest of the world passing by, Theo became Mark Anthony, and a small crowd of people even gathered around as he performed the speech.

Elizabeth stood back from everyone, no longer embarrassed once she saw the audience had recognized her husband, and was appreciating his impromptu performance; and she watched as he came to life in a way she had not experienced since seeing him as Romeo at Dunstable Hall.

His performance was mesmerising, and it alarmed her to the extent that she found herself wondering how he would ever settle for a life that did not include acting and the adulation of an appreciative audience. Although she was perfectly content with him having been a respectable actor with a prestigious Theatre Royal in the past, such as the Smock Alley or Crow Street theatres, or even with him performing here again if they came to Dublin during the season, it was not a career she happily envisaged her husband trying to continue in a town like Haverfordwest, which, without its own theatre, had to rely on visiting actors for its entertainment.

Her thoughts were interrupted by the crowd which was applauding and asking for more. Standing tall and proud like the performer he truly was, he looked at Elizabeth, seeking her approval. She nodded, and he became first Hamlet, then Henry V, before finally bowing out to his cheering audience.

Men came up to shake his hand and congratulate him, but mostly it was the women who crowded around him, obviously overjoyed to see their favourite back amongst them, some even touching him -- all begging him to return soon. One woman even saw fit to hug him!

Elizabeth continued to stay in the background. She could see her husband was completely comfortable in the environment in which he found himself -- as comfortable and enlivened by the experience as she herself felt alien and uncertain. "How different," she thought, "from when we walk around Haverfordwest where, if acclaim constitutes food for his soul, he must be cruelly starved."

The crowd dissipated, and apart from their driver and his

horses -- now impatiently pawing at the ground -- they were left alone once more in the still hot and dusty street. The performance concluded, the theatre behind them now stood lifeless and empty, like a backdrop of painted cardboard scenery, and as though to signal the end of the final act, the sun, sliding down behind a large house, gradually drew a dark grey curtain up over the facade. The show was over.

Theo helped Elizabeth back into their carriage, and they rode back in silence to the inn. She sensed a change in his mood, and wondered if they had done the right thing in coming to Ireland after all. Maybe this was why he had hesitated when she had suggested it. It was she who had persuaded him, and perhaps in doing so, she had rekindled a fire that may have best been left unlit.

"Did you know," said Theo later, "that I've been to Drury Lane and Covent Garden once already?"

Elizabeth was surprised. "You have!"

"Yes, my godparents, Sir Edward and Lady Manderson went to London for every season, and her son always accompanied them. I joined them too when I was sixteen, but after that they decided to stay in Dublin instead, so I went to London only that once with them, and I had really looked forward to accompanying them every year... I missed it greatly."

"Yes," said Elizabeth quietly, "I think that's obvious... but maybe we can go to London too," she added, knowing from their afternoon's experience that it was not so much watching others act, but performing himself that was his real need.

"Maybe..." His voice trailed off, and Elizabeth felt it was not something he wanted to talk about, so said nothing more.

He had little to say for the rest of the evening, and Elizabeth left him with his own thoughts, while pondering her own concerns for him at the same time.

For the next few days, the weather being fine, they drove around the countryside, and Theo introduced her to some of his favourite places.

He took her to the New Gardens, where she marvelled at the artificial fountain with its artificial moonlight, and on one evening they went to a concert in The Rotunda, a circular hall large enough to accommodate two thousand people. Another evening they went back there to attend a ball, where all were attired in full evening dress, and where Theo met more of his old friends and acquaintances, whom he introduced to Elizabeth, who continued to learn of the great affection his friends had for her husband.

Like many other fashionable Dubliners with their fine coaches, they drove around the North Circular Road, and when the first Sunday came, joined other onlookers to watch as all the great personages of the area gathered there in the afternoon, and made their own magnificent tour of the Road in their coaches and fours, and even coaches and sixes -- each complete with their retinues of beautifully-turned-out servants. One of these was Lord Howth, who liked to pretend he was the coachman, and was dressed as such, complete with a coachman's wig with lots of little curls on it, and an extravagant three-cocked hat, and chewing on a piece of straw.

On one day Theo took Elizabeth to the estate of Lord Trimelstown, who kept a magnificent, heated aviary of exotic birds such as parrots, macaws and Chinese pheasants, which wandered around among banana trees and other tropical plants. It was somewhere James had taken him as a child, and he had always remembered it with delight -- his Lordship himself almost as exotic as his birds, dressed as he was in scarlet, with full-powdered wig and black-velvet hunting cap.

On another day they went their separate ways, Elizabeth going with her personal maid on a purely female shopping expedition, which the presence of a bored man would have ruined, and Theo took the opportunity to visit a much-loved family whom he had not seen since the day before he left Ireland to go to Pembrokeshire. Here he was received with the warmth, love, hugs and kisses normally accorded a long-lost son, and afterwards went to find his friend, John O'Keeffe, the actor and playwright, who had left for London at the end of 1777. O'Keeffe had written to let Theo know he would be back in Dublin sometime during the summer. However, Theo was disappointed to discover he had not yet arrived. After that he spent the rest of the day taking care of some personal business that had accumulated during his absence, and needed his attention.

All in all it was a most satisfying week. However, after it had passed, and they still had not seen the estate on which Theo had been brought up, Elizabeth decided to suggest a visit. "Is it far to where you were brought up?" she asked one morning at breakfast.

"No."

"Is it somewhere we could visit in the day perhaps?"

"Yes."

"I'd really like to see it."

"Is it that important to you?"

"Is it not so to you?"

"No."

"But you spent the first twenty years of your life there. Why would you not want to go back to see it now that we're here?"

"The new owners would probably be in residence at this time of year, and I wouldn't want to inconvenience them." There was also another reason he had for not wanting to visit the new owner, but not one he was prepared to talk about. One day maybe.

"New owners? Did your cousin, as you call him, not inherit the property then?"

"Yes."

"I don't understand. Don't you want to see him again?"

"He's dead."

"Dead! But he was only two years older than you! How…?"

Theo stood up. "Very well. I'll take you there."

Elizabeth asked no more questions. Whatever else was told, would have to come voluntarily from Theo.

They set off later that morning, driving down the main road along the coast towards the village of Bray, but after a few miles Theo asked the driver to turn inland down a narrow lane that, after another few miles, opened out into wide open countryside. Finally they arrived before a pair of huge, black wrought-iron gates, each with the family coat of arms on it and the name of the estate, "Green Laurels". They looked as though they were left permanently open, as grass was growing around the base, and Theo instructed the driver to go on through.

Just inside the gates was a small gatehouse that gave all the signs of not having been lived in for some time. It had been a pretty little house at one time, and roses were still growing over its walls, but the windows were broken and dusty, and Elizabeth could see swallows flying in and out of the empty frames. "What a pity!" she remarked as they drove past. "It looks so sad and unloved."

"Yes."

They continued to drive along a winding road lined with lime trees, and after a while came around a bend, and there was the big mansion, standing on the crest of a hill. The driver stopped the horses, and they all stared at it.

"It's a beautiful house," said Elizabeth. "What a marvellous place in which to have been brought up!"

"Yes." Theo asked the driver to move on, and after a few

yards told him to turn off the road and onto a small side lane that curved off into a large wood.

"We aren't going to visit the big house?" Elizabeth had thought she had noticed Theo give a fleeting smile as he looked at the house, but it was too enigmatic for her to try to decipher what it might mean, and she did not like to ask.

"No. We won't be visiting the house... ever!"

The road became narrower and narrower, the trees closing in on either side. It was obvious it was rarely used, and Elizabeth began to feel an air of almost menace about it -- a chill stillness. The air was dank, and the sun barely filtered through the overhanging trees. Theo had said nothing, and all that could be heard was the clopping of the horses hooves and the occasional call of a woodpigeon. Even the two men accompanying them stopped talking to each other.

They had gone about a half mile when Theo asked that the carriage be stopped, and after helping Elizabeth alight, told the men to wait for them. They then continued walking until the carriage was far behind, and the sound of the men chatting again had faded away. Neither had said anything.

"It's eerie here," said Elizabeth finally. "I can't imagine Titania and all her elves coming here anon."

"'Our' elves," Theo said absent-mindedly.

Elizabeth ignored the correction. "More like hobgoblins and imps." She clasped her arms around herself.

"Are you cold?"

"No. it's just that..."

They walked on in silence until they came to a small clearing. A small breeze had arisen, and the aspen leaves rustled around them.

"Come," said Theo. He led her to a large rock that stood out amongst the grass and other wild plants. He looked about him. "This was a favourite place for Walter, my cousin as I called him, and me. We used to come here and play all kinds of boys' games, climb trees and pretend we were brigands." He bent over and picked up a stick which he threw into the woods, where it landed silently in the undergrowth. "We had a good life, and were the firmest of friends. Even when we grew up, we still did almost everything together."

"It sounds as though you lived well."

Theo gazed at the rock.

"For many years that's true, but then he went away to take up a commission in the navy when he was eighteen, but was back home again within the second year. He claimed he was on special leave in order to prepare for a clandestine mission, but he never went back, and over time began to behave in an odd manner.

"At first he'd make wild claims as to his importance to the navy, and say he was receiving secret messages, and would lose his temper with me because he claimed I was listening in, and trying to sabotage his mission.

"Then he'd get annoyed with me because I *didn't* listen, and would scream at me, saying I was deaf if I couldn't hear the voices... He even insisted he was being followed, and that someone was trying to harm him.

"I know his parents were worried about him, and even considered taking him to a physician in London to see what the problem might be, but before they could do this, they were both killed in an accident." Theo put his hand out and touched the cold rock. "It happened one fine afternoon like this, when they were out driving in their curricle, of which they were so very proud. No-one knew what happened, because no-one knew there had even been an accident until the horses came careening into the stable yard without my godparents. We went out looking for them and found them lying in the road. My godmother was already dead, and my godfather died a few minutes after."

"Oh Theo! How terrible!"

"Walter arrived home later, and everyone was perplexed because he didn't seem to understand the gravity of the situation... I was twenty at the time."

Elizabeth shivered. "Your poor godparents. What a sad thing to happen to you and your cousin too. Both gone at once."

Theo put his arm around her, and pulled her close to him before continuing. "Walter inherited the estate, of course, but many of the servants left because he'd become so capricious, and would accuse them of stealing his property, or spreading malicious lies about him. I couldn't leave because I still hadn't received my inheritance, and had no money with which to live anywhere else, but my life there began to change for the worse.

"Walter, as master of his estate, began accusing me of all sorts of things. He'd creep about the house, spying on the servants and on me, and on one occasion taunted me by telling me he'd seen the papers relating to my birth, and that I was really the grandson of John Potter, the Archbishop of Canterbury."

"Indeed? And is that true?" asked Elizabeth.

Theo shrugged. "I've no idea. He just said there were records, but when I begged him to show them to me, he simply laughed, and said he'd burnt them. Then he threatened to see to it that I'd be left destitute."

"But why would he turn against you like that?"

"I don't know. It was obvious to everyone he was a sick man, and a dangerous man too, because he wasn't so mad that he didn't sound believable to those who didn't know him well. Regardless, he succeeded in making my life intolerable, and I couldn't wait to leave what was once a happy, loving home, but which had turned into a cold mausoleum to which I was tied in misery and loneliness." He was silent for a while, and removing his arm from around Elizabeth, sat down on a large tree stump and put his head in his hands.

Elizabeth sat down next to him and took his hand, letting his head rest against her shoulder. "How did Walter die, Theo?"

He sat up straight, and pointed to the rock. "Even after we had grown up I often used to come and sit on there to read, or to daydream, mostly about the acting career I hoped to embark upon... I'd even act out scenes here by myself... And after he began to make life intolerable for me, I came here just get out of his way. And then one evening, I was sitting there as usual..." He pointed again to the rock. "I was reading... Oh God!" Theo threw his head back, looked up towards the tops of the trees, and shuddered.

"My dear Theo! What on earth happened?"

He held her hand so tightly it hurt. "He suddenly appeared out of the woods. He was dressed in dark clothes, and I greeted him before noticing that he was carrying a sabre, which he began to wave around. Then he started shouting at me. He said he'd already made his parents pay, and now I was going to pay too. He came towards me with the sabre raised over his head, holding it with both hands. I tried to escape, but the rock was in the way, and I was yelling at him that I was unarmed, and had nothing with which to defend myself. But he still kept screaming at me.

"I was lying back on the rock to get as far away from him as possible, while he stood over me with the tip of the sabre aimed at my chest. Then he brought it down, and it went right through my ribs on my side. He pulled it out, and raised it to strike again, but instead he fell on top of me, blood streaming out of his shattered skull..." Theo became silent, remembering the scene, unable to go on.

Elizabeth put her arm around him, smoothing his back with her hand.

After a while Theo continued. "A servant, who had seen him entering the woods armed with the sabre, decided to follow him, wondering what he was up to. He came upon us just after Walter had attacked me, and was about to strike again... I didn't know the man was there, nor did I see him pick up the rock and hit Walter with such force that he... he..." Theo put his head down between his knees and began to sob, his body shaking. "Oh God,! Oh God! I'd be dead if that man hadn't come!"

Elizabeth let him weep, and only Theo knew that the man was James.

She was only too thankful when he felt ready to leave. What had happened in the grove had transformed it from what one would normally think of as a calm and verdant sanctuary, into a foreboding jungle of grasping undergrowth and twisted trees, whose trunks had an air of sinister intent, and the echoes of what it had witnessed still seemed to reverberate from the shaking aspen leaves.

They walked back to where the carriage was still waiting, and then set off towards the entrance to the estate. When they reached the gates Theo signalled the driver to stop the horses. "You've heard most of it, but now I might as well tell you the rest."

Elizabeth looked at him in astonishment. "There's more?"

Theo nodded. "After my cousin died, the estate devolved onto a relative whom I'd never seen before, and who had never seen the house. However, within days of Walter's burial they arrived in their magnificent barouche, followed by a train of carts piled high with all their possessions, and they moved in at once.

"They'd brought with them many of their own servants as well, and summarily dismissed everyone they didn't want to keep, and when they discovered I was living there, and who I was, they told me I wasn't welcome, and turned me out. I was still recovering from Walter's attack, so they said I could move in and stay with the gatehouse keeper until I was fit enough to move on, but that I was on no account to enter the big house, for if I did, I should be treated as one of the servants." He pointed to the little gatehouse. "So this was where I spent my last days on the estate. Fortunately I came into my inheritance during that time, and so was saved from finding myself penniless on the streets... Home now if you please," he told the driver who, glad to leave the area, picked up the reins and slapped the horses' backs with them, forcing them into a fast canter.

Elizabeth looked back at the forlorn iron gates as they receded into the distance. Theo looked straight ahead. He never wanted to see his old home again.

That night, when they went to bed, it seemed as though Theo could not get close enough to Elizabeth, and hugged her tightly, fearful that she would be snatched away from him, and he would lose her. He kept whispering her name over and over, touching her, smoothing her hair and her cheeks. "You must never leave me, my beloved Bess. Please, please never leave me... My life without you wouldn't be worth living. I ache at even the thought of it."

It was as though he had spent his life starved of demonstrative affection, and Elizabeth soothed him as she would a child, and they eventually fell asleep, but when she woke in the middle of the night and reached out to touch him, he was not there. Startled, she sat up in bed, then noticed his outline against the dark indigo light of the window. He was sitting in a chair, motionless, gazing out over the city.

Having no idea what awful and confused thoughts might be churning in his mind, she worried that she had made things worse for Theo by encouraging him to come here against his will. What he had endured in his past had turned out to be far more harrowing than she could ever have imagined, and she regretted that in her ignorance, she had pressured him. There was also the experience outside the theatre on the first day of their visit. What a maelstrom of emotions poor Theo must be experiencing!

She lay awake wondering if she should go to him, or encourage him to come back to bed with her. She had already learnt enough about him to know that when he needed her comfort, he would seek her out and want to hold her, as he had done when they came to bed a few hours before. Now though, he did not, and she feared he may not want her comfort, and after much agonizing, she decided to leave him alone in the hope that he could come to terms with his past on his own.

For the rest of the night she pretended to be asleep, and it was dawn before he returned to bed and finally fell asleep -- and she did as well.

It was almost noon when they awoke, and even later by the time they were dressed and ready to face the new day. It was cloudy, not a good day for making more excursions into the countryside, and Elizabeth did not think Theo would have the desire for that anyway, so she wondered aloud if he might prefer some time to himself again. She could take her lady's maid and perhaps investigate some more of the fashionable shops in town. She wanted to know how he felt, but it seemed as though Theo was doing his best to pretend that all was well, and if he himself did not want to tell her, she could not ask him.

"No, no," he said. "I have an idea. As you saw, there are some fine bookshops in Dublin. Shall we go together, and spend what's left of the day choosing books for our library?"

"Yes, of course." In a way she was glad of the opportunity to wipe away yesterday's memories, but feared Theo's high spirits were assumed for her comfort only, and the only reason he was behaving this way was so as not to distress her further than he had already done. Having no other option but to join him in his present frame of mind, however, she set her mind to thinking of titles she could list. "I can already think of some of the latest authors whose works I'd love to read, and to have in our collection. I'm particularly interested in writings by women," she began. "We'd certainly buy Catherine Talbot's essays on various topics. Then there's Hester Chapone's Letters on the Improvement of the Mind. Oh! And, of course, we'd get Elizabeth Montagu's essay on the Writing and Genius of Shakespeare... for you," she added. "Oh, and Fanny Burney has just..."

Theo held up his hand, smiling, "Yes, yes. We'll buy whatever you want... just so long as there's a little room left for my own books as well."

Despite the clouds and Elizabeth's doubts as to the true state of her husband's mind, the gloom of yesterday's tragic revelations did seem to have lifted, and before they set off for the nearest bookseller's, her relief was immense when Theo put his arms around her, and held her close, kissing her. "You were right," he told her. "What happened yesterday was something I've dreaded and forced out of my mind all these years, but it's done now." He sighed. "I can't promise that it won't continue to come back to haunt me on occasion. What happened back then isn't something easily erased, but now I have you with whom to share it, I know it will all be that much easier to overcome."

Now happy again, and proud too, Elizabeth tucked her arm in his as they walked out of the inn, and he helped her into the carriage; and the rest of their sojourn in the fair city of Dublin passed pleasurably and without further incident.

Though it could not be said their visit had been emotionally uneventful, physically their time together had been altogether as pleasurable as it could be. In addition, no footpads robbed them; no highwaymen accosted them; no members of the Hellfire Club caused them to sweat with fear, or pinked Theo with their swords. If there were duels, they had not witnessed them, and if the Liberty or the Ormond Boys decided carry on their feud in the streets of the city, they did not do so while Theo and Elizabeth were in town. The dagger was returned to Mr. Flaherty unbloodied, having spent the entire time secreted in a closet in Theo's private and unused chamber, and apart from discovering that on occasion -- she did not ask how often -- her husband had visited Mrs. Margaret Leeson's select establishment, Elizabeth left Dublin thoroughly enchanted with everything the great city had to offer.

CHAPTER 14

Theo was in his library, sitting astride one of the many wooden chests that had arrived from Dublin, and singing to himself. Dressed only his breeches and stockings and his shirt, which had the sleeves rolled up, he was removing the contents from one of the chests, admiring each leather-bound volume, running his fingers down their spines, and opening their gilt-edged leaves to read a page or two here and there. Many were books from his own library back home in Dublin, that he had arranged to be shipped here to Haverfordwest, along with others they had bought together.

He assigned each book an area on the floor according to its size and subject matter, ready to be placed on the new bookshelves, then looked around for another patch on which to start a new section. Surrounded by mounds of books, he was contented for now with his new project and with assigning shelves on which to place everything. He was thinking also that, although he had been well able to afford the expense of binding all the books he had bought, it might nevertheless be an interesting art, which he could learn to do for himself, and save money at the same time.

"Mr. Potter, Sir." James was standing in the doorway. "Mr. Edwardes is here to see you."

Theo jumped to his feet. "Let him in James. Let him in."

Mr. Edwardes peered through the doorway and began to pick his way through the maze of books towards Theo, who was likewise heading towards his cousin of two months. They shook hands.

"Welcome home, Theo! It's so good to see you again! How was Ireland? How is my cousin Elizabeth?"

"Ah!" said Theo. "In answer to your last question, I'm afraid our Elizabeth isn't too well at this moment... Can I offer you some breakfast? I've not had mine yet."

Mr. Edwardes declined the breakfast with a shake of his head. "But Elizabeth?" he asked. "She's not ill I hope?"

Theo smiled. "Not at all, not at all," he repeated, grinning. "It's like this. We went to Ireland as two, and we appear to have arrived back as three!"

Mr. Edwardes was delighted, and the two men shook hands again. "Congratulations, my dear Theo! And do you know yet when the happy day will be?"

"We think next May, but it's early days yet." More congratulations followed, along with musings about the joys and tribulations of fatherhood, and James appeared with Theo's breakfast, which had to be set down on one of the unopened chests.

"Are you sure James can't bring you something to eat or a drink, Bill?"

Mr. Edwardes declined again, and Theo began eating his breakfast while his cousin explained the reason for his early morning visit. "Of course I wanted to pay my respects to you and Elizabeth, and to welcome you back home," he said. "But I was wondering as well if you would know of any way in which I can solve a small problem. You've shown yourself to be a practical and creative sort of man, so who best to discuss this with?" He waited while Theo finished his mouthful.

"Right," said Theo. "And thank you for your

146

compliment, although I'm not sure I'm worthy of it. So what's the problem?"

"Well, I'm on the Common Council as you know, and there are issues about which we'd like the citizens of the town to be informed, but, as always happens, we have no efficient way of broadcasting our message. Those of us on the council don't have the time or inclination to write out bulletins to be posted in all the areas where they're likely to be seen. There are many townspeople who are able to read, which is naturally why we want to put up notices, but there are few who can also write..." Mr. Edwardes, sitting on another unopened chest, slapped his hands on his knees. "So... I thought that with you having been with the theatre, you might know how you dealt with this problem when you wanted to advertise your presence in a town where you were expecting to perform, and there were no posters to announce it."

Although Theo did not like to point out that Haverfordwest was the only place to which he had ever travelled, that would require such advertisements to be produced by the players themselves, he did remember the fiasco with the printing press when he first arrived here, and a wry smile appeared. He took another mouthful of his breakfast, and Mr. Edwardes waited again for him to finish.

Theo finally pushed away his plate, and wiped his mouth and hands. "Ah yes," he said. "Well, if you'll remember, there *were* no printed notices in Haverfordwest when we came here to perform, and that, I'm afraid, was my fault."

"Indeed?"

"Yes." And Theo explained what had happened. "I'm not even sure if we still have the accursed printing press," he said. "James may have given it back to the other actors to take back to Dublin. It was their property after all."

Mr. Edwardes nodded. "And what if you *do* still have it?"

147

"I think the best thing would be to find out whether we do," and Theo stepped carefully over several piles of books blocking his way to the door, muttering something about the bell being somewhere. "James!" he called out. "James! Are you there?"

James appeared, rubbing his hands on his breeches. "Sir?" He looked at the mess, and did not attempt to enter, so stood in the doorway.

"James, do you know if we still have that printing press? You know, the one..."

"Yes indeed, Sir." James smiled. "I do indeed remember it, and yes, I think it's in the closet under the stairway."

Theo was not at all sure he was pleased that the object of so much frustration was still in their possession.

"Would you like me to get it, Sir?"

Theo looked around. "Yes please James... that's if you can find anywhere to put it."

Mr. Edwardes was pleased. "Capital! Capital!"

It was several minutes before James reappeared. "I had to wipe the dust and cobwebs off it, Sir," he apologised. He looked around. "Where would you like me to put it, Sir?"

Theo knew where he would like it put, but this was not the moment to say so. "Hmm," he pointed to yet another unopened chest. "Can you put it over there please, James?" He stood up. "Here, let me help you." He advanced towards James before realizing there was not enough space for the two of them to tread between the piles of books. Instead, he started to clear a path, and the printing press was finally set down.

"Thank you James... Oh! What about ink? I don't suppose we have any ink to go with it, do we?"

James thought there was, and went to look, coming back a few minutes later with something that might have been ink at some time, but was clearly no longer usable.

"Well, the printing press isn't much use without ink to go

with it," Theo commented.

Mr. Edwardes had come over to look at the machine. He ran his hand over it. "I've never seen anything like this before. How does it work?"

Theo sighed. "Well, I'm afraid I have yet to find out."

"But you're clever that way. If you're not rushed as you were before, I'm sure you could get it to work."

"Not without ink, I can't."

"No," agreed Mr. Edwardes, "But there must be ink available for it somewhere."

Theo was anxious to get back to his books, but recognized that he did need to exert himself on behalf of his cousin. "I don't know of any other printer in Pembrokeshire who'd sell me ink, so I'd have to get it from London," he said. "So, seeing that it takes two weeks for the request to be delivered, and two weeks for the ink to be delivered back here, it'll be at least a month before I can even start on it."

Mr. Edwardes nodded. "Can we go ahead and order it anyway? Even if it can't be used for our current project, it's something we most certainly need here in Haverfordwest in any event."

Theo was nodding in resignation when Elizabeth appeared in the doorway. She looked around at the jumble of books and chests littered over the floor, and put her hand to her mouth. "Theo! What *are* you doing?" She then noticed Mr. Edwardes sitting on a chest in the midst of it. "Cousin! How good to see you! But what a welcome we're giving you!"

Theo, not content with wending his way through the piles of books, leaped over the chests lying between him and the doorway, and stood next his wife, smiling. "I've told our cousin our good news."

"Oh Theo!" she scolded him. "It's such early days yet…Things can happen."

"Nonsense! Nothing is going to happen, and we're going

to have a son, and we'll call him John."

"It could be a daughter."

"No! It's going to be a son. I have decreed it."

It was well after noon on a frosty October day, when Elizabeth set down her book in her lap, and leaned her head against the back of the chair, smiling. She was happy and contented. She felt she had everything a woman could wish for: a handsome, amiable and wealthy husband who adored her and was universally popular, a comfortable and elegant home, all the books she could ever read, a lively and busy social life and -- she felt her stomach -- their first child was on the way.

She was still pondering over her great fortune, and wondering if there was anything else she could possibly hope for, when there was a light tap on the door of her sitting room. "Come in...Yes, Mary-Anne, what is it?"

Her maid curtsied, and stood at the doorway, embarrassed.

"Mary-Anne?"

Mary-Anne curtsied again. "Well, Ma'am. It's cook."

"Cook?"

"Yes Ma'am. You see, she needs to be able to use the kitchen so as to get dinner for four o'clock."

"And is there something that's preventing her?"

"Well, the master's using the kitchen, and her kitchen table is covered with..." She spread her arms in demonstration of the extent of the problem. "... all kinds of bits and pieces."

"Mr. Potter is using the kitchen, Mary-Anne? Why would he be using the kitchen?"

"Well Ma'am. I don't know Ma'am, but he's been working away in there since after breakfast, and cook has all these fresh apples, and she needs the table... and..."

Elizabeth stood up. "Well, we had better go and see. I

can't imagine..." She accompanied her maid down the servants' staircase towards the kitchen, but stopped half way when she heard her husband. The volcano of his temper had erupted, and he was cursing in a most ungentlemanly way.

"Thank you, Mary-Anne. You may go now."

Elizabeth arrived in the kitchen to find Theo, hands on his hips, staring down at parts of what appeared to have once been a machine. Cook's normally pristine kitchen table was littered with small, dirty fragments, and covered with large black stains.

"Theo?"

Theo looked up. He was furious. "This damnable machine! I ordered inks for it especially from London, and they took over a month to get here, and I've been struggling to get it to work all day, and now I know why it never worked from the start!" He took a deep breath, and Elizabeth went over and gazed down at the mess on cook's table.

"No wonder it wouldn't work!" he continued angrily. "There's a piece missing! And I've wasted all this time, and now it's never going to work, and I promised Bill..." his voice trailed off and he shrugged his shoulders. Temper spent, he looked down at the ruined table. "Cook isn't going to be pleased, is she?" He gave it a tentative wipe with his kerchief, but the stains had already set in the soft deal wood.

"I think that's quite probable." Elizabeth sent for James. "James, I think Mr. Potter no longer has a use for this printer. Would you please dispose of it."

"Yes Ma'am." James removed everything from the table, while Theo looked on.

"Should we get cook a new table, do you suppose?"

Elizabeth looked at the damage. "No, I don't think it'll make any difference to its usability once it's been thoroughly cleaned, although I have to say it most likely will never look quite the same again." She turned to leave the kitchen, suppressing a strong desire to laugh -- it was too soon for that. A rueful Theo followed her.

They went upstairs to the library and Elizabeth sat down. All the books had long since found their niches on the shelves; the room had developed a comfortable and dignified atmosphere, and for the moment, was silent.

Theo sat down also, his legs stretched out in front of him. He was thinking.

"I believe," he said after several minutes, "that if one does something, then it should be done properly, and I have this idea."

Elizabeth raised her eyebrows and waited. What new project had Theo in mind?

"The town needs a printing service, so what better than to fill this need?" He stood up and began pacing around the room, thinking aloud. "I'm sure it would be successful. We could even sell stationery and books. I remember Dublin had many such businesses, and they all seemed to thrive."

Theo had not mentioned Dublin since their return, and Elizabeth had contented herself with the thought that after their visit to Ireland, he had finally given up any idea of ever returning there to resume his acting career. It was something that satisfied her greatly, as she herself would never, ever want to leave her beloved Pembrokeshire, much as she had enjoyed her time in Dublin. Nevertheless, she felt she should remind him of something.

"Haverfordwest isn't Dublin, Theo."

Theo wanted to reply, "How can I ever forget that Haverfordwest isn't Dublin?" but he refrained. Instead he said, "I know, and it's true that Dublin is one of the most sophisticated cities outside London, but what is there to stop Haverfordwest being another Dublin? Like Dublin, it's thoroughly anglicized, is surrounded by enormous estates belonging to the nobility, who think enough of the town to have taken the trouble to build themselves townhouses here so as to take part in an elegant season..." He paused. "And the town is just as ideally placed as Dublin... I wonder even that it's not already become more vibrant."

"You must remember Theo, it's taken Haverfordwest longer than many places to recover, first from Mr. Cromwell, then from the big plague, from which it suffered more severely than almost anywhere else."

Theo walked over to the window, in front of which stood his large mahogany writing desk. He placed his hands flat down on it. "It's such a shame it doesn't have a theatre though... Still, I'm convinced there's hope for Haverfordwest in this regard, and then..." He turned and leaned back against the desk without finishing what he was about to say, and after a short silence, continued. "We'll of course need to buy the latest and highest-quality printing machine available... maybe even two." He looked at Elizabeth. "It'll be too large a service to provide it here in the house, so we'll need to find somewhere convenient in which to start the business."

Elizabeth was relieved her home was not to be turned into a busy place of trade; it was enough that the library, as another of her husband's ways of uplifting the culture of the town, was soon to open on certain days as a reading room and lending library for the local aristocracy and gentry. There was one other little impediment though to his latest project, and she felt it necessary to point it out. "Theo, you've forgotten; you can't open a business in Haverfordwest just like that. There are rules regarding residency, knowing your trade, being a burgess... and as far as I understand it, you don't qualify for any of them yet. I think you'd have to apprentice yourself to a master printer first."

Theo remembered his earlier idea of opening a coffee house, and the reasons why that had been impossible as well, and frustrated at continually having obstacles set in his way of achieving something, he snapped. "How can I apprentice myself to a printer when there's no printer in the town to apprentice myself to? That's ridiculous!" He swung round to face his wife. "Wait! I *do* know where there's a printer! A master printer too! That Welshman I met the night we performed *Romeo and Juliet* at The Blue Boar -- Mr. William Sutton!"

"But..." Elizabeth could understand all the problems still attending the idea. "Theo? How sure are you that you really want to set up in such a business? You don't need... A printing business?... You?..." She shook her head at the idea of someone like Theo running any kind of trade, let alone a printing business. "Are you really sure you want to set up a printing business? A trade is so... so..."

Theo knew what she was going to say, and did not want to hear it. "Bess, my dear. I *must* do *something* with my time. I can't live idly wandering around Haverfordwest, achieving nothing, going nowhere! I couldn't live with myself, and most certainly wouldn't be fit to live with. I can't be a real actor as long as Haverfordwest has no proper, licensed theatre, and if I can't carry on with my career, then I can at least have an excuse to do something with the written word: printing plays and books and other things seems to be the only alternative I can think of; I can't spend my life just reading."

Elizabeth was distraught at the extent of Theo's agitation, but still felt it necessary to point out to him her concerns as to the type of occupation he was proposing to enter. "But you aren't going to be printing many plays and books in this part of the country, Theo. It will, I imagine, be mostly what you refer to as 'other things': notices, brochures, and various publications put out by the council. I just can't believe that you'll not find it all so boring!"

Theo was silent. He was already bored. He had all this energy that needed to be expended, and this, coupled with his

154

conviction that satisfaction in life came only from achieving -- or at least working towards -- a goal of some sort, meant he needed to be gainfully occupied doing *something* worthwhile. He had plenty of money with which to acquire anything he wanted, but the satisfaction gained by admiring a new purchase was short-lived, and in the end, not satisfying at all. He had already said he did not want the responsibility of owning an estate, nor did a life of hunting and killing animals, shooting birds and spending hours waiting for a fish to bite appeal to him in the slightest. Even the thought of guns and killing caused a reflex response in him that opened his dreaded Pandora's box, and he shivered.

Seeing his mind was fixed on this new project, Elizabeth finally came up with an idea. "Let me talk to cousin Edwardes. He's on the council. I'll ask him to talk to one of my other cousins. He and his fellow councillors might be in a position to help you if necessary. Maybe something can be arranged. They might be amenable to making an exception, especially as what you'll be offering is something they all need... But first, you need to ask this Mr. Sutton if he's willing go into a business where he's the master, but you're the owner... it does all seem rather complicated Theo," she added, bemused at what seemed to her a most inappropriate path for him to follow.

Theo bowed to Elizabeth's reasoning, and went to see what Mr. Sutton's thoughts might be. Mr. Sutton could think of nothing he would like better.

Mr. Edwardes was approached, a meeting was held to discuss the matter, and by the new year, Theo had his printing machine, and had installed it in a large terraced house he had rented on High Street. By the end of that spring he and Mr. Sutton had more work than they could handle, and Theo, always a quick learner, wondered how it could possibly take years for someone to learn the trade. They also had hired an assistant, William, a boy of fifteen who was to be their errand boy. The Potter Printing Company of Haverfordwest was in business, and everyone was delighted -- and Theo had something with which to occupy himself.

Elizabeth meanwhile looked down at her stomach and wondered if Theo's son -- as Theo had determined that it would be such -- would take after his father. It was something to think about.

CHAPTER 15

It was now May, and Theo was alternately pacing back and forth along the wide corridor at Dunstable Hall, and leaning against the wall outside the blue room, the chamber in which he had spent so much time just over eighteen months ago, after being shot. Every now and then either Mrs. Edwardes or the midwife would emerge on some errand, and whenever they opened the door Theo would try to look in to see how his beloved Bess was faring. Her cries were putting him so much out of humour that the women tried to insist he leave and occupy himself elsewhere.

"There's no point in you upsetting yourself like this, Theo. We'll call you when the time is right," his mother-in-law had told him on several occasions.

"But it's been so long. She must be so weary. Are you sure everything is going well?"

"It's the first time, and the first time often takes the longest, and yes, your wife is bearing up well."

"Would it help if I came in and held her hand?"

"Theo! How could you possibly think of such a thing? It's not the place for men to be at all! This is a woman's domain! Now, be off with you! Surely you're tired and hungry! You've not eaten in sixteen hours!"

Theo, however, was not to be removed from his vigil outside the room. "Neither has Elizabeth. Isn't sixteen hours too long? Are you absolutely sure everything is progressing well?"

"Yes, yes." Mrs. Edwardes shooed him away, and Theo finally wandered off, not knowing where to go or what to do with himself.

He first made his way down to the home farm, hoping to talk to Mr. Griffiths, but when he got there he was told the farmer was in the ten-acre field beyond the woods, turning the hay. This was further away from the house than he wanted to venture at this time, so he turned back, and as the stables were on his way, went to where Hercules had been kept since his arrival the previous afternoon. He walked in through the high stone arch leading to the stable yard, and on into the large, cobbled courtyard, where the groom and three stable boys were carefully grooming the four Hanoverians. When they saw Theo they all stopped what they were doing, doffed their caps, and stood politely.

"Good afternoon. I... I..." Theo could not think of any reason why he should be visiting the stables. He looked around at the spotless yard. "I... I came to see how Hercules is doing," he blurted out. "I think he may have had a stone lodged in his hoof."

"Really Sir? He didn't seem lame when I took him out a while ago, but perhaps we should take another look." The groom handed to one of the stable boys the Hanoverian he had been grooming, and Hercules was led out of his stall and inspected, but no stones were found. There was an awkward silence. Theo, normally at ease conversing with almost anyone regardless of their status in society, was too agitated to think of anything but Elizabeth, and looked about him, wishing now that he had not come. He should have found himself a quiet corner of the estate where he would not have had to talk to anyone.

The groom, a sensible man in his late fifties, understood Theo's anxiety. Many years ago now he himself had experienced it. "How is Mrs. Potter, Sir?" he asked finally.

Theo, grateful to the man for giving him the opportunity to express his concerns, glanced over at the young stable boys still standing around, and the groom took the hint and sent them back to their work.

"I don't know, Thomas, if the truth be told. She seems to have been in labour for such a long time, and it's her first child... and I'm ignorant about such things... You, Thomas, you have children, don't you?"

The groom went over to the mounting block and encouraged Theo to sit down, then took the liberty of setting himself down next to him. "Yes Sir. My wife and I had seven children." He did not tell the anxious young father-to-be that two of these had died at birth, and that they had lost another two who had died during their infancy.

"Ah then! You know about these things. Is sixteen hours too long to be in labour?"

"It *is* a long time Sir, but it's her first, so I shouldn't be overly concerned at this time. I'm sure you'll be told if there are any developments."

The two men sat side by side on the mounting block in silence, and Theo twirled his hat around in his hands. "Hmm. It's all so worrying Thomas," he sighed.

"Yes Sir... May I suggest you take Hercules, and ride out onto the long meadow? You can be seen from there, and called if necessary."

Theo agreed; he was glad of any opportunity to be doing something, and Hercules was saddled up. Thomas went back to his grooming, and Theo was just walking the horse out under the arch, when James appeared, out of breath. "Sir! Mrs. Edwardes has requested I go to fetch Mr. Nash."

"Mr. Nash! The physician! What on earth has happened?"

"I don't know, Sir, but I need to go to Haverfordwest right now to fetch him."

"No, no! James. Let me go." And Theo set off at a gallop to fetch Mr. Nash, every step of the way fearing the worst, his stomach churning, making him sick with anxiety. To add to his panic Mr. Nash was not at home, and he spent a distressing hour searching for him all over town, unable to push Hercules lest he trip and tumble on the unforgiving cobbles.

At last he saw the physician coming towards him up Market Street, and within minutes the two men were hastening back to Dunstable Hall.

It was now eighteen hours, and Theo was beside himself, pacing up and down outside the blue room. It was all too quiet, and time had never passed so slowly. Even the bell of the great clock down in the hall seemed to have chosen to slow its striking of the hours, and still Theo waited.

Then Mrs. Edwardes appeared, looking distraught.

Theo rushed up to her. "What is it, Mrs. Edwardes? For God's sake, what is it?"

Mrs. Edwardes put her hand on Theo's arm. "Elizabeth will recover well, but the strain on the baby has been immense, and it's struggling. Mr. Nash is concerned about the heartbeat, which is irregular." She shook her head.

"What can be done to save him?... Her?... Mrs. Edwardes?"

"It's a boy."

Theo leaned against the wall, and banged his fists against it. "No! No!... And Elizabeth? You're sure she won't die too?"

The midwife appeared at the door, and whispered to Mrs. Edwardes.

"Theo, as I told you, Elizabeth will be all right, but it's been suggested you make another trip into Haverfordwest to fetch the vicar.

"You say my son is really dying?" He pressed his forehead against the wall in despair.

"We can't be sure at this stage if he'll survive, so it's best he be given a private baptism now at Dunstable Hall. If all goes well, he can be welcomed into the church properly at a later date." Mrs. Edwardes patted him gently on the back.

Theo, his face still pressed to the wall, shook his head. "James! James must go. I can't leave my wife and my son now!" He swung around to face his mother-in-law. "I have to see them." And this time there was no stopping him.

The vicar finally arrived, and Theo and Elizabeth's first son, John Potter, was privately baptised by the Reverend Ayleway, vicar of St. Mary's Church; and although the first few days passed in constant anxiety, gradually both mother and son improved, and Mr. Nash was able to declare young John Potter had survived the crisis.

CHAPTER 16

The Potter lending library and reading room had been open for several months, and was a great success, although not without its problems. It had been available to both gentlemen and ladies of the gentry, but the former had complained about this arrangement.

Their first complaint was the necessity for them to acknowledge the entrance and exit of any ladies to the library by being required, as manners dictated, to rise and bow on each occasion, thus disturbing the progress of their reading. Their second complaint was that the ladies, who never entered alone, but in at least twos -- as was proper -- were more in the habit of chattering annoyingly once seated, rather than engaging in the supposed purpose of their visit, which was to read or to select a book to borrow.

The problem was finally resolved by opening the library to gentlemen on the one day, and to ladies on another. Once this was achieved, the gentlemen then felt free to carry on their own lengthy conversations without the inconvenience of having any ladies listening in. This occupation indeed, after a while, became more the norm rather than the exception, so much so that, for the gentlemen at least, the Potter reading room became a private sanctuary in which they could get to discuss whatever they did not want anyone else to hear -- usually of a political nature. Theo, who enjoyed the camaraderie as much as the other gentlemen, was not averse at all to the arrangement, although he had to acknowledge it did little to raise the cultural awareness of those attending. It was something he had to accept, moreover, that some of the gentlemen in attendance, although literate and well-educated members of Pembrokeshire's finest families, were never even seen to open a book, let alone read it.

On one day in November, there were about half a dozen gentlemen seated around the fire in Theo's library. The weather was as dismal as Pembrokeshire can get at this time of year, with a strong wind from the southeast blowing before it heavy drifts of fine, soaking rain of the kind that seeps into every nook and corner of the clothing, something Theo had heard referred to as 'Swansea rain'. In the library, however, it was warm and comfortable, and as the daylight was already fading at four o'clock in the afternoon, the fire's leaping flames threw small orange darts of light around the darkening room and over the figures seated within it.

"It really was a moonlight battle." Young Lieutenant Foley, home on leave from the navy, visiting his father in Narberth, but now standing, leaning against Theo's library fireplace, was relating the story of his part in the taking of the Spanish Captain's ship off Cape St. Vincent at two o'clock in the morning last January. "And I was on Admiral Sir George Rodney's ship, and Don Juan de Langara was racing for home in Spain, and one of his ships, the Santa Domingo just blew up!" He whooshed his arms in the air, his young eyes wide with awe. "Then we raced after them, and our ships were faster, and..."

There was a knock on the door, and James entered.

"Yes, James?" James approached, and whispered in

Theo's ear.

"Sir, I'm sorry to interrupt you, but there's a young lad at the door. Says he must see you."

"Do you know who he is, James?"

James shook his head. "Although I think he might be the lad that works at the printing shop, Sir."

Theo stood up. "Excuse me gentlemen. I have some business that must be attended to." He turned to James. "Perhaps some refreshment can be found for the gentlemen... an aperitif before their dinners, perhaps?"

James nodded, and Theo bowed and left the room. As he entered the hallway, he heard Foley return to his story.

The young boy was indeed his errand boy. His clothing was soaked through, and he was shivering, still standing out under the porch.

"Come in, Bill... come in!" Theo ordered him, as the boy hung back. "Let's get you down into the warm kitchen, and dry you off."

He ushered the skinny little fifteen-year-old down the servants' staircase and into cook's cosy kitchen where a big fire blazed in the huge open fireplace, candles flickered, casting leaping shadows over the walls, and the odour of roasting chicken and baked apple pie filled the warm air. Cook was preparing dinner.

"My!" exclaimed cook. "What have we here?" She put down her rolling pin, put out her hands, and pulled the boy towards the fire, tutting and clucking like a hen over her chick.

"I know you're busy preparing dinner, cook, so perhaps you can find someone to take care of this young man... find him some dry clothes, and..." Theo looked at the boy. "Find him something to eat."

"Sir, Sir!" William protested. "I didn't know who to go to. I need to tell you..."

"Is anyone badly injured or dying at this moment, or is

164

anyone's home burning down right now?"

William shook his head. "But…"

"Then it can wait until you're taken care of." Theo turned to leave the room, telling William on the way, "I'll return within the hour, and we can talk then."

As promised, Theo returned fifty minutes later. William was wearing some clothes belonging to someone much larger, while his own sent up wisps of steam before the fire.

"Cook, you can serve dinner as soon as you're ready. Please have someone tell Mrs. Potter I'll join her at the table as soon as I can… Come, Bill." He put his hand behind the boy's shoulder, led him upstairs to his private sitting room, and pointed to a chair. "Sit down, Bill." He himself stood resting one elbow on the fireplace, ready to listen.

"Sir, my father's in prison… He owes someone some money, and couldn't pay him because it's his knees you see… No-one would hire him at the fair this year because of his knees, and he can't get out of gaol because he owes the gaoler fees, so the gaoler won't let him out… My mother's in labour and my fourteen-year-old sister doesn't know what to do… The midwife won't come and I'm afraid…"

Theo put up his hand. "Your mother's in labour? Right now? This minute?" He cursed himself for not having thought of more reasons why he should not have kept the boy waiting.

William nodded.

Theo moved towards the door. "James!"

"Where do you live, Bill?"

"Over in Prendergast, Sir."

"This side, or the farthest side?"

"On the farthest side, out on the road towards Fishguard, Sir -- just past the Withy Bush estate."

James had appeared. "James, I'm sorry to get you out in this weather, but I need you to go to Mr. Nash, and tell him I'd be grateful if he would follow me to the farther side of

Prendergast. I'll be outside his house as soon as I can."

As soon as James had left, Theo put on a heavy coat to keep out the rain, and found one for William. It was way too big, and enveloped his slight frame like an enormous cocoon. He called for Elizabeth's maid, and told her to tell her mistress he was out on an errand, and would be back as soon as he could. He then ushered William out of the door into the driving rain, and the two ran to the livery stable. Within minutes they were both mounted on Hercules, and hastening to the doctor's house, where Mr. Nash was already mounted and waiting.

"I'll explain later," Theo called over to him and the two horses set off down High Street as fast as was possible without the horses falling, across the bridge, and up Prendergast hill, heading towards Fishguard.

They passed by Mr. John Phelps's seat, Withy Bush, and about a half mile out of town, the boy shouted to Theo to turn off down a small lane leading off to the right, and after a few hundred yards along a narrow path where the overhanging, water-laden branches lashed them as they rode past, they came to a tiny whitewashed cottage. They had arrived at William's home.

They dismounted from the horses whose necks and flanks steamed with sweat, and walked towards the cottage, water dripping from their hats and down their necks. It was dark by now, and they were met at the door by a young girl holding a small child on one hip, and carrying a guttering candle in her free hand. They stepped over the threshold, behind which a carpet of straw crunched under their feet. The cottage was identical to those Theo had passed that day back in spring on his way home from his first gallop along Druid's Town beach.

The girl led them to an area off to the right, where, in the gloom, they could make out the figure of a woman lying on a bed of sack-covered straw. Several children in threadbare

166

clothes hung around in silence, bare feet on the hard-packed earthen floor. A small fire glowed at one end of the room. It gave out no smoke, and at first Theo thought there were potatoes roasting on it, but then realized they were not potatoes, but slow-burning coal balls, fashioned out of a mixture of local coal and clay, and piled up in rows in the fireplace. They gave out a good heat, but the only other light came from a single candle. From somewhere off in the corner there was the sound of water drip, dripping through the worn-out thatch.

Theo looked around in horror at the poverty and squalor. He had never seen anything like it before. He pulled himself together, reminding himself of the purpose of their visit. Mr. Nash had already gone over to the woman, who was loathe to let a man look at her. "It's all right," he told her. "I'm a physician, and I'm here to help you deliver your baby."

The woman lay back exhausted, and within an hour a baby boy was brought bawling into his wretched world.

After doing as much as they could for the mother and baby, Theo and Mr. Nash left in silence, Theo first telling William to stay home and help his family for the next three days, and he would still get his wages. On arriving back in Haverfordwest, Theo asked the physician to check on the woman and her child the next day, and Mr. Nash agreed; he knew he would be well rewarded for his time, and the next morning Theo contacted St. Mary's Church charity, asking that special consideration be given to this family on the outskirts of town. He then went to his bank where he made arrangements for a specific amount to be deposited anonymously into the charity every New Year.

CHAPTER 17

It was December, and the height of the social season in Haverfordwest. Theo and Elizabeth had attended several balls, and had spent enjoyable evenings at parties at the townhouses of the county's nobility and social elite. It had originally been Theo's plan to take Elizabeth to Dublin for the theatre season, giving him the opportunity to act again in his old theatre. He loved it so much, and had sorely missed acting, as well as watching it, and when he had managed to arrange for another brief visit to Haverfordwest from the Dublin Theatre over the summer -- a visit in which he himself had taken part in the performances -- it had made him realize even more that a large part of his life was missing.

It was not that he was unhappy. He had a wife whom he loved more than anything, and who formed a perfect, more generally tranquil complement to his own ebullient personality; and he had a son who, having survived the initial trial of his birth, had grown into a healthy, happy baby.

Elizabeth was contented with her life. Apart from spending time with her friends and loving the town in which she was born, she was also happy with her role as mother, even to the extent of breastfeeding her child, something that other mothers of her social status never did, at least, not in

Haverfordwest. In this respect, most families of their social status were like those in Ireland, and fostered their children out until they were weaned. Elizabeth, however, loved nothing more than to spend as much time as possible with little John during the day, and after dinner he was always brought down from the nursery to spend time with her and Theo.

As with the previous year, however, Theo's plans to go to Dublin were thwarted as Elizabeth was once again expecting a child. This one, like little John, was due in May; and although they could have taken steps to avoid this pregnancy, it was Elizabeth herself who, loving to have children always around her and, as she insisted, always wanting to have a baby in her arms, had said she wanted as many as possible, a desire Theo was not averse to fulfilling, although their timing did spoil his other plans.

He was still, technically, apprenticed to Mr. Sutton, as the apprenticeship was for seven years, but he already found he could do most of what was required where printing was concerned. Learning how to bind books properly, however, was a much more difficult task. Unlike printing, which he found incredibly monotonous -- as Elizabeth had predicted -- each new book to be bound was a new project in itself, making the task more interesting because it gave him the opportunity to be creative and imaginative, and to produce a finished book in a way that would tell people that he, John Theophilus Potter, had created the finished product. His problem was that, once he had spent so much time and effort in binding a book in the finest leather, and etching its details in gold on the spine, he was loathe to sell it, and it would more often than not find a place in his own private collection at home.

Despite his interest in the art of book binding, however, it was still a sedentary occupation, and Theo was not a sedentary man. Full of energy, he needed the stimulation of drama and activity in his life. Acting had satisfied this need, whether it

169

had been by pacing impressively around a stage, and gesticulating as or if the role demanded, engaging in fencing displays, or making the annual pilgrimage to Cork and Limerick. The reward of the constant motion and the appreciation of an enthusiastic public had added a lustre to his life that was currently missing, a lustre which sitting, binding books could not supply, and he needed to explain to Elizabeth how he felt.

He had gone to see her in her own little sitting room, where she liked to retreat to do her embroidery, attend to her correspondence, or to read. It was mid afternoon, and she was seated in her favourite chair, dandling baby John on her lap. She looked up as Theo marched in, snatched up his son off her lap, and held him over his head, swinging him to and fro. Little John, happy, gurgled and drooled all over his adoring father.

"Gently, Theo! Gently! He's only very little!"

"He's fine! You're going to grow up to be a big strong man, aren't you, my son?" And the baby continued to gurgle.

Theo sat down, put the baby on his knee facing Elizabeth, and jiggled his knee up and down. "Come on John! Ride Hercules!" The baby laughed out loud, his head swaying from side to side as he went up and down.

"My beloved wife..." Theo stopped jiggling his knee, and the baby continued to try to rise up and down on his own. "Bess...You remember that my theatre agreed to employ me again, were I to return to Dublin?"

Elizabeth stood up and went over to the baby. She picked him up off Theo's knee, held him close to her, and sat down again, cuddling him, smoothing his hair and kissing his head. She then looked across at Theo, displaying none of the alarm she felt. "Yes."

"Well, I've been wondering. Have you ever thought what it would be like if we left Haverfordwest and went to live in Dublin?... No?" Theo added when Elizabeth did not answer at once.

"Yes. I've given it *considerable* thought, as I sometimes feel you're not altogether contented with your life here. But, my dearest Theo, I do hope your life isn't so unhappy that you can't consider spending the rest of it here."

Theo said nothing, and Elizabeth continued. "I couldn't bear the thought of you thinking such a thing... I know you're an active man both mentally and physically, and perhaps Haverfordwest doesn't always appear to supply the stimulation or opportunities you need, but it's early days yet... you need to give it time... You're not yet settled into life here the way I am, but please, do tell me what it is that has led to this... this idea of moving back to Dublin."

Theo shrugged. "My stupidity in not being able to find a fulfilling substitute for the career I appear to have abandoned, I imagine. My mind tends to run away with itself when it has nothing else to occupy it... and no, my sweet Bess..." He went over and kissed her. "My life isn't terrible at all. I'm well aware that I'm a most fortunate man. No man could be more happily married, or blessed in having a more loving wife. As I've told you before, you're everything to me; I'd be lost without you, and would never do anything to make you unhappy, and if that means spending the rest of our lives here, then we'll do that..." He leaned over the back of her chair and kissed her again. "And perhaps I'm not the easiest of men to live with either..." to which Elizabeth responded by smoothing his cheek, and smiling.

"I'm thinking though," he said after a moment, "that if we can't go to Dublin -- at least to visit this season -- is there any reason why I can't produce, and act in a play right here in Haverfordwest? The citizens here are appreciative of a well-acted play, and now the laws have been relaxed regarding the licensing of theatres, it would seem not an impossible task to create something right here, don't you think, even if we don't have a proper theatre?... I can't understand it," he went on. "Theatres are being built in provincial towns all over the country now. Why not here in Haverfordwest?" He returned to his chair. "If ever a town would benefit from... However, as you say, I'm still a relatively new arrival here, so am aware that I need to be careful how I tread; I don't want to remove myself from favour by being too demanding in pushing for a theatre to be built... or anything else for that matter... yet..." He thought for a minute. "It does take a long time to be truly accepted here, doesn't it?"

Elizabeth said nothing.

"I could still put on a play though, don't you agree? There's nothing to stop me doing that, and I'm sure Stephen George wouldn't mind at all if it could be performed at The Blue Boar -- that's if the town hall isn't available -- although that would be better..."

"But where will you find trained actors? Besides, as you've said yourself so often, you abhor amateurish performances, and if the gentry won't patronize the show because it's amateurish, you certainly won't make any money."

Theo knew Elizabeth was right, but was so desperate to be doing something whereby he could put his own real talent to some use, he chose to ignore her arguments.

"Oh Bess! Now you're looking for obstructions. There are plenty of people hereabouts who would welcome the chance to learn how to act; there have to be some good amateurs around. What's to stop me from trying at least to bring them up to acceptable standard? As far as making money is concerned, it doesn't matter to me whether we make a profit or not. There's no reason at all why I couldn't produce a play."

Elizabeth did not know what to say. While she had felt proud of Theo as a respectable member of the great theatre in Dublin, being a small-time actor with amateurs in Haverfordwest was, in her opinion, not worthy of him, and she felt sad his need was so great he would degrade himself this way. She sighed. First he had opened a reading room, to which she had had no objection, but then he had entered into a trade, which was certainly not befitting his gentleman status. Now he wanted to promote an amateur performance of something or other in Haverfordwest. She loved her husband's high spirits and enthusiasm for life, and could not bear the thought of herself being the one to in any way depress those high spirits, or extinguish that enthusiasm, but... She had learned to a certain extent to come to terms with his idiosyncratic ways, but her upbringing as a gentlewoman was often at odds with his ideas, and she was forever wondering what he was going to do, or in which direction he would lead them next.

Receiving no comment from his wife, Theo was annoyed, especially as he had not even managed to convince himself with his own arguments. "Right then," he said, his voice flat. "I think that's what I'd like to do anyway," and walked out.

He made his way down the road towards the printing shop, and soon caught up with William Evans, his errand boy's father, who was hobbling along, using a stout hazel staff to help take the weight off his arthritic knees. Theo had not seen him since he had been able to effect the man's release the day following the birth of William's baby brother, when he had gone to the gaol himself to see what could be done.

There he had found a building which, in his own opinion, was unfit for human habitation, yet it had been built in the grounds within the castle walls a mere three years previously. How, he had wondered, could conditions have deteriorated in so short a time? He then discovered that the person in control of the prison, the gaoler, was himself earning a sizeable income from the inmates by charging them for everything, and when they could not pay him, would not allow them to leave, even though they had finished their sentence. He found this to be the same problem facing Mr. Evans who, being a debtor to begin with, had become ever more in debt the longer he stayed in gaol, and although his own sentence had been served, he was just as much in debt to the gaoler as he was to the man who had put him there in the first place.

Theo had paid off all Mr. Evans's debts, then offered him work in his own garden doing odd jobs. He already had a gardener, but this was a way of allowing Mr. Evans to work off his debt to Theo without losing whatever little pride the poor man had remaining.

Overtaking Mr. Evans in the street, he greeted him, asked after his family, wished him the time of day, and walked on. As he walked his thoughts turned from his own present dissatisfactions to the much greater problems faced by poor Mr. Evans, and not for the first time he wondered at the inequities visited upon people simply by reason of their birth. On his own level, he himself had suffered, but nothing that could in any way equate with Mr. Evans's problems. What hope had this man? Soon he would be forced to cease working because of his infirmities, and what would he do then? His most likely future would be to be separated from his wife and family, and sent to live in the new workhouse due to open in Haverfordwest in the near future.

Theo then contemplated with chagrin his own situation, and how he was feeling frustrated simply because he was unable to follow his ambition to be a successful actor on the stage of a proper theatre. But he was also a pragmatist. He could not return to Dublin without his wife and son. He would not even want to; he loved them far too much for that. He was not a burgess of the town of Haverfordwest, nor would he be able to apply to be one for another six years, and until he was accepted as such, there was nothing he himself could do to even try to effect any changes within the political system of this county cum town, because he could not vote.

There were small things, however, he could achieve on his own in the meantime. He had helped the Evans family in one way or another, but he was still concerned as to what was going to happen to them all when Mr. Evans was no longer able to support them. Right now they had only the money they received from St. Mary's church charity, along with William's wage as an errand boy. It was not enough.

As he walked, he formulated a new idea. What if William were apprenticed to Mr. Sutton, and so became a printer in his own right after the required seven years? William would then have no problem supporting his family. Then he remembered that apprentices receive no pay during their apprenticeship, so that would not do. However, by the time he arrived at the shop, he had come up with yet another solution. With William out on a delivery errand, Theo approached Mr. Sutton with his idea. "Would you be willing to take on William as an apprentice as well as me, Mr. Sutton?"

At first Mr. Sutton was sceptical, but then on reflection thought it was indeed a possibility, especially when Theo promised him an increase in salary to cover the extra work. "Then," Theo persisted, "is there any reason why he can't be an apprentice and an errand boy at the same time?"

Mr. Sutton did not see why this should not be, and so it was decided that William should become Mr. Sutton's unpaid apprentice and Theo's paid errand boy at the same time. Theo then turned his mind to holding auditions for his play, which he was determined to produce, regardless of any arguments against the wisdom of such a venture.

CHAPTER 18

Mrs. Carswell had just arrived at Mrs. Pollard's house, and the two ladies lost no time in entering into their favourite arena of conversation: the latest local gossip.

"My dear Mrs. Pollard!" Mrs. Carswell gave her dress an extravagant swish as she settled herself into her chair. "My dear Mrs. Pollard! I know you were out of town last week, but did you hear what happened in church on Sunday?"

Mrs. Pollard had not, and leaned forward.

"Well, Lady Marchant was wearing this enormous hat...the latest fashion of course, for as you know, Lady Marchant has an enviable flair for fashion. As I'm always telling Mr. Carswell: 'After myself'... and you too of course, my dear Mrs. Pollard...'there's no one who has such an excellent sense of taste and fashion as Lady Marchant...'"

Mrs. Pollard waited.

"Well, as I was saying, Lady Marchant was wearing this enormous hat, decorated with the most beautiful ostrich plumes, which reached out well beyond her shoulders. I do declare, my dear Mrs. Pollard, her poor husband had to sit at least two feet away from her to avoid having his face enveloped in feathers. It really was quite amusing as whenever she turned her head to the right, he would be obliged to lean over to his right to avoid being tickled. Everyone noticed, of course, and were looking more at Sir John and Lady Marchant than they were at Vicar Ayleway during his sermon." Mrs. Carswell paused while she extricated her fan from the folds of her dress, and gave herself a few brisk swats with it. "Then what happened was this. Lady Marchant, for some reason only she herself could explain, decided to look up at the roof of the church. Goodness knows what she saw up there, but she stretched her head farther and farther back until, before he had time to get out of the way, one of her ostrich feathers tickled the nose of Sir Thomas Sinclair, who was sitting directly behind her, and he began to sneeze. Well, my dear Mrs. Pollard, he couldn't stop sneezing, and in the end he had to get up and walk out of church, sneezing all the way! I declare, my dear Mrs. Pollard, the whole congregation would have been laughing, had it not been for the vicar looking so sternly at us all."

"Poor Sir Thomas! Did he ever come back into church?"

"No, and according to Lady Sinclair, his eyes were watering and he was sneezing right through dinner!"

The two ladies sat in silence for a few moments of sympathy, contemplating poor Sir Thomas's discomfort.

"I have a piece of news also!" Mrs. Pollard announced after a respectable interval.

It was Mrs. Carswell's turn to lean forward.

"Have you heard? Our Mr. Potter is going to be producing, directing... and acting in... a play!"

"Producing a play, and *acting* in it!" Mrs. Carswell was incredulous, and raised her fan to her face once more.

"Well, yes... He's performed before if you'll remember."

It was something Mrs. Carswell was unlikely to forget.

"Yes, indeed! But he's now a respectable, married gentleman. Anyone in his position should behave more decorously than prancing around on a stage like... like..." Mrs. Carswell was at a loss to describe what such an activity was like. "But," she sniffed, "he *is* in trade in town, of course, so I suppose one has to expect... All I can say is, he certainly doesn't act like a gentleman, at least not any gentleman with whom *I've* ever had the pleasure of being acquainted... And who else, I may ask, is he expecting to perform with him? I declare, no one of his own social status would be seen behaving in such a manner, unless he's considering amateur dramatics for the gentry -- for charity -- and there aren't enough of them in town at this time of year for that, even if they were willing. He'll have to find people well beneath him, people I'm sure he, and most certainly his wife would never normally associate with, she, in particular, being one of the Edwardeses."

"I heard he's going to be posting notices around town offering auditions to anyone who would like to join his theatre group."

Mrs. Carswell rolled her eyes in disbelief. "I can scarcely believe it! All I can say is that *I*, for one, shall not be attending any such performance. And I doubt anyone of quality will do so either... And, anyway, what play does he plan to produce and act in may I ask?"

"*The Taming of the Shrew*, by Mr. William Shakespeare, I understand."

Mrs. Carswell raised her eyebrows. She had never seen the play herself, and had no idea what it was about, so, unable to offer any comment without displaying her ignorance on the matter, she showed her disapprobation of whatever it might be, by giving an indignant sniff.

Other items of mutual interest occupied the rest of Mrs. Carswell's visit, but, as she finally took her leave, and was helped aboard her chaise, it was the folly of Mr. John Theophilus Potter that was foremost in her thoughts, and it was not until several weeks later, by which time she had had the opportunity to disseminate her opinions on the subject to everyone she met, that she learned that Sir Thomas and Lady Sinclair -- themselves friends with a number of actors belonging to the Drury Lane theatre in London -- were so impressed with Mr. Potter's initiative, they had given their daughter permission to audition for the part of Kate.

With his usual predilection for getting things done as quickly as possible, Theo set about making all the necessary preparations for the production of the play. An efficient man himself, he was frustrated, therefore, to have to wait for the wheels of officialdom to grind their slow way through whatever was required for his plan to proceed. It all took so much time that when he was finally ready to begin auditioning for the parts, it was well into the month of May, and on the day selected to start this, Elizabeth, who had had no option but to come to terms with her husband's latest project, had already departed to Dunstable Hall in expectation of the arrival of their second child.

The auditions were to be held in the library of the Potter home, and the first day was to be devoted to finding someone to play the part of Kate. Theo, liking the spirited, rollicking role of Petruchio, had chosen to play this character himself, so he was looking for a young lady who would complement his own role, and whom he would feel comfortable tossing over his shoulder as the part demanded; and indeed a young lady who would herself feel comfortable being thus treated. Of course, it was desirable that she could act as well.

It was with some alarm then that, on the appointed day, Theo looked out of an upstairs window, and failed to see any end to the line of people stretched down the street. What he *did* see was a large number of women of every shape, size, age, state of dress, or undress, and cleanliness. There were also several smart chaises lined up along the street, their occupants presumably wishing to take the test as well.

Having had no experience whatsoever with this aspect of the theatre world, he began to wonder now if he had taken on more than he could cope with. He left the window, and called for James. "James, I know you're a tactful man, and I'd take it kindly if you would do something for me." He then described the character and age of Kate to James, and asked him to tell, with as much tact as possible, those who were obviously not right for the part, that they would not be needed. He then went down to the library, took a deep breath, and waited.

He had chosen for the audition Act II, Scene 1, in which Petruchio first meets Kate, and in which she "the shrew," is on her worst behaviour: bad tempered, rude and behaving disgracefully towards her would-be husband, Petruchio. As this had been stated on the notices, it was expected that the applicants would be ready to play their part and know their lines.

The first young lady was ushered into the library. She was shy, sweet-natured and pretty, but as soon as she started speaking, it was clear she would not do. Her thin, flat little voice did not carry even as far as Theo, who was standing right in front of her, let alone across a large room. He thanked her for her time, and she made a tearful departure, which he found most disconcerting.

As the various applicants made their way in and out of the library, it became clear that some of them had come only because they wanted to see the inside of a gentleman's house, and were so little interested in securing the role, they had not even bothered to learn any of the scene at all. Some other young ladies, having heard that the gentleman holding the auditions was tall, young, and of excellent appearance, appeared to have in mind a role of a different sort, and Theo was glad his housekeeper was in the library acting as chaperone. One young lady was so overcome when she found herself standing looking up at this man -- whom she later described to her friends as the most handsome and appealing man she had ever seen -- that she collapsed at his feet in a complete faint, at which Theo hurriedly left the room, and waited until the housekeeper had dealt with the situation, and the young lady escorted outside to her waiting mother.

It was well into the afternoon, and Theo's spirits no longer retained their initial enthusiasm. He had kept the names of the small number of possible candidates, but had not yet found anyone about whom he could definitely say, "Yes. She's Kate." He was even beginning to think Elizabeth was right all along, and such a venture ought not to be attempted after all. Right then another young lady was ushered in. Theo, who had his back to the doorway when she entered, turned and found himself looking at Miss Martha Carswell.

He bowed. "Miss Carswell. I'm afraid my wife, Mrs. Potter, isn't here today, and she won't be back...well, I'm not sure when she'll be back at this moment. You see, she's..."

"I'm not here to see Mrs. Potter."

"No?"

"No."

"I'm sorry, I don't understand. Is there something I can do to help you?"

"Yes. You can audition me for the role of Kate in *The Taming of the Shrew!*"

"*You!*... I'm sorry. *You* want to play the part of Kate... on the stage... in public?"

"Why would I waste my time and yours in coming here if I didn't?" Miss Carswell raised her head and pulled in her chin.

"I... ah... Your mother..."

"What has my mother got to do with it? I'm of age, I can

do what I want. Besides, it was she who suggested it."

"Your mother!"

"Please don't look so askance at me, Mr. Potter. As I said, I'm here to be auditioned, and should appreciate it if you'd waste no more of our time in quizzing me, unless of course I don't look right for the part -- although I can't see why not. I'm of the right age, and consider myself to be of passing looks and dimensions."

Theo, bemused by this unexpected situation, shook his head in disbelief, then finally gathered together his senses. "Yes, yes. Excuse me. I apologise. It's just that I wouldn't have expected you to have ever come. However, now that you're here, yes, of course I'll audition you."

Theo was so astounded by the direction the afternoon had taken, that it was he who then fluffed his lines, and they had to start again. Then it was not clear to him if she was indeed acting, or in reality using the opportunity to be as rude to him as he was sure she had wanted to be ever since they had last met. Either way, she was both convincing, and word perfect. To make sure, he asked that they do the scene again, as it was unlikely she could be as venomous in her delivery twice running unless she were truly acting. Her performance was once again, convincing.

"Well!" said Theo. "If you can play the last scenes as well as you played the first ones..." He smiled. "Do you think you can be as nice to me as you've just been horrible?"

"I can be whatever I want to be, regardless of how I feel." Miss Carswell again tucked in her chin in characteristic disdain.

"An actress after all then," Theo thought. That Miss Carswell was not here out of friendship, was certain, and he felt rather relieved. He would give her the part, but this would still allow them to continue to despise each other as much as ever -- and, he mused, he would take particular pleasure in tossing her over his shoulder, and carting her off the stage at the appointed time, as the script demanded.

CHAPTER 19

At Dunstable Hall it was considered fortunate that Mr. Potter had been busy with his auditions during the day, as while he was thus occupied Elizabeth had gone into labour, and again it had been a long and difficult delivery. Once again it was not certain at all if the baby, a girl, would survive the ordeal, and it was this news that greeted Theo when he finally made his way over to his cousin's estate late in the evening, just in time to be present when Mr. Ayleway, in a private ceremony, baptised the little girl 'Elizabeth', after her mother.

Once the vicar and the midwife had left, and the baby taken to the nursery to be cared for, Theo sat on the edge of the bed, and held his wife's hand until she fell asleep. Then, himself overcome with the trials of his own long day of auditioning, he lifted his still booted feet onto the bed, and laid his head on the pillow, where he remained until the morning, oblivious to whatever might be taking place around him.

As it happened, Elizabeth herself became a cause for concern during the night, as she was bleeding more than was considered normal, and in the early hours of the morning her mother had felt the need to call Mr. Nash to the house to see to her. The exhausted physician had finally appeared at daybreak, by which time the bleeding had stopped of its own accord, and, after assessing the patient's condition, he was able to assure the family that Elizabeth, while weak, would most certainly recover.

On his way out, and still able to summon up some humour, Mr. Nash looked down at the fully-clothed and sleeping Theo, and, after taking the trouble to remove some blades of muddy grass still adhering to the boots of the peaceful and inert father, pronounced that he too was most likely to survive whatever ordeal he himself appeared to have suffered the preceding day. He then went to see the baby Elizabeth one more time before returning to Haverfordwest and his own bed.

By the time a week had passed, both Elizabeth and the baby were recovering, and Theo had completed the selection of the cast for his play. It had been a trying time for all, and at the end of it, they decided to stay at Dunstable Hall for a few weeks, and forgetting everything else, to enjoy walking through the woods and meadows of the estate, just as they had done before they were married.

It was during one of these walks that Theo told Elizabeth the tale of Martha Carswell, and her audition for the role of Kate. Elizabeth was as amazed as Theo had been, and they both speculated as to why Mrs. Carswell, who had entertained such a disdainful view of actors in general, had not only agreed to her daughter taking part in the play, but had even suggested it. Having heard the daughter of Sir Thomas and Lady Sinclair audition for the part of Kate, Theo wondered if perhaps Mrs. Carswell, having discovered this, had concluded that whatever was acceptable behaviour for the daughter of Sir Thomas and his wife, was also acceptable for her own daughter. Elizabeth agreed that this was probably the case.

Mrs. Carswell was indeed delighted at her daughter's success, especially as it had meant that, by securing the part of Kate, her own daughter had outshone that of Sir Thomas and Lady Sinclair, and she lost no time in making sure all her friends and acquaintances were fully aware of it. She had even contemplated having the Potter Printing Company print up announcements to proclaim that Miss Martha Carswell would be playing the part of Katharine in the production of *The Taming of the Shrew* in Haverfordwest for two weeks during the upcoming season. However, even Mr. Carswell had considered this as taking his daughter's accomplishment to excess, and had refused to pay for such publicity, thus putting an end to the idea.

Mrs. Carswell, however, not content with her daughter's expected fame and future fortune in the theatre, decided she herself would like to take part in the forthcoming limelight. Although there was no acting role available to her -- and she had to take into account that she herself was unable to read a script -- she set about finding out what part she could play in the production process: a significant part, of course, which would need to have a glamorous ring to it, and result in having her own name imprinted on the play list. Her research yielded the title of 'Wardrobe Mistress'.

"Wardrobe Mistress!" she told her daughter. "That would suit me perfectly! With my superior sense of style and fashion, I'm sure no better person could be found." So she applied for the position, and was delighted when her offer was accepted.

Unfortunately, having taken up the challenge, and having let it be known that her name also would be listed prominently in the printed playlist, she discovered that her knowledge of fashion and style had nothing whatsoever to offer where the task ahead was concerned. To her consternation she learned that, instead of sashaying into the best shops to select the latest Paris designs for the cast, she had undertaken to produce one way or another the costumes for a period that not only had nothing to do with modern fashion or style, but in some cases were even peasant-like.

The revelation caused her considerable alarm as not only was she disinclined to take on such a task herself, but so also was everyone else in her circle, thus forcing her into the degrading position of associating with common people in order to provide the necessary outfits, something she found insupportable. She therefore summoned her housekeeper and transferred the obligation to her and whomever she could find to complete the task, after which she swept the whole unfortunate affair from her mind, having first made certain that her name would still appear on the playlist.

A summer of rehearsals passed, and Theo was as satisfied as was possible with the quality of the acting, although it remained in his eyes amateurish. Elizabeth had been right, you could not expect to make proper actors or expect perfect performances out of townsfolk who also had to work long and arduous hours at their normal tasks just to have sufficient income to be able to feed their families. Expecting them to have enough energy left to pour into their roles at the end of the day, was asking more than they could give.

There were other problems to be overcome as well, leaving Theo on several occasions, ready to toss the script in the air, storm out and abandon the project. One of the more serious of these arose when two of the actors decided they did not want to take part after all, making it necessary to use his understudies even before the play was staged. Then, late in October, after the notices had been printed and posted around town, it was discovered that those involved with scheduling the use of the Town Hall, where the performances were to be held, had omitted to notify Theo that there was a not inconsiderable number of nights on which the building would be needed for other purposes, making it impossible to perform the play there on those occasions.

Then it turned out that none of the county's elite would be willing to attend a performance at the Town Hall anyway, because, unlike in church, or at a proper theatre, there were no seats available that would separate them from the common citizens, so in order to satisfy their requirements, a special performance would once again have to be held at Dunstable Hall. During the process, there came times, even, in which Theo felt that should his play be successful, it would be despite the cooperation of those in power in the town, rather than because of it.

However, it was in the end successful enough to satisfy most, and Theo was glad he had made the effort, although by the end of his brief, two-week season -- which was all the small population of Haverfordwest could support -- he was not sure it would be an endeavour he would like to repeat, at least not until Haverfordwest had a theatre of its own, something he hoped to persuade the town to provide in the near future.

CHAPTER 20

Although Theo was amiable and happy to sustain his share of conversation and amusement at any gathering, he was, nevertheless, someone who found it necessary to replenish his spirits by spending many hours in his own company. This he accomplished by either sitting alone in his library reading, or by taking Hercules out for long rides in the countryside, trips that would often have him disappear from his family from early morning till sundown, although he always tried to be home before dark.

At first Elizabeth had been concerned for his safety during these day-long absences, and with her dear father's sad and unforeseen accident and resulting death as a constant reminder, had always worried that some similar accident would befall Theo. Time had passed, however, and he had never failed to return home refreshed and ready to be his usual congenial self once again. So now, with children to think about as well, she no longer worried about his safety on these trips, but was just relieved and delighted to see him once he did return home unharmed -- although she might not have been so sanguine about it, had she known how many times Theo removed the saddle from Hercules, and raced bareback along Druid's Town beach.

On this particular day in late October, there had been frost on the ground when he had set out, but there was still enough warmth in the sun during the day to make it so that heavy clothing was unnecessary, and he had taken no coat with him. He had not been to Druid's Town beach for a while so decided that, although it was too cold for swimming, a good gallop would be just what both he and Hercules needed.

He picked up the horse at the livery stable, an event that never failed to inspire comments of admiration and wonder, so obvious was the affection between horse and man. Both seemed to understand each other, and their interaction was a joy to watch. On this day the groom saw them off a little later than usual, Theo having been detained earlier in the morning.

He left the town behind and headed out across Portfield Common, past the Whale Inn, and out towards Broad Haven, passing on his way groups of half-starved horses, cows and donkeys, left to fend for themselves as best they could among the gorse and the heath.

As he rode he thought over the past year, the most recent event being the birth of another, this time healthy boy who had been named -- as was customary for the second son -- after his maternal grandfather, Joseph; and it had been in this October of 1783, that Joseph, along with his older siblings, who had not yet been publicly welcomed into St. Mary's church, had all been baptised together in front of the whole congregation.

He meandered along, taking the time to observe the countryside around him. The shifting clouds flowed over the common like grey silk mantles, but where the sun broke through, all the plants burst into colour, revealing golden wisps of dying grasses against backgrounds of russet bracken and deep green clumps of gorse, twinkling here and there with its few remaining saffron flowers. Other areas shone with speckles of pure white where the spent blooms of thistles had turned to down.

The common was high enough above the surrounding countryside that, off to his side, he could see it fall away and stretch in one expansive vale as far as the Preseli Mountains, standing guard on the distant horizon. Here and there, flocks of goldfinches, frightened away from their autumn feast of thistle seed, flew away like colourful little toys, jerked through the air by some unseen puppeteer.

When he reached Druid's Town he noticed some people swimming in the sea, and on closer inspection could see it was a small group of young women. Being the only man around, he thought it would be ungentlemanly to ride down to the beach while they were still there, cavorting in the waves in their birthday suits. His presence might deter them from coming out of the water to retrieve their clothes, revealing more of themselves than was ladylike, yet they could get overly chilled remaining in it.

He stood at the edge of the cliff for a few minutes, wondering what to do, then decided to wander further down the coastline and return later, by which time they would surely be gone, so he made his way to Nolton harbour, through the marshy valley surrounding the stream and out onto the path towards Newgale.

It took him longer than he had expected, and by the time he returned to the beach, not only had the young women long-since gone, but the sun was nearing the horizon, and without its heat the clear air already held a crispness that spoke of another frosty night to come. Theo knew it was already so late he would not be home before dark, and this being so, he reasoned he had nothing to lose by having his gallop anyway, and it was another half hour before he was back on the path to Haverfordwest.

Now he began to wish he had not waited around for the women to leave the water, then added further to his lateness by going for the gallop. "You should have gone straight home," he told himself. "Bess is going to be worried... should have brought a coat too," he remembered, starting to feel the temperature fall around him, and he scolded himself for his stupidity.

There was no moon tonight, and soon it was so dark he could barely see his way ahead, and although the Milky Way was bright in the sky, its faint glow was not enough to light up the path.

Horse and rider plodded on, and Theo, with only his shirt and sleeveless leather jerkin to protect him, began to feel the bite of the still, frosty air, but not being able to see clearly where he was going, could not go faster without risking an accident. They could easily wander off the path, and disappear down one of the many abandoned mineshafts scattered around the area -- mineshafts that were treacherous even in daylight, because they were overgrown with grass and shrubs. The danger posed by them was not to be ignored, as he had heard of people who, along with their horses, had tumbled into them and been killed.

He began to feel nervous too, because he was travelling alone. Only last week a man walking home in the dark had been accosted by some men who had relieved him of his possessions -- and they had been rough about it too. A hue and cry had been raised, but the robbers had not been found. Theo tried to comfort himself with the knowledge that this attack had taken place on the other side of town, on the road to Slebech, but even so, every time he heard a noise, he peered into the darkness, expecting someone to jump out at him. Several times he heard a barn owl screeching in the distance, always an eerie sound, but its innocent call seemed menacing in the still, black iciness of tonight, making him feel as though he were taking part in a re-enactment of some grim, gothic tale.

Once out on the common again, and out of the shadows of overhanging trees, he was able to move along a little faster, and was three miles from the outskirts of town when a man limped out into the road, waving his arms. "Oh Sir! Heaven be praised that you've come along, kind Sir. I was sure I'd be freezing to death out here this cold night."

It was not a night for anyone to be stranded out in the inhospitable wilds of Portfield Common; he could perish from the cold, and as the man approached, Theo reigned in Hercules, stopping in front of him, prepared to help.

The man put out his hand and patted the horse on the nose. "No indeed, Sir, your coming along is a miracle to be sure."

"Ah!" said Theo. "You've hurt your leg too, I see. Come on, just jump up behind me here, and I'll take you into town." He put out his arm to help the man up.

While he was talking, he did not notice the man's hand sliding across Hercules's nose towards his bridle. He wrapped his fist around the side strap, grabbing hold of it. "All right boys, I've got him," he shouted.

Hercules shied and jerked his head as two men jumped out from behind a gorse bush at the side of the path, but the man held onto his bridle.

Theo did not say anything. All that was going through his mind was that he should have known better than to have stopped. "You damned fool, Theo!" he berated himself. "You stupid, gullible fool!" It was one of the oldest tricks, and he had fallen for it. It was not even as though he had not been expecting something like this to happen. Had not such a possibility been foremost in his thoughts all along the way? Too late now though. He was about to be robbed, and it was three against one.

"Off!" one of the two men ordered him. "Off!" he shouted again, when Theo did not move.

Theo's temper erupted. "No! I'm damned if I'm getting off my horse for three thugs like you!" He put his hand in his pocket and pulled out whatever money he could find -- it was not much -- and threw it at them. "There! You want my money. Take it. Now let go of my horse!"

"We said, 'off!'" the man repeated. "Now! Or we'll drag you off." He made to grab hold of Theo's foot, but Theo lashed out, the toe of his heavy boot catching the man high on his cheekbone.

The man gave a howl of pain, and putting his hand to his head and feeling the stickiness of blood running down his face, became enraged. "Goddam you!" he screamed at Theo. "Goddam you! You've asked for it now. I'll get you for this," and grabbed hold of Theo's leg.

Once again Theo berated himself, this time for allowing his temper to get the better of him. "What did you think you were going to achieve by putting up a fight against three men? You fool, Theo. Now, you're not only going to be robbed, but beaten up too."

Defeated, he put up his hands. "All right, all..." He prepared to dismount, but now the other man as well had caught hold of his leg, and before he could get off by himself, they dragged him off.

Hercules was a tall animal, over seventeen hands, and Theo fell heavily, the side of his foot landing on a large stone, which slipped away from under him, forcing his ankle into an awkward twist as he hit the ground. The men held him down while they searched his pockets and removed whatever they could find of value.

"Don't carry much worth taking, do you?" One of the men clipped Theo over the ear. "Ah! Here's a nice piece though." He held up Theo's valuable pocket watch, and placed it in his own pocket, acting out the role of fine gentleman as he did so.

Theo looked up. It was the watch his godparents had given him for his eighteenth birthday. "No. Not that." But all he received in response was another clip on his ear. "Put your head down, damn you, and stay there."

They searched him, and finding nothing else worth taking, prepared to leave, but before departing, the one Theo had kicked in the face took the opportunity to get his revenge.

"And that's for what you did to me," he shouted, and gave him a sharp kick in pit of his stomach, winding him.

Theo lay there, curled up, trying to catch his breath, and after delivering one last kick, the three men mounted Hercules and set off down the road, back towards Broad Haven.

"No! No! Not my horse! Please, not my horse," he tried to shout after them, but no sound came out, and he laid his head back down on the path. "No, not my horse," he whispered to the icy ground beneath his face. "Anything but Hercules."

When he could breathe again, he tried to stand up, but found he had sprained his ankle so badly in the fall, it was already swelling up inside his boot. He got up onto one leg, then put his other foot to the ground, but it was so painful he was able only to hop to the edge of the road, where he sat down. He looked up and down the empty path. The whole common was silent. Hercules and the men had already disappeared, and it was freezing. Frost was already forming on the blades of grass around him, and he began to shiver, from fear now, as well as from the cold.

Apart from the sound of his teeth chattering and the icy glitter of millions of stars in the hollow blackness of the sky, the world around him was dark, silent and still, and he became colder than he had ever been in his life. In addition to this, Hercules was gone, and he had no way of either following the robbers to try to get him back, or now even of getting home. His only option was to sit there and hope someone would come by soon, and he waited, but nothing moved, no light shone, and no-one came.

When her husband had not returned by dinner time, Elizabeth, thinking perhaps she was, as usual, worrying unnecessarily, waited an hour before calling James and asking him if Mr. Potter had told him he intended to be late. "He'd said he'd be back by dinner time," she told him. "He always tells me when he'll be back, James, and it's not like him to be late as you know." She tried not to show her anxiety. "It's cold out tonight too, and…"

James was equally concerned. "Don't worry, Mrs. Potter, Ma'am. I'll round up some men and we'll soon find him I'm sure."

"Thank you James."

Given James's lifetime of concern for his master's welfare, he was now extremely worried. As Elizabeth had said, it was not like Theo to be late, especially when he had said he would be home in time for dinner; and dinner had been over two hours ago.

He went out, and prevailed on some willing neighbours to help in his search, all the time imagining the possible dangers that lay out there on this frigid and dark night; and he did not even know where to start looking, although having seen him ride past the house towards Portfield Common earlier in the day, he suspected he might have gone to Druid's Town.

Not expecting any late arrivals, the livery stable had closed for the night, and the owners, who did not live on the premises, were nowhere to be found, so with only three horses available, some set out on foot in one direction, while those who were mounted, set off in another. James, following his own intuition, set out on foot with the remaining two men towards the common.

The anxiety Elizabeth began to feel once James had set off in search of her husband was nothing like any other worry she had ever experienced. She first felt a strange emptiness in her stomach, which turned into a gnawing pain, and then her heart began to beat irregularly, making her feel light-headed. She could not catch her breath, and found the deeper she tried to breathe, the more difficult breathing became. Scared, she started gulping for the air which would not fill her lungs, but collected in her chest instead, causing additional pain and, pressing on her heart, made its palpitations even wilder; and the combination of all these frightening sensations increased her level of anxiety until it reached such a pitch she felt as though, if she were to sit down, she would die.

She began pacing around the house, trying to fight whatever was happening to her, but without success: upstairs, downstairs, into the library, into her chamber, down to the kitchen, into the dining room, then upstairs again, over and over again, trying to rid herself of the panic consuming her, and all the time she called out for Theo.

James and the other two men walked out onto the open common. There was no-one around, and everything seemed frozen in a tableau of immovable black statues of gorse and heather. There was light coming from the Whale Inn, and they could hear voices inside, but when asked, no-one there had seen or heard anything of Theo or his horse. The temperature was now well below freezing, and the common was bleak and threatening in the darkness. They walked on, not knowing even if they were going in the right direction. Maybe, they thought, someone else had already found him, and he was now safely back home.

Although James did not say it, his fear was that somehow a cliff edge had given way -- the cliffs around Druid's Town being prone to crumble without warning -- and that Theo now lay down on the rocks, maybe even washed out by the tide, and they would never find him. Not a man to panic, James nevertheless loved Theo like a son, and could not control his anxiety, and he pushed the men to walk faster.

After covering a couple of miles, the other two men thought they should turn back. "What's the point of going on?" they argued. Theo, they quite rightly pointed out, could be anywhere, and trying to find him on such a dark night was fruitless. But James refused to give up, and persuaded them to go just one more mile, so they trudged on, small, frozen puddles breaking the silence with their tinkling cracks and pops as the men's heavy boots stepped on them.

While the men were still out searching for Theo, Elizabeth's panic continued unabated, and Mary-Anne, her personal maid, became so alarmed at her mistress's bizarre behaviour, she went to find the housekeeper. Mrs. Kelly, unaware anything was wrong at all, was sitting in her private apartment, eating a late evening meal, but when Mary-Anne related to her all that had happened, she went with her at once to see Elizabeth.

Neither woman had ever seen anyone behaving in such a manner; it was as though Elizabeth had lost touch with reality, and was locked into a mysterious suffering which they could not understand at all. Mrs. Kelly, being the only person left in the household with any power of decision-making, decided that Mr. Nash, the physician, needed to be fetched. However, there were now just three women, apart from Elizabeth, left in the house, cook having gone to visit her parents for the evening, so Mrs. Kelly left a scared personal maid to look after her mistress, while she and the scullery maid set off to fetch Mr. Nash.

Mr. Nash was relaxing in his library after a long day, his legs stretched out in front of a fine fire, dozing, so was surprised when two of the Potter family servants were ushered in. He jumped to his feet. "Come in! Come in! What brings you here in this weather at this time of night? You both look scared out of your wits." Before waiting for a reply, he rang for his butler, and asked him to bring him his coat, and while waiting for this to happen, listened as Mrs. Kelly explained, first that a search party was out looking for the master of the house, then that Mrs. Potter was causing them great alarm by behaving in an unnatural way.

The poor scullery maid, meanwhile, hung back near the door, trembling -- the master was missing, no doubt dead by this time, and the mistress had lost her sanity. Her comfortable and secure existence as part of the Potter household had, she was convinced, come to an end, and her own life ruined.

Mr. Nash's coat was brought, and while he put it on he asked, "In what way is Mrs. Potter behaving?" Mrs. Kelly explained, and Mr. Nash nodded. He then went over to a corner of the room where he kept his potions, liniments and tinctures, and selected a small bottle which he put in his pocket.

"Right. Shall we go?"

A few minutes later they arrived back at the house, where Elizabeth was still pacing around, holding her chest and gasping for breath, but when she saw Mr. Nash, she became calmer, especially when he made her sit down. "It's all right, Mrs. Potter," he said in a soothing voice. He took her hands and held them. "You're all right. There's nothing wrong with you, I assure you."

Elizabeth looked at him.

"That's better," he told her. "Now, hold your breath for a bit, then breathe in slowly. Here..." He took her hand and laid it on her stomach. "Breathe in slowly, and just feel your stomach going up and down. That's it. Slowly, in, out...You know," he told her as her breathing became calmer, "my wife suffers from these attacks too, and I agree, they're frightening, but she's learned how to control them, and when you're ready, you and she can get together and talk about it." He went on chatting, and as Elizabeth's breathing returned to normal, he continued talking about anything he could bring to mind.

It was well over an hour after leaving home that James and the two men came across Theo, who was by this time lying curled up on the grass at the edge of the road, unable to control his shivering after trying to walk home, but forced to stop after having gone fewer than a hundred yards. James, overjoyed at finding him alive, fussed over him, feeling his ice-cold face, and rubbing his hands between his own. Then the men pulled him to his feet, and over the three-mile journey back to Haverfordwest, took it in turns to wrap him in one of their coats, and with one on either side of him, and with his arms round their shoulders, they eventually arrived back home just after midnight.

Mr. Nash was still there attending to Elizabeth when they heard the commotion of their arrival, and as they had happened to be in the entrance hall sitting at the bottom of the stairs all this time, when she saw Theo, instead of rushing up to welcome him, she began sobbing, releasing all the tension that had caused her so many hours of deep anguish.

James hastened away to prepare a warm place for Theo to spend the night, while the other two men stood in the hallway waiting for instructions as to where to take him, but Theo, looking across the hall at Elizabeth, hobbled over, and set himself down on the stairs next to her, putting his arm round her. Her sobs came in great heaves, and he pulled her head towards him, leaning it against his shoulder, putting her face next to his.

They did not hear or see his rescuers leave, but in leaving, the men knew this was not the moment to expect expressions of gratitude; they would come later, and they went home satisfied to have helped save a man's life.

Mr. Nash let Elizabeth and Theo have a few minutes

together, before taking charge. Elizabeth would be fine, but Theo certainly needed his attention, and the rest of the night was spent in looking after him. He was wrapped in warm blankets, given hot soup, and put to bed after James, under Mr. Nash's supervision, had had to cut away his boot with a knife, but it was quite a while before Theo was able to tell them what had happened.

With all the activity throughout the night, there was little sleep for anyone, including Theo, whose ankle -- giving him no relief from pain -- combined with his concern over the loss of Hercules, kept him awake despite his exhaustion. Even so, he could not wait until daylight should break, at which time he was determined to join all those who would be taking part in the hue and cry after the thieves.

By mid morning a group of burgesses had gathered, along with Mr. James Evans, the sheriff, and having learned from Theo that the thieves had not doubled back towards Haverfordwest, set off in the direction of Broad Haven in search of the horse and the men who had stolen him.

Theo meanwhile, insistent that he should accompany them, would not listen to anyone's advice, so it was decided Mr. Edwardes's curricle and pair should be brought into town, and Theo would follow the rest of the group in this. He had insisted as well, that he was perfectly capable of handling the curricle on his own, but for once, James refused to follow orders, and with Elizabeth's approval, would not let his master out of the yard unless he accompanied him. Theo was obliged to comply.

Elizabeth, although recovered from her frightening experience of the previous night, nevertheless suffered from its after-effects, as it left her feeling weak and debilitated. As a result she spent the whole day in bed.

As for the search for Hercules and the men who had

stolen him, the day spent covering the area failed to reveal anything, and Theo spent a second night worrying about his horse, and speculating about what they might have done with him. He was a valuable animal, so he doubted they would have let him come to any harm, but if they had already sold him on, there was no knowing where in the whole country he might be by this time, and he was afraid he would never see Hercules again.

The days passed, and there was still no word on his horse's whereabouts, and the effect on Theo was severe. There could be no man who had ever loved his horse more than Theo loved Hercules, and he knew that if the animal were free to come home, he would, so every day he went to the livery stable, hoping to discover his horse had somehow found his way back home. The men at the stable hated to witness this daily pilgrimage; in their opinion the horse was gone, and they would never see him again, so were sad to see Theo turn away each day after hearing no good news.

The weeks passed, and Theo was becoming resigned to his loss. Even so, he knew that, without Hercules, he would never want to go again to Druid's Town beach, or to any other of their favourite places. It was as though not only had his horse gone, but all the haunts he had grown to love had gone with him, and the realization saddened him. And as the winter went by, followed by the spring and then the summer, Theo knew Hercules was gone forever.

CHAPTER 21

The spring of 1785 was not a happy time for Theo and Elizabeth. In November of the previous year Elizabeth had given birth to a boy to whom they had given the name Edward. Normally, the third son would have been named after his paternal grandfather, but as Theo had no idea who his father was, he wanted him to be named after his godfather, Sir Edward Manderson, so the child was duly baptised Edward.

Little Edward was a bonny child who thrived and grew, and at the age of three months was bright-eyed and happy. One day in the following February, however, he was not his usual self, and became irritable and restless. That evening he developed a cough, and seemed to have some difficulty breathing. Mr. Nash was sent for, but was out of town, so his medical-student son came instead. He looked at Edward's flushed face, and felt his forehead which was hot, and noticed the child's heart was beating fast. But the young Mr. Nash was not well along in his studies, and after prescribing the usual care for a child with a fever, assured them Edward would be all right, and he would return in the morning. In the early hours of that morning, however, little Edward was suddenly unable to breathe at all, and within minutes he died, cradled in Elizabeth's lap. Theo watched, distraught at his inability to do anything to save his child.

With his various projects to occupy him, Theo was able to cope with the loss of Edward more easily than Elizabeth, whose whole life was almost exclusively devoted to her children, and he was at a loss to know how to help her recover from her misery, and even talked of his concern among his friends at one of their gatherings in his library.

"My dear wife is usually so cheerful and contented," he told them, "but now I find her crying day and night. She's inconsolable, and even her women friends, several of whom have also lost their babies, have been unable to raise her spirits." He shook his head, perplexed, and looked at the half-dozen men gathered together. "Looking around now though, I suppose I can get no advice from any of you as I see not one of you here today is even married yet. It is then a subject with which I should perhaps not presume to concern you... but it's on my mind."

"That doesn't stop us from sympathising with you," said Sir John Campbell. "I'm sure none of us would want to endure what you and Mrs. Potter are suffering." Sir John being just a year younger than Theo, and the two men being of similar temperament, energy and way of thinking, they had become firm friends.

The other men nodded in sympathy.

"Have you thought of going on an excursion somewhere?" suggested one. "It would seem a change of scenery might be beneficial for both of you."

Theo shook his head. "I did suggest perhaps we could visit the Lake District, but Mrs. Potter wouldn't hear of travelling so far away from her children...Well, I'm sure she'll improve before long," he said after a few moments of silence, and changed the subject.

For a while they discussed Mr. William Pitt's candidacy

at the upcoming general election, then Theo mentioned a new journal just published called, *The Annals of Agriculture*, both subjects normally of particular interest to his friend, Campbell. The latter, however, had been staring out of the window during the whole discussion, apparently absorbed in thoughts of a different nature. Finally he turned round.

"May I return a minute to the subject of your bereavement?" he said. "I've been thinking; I'll be at Stackpole Court for the summer, and should like nothing better than if you and Mrs. Potter would come and share your company with me and some other guests for the duration. It's not so far that you couldn't return home quickly if needs be, nor so far that frequent reports of your children's welfare couldn't easily be delivered. What say you, Potter?"

Theo was overwhelmed by the invitation. "My dear Campbell! What can I say? For myself I'd be delighted to accept your invitation, and I'll most certainly do my best to encourage my dear wife to accept. There can be no objection I can see for her not doing so." He stood up. "Do please excuse me gentlemen. I'll go right now, and see what she has to say... I'm sure she'll say 'yes'." And he rushed from the room.

While he was gone, Campbell returned to what had been his ongoing progress report at the group's meetings ever since he had inherited the Stackpole estate. It concerned a project that would have daunted a less capable and enthusiastic spirit; it was a project that consisted of the conversion into a lake of three separate and converging valleys some way down and to the front of his mansion house. As the project was near Bosherston village, the resulting lake, or series of lakes, would be called after the village.

A little while later Theo returned, smiling. He and Mrs. Potter would be happy to accept the invitation.

Theo guided the horses with his one hand, and put his other round Elizabeth's waist. It was his sincere hope this visit to Campbell's estate would cure her of her depression. Mr. Edwardes had been only too happy to let his cousins have the loan of his curricle and pair for the summer, and on a warm, sunny morning at the beginning of June, Theo and Elizabeth had set out on their trip to Stackpole Court. In the intervening time Elizabeth had tried to accustom herself to the idea of leaving her children at Dunstable Hall in the care of their nurse and her mother for the following weeks, and had even allowed herself to look forward to the prospect of relaxing in the soft air and gentle landscape of south Pembrokeshire.

The hawthorns had just started to shed their tiny white, sweet-smelling petals, forming a carpet for them to ride over that was reminiscent of their wedding day, when white petals had been scattered in front of the entrance to St. Martin's Church.

The drive would take them most of the day, and cook had prepared some cold cuts with bread and cheese to be eaten along the way, while James and Mary-Anne had left the previous day so as to prepare everything ahead of time, to transport the necessary baggage, and to acquaint themselves with the mansion itself as well as with the household staff and routines.

In Canaston Wood they turned off at Blackpool Mill, and as they were climbing the hill, Elizabeth started to worry that she had not left sufficient instructions for nurse regarding the children, nor had she been able to bring some likenesses of them with her because Theo had said "no" in such a way she had not dared to mention it again.

Now, as she already began worrying, Theo repeated to her what he had been forced to tell her ever since the trip to Stackpole had been decided upon. "Bess, my dear, you know your children are in excellent hands. There's no better nurse than the one you selected three years ago to look after John, and since then you've had no reason at any time to question her competence or her regard for our children. Besides, your mother is there should any emergency arise. Other than turn around now, and go home, there's nothing for you to do, so please, my dear, allow the nurse to do what she's trained to do, and what you've hired her to do… Please?" He pressed her hand lovingly, but his voice was decisive. "It's time to let go."

They travelled in silence for a while, Elizabeth thinking of her three children back in Haverfordwest, and Theo thinking about the town itself, and once again about the stark division between the lives of the gentry and those of the common people.

"We lead a privileged life, you and I," he announced with a suddenness that raised Elizabeth out of her own reverie. "We live in a beautiful house in a fashionable part of town. We ride in sedan chairs to entertainments and other fine functions that we attend. We enjoy the balls that are held for the county's nobility and elite. We're invited to exclusive parties and gatherings. We don't want for anything." He paused.

Elizabeth looked at him in surprise. "Here we are, driving through beautiful countryside on a lovely day in June. What on earth has brought such thoughts into your mind right now?"

"Not many minutes ago we were trotting through parts of Haverfordwest in which you and I would find it inconceivable to live. Yet so many people do live there, and I find it hard to reconcile my own life of luxury with the poverty and squalor in which they're forced to live." He slapped the reins on the horses' backs. "I wish it were possible to improve their quality of life in some way… provide lighting, water, sewers. I'm sure much of their sickness comes from their surroundings, and unlike some -- our friends even -- I don't think the townspeople would choose to live in squalor like that, regardless of what was done for them; they have no option the way things are."

"Well, I really don't know what *we* can do about it, my dear. You and I, we walk a fine line in society, you must remember. The members of the Common Council are the only ones in a position to carry out the changes you'd like to see, and they're also the ones who are our friends, one of whom we're on our way to visit, and another, a cousin of mine. If you were to nag them about what you consider to be their social obligations, how long would they continue to consider us our friends and seek our company? Besides, you can't complain that many members of the council are not charitable; so many make bequests in their wills to charities, and give during their lifetimes too, as does my cousin."

"I know, but that's not the same. In that they're acting as private citizens, and helping individuals here and there -- I've done it myself -- but as council members they sit there at their meetings in their little room in St. Mary's Church, to my mind doing little other than passing resolutions such as offering from the public coffers *one hundred guineas* reward to catch the vandals who've set fire to a couple of *their personal* haystacks, or damaged other *personal* property of theirs. Think what could be done for the community as a whole with *one hundred guineas*! At the same time they pass a resolution to give some poor widow, again out of the public coffers, a mere forty shillings a year in charity to keep her from starving. Is a haystack worth more than fifty times a human life?"

"Theo. I don't know what to say to all this. You're right of course, but here we are, you and I, as I said, on our way to spend several weeks at the home of one of those council members. What do you want to do? Destroy our own lives by chastising them and speaking out against something we know neither you nor I can change anyway? Neither of us has the power to vote. I, as a woman, shall never have that power, and you yourself will *never* get it either if they suspect you of planning to upset their apple cart... Besides, I think you've chosen your particular friends well. Knowing Sir John Campbell as we do, I think he most likely thinks as you do, but he's only one on a council of twenty-four men."

Theo gave a big sigh, gathered up the reins with both hands, and slapped them on the horses' backs again setting them into a fast trot. He was annoyed with himself. He had complained about his wife spoiling their journey, worrying about their children. Now he had more than compounded the depressed atmosphere by voicing his own thoughts about the inequities of society. Elizabeth was right though about Campbell: he was sensible, forward thinking, and he was also a man he could talk to. Hoping to lift them both out of their current sombre mood, he said, "Do you think I'll ever be on the council, Bess?"

Elizabeth patted him on the arm. "No, my dear Theo. There are conditions you have to meet in order to be elected to the council, and I'm afraid you'll never meet some of them."

"You mean I'll never get to be mayor then?" Theo was smiling now. "Just think: if I'm never to be mayor, then whenever the council agrees to the rental of one of their properties, I'll never get my commission of a couple of fat hens annually from the renter of that property!... How *shall* we survive?... And when you think of the number of properties the council owns and rents, the mayor, by the end of his term of office, must be thoroughly sick of being served chicken for his dinner!" And they both laughed.

"Oh!" Theo added after a short silence. "I've just remembered! I need to pay my own rent to the council next month... for the house and for the business property... And I suppose that means I'll need to ask cousin Edwardes if he can let me have four chickens to give to Mr. Fortune. In truth, I do wonder what the mayor does with them all."

"I imagine that in Mr. Fortune's case, at least, he gives them to the poor. On his estate I'm sure he has more chickens of his own than he can ever eat."

"Oh? That makes me feel much better about it then," Theo laughed.

CHAPTER 22

Theo, by nature a man who rose early, was up and dressed in time to see the sunrise. Elizabeth's chamber -- for each had been given their separate apartments -- which Theo shared with his wife as a matter of custom, looked out over a steep, tree-covered valley, beyond which the sea reflected the shades of the lightening sky. Several hours remained before breakfast would be ready and laid out along the buffet in the breakfast salon, so he reasoned a walk would be an uplifting way in which to fill the time.

With this in mind he crept out of the room, and apart from passing a servant already at her task of dusting and polishing, the family area of the huge house was silent as he made his way down to the great entrance hall, out under the lofty portico and onto the driveway of Stackpole Court. He then set off in a cheerful mood across an intervening lawn towards a pathway that led towards the beach.

The lawn was providing breakfast for a multitude of rabbits which scattered as he walked past, and as he entered the path, he could hear the sad, mewing call of buzzards circling above, their lonely cry haunting the tall, hilly banks on either side of him. He breathed in the cool morning air, feeling refreshed and not in the least tired after the lively party that had welcomed them and the other guests the previous night.

They had arrived about an hour before dinner, and their host had greeted them warmly, and introduced them to other guests who had already made their appearance. Many of these were already known to them, being friends and acquaintances from Haverfordwest, among whom were Mr. Francis Edwardes, brother of Lord Kensington, and a distant cousin of Elizabeth's. Sir Thomas and Lady Sinclair were there, as was the mayor, Mr. Joseph Fortune -- and the subject of chickens avoided. Others from England they did not know, such as the Earl and Countess of Carlisle, and Mr. Arthur Young, a man the same age as Theo, who was an expert on agriculture, and from whom Sir John was hoping to receive useful information regarding the Stackpole estate. One thing all guests had in common was that they were interesting, excellent and witty conversationalists, talented, and of lively spirits. Moreover, with the exception of Mr. and Mrs. Fortune and Mr. Francis Edwardes, who were older, all were in their late twenties and early thirties, an age at which, even after a heavy dinner, they could all still find the energy to entertain and be entertained until the early hours of the morning.

After a while Theo came to the end of the valley, where a small river meandered through a soft, sandy delta, out onto a wide beach and on into the sea. There were already visible signs of Sir John's plans for a lake taking shape, as earthworks were gradually creating a dam from one side of the valley to the other. Once the dam stopped the river, he could visualize the lake behind it, and with three large prongs to it, it would, he thought, look rather like Neptune's trident.

He walked out onto the wide beach with its golden sands, beautiful and unspoilt, and with a large picturesque rock rising like a steepled church out of the bay. Instead of walking along the beach however, he climbed up the nearest cliff, and walked along the top until he came to the tiny cove they had passed yesterday on their way to the Court, and which had recently had a new quay built so as to provide access from the sea. A small fishing boat was tied up next to it, and there were fishing nets and lobster pots neatly laid out in the sun. The tide was out, and the air smelled of warm, wet seaweed and the faint smell of rotting flesh that came from the lobster pots, a smell that, on closer inspection, turned out to be from the body of a dead puffin -- or sea parrot as he had heard the locals call them -- that lay in each pot, as bait.

Theo turned back inland towards the mansion, and finally passed the big arch leading to the stable yard. It reminded him of the stables at Dunstable Hall, and he spent the rest of his walk wondering where Hercules might be. Was he even still alive? He grieved for his loss. It was, of course, nothing like the grief of losing his little son, but he nevertheless still felt a wave of sadness wash over him whenever he thought about his horse; and now in a sombre mood he finally arrived back at Elizabeth's chamber where he found her ready for breakfast, but equally agitated.

"There has been no word sent of the children. I do so hope they're all right."

"My dear, if anything were wrong, you would have heard about it I'm certain, so please don't concern yourself... and it was only yesterday that we left them!" Theo put his arms around her. "My dear Bess, you're here to relax and think about enjoyable pursuits, meet new friends and take your mind off your children."

"Yes, but when you've lost one, you're in constant fear for the others."

"I once heard that worry is interest paid on trouble before it's due, and your worrying can make absolutely no difference to what's going to happen anyway, so why distress yourself by doing it? My dearest Bess, do please set such thoughts aside I beg you. Come..." He took her hand. "Let's have breakfast.

213

You'll feel better afterwards." And he led her downstairs to the breakfast parlour.

It being summer, there was no hunting available for the men, apart from taking pot-shots at the rabbits out on the lawn in front of the mansion, so various outings and excursions had been arranged for everyone's amusement, and early on in their stay, Campbell had suggested it would be fun if he and Theo and one of the ladies could get together and produce a sketch all could enjoy at some time during their visit.

Not being able to call to mind, let alone remember the script of any such sketch, Theo found himself having to spend a considerable amount of time creating one, even staying home on some days while everyone else went out. He did not mind, however. It was something he enjoyed doing, and even found himself -- at the prospect of performing again -- rather like a corn-fed hunter champing at the bit at the sound of the huntsman's horn.

It was to be a farce, of course, after the type written by his friend, John O'Keeffe, with whom he was still in touch, and once the script was to his satisfaction, rehearsals began, with Lady Carlisle having been persuaded to take the part of the hapless damsel -- in distress, of course. Theo could not think when he had last had so much fun, and with Sir John overacting and sounding like a fairground ranter in his attempts to speak out to his audience, Theo often ended up on the floor, laughing helplessly -- all of which was taken good naturedly by his friend, as he knew it would be. Lady Carlisle, being naturally quite prim, was herself unintentionally funnier even than the part called for, so by the time the evening arrived on which their performance was to take place, there was no guarantee at all that the whole sketch would not fall apart, with Lady Carlisle standing bemused in centre stage, with both of her would-be rescuers on the floor, disabled with laughter.

As it happened, it did not end quite like that, but there were sufficient incidences along the way to keep the audience laughing, regardless of whether it was as a result of Theo's script, or not.

Another entertainment, provided this time by Theo and Sir John, had been found possible just by chance. Sir John was telling Theo at breakfast one morning about a duel he had witnessed some months before, and began explaining some of the technicalities of fencing to him. However, it quickly became clear that Theo's knowledge on the subject was equal to that of Sir John himself. "You can use a sword?" he asked Theo in surprise.

Theo smiled. "Yes, I think you could say I can."

"I say! Would you care to have a bout with me? I like to keep up my skill, but there aren't too many around here with whom to practise... I promise not to kill you," he added laughing.

"That's good to know." Ever since his recovery from being shot, Theo had made sure he constantly re-honed his fencing skills, and those of James too, and the two men frequently engaged in friendly fight, just as they had done since Theo was a teenager. He was therefore confident he could at least not make a fool of himself in a duel with Sir John, regardless of Campbell's level of expertise.

"Where better then, than right outside the front of the house, on the lawn? How about later this morning?"

"I'm game, if you are." Theo could not help but show his enthusiasm, and word soon spread that Mr. Potter and Sir John were to engage in a friendly duel out on the lawn, and by the time the two men were facing each other, their swords raised in salute, there was quite a gathering, including servants, who looked out of windows, all expecting the visitor to be floored in the first few seconds, with Sir John's sword pointing at his heart.

It did not take Theo long to discover that although Sir John was an excellent swordsman, his own level of expertise was much greater, but he was too much of a gentleman to make a fool of his host, and the two men fought until a draw was declared. It was a good fight, and pleased all the spectators, who were amazed at the skill of someone whom they had not expected to know how to even wield a sword, let alone conduct a reasonable duel.

At the end, Sir John shook Theo's hand, and gave him a quizzical look. "Thank you," he said, and started to walk away, but then turned and came back. "Where did you learn to be the expert you obviously are?"

Theo pointed to James, who was standing nearby. "There's the man who taught me everything I know."

Sir John turned to look at James in amazement. "Your manservant taught you?"

"Would you like an exhibition?" Theo asked him.

"I most certainly would!"

As everyone was still around, Sir John announced another friendly fight that might be well worth watching. Theo still had his sword, and everyone was amazed to see Sir John hand over his personal sword to Mr. Potter's manservant.

The fight that followed was of the same calibre as that which had drawn the men to the Smock Alley Theatre, and which now drew cries of fear, wonder and excitement as Theo and James exhibited the full extent of their dazzling fencing skills. At the end, pouring with sweat, the two men shook hands, bowed and grinned at each other, as everyone, even the servants hanging out of the windows, cheered and applauded. Theo, the performer, was in his element.

"Well, well!" said Campbell. "You entertain us with your wit; you entertain us with your acting skills; you entertain us with your fencing skills. What other skills have you got hidden up your sleeve, Potter?"

"Get me two horses, and I'll show you."

"Indeed! What? Right now?"

"Why not? Everyone is out here, and the weather is fine."

"What sort of horses?"

"A couple of cobs ones will do... Oh, and only one to be saddled, but both to wear bridles."

Campbell sent down to the stables for two horses, and everyone waited around until they arrived twenty minutes later. The servants were still hanging out of the windows, wondering what was going on when they saw the horses being handed over to Theo, Campbell being a bit worried about what was going to happen to them. He had no idea how good or bad a horseman his visitor was, and his horses were valuable. He was even more worried when Theo handed them both over to his manservant, who leapt onto the saddled one, and taking the other in hand, proceeded to ride off to the right of the house, about two hundred yards away, at the far end of the long lawn, where he turned around and waited, looking back towards the Theo.

In the meantime Theo had told everyone to line up along the front of the house, and there was a lot of whispering and conjecturing amongst the onlookers as he then walked about seventy-five yards towards his servant, then also turned around and stood facing back towards where the onlookers were craning their necks sideways to see what was going on.

A few seconds passed, then James yelled, "fly past," and set the horses into a controlled gallop, while Theo began to run as fast as he could away from them and back towards the spectators. Then, as James came alongside his master, Theo, still running at full speed, reached up, and with his left hand seized hold of the riderless horse's mane and vaulted onto its bare back. The two men then continued galloping past the cheering spectators until they reached the far end of the lawn where they came to a stop.

217

But Theo had not finished. He then swung his horse around, and raced flat out past the amazed onlookers, bringing the horse to a skidding stop right in front of the horse's astonished owner. Everyone clapped and cheered again, and Theo jumped off, and with a big smile, bowed around to his audience, while Campbell stood there, shaking his head in wonder.

"That could prove to be a useful manoeuvre in an emergency," he commented finally. "And did your manservant teach you that as well?"

"Yes, he did, and that trick *did* save my life once."

"That's a most unusual manservant you have, I must say. How long has he been with you?"

"Since I was five years old."

"He'd appear to me to be more of a trained bodyguard than a servant."

Theo did not answer that.

Where planned excursions were concerned, on one day the men walked, and the ladies were driven over to the Stack Rocks to see the thousands of guillemots nesting, and a fine picnic was enjoyed near the cliff edge, although Sir John had to keep warning his guests that what may look like solid ground on those cliff edges, was all too often merely a thick sod of grass overhanging the actual cliff, as many an unfortunate sheep and cow -- and not a few people -- had discovered.

On another day they left early in the morning to make a trip to Freshwater West. It was a perfect June day, sunny and with no wind at all. The men rode as usual, and the women went in an open carriage. The servants had set out earlier with everything necessary to make sitting around and eating on the sandy dunes as comfortable as possible. Everyone was in high spirits, and after an excellent lunch, some of the men lay back, closed their eyes, and enjoyed the warmth of the sun, while the ladies chatted and laughed.

Although Theo was happy to hear and take part in chatter and small talk when indoors, where without the constant buzz of human voices, the only sound would be of clocks ticking, out here he found it irritating, and did not want to listen to it, so he got up and wandered off on his own. He went over the dunes with its reedy marram grass, and eventually came to low hummocks of meadow grasses mown short by hundreds of resident rabbits, and riddled with their warrens.

He sat down and listened to the natural sounds around him. High above, larks were singing, their songs increasing in beauty the higher they flew, and he lay back and gazed at the cloudless sky, watching how the birds rose into the blue with almost vertical spurts of energy.

After a while, not wanting to be impolite by being absent for too long, he got up and started to walk back in a roundabout way, but came across a lone rabbit, lying in front of its hole. Unlike all the other rabbits, which had scurried away at Theo's approach, this rabbit stayed motionless, and only when he was looking down on it did he notice that its front leg was caught in a heavy, rusty gin trap. Theo bent down. He knew that for the local people rabbit was a major source of food, but he could not bear to see the animal suffering. Its leg was broken, the ends of the bone sticking out, raw and pink, and he stamped his boot hard down on the long bar to release the strong iron teeth that clamped tight over what was left of the animal's leg.

The rabbit, in shock, did not move, and still keeping his foot on the bar, Theo bent down and lifted it out of the trap, his left hand under the rabbit's chin, but as he did so, the poor animal in its fear bit him hard on the fleshy part of his thumb, its sharp incisors cutting quite deeply. He laid it down on the ground, and while he wrapped his hand in his kerchief, waited for the rabbit to move, but instead it lay down on its side, panting, its mouth open. It was going to die, and Theo could not watch it, nor yet leave it there like that, so avoiding being seen by the group, he ran down to the beach and picked up a large rock. Returning to where the rabbit still lay dying, he hit it sharply on the head, killing it instantly.

Afterwards, he returned to the others, and asked if anyone wanted to come down to the sea with him for a walk. Sir John stood up. "Yes, I will." Mr. Young would accompany them also, and the three men walked down to the water's edge where Theo -- as usual not wanting to make a fuss or be fussed over -- pretended to test the water's temperature, while taking care to flush out the bite with seawater. It had not quite gone down to the bone, but it still stung sharply in the salt water.

The tide was way out, and after marvelling at the ancient forest that on this occasion could be seen rising out of the sand, the men then wandered over towards the low rocks, where earlier they had seen a man collecting laverbread seaweed, and had stopped to watch him carry each load up to the tent-shaped drying huts on the hill. They had not noticed him leaving the beach, but now he was nowhere to be seen, and as they approached the rocks they heard a voice calling for help.

Sir John saw him first. The man had stepped into one of Freshwater West's small, but treacherous quicksands, and was already up to his waist. They raced over, and while Theo and Mr. Young held Sir John's feet, Campbell lay down flat on his belly to spread his weight, and reaching out, grabbed hold of the man's arms. By now, everyone on the sand-dunes had noticed the activity, and were standing up, watching. While the other two men held on tightly to his feet, Sir John gradually hauled the man out, finally pulling him to safety, to the accompaniment of much cheering and applause from the dunes.

As Theo walked up the beach with the other men, he did not hear the man's profuse thanks for their having saved his life; he was thinking instead how it was that, but for a small wild rabbit, the man happily and gratefully returning home to his family in Angle, would now be lost forever beneath the shifting sands of Freshwater West beach.

CHAPTER 23

In the evenings, when the men joined the ladies after dinner, tables were set up for those who enjoyed playing whist, loo, or other card games, while those who did not, chatted, read, or played the spinet that sat in the corner. Elizabeth, not only accomplished at the spinet, but also having a sweet, if not strong singing voice as well, was often called upon to display her talent. It had been noticed that Theo too had a good tenor voice, and so when Elizabeth played and he sang, or when they sang a duet, everyone stopped whatever they were doing, and listened.

On this particular evening, when the afternoon's drama at Freshwater West had been told and retold, marvelled at and analysed until no one could think of anything more to add to the subject, and Theo and Elizabeth had just finished singing "Johnny's so long at the fair," some visitors were announced.

"Mr. and Mrs. Carswell and Miss Carswell."

Everyone looked up in astonishment, and all who knew the Carswells wondered, not only what they were doing in this part of the county, but why they had chosen such an unconventional time of day in which to visit -- and considering they were not at all well-acquainted with Sir John, were exhibiting a decided lack of good breeding.

The gentlemen all stood up and bowed, and Sir John walked forward to greet them. Not even recognizing the Carswells, he was glad the footman had announced their names loudly and clearly, because otherwise he would not have known who they were.

Mrs. Carswell swept before her husband who, embarrassed because he knew it was inappropriate for all of them to visit in this manner, but had failed to dissuade his wife, slunk forward, his hands behind his back, yet trying to look jovial. His wife had no such qualms.

"Good evening! Good evening! How delightful!" And she stood waiting first for her husband to introduce Sir John to her and her daughter, then for Sir John to make all other necessary introductions, which he did. Once this was accomplished, and she and her daughter were seated, Mrs. Carswell felt at ease to attract the attention of everyone in the room, regardless of what they were doing before her arrival.

"I take the greatest pleasure in telling you," she announced, her shrill voice eluding no one's ears, "that close friends of ours -- a highly respectable family from Herefordshire -- have had the excellent good fortune to secure the rental here of Bosherston Manor for the summer season. We are also fortunate enough to have been invited as their guests, and as we arrived here only this afternoon, we felt it our duty, naturally, to pay our respects to you, Sir John, at your beautiful home as soon as possible."

Having achieved all this in a single breath, she paused, and surveyed the large drawing room.

A few polite nods greeted this monologue, followed by an awkward silence until Mrs. Carswell had regained sufficient breath to continue.

"What a delightful room, I do declare, Sir John. So well appointed, and so well-situated so the afternoon sun doesn't disturb you. You must be so happy to be here! It's such a delightful area, don't you think? And I've never visited this part of the county before -- so different from the north... I said to Mr. Carswell, 'We must visit Sir John while we're in the vicinity'. Did I not, Mr. Carswell?"

Receiving no response, she relaxed into her chair, and waved her plume fan around to encompass everyone in the room. "Now, don't let us interrupt whatever it was that you were doing." She looked about, and despite seeing Theo standing beside his wife -- who was still seated at the spinet -- the obvious conclusion as to what they had been doing before her entrance escaped her. "Ah! Mr. and Mrs. Potter! I see you were entertaining everyone with your talents. Were you performing an act from a play, Mr. Potter?... Let me guess, *The Taming of the Shrew?*... Oh no! I see you were attending your wife at the spinet. Well..." She waved her fan at them. "Please don't let us interrupt you. Do please continue. Don't mind us."

She sat back, but as great at the art of conversation as the rest of the guests were, everyone was so taken aback that none could think of any subject with which to start.

Theo, being the only one still standing at this moment, took it upon himself to put everyone at their ease. "I suggest it's time we have some dancing. What do you think, Campbell?"

Sir John agreed and leaped to his feet in relieved anticipation. If everyone were dancing, it would be hard to be interrupted by Mrs. Carswell, whom he had suddenly remembered the instant he had heard her voice, and recognized its peculiar and distasteful resonance.

They prevailed upon Elizabeth to play some lively tunes, and, relieved on occasion by the Countess of Carlisle, she was able to dance with her husband. During one of the lulls in the dancing, however, while Elizabeth and the Countess were exchanging places at the spinet, and there were a few minutes of quiet while everyone waited for the music to begin again, Mrs. Carswell could not help but fill it by telling all how proud she had been of her daughter's performance in *The Taming of the Shrew*, something she never failed to mention at every opportunity -- whether the recipients of this news had heard it before or not -- and how there were great expectations that she would be going on to greater things. The name of Drury Lane was mentioned also. On this occasion, however, she went even further. "Mr. Potter," she called across the room from her seat. "I know it's quite a while now since the play, but I still can't help but mention it. I'm sure you were as delighted with Miss Carswell's performance as we all were on that occasion... Such a *great* Kate to your Petruchio, don't you agree? You performed so delightfully together; it was almost as though you were made for each other! We have great hopes that you'll see fit to encourage her in her future endeavours -- you being such an excellent and respectable actor yourself."

Theo did not know where to look, or what to say. His face flushed with anger, he looked down, mortified at this woman's presumptuous behaviour, and was never more grateful to his wife who, pretending she had not heard anything that required a response, began playing another lively air, signalling everyone to rise and dance -- a signal all were delighted to attend to with haste and gratitude. Theo meanwhile was thankful they were not in the middle of performing the sketch they had produced the previous week; there would be no knowing what Mrs. Carswell's reaction to that would have been.

Her impression made, it was not long after that Mrs. Carswell, assured in her own mind that not only had they paid their respects by visiting, but had also impressed everyone favourably thereby, instructed her husband and daughter that good manners dictated it was time for them to take their leave, which they did. And not long after that interruption, everyone else -- overcome by the combination of fresh sea air and the day's events, not to mention that the party spirit prevailing before the arrival of Carswells, had been so dampened that it had failed to rekindle itself -- took their leave, and retired to their apartments for the night.

Nobody had seemed to notice that Theo had kept his hand in his pocket all the evening. Every time he had tried to remove his kerchief, his hand had started to bleed again, but at last inspection it had all finally dried, so once back in their chamber, he had planned to tell Elizabeth the whole story of the rabbit. Before he had the chance, however, Elizabeth started to tell him her own story, which was that while Theo had been off on his own during the afternoon, she and the Countess had sat together, away from the others, and had talked about their children.

"You know, she's only two-and-thirty years old, and already has a fourteen-year-old daughter, the Lady Isabella Caroline Howard. It's such a pretty name, Isabella, don't you think, Theo?... Although I think they call her Caroline."

While his wife recounted her story Theo had gone over to the window, and had his back to her as she spoke. He was trying to remove his kerchief, still firmly stuck to his hand. "Yes, I'd heard she was married young." He pulled at the kerchief, but it was still stuck.

"And while we were sitting there she took out from under her bodice a beautiful miniature of a large portrait Sir Joshua Reynolds had done of the Lady Isabella when she was only six years old. Such a pretty child, such lovely dark hair and beautifully fair skin!"

"Hmm." The kerchief refused to come off without the bite starting to bleed again, and Theo knew that if Elizabeth were to see it as it was, she would start to fuss over him, and he had had enough of women's misguided attentions for one day.

"I was so sad, Theo, that I didn't have any likenesses of our own children to show her. I do so wish I'd brought them... I wonder how they are," she sighed. "I do so worry about them. We really should have heard by now. I can't bear the suspense of not knowing... I think we should send James back to Haverfordwest to see if all is well. I really do, Theo. There's no knowing what might have happened to them."

Theo put his hand back in his pocket and turned round. "Elizabeth, your children not only have their nurse to see to them, they're safely at Dunstable Hall under the watchful eyes of your mother and your cousin. I assure you, *nothing* has happened to them."

"I can't stop thinking of what happened to Lady Lucy Moriarty."

"*What* happened to Lady Lucy Moriarty?"

"It happened just two months before you arrived in Haverfordwest in the October. Her little son was just eighteen months old when she went to Ireland with her husband for just a short visit, leaving the child at home in Haverfordwest in the care of his nanny. When she returned, she found that during their absence the little boy had fallen in the fire and had been burnt to death!... It was a terrible tragedy, and Lady Moriarty is still so upset, she can't bring herself to even write a little epitaph for him on his grave." She began to cry. "Please, Theo, please can we send James to find out if our children are safe? I can't bear it."

Theo went over and sat next to her on the bed, and she put her arms around him, burying her face in his chest. "Oh Theo! I'm so full of fear. When little Edward died, it was so sudden. It was the last thing I expected. Some things I *do* expect, but while the things I expect to happen, don't, the things I *least* expect -- things that I've not thought of even -- do happen. It was so when you were attacked that evening, and Hercules was stolen. I wake up at night with a sudden intake of breath, and think, 'What if Theo hadn't been found so soon?' You would have frozen to death, and I'd have lost you! And now I find myself constantly trying to think of all the things that could possibly go wrong, as though by listing them all to myself, this will ensure they won't happen... Everything is bearing down on my mind. It's eating away at my soul, Theo."

Elizabeth was weeping now, and she clutched hold of him. "Theo, don't ever leave me, will you? I see the other women with their husbands, and I wouldn't exchange you for any man in the world. I love you beyond all else. If something happened to you, I'd feel as though a part of my body had been ripped and torn away from me."

Theo took her in his arms, holding her, letting her cry away sorrows that seemed to continue building, and telling her that trying to forestall tragedies in the way she was trying to avert them, would make no difference to whatever life's fortunes were going to deal out to anyone; it was better to enjoy life while it was good, and only mourn if and when it chose to visit misfortune on them. As he spoke, his words sounded like platitudes even to him, but he hoped maybe just talking to her, regardless of what he was saying, would help to soothe her.

He removed his arms from around her, took hold of her hands, and held her away from him. "Look at me, my sweet Bess. Look at me."

She raised a tearful face, and caught sight of Theo's blood-stained kerchief still wrapped around his hand.

"Theo!" She stood up abruptly, looking at the hand which held her own. "What happened? When did you do that? Did it happen on the beach this afternoon?"

"I was going to tell you, but you haven't given me the chance." He smiled, hoping to receive one in return.

"Oh my dear Theo! I'm so sorry! I've been thinking only of myself. Let me see it." She wiped her eyes, and tried to remove the kerchief, but as Theo already knew, it was stuck. "It really isn't anything," he said. "It has all dried perfectly. It just bled a bit, that's all."

"Oh but we must get it seen to!"

"Bess, my dear, it's well past midnight, and everyone is asleep. When the maid brings us hot water in the morning, we can soak it off. There's no problem, I assure you," and he told her the story of the rabbit.

"I still think it should be taken care of. A bite from an animal isn't safe. It could get infected. There's no knowing what was in that animal's saliva!"

But Theo was adamant. It could wait until morning, and that was his final say on the matter.

By the end of breakfast, despite his hopes to the contrary, everyone in the whole household, including the servants, knew about his rabbit bite. This was because Elizabeth had expressed her concern to Sir John regarding possible infection, and he had insisted that his housekeeper, Mrs. Williams, should attend to it, Mrs. Williams being well known in the area as being expert at concocting many herbal remedies for all kinds of maladies. Mrs. Williams had been called for, and she had covered the bite with a dark orange, oily substance that smelt of some pungent plant.

While she was attending to the bite, and they had been chatting about Sir John's love of his gardens, Theo mentioned the number of hawthorn trees he had seen around the property. "The whole estate must turn white in the month of May," he commented.

"Oh yes, indeed, Mr. Potter. And the perfume from them too, as you must know, is enchanting."

"I've seen hawthorns all over the county, but never so many as here. Sir John must be particularly enamoured of them to allow so many to almost take over the property!"

"Ah! You should know there's a story attached to the hawthorns of Stackpole Court." Mrs. Williams took great care in washing the wound, squeezing it gently to drive out any poisons that may have accumulated.

"There is?"

"Yes, the story goes that one of Sir John's ancestors, a Thane of Cawdor in Scotland, was able to hide in a thicket of hawthorns which protected him, and so allowed him to escape from his enemies. Because of this, Sir John is solicitous of every single hawthorn on the property."

Theo smiled.

"It has medicinal qualities too, you know," Mrs. Williams added. "It's excellent for ailments of the heart, especially for those people who suffer palpitations and irregular heartbeats."

"It's amazing, isn't it, how many of the plants we see around us and generally ignore, can help alleviate so many ailments and restore our good health."

"Yes, indeed, Mr. Potter." She patted his hand as she finished treating him. "Even the humble marigold here, you see."

Then she had insisted he come to her every day until she was satisfied no infection was likely to set in. None did, and within a few weeks, all that was left was the scar.

CHAPTER 24

Theo and Elizabeth had been in Stackpole for nearly a month, and soon it would be time for them to leave. All the other guests had already left except for the Countess, although another couple was expected to arrive the following week. During this time when they would be the only guests, Sir John had suggested he should teach Theo how to sail. It would, he said, be his birthday present to Theo, who would be three-and-thirty years old the following week, on July 1st. Sir John kept his little sailboat down at the quay, and liked to go out fishing on his own, so it would be perfect for the two of them to set sail together, and he could show Theo how to handle the boat.

Ever since he had crossed the Irish Sea to Fishguard, and had watched the captain's skill in handling the sloop, Theo had wanted to learn to sail, so to be given this opportunity was a source of great excitement and anticipation to him, and he could not wait to begin.

By this time though, the weather had turned, and the following three days were blustery, with heavy downpours, not good sailing weather even for the experienced on that part of the Pembrokeshire coast where, not far from shore, it was too deep for a small craft to put down anchor. It was not until the evening of the third day of rain, that the sky cleared, the wind veered out of the southwest, and a brilliant red sunset predicted a fine day on the morrow.

That night Theo went to sleep looking forward to the only few days left in which to gain some experience of sailing. If he could only learn, he thought, he would buy his own boat, and have the pleasurable freedom of going out on his own. It would be an activity requiring all his concentration and his newly-learned skills, but with the prospect of the exhilaration of racing along through the surf, driven by a wind he could control, he knew it would be just the occupation and sport to which he would be well suited. It might even fill the emptiness he had felt ever since losing Hercules, and his anticipation as he fell asleep was great.

He had been asleep but a few hours when he was woken by Elizabeth; she was crying again. This time he was unable to find anything to calm her fears that her children were in danger, or that he would be sure to be drowned if he went sailing, and she insisted that nothing would do other than to return home the next day. This time no amount of persuasion or soothing would convince her, and Theo had nothing more to offer her. He was, moreover, so fearful of his wife's mental state, he eventually agreed to do as she wished, although with an ill-humour that revealed his displeasure.

Satisfied that she would no longer have to worry beyond the next day, Elizabeth soon fell asleep, but Theo lay awake, his own emotional turmoil leaving him in such a state of irritation and regret, that he went to his own apartment to spend the rest of the night for the first time away from his wife's bed.

For the first few hours he thought only of his own disappointment, and of what he perceived as Elizabeth's lack of understanding and unnecessary anxiety, but as the night wore on, and reason took over, his conscience told him that while he had agreed, albeit grudgingly, to go home this coming day, and in this he had acted properly, his mental reaction had been selfish, and he felt ashamed of it.

It was little over three months since Edward had died. How could he have possibly expected a mother to set aside all grief over the loss of her child in just three months? How in a lifetime? It was not even as though the baby had died at birth, and they had never known him or had the time to get to love him. In his short life he had grown plump and happy. He had smiled at them, recognized them, and put out his little hands to reach towards them. And then, in the space of twenty-four hours, he was gone. Theo felt the tears coming. "Our little Edward. What a beautiful little boy he was! And what is it that to me is so important? I want to learn to sail!" He leapt out of bed. "How could you have been so self-centred? Yes, you did try to comfort her, but all the time you were thinking about your own petty disappointments." He left his apartment, and crept back into Elizabeth's chamber. She was still asleep when he slipped in beside her and drew her towards him, cradling her body next to his.

On the morning of their departure from Stackpole Court, the weather was at last perfect for any type of amusement appropriate for July, and Theo sighed with regret about his birthday present that was not to be. After breakfast they said their goodbyes, and thanked their host for his hospitality, and set out on the road for home. This time they intended to take the ferry across the river, rather than go through Canaston Woods, as this would shorten their journey by almost twenty miles. They trotted along at a leisurely pace, warmed by the summer sunshine, and surrounded by the gentle countryside of south Pembrokeshire, arriving back at Dunstable Hall in late evening.

The children were already in bed asleep, but after all the greetings were over, both Theo and Elizabeth ran upstairs to look at them. John, Elizabeth and Joseph lay curled up in their beds, rosy-cheeked and in perfect health. Elizabeth took hold of Theo's hand; no harm had befallen her children; they were all at home together again. All was well.

CHAPTER 25

Now Elizabeth was back in the comfort of her own home and surrounded by her family once more, her high level of anxiety diminished, although she was still overprotective when it came to allowing anyone to take what she considered risks, and this included Theo, who found himself being warned to take care of himself even though, now that he no longer had Hercules, rode only when necessary, and then on a horse borrowed from cousin Edwardes.

This Christmas Elizabeth was not expecting a child, so Theo once again suggested they go to Dublin, if even only for a few weeks. Yet again, however, there was a reason for their not going.

"Theo, crossing the Irish Sea at this time of year can be extremely dangerous, and I can't bear to think what would happen to our children if, by some terrible chance, we were swept to our deaths as the result of a storm... They're so frequent, you know. Why yesterday even, the wind was at a gale, and I'm sure it was bad enough so no ship would have even left the harbour!"

"If that were the case," said Theo, his irritation showing, "then we'd have had no need to worry, because we wouldn't have even left the shore."

"But storms can flare up so quickly; we could be out there, out of sight of land even… and, as I said, what would our poor children do without us? My mother is getting beyond the years now when she could care for them, and…"

Theo raised his hand for her to stop. "Before you think of any more reasons, do I take it there is *no* way in which you can be persuaded to go?"

Elizabeth shook her head. "I'm sorry Theo, but we are parents, and must act responsibly."

"And I don't?" Frustration was welling up, but Theo had never yet lost his temper with his wife, and would not allow that to happen now.

Elizabeth made no reply.

"Very well," he said. "Then that's the way it must be," and left the room before any further aggravation could occur.

In the past he would have acted as he had always done on such occasions; he would have gone to get Hercules and raced out his frustration on Druid's Town beach. Instead, he went to his library, shut the door, sat down and gazed at the ceiling, not yet ready to admit that Elizabeth was right. It *was* dangerous to cross the Irish Sea in winter, and he reminded himself once again of Theophilus Cibber, who was drowned in a shipwreck on his way to perform at Smock Alley back in '58. For now though, he was not prepared to consider any reasons for not going there, knowing deep down, that the true cause of his aggravation was Elizabeth's consistent refusal to go anywhere, at *any* time of year, and he was annoyed at himself for even mentioning the subject, knowing in advance he would be once again frustrated by her reply.

Another source of frustration, which had a habit of reopening his old Pandora's Box at times like these, was the recognition that his illustrious career as an actor was gone forever, and he had thus far found nothing to provide him with the same fulfilment -- and life was passing him by.

Depressed, he sat and fretted that it was now seven years since he had last had the pleasure and satisfaction of acting on a real stage himself, or of sitting in a proper theatre and seeing the first-class performance of others -- and it was unlikely he would do even that again either. Some acting troupes visited Haverfordwest, but to Theo, not only were the venues uncomfortable and inadequate -- the performances being held for the most part in taverns or inns -- but their acting lacked polish, and he found watching them often embarrassing, sometimes excruciatingly so, and he had long-since lost interest in attending them. He had invited the Dublin theatre troupe from Smock Alley, but the theatre, without Thomas Sheridan -- and without him too -- was not prospering, and they could not come; and although Mr. Ryder was still there, actors had moved on, and their replacements did not know Theo, or he them.

He put his head between his hands, feeling isolated because no-one, not even Elizabeth, would understand his yearning and how it ate away at him, and there was no-one in his life anymore with whom he could even discuss those longings. He adored his wife and children, and would never leave them, but he had paid a high price in choosing his love over his chosen career -- he would never again have the opportunity to follow it, or even watch others follow theirs.

If they were to visit Dublin now, after all these years people would no longer even recognize him, let alone want to stop him to pay their respects. He had been gone too long, and he would have been forgotten. It was all too late. His chance was over, and the realization filled him with deep sadness, and he sat there, remembering his truly illustrious five years, when for it to be known that he, John Theophilus Potter, would be performing, was to fill the theatre, whether it be in Dublin, or Cork. It was a life he had loved so much, crazy though it had often been.

237

Dispirited, he turned his thoughts to Pembrokeshire and to the town of Haverfordwest. As far as the county was concerned, he had to admit its countryside and coastline were beautiful, and he enjoyed it as much as anyone. However, whether it was due to the air or not, he could not tell, but there was a feeling of languor that permeated the area, a languor that extended into its county town of Haverfordwest, and he sometimes felt as though he would like an enormous storm to blow through it, leaving it clear, lively and optimistic about a future which it surely could have if those with the necessary power would use it to breathe life into it.

"Haverfordwest has such a noble past," he said to himself, "and the nobility still think enough of it to build their townhouses here -- and even spend the season here -- but I fear that soon, if no provision is made for cultural pursuits and a few other trappings of progress and sophistication, those who are wealthy enough to go to London or Bath to satisfy their cultural needs -- and most of them already own homes in these cities -- will eventually abandon Haverfordwest and leave it to its slumbers."

The problem, he concluded, was that the Common Council, which alone determined which way the town moved, was made up of people who ran it to suit their own purposes, and theirs alone. To them Haverfordwest was a convenient gathering place, somewhere they could all get together when they were not in London, or on their estates. They would, he realized, only spend money to alter and improve it if it helped make their own lives more comfortable, and, sadly for all the common folk of the town, who had to live there regardless, it seemed as though the Council had already achieved all they were ever likely to want from it.

Theo was still there an hour later, drowning his spirits in maudlin contemplations, when he heard a knock on the front door, and James came to tell him there was visitor to see him.

"Send him in James." His voice was flat, dejected, and he pushed himself wearily to his feet.

To his surprise, it was the owner of the livery stable, Mr. David Jones. Theo had not seen him, or been near the stable, since he had given up hope of ever finding Hercules, and for a moment he wondered if, in his distress at the time, he had forgotten to pay his bill, and owed the man money. The two men bowed briefly, and a bit belatedly Theo invited his guest, who looked agitated, to sit down. Maybe he was embarrassed at having to ask for money owed, Theo thought.

"Oh excuse me please," he apologised. "Do sit down. How can I help you, Mr. Jones?" Maybe he should bring up the subject about not having paid any bill; it would be inexcusable for him to put the poor man through any further embarrassment. "I do regret it sincerely, if I've forgotten to pay you. I'm afraid my distraction over losing Hercules must have put it out of my mind. You should have approached me sooner about it, and…"

"Hercules is back!"

Theo who had himself sat down, jumped up. "He's back! How? When?" He was already on his way to the door. "Come. We can talk about it on the way." And within seconds they were hurrying back to the stable, Theo even having forgotten to put on his coat.

On the way, Mr. Jones told him how a man had arrived late last evening, riding a fine, large horse, and had left him at the livery stable, paying in advance for stabling the animal while on a three-day sojourn in the town.

"Why did no-one come to me at once?" Theo asked, afraid the man might have already left town again.

"It was very late, and in the darkness the stable boy on duty didn't think to look at the horse closely before closing for the night."

Theo was rushing ahead so full of anticipation, that poor

Mr. Jones, a man of portly build and small stature, was out of breath trying to keep up with him.

"Yes, yes, go on." Theo stopped long enough for Mr. Jones to draw in a few deep breaths before continuing.

"It was only this morning that they... saw it was Hercules when they took him... out into the yard," he panted. "There was... no mistaking him, of... course, and he... knew exactly..." He stopped again. "Where he was because when... we went to put him ... back in the stall, he balked, and... made straight for his... old stall."

Theo's excitement was such that he ran the last fifty yards to the stable, almost tripping on the cobbles as he did so, and leaving Mr. Jones stalled behind, head bent, hands on his knees, trying to catch his breath. He rushed straight to the stall. "Hercules!" And Hercules, who knew his master's footsteps well, was already snickering, straining his head over the door to welcome him. Theo slid open the bolt and went in. "Hercules! Oh Hercules!" and as Hercules bent his huge head to nuzzle Theo's neck, Theo buried his own head in his horse's mane. When he looked up, it was to see all the stable staff craning their necks over the stall door to see the happy reunion.

It was several minutes before Theo, not willing to leave his horse's side, came to the distressing realization that whoever rode him in, must be under the impression that he also owned him, and might not want to part with him. The prospect of still not being able to have his horse back caused a sudden, overwhelming emptiness in his gut, and he slid down into the corner of the stall, his back against the wall, his head in his hands. Hercules followed him and stood over him, still pushing his nose into his neck, as though he understood the turmoil in Theo's mind.

"This man," he said finally, looking up and peering out from under his horse's head. "Do you know who he is? What sort of man is he? Is he a gentleman? What age man is he?

What sort of character do you consider him to be?" He ran out of questions, and as Mr. Jones opened the door to join Theo in the stall, Hercules moved forward, placing himself between Theo and the stable owner, as though to protect his master.

Mr. Jones leaned his back against the door, ignoring the horse. "There was something about him; I don't think he's a gentleman, more like a businessman of some sort, perhaps." He shrugged. "Quite abrupt in manner, he was. I don't know how he'll react to your claim that he's your horse."

Theo nodded, and looked down. He was still slumped down in the corner, his hands between his legs. "Do you know when he's coming back?"

Mr. Jones shook his head. "He didn't say. It could be that he doesn't want Hercules till he leaves in three days. He could be anywhere in the meantime."

"Three days!" How could he possibly endure waiting for three days, not knowing whether he was to get Hercules back, or not? Other than the sound of a horse in another stall clopping around on the cobbles and pawing at the straw with its hooves, there was silence.

Mr. Jones slapped his hand on the side of his head. "Of course, he'd have left the name of the place where he's staying," and he rushed off to find the record, coming back a few minutes later. "He's staying at the Traveller's Rest." He pointed down the road.

"Yes, I certainly know where that is," said Theo getting up and remembering his own stay there seven years ago. He dusted himself off. It had seemed as though his powers of logical reasoning had left him for a while, but he was now beginning to think again. "Can you put a lock on the stall door?" he asked.

Mr. Jones was dubious. "Yes...well... I can I suppose, but..." He was thinking they could not refuse to let the man have his horse if he asked for it, especially as he was fully paid

241

up for three nights.

"Please do it, and if the man does come back within the hour, use any excuse to keep him waiting -- lose the key, or whatever it takes." Theo was now almost out of the stable altogether. "I'm going to get the sheriff," he called back.

There followed an anxious search for Mr. Thomas Tucker, the sheriff. He lived as far away from the stable as it was possible to be without being outside the town itself, and when Theo arrived at his home, he was not there. Did Mrs. Tucker know where he might be? She had shaken her head, but thought maybe he might be with the magistrate. Another walk to the magistrate's office proved equally fruitless; he was not there either, and the magistrate had no idea where he might be at all. He had not seen him since the preceding day and could be out of town altogether. There was no sign of him at the prison either, and Theo was about to give up the search when he saw the sheriff on his horse, coming from the direction of Merlin's Bridge. He had been at the blacksmith's for the last two hours, and was not in a good mood. For reasons unexplained, he had had to take the horse himself, but all Theo wanted to know was if he was willing to return with him to the livery stable.

"Where else do you think I'm going right now? I keep my horse there too, you know."

It was well over an hour since Theo had left the stable, and every minute his fear increased that the man would have returned, demanded his horse, and Hercules would already be gone. It took another fifteen minutes to arrive back there, during which Theo explained the situation, and during which time, Mr. Tucker became less grouchy, and more sympathetic to Theo's situation. He himself had been with those out looking for Hercules after he had been stolen the previous winter, so was quite prepared to accept Theo's claim; the horse, after all, had that distinguishing white line down his foreleg.

The stable boys had gone back to their work, so now it was only Mr. Tucker, Mr. Jones and Theo left to discuss how the problem could be resolved. However, they had no sooner begun this when the owner appeared.

He strode into the stable yard, already in a state of high irritation. He snapped his fingers at one of the stable boys. "Get me my horse," he demanded, and stood, legs apart, slapping his riding crop against his thigh, expecting instant attention.

Mr. Tucker stepped forward. "Excuse me, Sir..." he began.

The man looked him up and down, his mouth set in sneering distaste. "Yes?" he snapped.

"Um... ah, I'm afraid there's a problem, Sir."

"A problem? What sort of problem?" He began to stride towards the stall, with the three other men in pursuit. "If anything has happened to my horse, I'll..."

Mr. Tucker caught up with him at Hercules's stall.

The man saw his horse appeared to be unharmed, but then noticed the lock on the sliding bolt of the stall door. He flipped it with his crop. "What's the meaning of this?"

"Let me explain, Sir."

"Yes. Do. And quickly. I'm leaving this God-forsaken town... and I want the rest of my money back too," he demanded of Mr. Jones who had, along with Theo, joined the them at the entrance to the stall.

Hercules, on seeing Theo again, strained to reach him over the door, and the man hit him sharply on the nose with his crop. "Get back!" he snapped. Hercules showed the whites of his eyes before retreating, and began pacing around the stall, shaking his head up and down and switching his tail in anger. Theo restrained his own anger by turning away; he could not watch his horse being mistreated, and from a distance, heard the sheriff explaining that the horse had been stolen.

"Nonsense! I paid good money for that animal."

"I'm sorry, Sir, but that horse was stolen from that gentleman there late last autumn." He pointed to Theo.

"Well, it's mine now." He turned again to the lock on the gate. "Open this right now, or I'll have the sheriff after you."

"I *am* the sheriff, Sir."

The man nodded his head as though comprehending the situation, his sneer increasing. "Oh! I see. That's how you run affairs in this town is it? See a good horse, then collude to claim it's been stolen."

The sheriff kept his temper. "No Sir. That's not how it is, and I should ask you to be careful how you address me. Now, I have to inform you that the horse is indeed stolen property, and if necessary, it can be proven that it belongs to this gentleman." He pointed again to Theo.

The man folded his arms, and leaned with his back against the stall door. "Then I suggest you *do* prove it, and soon, because I'm not leaving here without that horse otherwise."

Theo had grown nervous when the sheriff had claimed he could prove the horse belonged to him. He had, of course, bought Hercules from cousin Edwardes, and the sale had been sealed with nothing more than a spit and a handshake; he had no bill of sale, nothing at all to prove Hercules was his.

The sheriff meanwhile was looking at him, expecting him to at least nod in agreement, which Theo could not do if a bill of sale was what was required.

For a minute nobody said anything, then Theo stepped forward. "I *can* prove he's my horse," he said. "Take him out into the yard and I'll show you."

By now the stable boys had stopped their work again, and were standing, watching.

"Yes. Well then, I suppose…" said Mr. Tucker, not sure what proof could be offered by doing nothing more than taking the horse out into the yard. "Uh… Mr. Jones. You have the key to this lock, I assume."

Mr. Jones removed the lock, drew back the bolt and began to open the gate, at which Hercules started to come forward, but the man rushed up waving his arms, his riding crop swatting at the horse's head. "Back! Back Sailor! Watch him! Watch him!" he cried out to everyone, stretching his arms out wide to prevent the horse's escape. "He'll be out of here and gone before you can stop him." He slammed the gate shut. "If you're going to take him out of this stall, I want a halter on him, and you'll need to shut the stable-yard gates too... I know that horse!" He pointed his crop towards Hercules. "He'll run away if given the slightest opportunity, and I've nearly lost him on several occasions already... He's a dammed nuisance," he added.

Theo stepped forward. "Sir, if that horse escapes, I promise you here and now, and in front of everybody, I'll pay you five hundred guineas."

The man laughed, and opened the stall gate wide. "You heard him everyone! Five hundred guineas, eh?" He looked at Theo. "You're a fool, Sir." He waved his crop towards the open gate. "Let the fun begin."

Hercules had already started to come forward, but stopped when Theo stepped towards him. There was no halter, no form of restraint at all, and Theo took hold of his ear and caressed it gently, pulling his head down, and calming the horse which had become agitated with all the commotion, and having been slapped around the head with the man's riding crop. Everyone had stepped back, waiting, and after a couple of minutes Theo left the stall, and began to walk towards the stable yard where the gates still remained wide open. Hercules followed him, and once out in the centre of the big yard, they came to a stop. Everyone followed quietly, the man now looking unsure, but still maintaining his swagger of superiority.

"Any minute now!" he shouted out. "Just wait for it!" He

slapped his riding crop several times against his thigh, hoping to frighten the horse into bolting, but Hercules, although he tossed his head and put back his ears at the sound, remained standing next to Theo. Theo patted him on the neck, then moved away from him, so that he stood out in front of Hercules, several yards away.

Everyone waited, then were amazed to see Theo, with deliberate and immense dignity, swing his right arm across his midriff and bend over, making a deep and elaborate bow to his horse, a bow fit for the king himself. Still bowing, Theo said to Hercules, "Bow Hercules. Bow." and Hercules bent his one foreleg back so that the tip of his hoof was resting on the ground, leaned back so that the other foreleg was stretched out in front of him, and lowered his head in a perfect bow.

"Thank you Hercules." Theo stood up, moved forward and patted the still bowing horse on the neck, and everyone applauded, while the man looked on, curling his lip into his now familiar sneer.

Theo released the horse, and stood next to him. It had been a trick he had taught Hercules a few years before, and with which he had amused his children on many an occasion. He led the horse back to the stall, and as he passed the man, said, "And his name is Hercules, *not* Sailor. Sailor indeed!" he muttered to himself.

But the man was not finished. "So you can make the horse do tricks. That does nothing to prove your ownership of him."

Theo stopped. He did not turn around, but his shoulders sagged. He then continued to Hercules's stall and put the horse in, shutting the door and sliding the bolt. Without a bill of sale he could prove nothing, and although all present knew that Theo alone had ever had anything to do with Hercules, none could swear it was, indeed, his horse. He turned round. The man was standing in the entrance way, still sneering, still slapping his thigh with his crop, waiting for a reply, and Theo had none to give.

At this moment it would have given him some satisfaction to have snatched that infernal crop from the man's hand, and beaten him around the head with it. Instead, he leaned on the gate of the stall, looking at Hercules, feeling an emptiness in the knowledge that this man was going to take his horse after all; losing him for a second time was unbearable, and he began to wish the man had not brought him to Haverfordwest at all.

"Theo! What are *you* doing here?" His cousin Edwardes had at that moment arrived at the stables, and not having seen Theo there since his horse was stolen, was wondering what had brought him here now. Then he saw Hercules. "Hercules! This is indeed a great occasion! I'm delighted for you, Theo!" He slapped Theo on the back, and getting no response, stood back and looked at his cousin's sad expression. "But why the low spirits?"

Theo explained his dilemma.

"But *I* can prove you bought the horse from me!" Edwardes cried.

"Indeed! How?"

"Mr. Edwardes slapped his cousin on the back again. "My dear Theo! You can't think I run an estate without keeping meticulous records of my income and outlay! We can go back to Dunstable Hall right this minute, and I'll show you!"

Theo could not wait, and taking his cousin by the arm was almost dragging him out of the stable. "If you wait here," he shouted back to the man, "I'll be happy to go with this gentleman and bring back his ledger which will show when and how much I paid him for this horse which I bought from him. I'll be back within the hour." And they were gone.

The two men set off for Dunstable Hall in Mr.

Edwardes's curricle, where they picked up the ledger and hastened back to the stable, but when they got there, the man had gone -- without Hercules. He never returned.

Sometime later Theo learned that, after several more horse thefts, one of the animals was discovered hobbled along with a number of nags on Begelly Common, where there was a gypsy encampment. The men responsible for the thefts were caught, and having nothing further to lose, admitted to having been the ones to have stolen Hercules as well. They pleaded guilty also to having sold him to the man for a mere ten guineas.

Theo was glad the robbers were found and punished for their crimes, but grateful too that Hercules would never suffer the indignity of knowing the paltry sum for which he had been sold.

CHAPTER 26

The season had started with Hunt Week in early November, and from that time on, private parties were being held all over Haverfordwest at the gentry's townhouses. Such houses rarely contained a ballroom, so balls were usually held at another appropriate venue, although plans were being drawn up for new assembly rooms to be built up near St. Mary's church.

The Edwardses, being delighted to have any excuse to act as hosts, and Dunstable Hall, being one of the few estates close enough to permit easy access to those staying in their townhouses, therefore offered up their home for an upcoming ball, and decided on something new; they would hold a masquerade ball. Such balls had been much in vogue in London and Bath for a number of years already, but this was the first time one was to be held in Haverfordwest, although it was believed that many years ago, in 1716, Joseph Addison had met the Countess of Warwick at such a ball held by the Lady Elizabeth Rich, at Haroldston Hall.

There was great excitement and anticipation at the prospect of this one, and Elizabeth, like everyone else, could not wait to choose her disguise. This time, however, it was Theo who was not willing for them to participate in a plan.

"Bess, my dear. Have you not noticed you're almost seven months pregnant? How are you going to wear any disguise in which you'll not be recognized? It would not be proper at all." He shook his head.

"But there are plenty of women in town in my condition, and as you know, with a masquerade ball, there's a strong likelihood that townsfolk, even pregnant ones, will take the opportunity to attend, so nobody will know me from anyone else."

Theo knew from hearsay that in London, not only townsfolk but even whores and other undesirables frequented masquerade balls, and that this was one of the few occasions on which all classes mixed without reservation, and being unrecognizable, servants could speak to the king himself in a manner unheard of under normal conditions. It was a strange concept to him -- not that he was averse to mixing with the lower classes at all -- but rather that there were, regardless, people with whom one would not want to associate under any circumstances.

"Well, I suppose so then," he relented. "It could be an amusing way to spend an evening."

Thus persuaded by his wife's enthusiasm, he entered into the spirit of the upcoming ball, and having agreed not to reveal their own disguises to each other until the minute they were ready to leave for the ball, he began take an interest in what he himself would wear.

The agreement was kept, and as Theo and Elizabeth met in the entrance hall, all ready to be transported to the masquerade, they had the first opportunity to pass judgment on each other's choice of costume.

On first seeing his wife's disguise, Theo was glad he was wearing the obligatory mask, as he felt a strong urge to laugh, so absurd did she look. Instead, he gave her a deep bow of respect. "Ah! The goddess Athena, I presume," he announced with the strong Irish brogue with which he intended to disguise his own, easily recognizable voice for the evening. As he bowed, he was forced to conclude that had his dear wife been thus attired for the previous month and more, there would have been no need for her to have resisted -- with complete success -- all his advances during that time, as he doubted any would have been made. There was one consolation though, he mused: if he himself did not find his wife attractive in her present outfit, then he could attend the upcoming ball in the comforting knowledge that no other man would either.

"Theo! What a magnificent Caesar you make!" Elizabeth approached to take a closer look. Taller by far than his wife, he towered above her, the armour on his upper body making him look even more impressive than usual.

"Where did you get that wig?" Elizabeth put her hand up and touched his head. "I never imagined Caesar with white hair, and you don't possess any wigs."

"I found it at a pawnbroker's."

Elizabeth stood back. "Ugh! How could you?" She shivered. "It could be full of vermin!"

"Well, it did smell a bit of mouse, and there were a few bits of nest and ..."

"Theo! Stop it! That's revolting!"

He laughed. " No, but I did take it to Mrs. Kelly who said she'd had years of experience dealing with such problems, and I assure you, it is now pristine." He bent over. "Smell it. I have to say it smells quite pleasant."

Elizabeth turned on her heels at the invitation, and had nothing more to say about the matter, and they finally arrived at Dunstable Hall where, like everyone else on this occasion, they walked in unannounced. The dancing had already begun, and it was clear from the numbers already there, it was not only the county's elite in attendance.

Theo found his wife somewhere to sit, then looked

around in doubt, not sure he was going to enjoy this after all. Elizabeth was not able to dance at this late date in her pregnancy, and he wondered what one did when everyone was not only a stranger to start the evening, but would remain so until late in the night when, after dinner, masks would finally be removed. He stood off to one side, feeling rather foolish, especially as he appeared now to be on his own. Elizabeth, despite her earlier protestations, had been recognized at once by two of her closest friends, and was engrossed in conversation with them, leaving him standing there in majestic and embarrassed isolation, and now of the opinion he looked more than just a little ridiculous in his Caesar-as-warrior costume.

He had not stood there many minutes, and was about to escape to the library -- where he intended to hide himself away for the rest of the evening -- when a woman approached him, took his hand, and said, "Do I know you?"

Theo, unacquainted with all the formalities of a masquerade ball, replied, "I hope not," and made to remove his hand along with rest of himself from her presence.

The woman, unabashed, kept hold of him, and tried to lead him towards the dance floor. "Ah!" she said, "I see you're unacquainted with masquerade balls, and so I'll teach you. Come. Dance with me."

When he continued to hold back, she repeated, "Come dance with me. It's not only safe, I assure you, but even acceptable tonight for a lady to ask a man to dance with her... even one she's never met before."

Theo looked back at Elizabeth, but she was in earnest discussion with her friends, and did not see him, so he acquiesced -- although with less grace than was normal for him -- and danced with the woman, whose performance was good, but not as elegant as his wife's would have been. Even so, he was glad not to be standing alone at the side of the ballroom looking foolish, and soon found himself warming to the mood of the unaccustomed atmosphere and strange mode of behaviour; and as Elizabeth was otherwise occupied, he allowed himself to join in, and even began to ask other women to dance, not having the slightest notion as to who they were, and hoping the same applied to himself.

The evening progressed, and between visits to Elizabeth to make sure she was well attended to, Theo was now enjoying himself, even feeling light-hearted and at his ease -- masquerade balls were fun and entertaining after all.

He had just finished the most recent of many dances, and both he and the air in the ballroom being now so warm, he moved to the open French doors, and stepped out onto the edge of the terrace, where he leaned against the waist-high parapet, and looked out towards the dark meadow below. Unaware he had been followed, he jumped when a light hand touched him on the shoulder. He turned round. Standing there was a tall, elegant woman dressed in the domino disguise, enveloped in black from head to toe, her face hidden behind a heavy black veil. "Do you know me?" she asked, using the accepted form of introducing herself on this occasion.

"No, I don't."

She held out a refined hand from under her black cloak. "Come with me." She beckoned to him, and began walking backwards towards the ballroom. She had a beautiful voice, low, melodic and sultry, which Theo found most alluring.

"I would have you dance with me," she said. "And alas, although I've watched you invite so many other ladies to dance with you, you've ignored me all evening." She was still stepping backwards, and still beckoning to him.

Theo stepped forwards. He did not remember seeing her before, but then he had not heard her speak either, and finding her seductive -- even disguised as she was -- had no problem accepting her invitation, and let her take his hand, and lead him to the floor.

It was a dance like none other he had danced that evening, and Theo was well aware she was trying to seduce him. Without seeming to touch him, she nevertheless managed to caress him with both her body and her provocative voice, and Theo, starved of making love for longer than was good for him, was aroused. At the end of the dance he led her back to her seat, but she rose again, her body sinuous, like a cat's, and begged him to dance with her again -- and again. And he did.

Theo knew that what was happening was unacceptable behaviour for him, but at the same time was so enchanted by this woman, he found himself rationalizing his willingness to participate in what he succeeded in persuading himself was *her* charade. For himself it was, after all, like performing in a play in which he was not Theo, but rather an actor playing a role. He had played love scenes before, and could he not easily control his mind and body's responses in such situations? But this was not a play, and he was not acting. He was Theo, and he had a wife he loved, yet was allowing himself to be seduced, and was revelling in the thrill of it.

Such a progression of his evening's entertainment had been the farthest thing from his mind when he had first entered the ballroom several hours ago. Now though, he was so aroused he could think of nothing else. Maybe he could...would... let it go just so far. There would be no harm in that, and when she took his hand and began to lead him, first to the far end of the ballroom, then out of it altogether, he let her, and they went to a part of the house where he himself helped find somewhere where they would not be discovered.

They lay on the bed, and the lady put out her hand to remove his mask.

"No!" He snatched her hand to prevent her. "No. Whatever else we remove, it won't be our masks..."

She laughed, and Theo watched as she stood up, lifted

her black gown as far as her knees, and began to remove her white stockings -- one by one -- pointing her delicate toes as she did so. She had beautiful feet, and Theo imagined her naked. He was mesmerized, and when she had removed each stocking with a deliberation that provoked him into even further arousal, she leaned over and touched him, and Theo hastened to pull her towards him, but she drew back, tantalizing him.

"Now you. It's your turn to remove something... slowly, slowly," she rebuked him as he rushed to remove first his wide, leather, Caesar belt. This achieved, Theo was ready to rip off more of his clothing, much more -- and the more quickly, the better -- but was prevented when she sat on top of him, pushing him onto his back, taking his hands and bringing them to her lips beneath the veil.

"I'm not yet ready...Wait...You're too hasty. Let me just look at you." Her body was light, and smelled of spicy perfume -- erotic.

He released his hands from her grip, intending again to draw her down towards him, but once more she drew back.

"No!" She sat there, her head to one side, looking at him, studying him, and Theo had difficulty containing himself. "All right. You may remove more of your costume now," she told him after a while, and moved to his side, to allow him to remove his clothes, all the time looking at him through the veil.

"What about you?" All he had seen of her thus far were her elegant feet and hands.

"Ah no! You first. How can I feel Caesar's body under all that armour? Pray, do remove it... now."

Theo had never heard a voice that had such an effect on him. He sat up and under her gaze, removed his armour.

"Now your tunic." And Theo did as he was told.

She put out her hand and gently pressed him back down on the bed again with her fingertips, then kneeled astride him, studying him again.

He knew this woman was controlling him completely, but felt quite helpless to let it be otherwise. "Isn't it now your turn to let me see more of you?" Her feet and hands were not enough; he was now desperate to see more -- everything. "If your body is like your irresistible voice... I need to see you out of that ugly, all-enveloping shroud of a disguise. Please? Please," he repeated, when she remained motionless.

She did not answer, but drew her index finger down his bare breast bone to his navel, the movement slow and deliberate, expert. "You have an extremely handsome body and a wonderful voice." Even her voice was slow and deliberate, each word serving only to heighten Theo's desire even further. "And that soft Irish accent is so alluring... You'd make a great actor."

"You think so?" Theo put out his hands again, needing more than anything to embrace this woman, to make abandoned love to her, but she took hold of his wrists, and bending over, held him down, her grip gentle, but firm. She put her face to his chest and kissed it, her warm breath on his skin, and Theo could not resist.

He did not know what it was: a noise somewhere, his conscience, a feeling of momentary fear, but whatever it was urged him to release his hands from her grip and push her off. Aroused as he was, there was no explaining to himself why he wanted her away from him, needed to get away from her. He leaped off the bed. "I'm sorry... I... I can't do this." He bent down to reach for his clothes lying on the floor beside the bed, and when he stood up, she reached out to him across the bed and put her hand between his thighs. But the moment had passed, and all he wanted was to leave the room, to find Elizabeth and take her home.

The woman did not beg or berate him, but sat on the side

of the bed, her hands in her lap, calm, watching him as he dressed as fast as he was able, bowed to her with almost insulting haste, and raced back to the ballroom, leaving her to find her own way back.

Elizabeth was still chatting when Theo marched up and offered a hasty bow to the ladies. "I think it's time we left now my dear you must be tired and I've certainly danced until I don't think I have another dance left in me." His words tumbled out, and with much greater haste than was normal for him, or even seemly, he reached out, grabbed his wife's hand, and pulled her to her feet.

Elizabeth smiled at him. "I'm so glad you've been able to enjoy yourself Theo. I shouldn't have liked it if you'd been obliged to sit next to three married women all evening; it would have been so boring for you." She squeezed his hand, and he raised and kissed it. "I *do* love you, my Bess."

"I know you do, Theo. And I love you too."

CHAPTER 27

Acknowledging that he was not going to be returning to Dublin, and was in Haverfordwest to stay, Theo had a few years previously bought up the properties he had thus far been renting, and this, together with his being now a master printer, made him eligible to become a burgess of the town.

Thus it was that late in 1786, and at the age of thirty-five, he wrote his application to the Common Council, but it so happened that Lord Kensington himself had also put his name forward, making the application unnecessary, so in the February of the following year he received notice he was now a burgess.

This status gave him several rights and privileges: he could vote and hold certain offices, as well as share in the use of common land. It did not come without its obligations however. He had to promise to be an upright and honest citizen, to help those in need, and to be ready to help defend the town if necessary. He was beginning to feel he belonged at last.

In that same month Elizabeth gave birth to a girl, whom they named Ann, after Theo's godmother. Also, in that same month Theo found he had to help out at the printing shop as Mr. Sutton had not been well, and had been unable to come to work for several weeks, making it necessary for Theo to stand in for him. They had been busy too, and William, who was himself making significant progress towards becoming a master printer, had been a great help. Lately, Theo had needed to print so many books, he was glad the majority of them left the shop with a simple paper and card wrapper, not needing to be bound, as he did not have the time to do it. Most of the books were sold unbound, but other buyers would leave instructions as to the type of binding they wanted, and Theo would do this for them, as required.

On this cold morning in February, Theo set off towards his printing establishment on High Street, intending to call on Mrs. Anne Evans, the paper maker, on the way. This he did, but after placing his order with her, they continued chatting well after their business had concluded. At length he finally took his leave, but then saw his friend, Stephen George, standing at the door of his inn, The Blue Boar. Once more he stopped to chat, this time about politics, and before long Mr. George was inviting him in for a tankard of ale in his parlour, where the discussion continued for another half hour.

During this discussion two small heads appeared around the door. They belonged to Stephen George's son, John, and Theo's own son, John. The two boys, born in the same year, and now seven years old, were the best of friends, and if either could not be found at any time, their parents always knew where to look for them, as they would be either at The Blue Boar, or at the Potter home.

Theo looked at his son. "So this is where you are! Your mother's been looking for you. It's time for your lessons, so off you go." There were moans and groans from both boys, but Theo was insistent, and young John set off for home, complaining about the need for him to learn anything.

Having himself taken his leave from Stephen George some time later, Theo once again headed for his shop, stopping only twice more to pass the time of day with acquaintances, and on his arrival apologised to William for leaving him all this time to handle the business on his own.

"I fear it's impossible to walk through this town without finding myself being forever delayed by falling into conversation with someone or other. I call it 'the Haverfordwest Disease'. It seems that for every quarter of an hour I spend walking, I spend at least twice that time talking!"

William who was at the back of the shop printing up some notices for the Council during Theo's observations, smiled and nodded in agreement about this phenomenon.

Theo took up some work, and seated himself near the window, where he began putting the finishing touches to a tome he had just bound in beautiful leather for Lord Kensington. "It's the same when I take Mrs. Potter and my children for an evening stroll along the Parade," he continued. "Inevitably we meet friends and acquaintances along the way, and we stop, and the ladies begin chatting, and from what I can hear, it always seems to be about someone's ailments, while we men launch ourselves into the ever-absorbing gossip about the latest intrigue, skirmishes and power struggles between the Owenses of Orielton and almost all the other of the county's first families."

William was a quiet young man with little to say. Other than the knowledge of printing he had acquired in recent years, along with the necessity of first learning to read and write, both of which Theo himself had taught him, his education had been non-existent, making his contribution to a conversation negligible. He did know, of course, about such important men as Lord Kensington of Johnston, Lord Milford of Picton Castle, Sir Hugh Owen of Orielton and Sir John Campbell of Stackpole, but as he had no say in anything that could in any way improve his own quality of life, he did not bother to take much interest in them or their politics -- although he knew most of them by sight, as they did a large amount of business with the Potter Printing Company.

The day passed, and with the one book ready for the owner to collect, or for William to deliver, and not wanting to start on another, Theo spent his time looking over orders and various receipts, and was bored. Trying to converse with William had proved fruitless, and as it was a cold day, with a sharp wind out of the northeast, there had been few customers, so he went to sit again by the window, looking out onto the almost empty street.

Half moons of frost sat in the inside corners of the mullioned window panes, and with nothing else on his mind, he set about drawing the profile of a horse's head on the nearest one with his finger nail. First he gave it a fine, crested neck with flying mane. This was followed by a noble, curved nose and deep neck. He then gave it a spirited eye, and completed it with a flaring nostril. Although he had had no particular horse in mind when he started, now, when he looked at it, it was, of course, Hercules. He was still adding final touches to his design, when the bell on the door tinkled, and a young man entered. Theo was delighted. Conversation at last!

From his bearing, the young man was obviously a gentleman, and was immaculately dressed, although with a few more frills than Theo was in the habit of wearing, preferring himself a plainer style of dress. Once having carefully closed the door behind him, shutting out the cold blast of air that would enter with him, the young man stood there, one ankle casually crossed over the other, his silver-topped ebony cane stylishly held out some way from his body.

"A bit of a dandy," was Theo's first impression, and for an instant, his mind cast itself back to the time when he himself had revelled in playing such a role on the stage -- when he had thrilled his audience with his ability to play the consummate English snob, the ultimate fop, the biting wit tripping off his lips so as to delight, and be hated by all. Tall and elegant, with fine aristocratic hands perfect for foppish gestures, and coupled with the true comedian's sense of timing, he was made for such a role, and it had constituted some of his most brilliant acting. The memory vanished, and Theo looked at his customer.

The winter sun was low in the sky, and the light in the shop was such that William had needed to light some candles, so as to be able to see the type he was setting. Theo approached the customer, and both men greeted each other with a slight bow, but with the man's body silhouetted against what light there was, Theo could not make out his features. "Good afternoon Sir," he greeted him. "A cold, raw day, is it not? How can I be of service?" He led the man over to the mahogany counter, where he held out his hand, indicating a chair where the customer could sit, and dipped a quill in the inkwell, ready to make a note of whatever it was that was wanted, and hoping to relieve his boredom with some pleasant conversation at the same time. Before waiting for an answer, however, he put down the quill. "Just one minute, Sir. The light is such that I need to get a candle... need to be able to see what I'm doing," he laughed, and went to the back of the shop where he borrowed one of William's candles. When he returned, he found the young man still standing in front of the counter, but having already offered him a seat once, Theo saw no point in repeating it, so sat himself down on the high stool behind the counter, where he could more easily write whatever needed to be written.

He smiled up at the silhouette standing up before him and picked up the quill again. "There we are. That's better. Now, what would you like, Sir?"

"Well, I and some of my friends are planning to hold a *very* special party in about a month's time, and we'll be needing some invitations about so big." He held out his hand to indicate the size. "And..." He paused, startled because Theo had dropped the quill on the counter and was sitting still, as though overcome by some form of slight seizure, causing him to cease all activity, leaving him immobilised.

"Sir?" the young man said tentatively. "Sir? Are you all right?" he repeated when Theo remained unresponsive.

"Excuse me... I apologise." Theo blinked, recovered himself, and stood up, but his voice was unsteady and hoarse. He coughed. "I think I'll let my assistant attend to you... he... he's ..." He coughed again. "Better qualified than I." And with a quick bow he rushed to the rear of the shop, telling William in passing to attend to the gentleman.

William looked up, alarmed, but hastened to do as he was told.

Theo escaped to the rear door, opened it, and went outside where he leaned his back against the wall. His knees felt weak, and he shuddered. He put his hands over his face. "Oh God, no!" he whispered from behind his fingers. Theo was not a deeply religious man; he had on occasion, and in the privacy of his own mind, even asked questions that most people dared not ask. Even so he was not given to taking the Lord's name in vain, and on this occasion was unaware that he just had.

That voice! That melodic, sultry and erotic voice! He would recognize it anywhere! It was the voice of the young "lady" who had tried to seduce him at the masquerade ball -- and he stood there, leaning against the wall in mortified shock.

After William had dealt with the customer, and taken his order for printed invitations, he went looking for Theo, whom he found still leaning with his back and head against the wall. "Are you all right Sir?"

Theo's emotions were in turmoil at the thought of his encounter at the ball and where the young man had intended it should lead, but there was nothing he could say to William or to anyone about his humiliating experience. He pushed himself away from the wall, lifted his head and put his shoulders back in an attempt to behave normally. "Yes thank you, Bill. I suddenly didn't feel well; that's all, but I'm all right now."

They went back into the shop, in which Theo could not face spending another moment today. "It's gone four o'clock, Bill. What say we close up now?"

William of course was agreeable to this idea, and the shop was closed, and each went his separate way back home. Theo, fearful he might encounter the young man again, was glad it was now dark. Even so he worried that he might have been recognized, which he realized he most certainly would have been had he not disguised his voice by adopting a heavy Irish brogue on that dreadful occasion.

On arriving home he found Elizabeth in the library, where candles lit up the room with a warm glow. She had just found the book, *The Social Contract*, by Jean Jacques Rousseau, about whom she had heard Theo talk so much. "I've just begun it," she started as he entered, "and... What's the matter? You look like you've seen a ghost!"

"I have," he said, and fetched himself a large glass of whiskey from the Tantalus. Elizabeth did not ask about the ghost, and Theo did not tell.

His bad day was not yet over, however, for there was a letter waiting for him. It had come from an old friend in Dublin, who had written to tell him his manager, Thomas Ryder, had finally given up, and Theo's beloved Smock Alley Theatre, which had closed its doors, was now a warehouse; those boards on which so many actors like himself had trodden and achieved fame, were now used to support lifeless dry-goods. He sighed, crushed the letter and threw it into the fire, where he watched it crumble and fade away. "Much like my acting career," he sighed. It was as though an immense door had finally slammed shut on his fame as an illustrious actor in the sophisticated city of Dublin -- never to be opened again.

That Theo was gone forever. John Theophilus Potter, a solid and reliable burgess of Haverfordwest, was a printer and bookbinder.

CHAPTER 28

Theo strode home. He was annoyed, and wanted to share his bad news with Elizabeth, but when he knocked on the door of her private sitting room and marched in, he found himself faced by half a dozen ladies, sitting, working together on a tapestry.

"Oh, please excuse me ladies! I had no idea..." And before anyone could say anything, he had bowed hurriedly and retreated, shutting the door behind him.

He stood in the hallway and swore quietly. That Elizabeth was always willing to listen to him and to talk things over with him was another of his wife's endearing attributes as in contrast to his own fire when out of temper, she was calm -- unless someone's safety was concerned -- always listened to what he had to say without interrupting, and was always ready to offer a reasoned opinion, even if it meant her having to play Devil's advocate on occasion.

It was still quite early in the day, and there was no reason to suppose the ladies would be quitting their handiwork any time soon, so after pacing up and down the hallway for a few minutes, Theo left the house again and went to the livery stables to fetch Hercules. He was soon setting off towards his usual destination in times of agitation, Druid's Town beach.

He had not yet reached the turnoff when he saw another rider ahead of him. The man was moving at a much slower pace, and as Theo drew near he recognized him as being the most likely source of his present ill-humour -- it was Lord Kensington.

Like Members of Parliament representing the county of Pembroke as a whole, his Lordship, as MP for the county of Haverfordwest, needed to know his power base was secure. To this end he made sure as best he could, that those who could cause him problems by supporting his rivals, were kept out of positions where they could achieve this, most notably the Common Council on whom he depended entirely for his position.

He liked Theo, and knowing his wife was, like himself, an Edwardes, assumed he could count on Theo's loyalty at all times. He had, therefore, done what he could to see that out of the three men whose names had been submitted by the burgesses for the post of sheriff for the upcoming year, Theo was the one whose name would be pricked by the Council for the position.

Theo came alongside Lord Kensington and doffed his hat. "Good morning, your Lordship." Kensington was old enough to be Theo's father, and Theo would never dream of calling this peer 'Kensington', as he did his friend at Stackpole Court, 'Campbell'.

Lord Kensington, despite his advanced years, sat well in the saddle, and still rode regularly to hounds, negotiating all pitfalls of the Pembrokeshire countryside along with the best of them. "Good morning Potter! Good morning! And where are you off to this fine day?"

"Every now and then, your Lordship, I like to take my horse for a gallop along Druid's Town beach, and today is one of those days."

"Indeed! Then I'd like to accompany you. Captain here

could do with a good gallop."

Theo concealed his disappointment. He was not in the mood for company, especially his Lordship's. The two men turned down towards the coast, walking abreast along the path.

"I see you've been pricked for sheriff next year."

"That I have. I found out about it only this morning, moreover. I was surprised, considering I've been a burgess for such a short time -- so surprised, I demanded to see the form. And yes, there it was, the stylus prick was right there, next to my name, no argument about that."

Lord Kensington nodded. "It's true you've been in a position to have a vote for only three years, but you're well-known and respected in town, and it was time you joined the club." His Lordship looked at Theo.

"Yes your Lordship." Theo knew well how the system worked.

The conversation moved on, and Kensington took the opportunity to enlighten Theo on many of the less public aspects of Pembrokeshire politics, information Theo would have preferred not to have heard. He himself was not partisan; he did not like confrontation, and was not competitive in that way. However, he had learned enough about local politics to know the heads of the county's leading families ran for the office of Member of Parliament, not because they cared about what happened in Parliament -- unless it was likely to adversely affect their own personal rights or powers -- but because the winner would be the most powerful man in the county, giving him the right to appoint his own followers into all the other influential posts. It was, in effect, all about local power, not about national policies, and was what Theo like to call, "a closed shop."

They reached the beach, and Lord Kensington looked at Theo. "Are you up to a race?"

Theo gathered up the reins. "That I am." And the two

horses flew down the dark sand, neck and neck. As it happened, Hercules was the faster horse, but Theo held him back, allowing his lordship to win by a head.

"Capital, capital!" Lord Kensington seemed to be almost as out of breath as his horse.

They walked back along the beach, allowing their mounts to cool down, and on the way home Lord Kensington, who had recently returned from London, regaled Theo with reports on the latest concerts, plays and other entertainments being offered this season in Town, as they called London. Theo listened enviously, and wishing to know as much as possible, asked many questions his lordship was only too willing to answer.

"How often do you come to London for the season?" he asked Theo.

"I'm afraid we've not had the opportunity since I arrived in Haverfordwest. My wife is of an age where she's still bearing children, and it seems our timing is such that she's never in a fit state to make the journey."

"That's indeed a pity. I couldn't survive without the intellectual stimulus of the Town to boost my spirits on a regular basis. The country is wonderful, and Pembrokeshire is where we as a family belong, but while Haverfordwest is a most pleasant venue, where those of us of similar tastes and background can meet up and entertain one another, it offers us little beyond our own camaraderie, don't you agree Potter?"

Theo agreed more than he was willing to admit to, but Lord Kensington had said it all for him anyway.

"Well, expecting an addition to the family or not, you'll be unable to wander too far afield next year because you'll have your sheriff's duties. However..." Lord Kensington paused. "Lady Kensington and I should take it as a great honour if you'd come and spend some part of a season with us in London some time. I'll leave the invitation open, and whenever the opportunity presents itself, send word, and we'll be happy to welcome you as our guests."

Theo was overwhelmed. "Your Lordship! I can't think of an invitation Mrs. Potter and I would have more pleasure in accepting. You may be assured you'll be hearing from us in the very near future."

They arrived back at the livery stable where both men kept their horses, and after a few polite exchanges, went to their respective residences, and when Theo finally found himself alone with Elizabeth, and in a position to discuss his day, he did not know where to start, and said so.

"Why not start at the beginning? You obviously were ready to tell me something when you came in this morning, so why not start with that?"

Theo explained how he had been pricked for sheriff, and how he was not looking forward at all to spending a whole year carrying out this duty. "I know some feel proud to be sheriff, and get quite puffed up with all the power and prestige it gives them, but I can't see myself in the role at all. I'm not the sort of man to enjoy meting out punishments to sinners in our community."

Theo was pacing around the room in agitation. He turned to face Elizabeth. "Can you see me executing a punishment such as I had the misfortune to witness just the other day? This poor woman was being marched down the street, covered in blood from the public flogging she was receiving! I couldn't do it, Bess." He shook his head. "I couldn't do it, nor could I order someone to do it." He sat down and put his head in his hands. "No more could I see to it that a man is hanged from the gibbet. I can't stand by the side of the road and watch such exhibitions, let alone order them to be carried out!"

"Punishment is given to those who have broken the law, Theo. Would you have them patted on the head and told, 'You've been naughty; don't do it again please'? Public

270

humiliation is a strong deterrent."

"Humiliation is one thing: physical beating until the blood flows is something else."

"I do think such sentences are quite rare though, and you may find you have no such obligations to carry out under your watch."

"Another obligation will be to make sure all those who have been fined, pay their fines to me. If they don't, then I myself will have to pay what they don't pay... Some of these people are so poor, Bess. Can I be the one to throw them in gaol if I can't exact the fine from them?"

"One thing is sure, my dear: you can't refuse this obligation. You yourself would be breaking your oath as a burgess, and I do remember hearing of one man who refused the post, and he was fined forty shillings -- money that was used to whitewash the shingles on St. Mary's church steeple," she added.

Theo remained silent for a minute. "Then there's the expense too. What about the Whit Monday parade? I have to provide a magnificent breakfast for all the local dignitaries out of my own pocket -- and that has to be for at least fifty people!"

"Oh Theo! Please try to think of the positive side. You know you'll enjoy acting as host, and it's not as though you can't afford it. Another complaint I've heard from you is that the gaoler makes a tidy living out of his prisoners by unfairly overcharging them for the smallest favour or item. As sheriff you can choose your own gaoler, someone you trust to act fairly towards his charges. You've said you're a great admirer of Mr. John Howard, the prison reformer; maybe you could try, as he is trying, to effect some changes in the way our prison is run and the prisoners are treated."

"Maybe...There's one good aspect at least: there are no elections next year, so I shan't be put in the position of having

271

contestants try to bribe or intimidate me into influencing the outcome. The tricks they'll resort to! I wonder that seemingly law-abiding citizens can be so devious and duplicitous..." He shook his head. "Well, it's good too that Mr. Sutton is now better because from what I've heard from others who have been sheriff, your time isn't your own, and you can be called upon at any time of the day or night. And maybe Stephen George will help with the breakfast at the Blue Boar, because we can't expect poor cook to do it, and The Blue Boar has an excellent chef..."

Theo paced about the room, muttering to himself. Finally he said, "Oh Bess! I don't look forward to next year at all! And I know Lord Kensington thinks he's doing me a favour, as well as himself of course, by helping to push me into the small enclave of Haverfordwest's political arena, but I don't want any of it. I'm not a political man; power and influence are not what I myself look for in life... If I have any political instinct at all, it's to try to remedy injustices, not perpetuate them."

"So it's Lord Kensington we have to thank for this?"

"Oh yes! I should tell you..." And Theo recounted the story of his hours spent with his Lordship.

Elizabeth smiled. "I'm glad at least you let him win the race."

"Yes, but what about his invitation to stay with him and Lady Kensington in London? Think what we could do! Concerts we could attend! Plays we could see! It'll be wonderful, won't it?" His spirits rose as he imagined the two of them there together, and when Elizabeth made no response, he allowed his thoughts to run on. His old mentor from Smock Alley, Thomas Sheridan, had died two years ago, but he knew his son, Richard, who was manager of the Drury Lane Theatre. How great it would be to see him again! Perhaps he could even take on some acting roles while there! His excitement grew as he imagined the possibilities. And his good friend, John

O'Keeffe, was having his comedies and farces produced successfully all the time now at the Haymarket Theatre. He would give anything to see Jack again. Maybe also, they, like so many of the gentry in Pembrokeshire, could even buy a second home of their own in the Town, somewhere to which they could escape in the season to be intellectually stimulated and entertained in a way that Haverfordwest most assuredly was unable to do for them.

"Let's not get too thrilled at the prospect until we know we're able to accept their offer." Elizabeth brought him out of his reverie. "Right now and for the foreseeable future I can't see how we can possibly just leave the children and take off for London for a couple of months..."

Theo's spirits sank again. He should know by now the response to any suggestion they leave Haverfordwest for even the shortest time, would always be "no". It was not as though there were no close relatives at Dunstable Hall who would be more than delighted to have the children around for a while, but they had been through this so many times before. Yet Lord Kensington's descriptions of all the delights and allures of the big city had reawakened his yearning, and he felt sufficiently angry at this latest refusal to know that, should he stay in the room any longer, he would lose his temper and say things he would later regret. Even so, he stood there in silence for a few moments before raising his arms in frustrated resignation, then turning swiftly and striding out.

CHAPTER 29

Theo's term of office as sheriff began quietly. It was a cold winter with plenty of ice and snow, and would-be troublemakers were deterred from carrying out any crimes on Haverfordwest's already dangerous, steep and uneven streets that might involve trying to execute a quick disappearance from the scene.

Drunken behaviour was as usual, with one large and belligerent man, Thomas Haggerty, who frequented the many Shut Street taverns, finding the need to get into as many fights as possible. For such disturbances, however, Theo could usually rely on his two constables, except on one darker-than-usual night, when they had to call upon his help as Haggerty, rendered even stronger by the over-consumption of the pubs' home-brewed ales, was more than the two constables could handle alone.

Theo could hear the commotion almost as soon as he left his house on Tower Hill, but it took him several more minutes to arrive at the scene than it would normally have done, on account of the ice-covered cobblestones, which could turn an ankle in a second. There being only the odd candle in the windows of one or two houses to guide him, the going was even more treacherous, and he wished he had asked James to accompany him with a lantern. One thing he could do, however, was smell the putrid dung heaps outside the hovels at the top of Shut Street, from whence the noise came.

On finally reaching the gathered crowd, he made his way to the centre of activity, where one of his constables was nursing his jaw, while the other was engaged in a dangerous boxing match, which the crowd was only too happy to witness -- cheering the drunk more than the constable.

Theo, at least as tall as Haggerty, but much younger and fitter, pulled the man away from his constable, at which Haggerty turned his attention to Theo. Theo was not a fighting man, but when the drunk hit him in the chest, his famous temper flared, and he hit the man on his chin with such force he knocked him out. It was all over in a second.

His first thought was that he must have broken his hand -- it hurt so much -- but as he rubbed it with his other hand and wiggled his fingers, was relieved to discover that all appeared to be intact. He then noticed that the crowd was cheering him, so, much to their appreciation and amusement, he gave them an exaggerated and humorous bow, and as he walked back home, leaving the constables to transport Haggerty to the gaol in a hand-cart procured from somewhere, he would have been gratified to learn of the level of awe and respect with which the new sheriff was now, and would continue to be viewed.

There was one major event in this year to which Theo *was* looking forward, and that was the annual Shrove Tuesday football game. This used to be celebrated with cock-fighting and bull-baiting events, but had more recently been replaced by this football game, it being considered a less violent and bloody way of celebrating. This year it was Theo who, as sheriff, would hold the new football in his hands and kick it into the air, a kick that would start the free-for-all. It started at noon, and then it would be kicked all over town until night fell, and it was too dark to see. Theo, still in his thirties, could not wait to take part in the mêlée. He had heard that on one occasion the ball had been kicked so high it had flown all the way down Market Street, landed on St. Mary's steeple, then bounced off, ending up in Dark Street.

By February the snow and ice had gone, and on Shrove Tuesday the weather was perfect for such sport, and as he had walked through the town that morning, Theo had seen the shop owners preparing for the fray by barricading their windows with ladders or whatever else they could find to protect them from both the football and from those who might fall against them. He had wondered about letting his older sons take part, and had decided that, although Joseph was still too young at seven to be allowed to enter the game, John, at ten, should be allowed to enjoy the fun.

Elizabeth, however, did not approve at all. "He came to me, so excited about taking part because John George is going," she told Theo. "I can't believe Stephen George would let a ten-year-old loose in that mob! He could get killed! No! We can't let our John take part, Theo!"

"Have you told him already he can't go?"

"No, I haven't. I thought it better it came from you."

"Well, I'm glad you didn't say 'no', because then I'd have had to stand by your decision, but John is a big strong boy, well able to take care of himself, and we have to let our boys grow up to be boys. It's not healthy for them to be missing out on things that all the other boys do, just because we're afraid they might get hurt. I'm sorry, Bess, but I must go against your wishes on this occasion. He can go, and I'll keep an eye on him."

Nothing Elizabeth could say would make him change his mind, and so, at noon on Tuesday, February 2nd, 1790, John joined his father in St. Thomas's Square, where the kickoff was to take place, leaving Elizabeth in a great state of motherly apprehension, fearing the dreadful violence sure to befall her eldest son. During the whole afternoon she could not settle to anything, and the hours passed so slowly that by the time Theo arrived home, she had worked herself up into a state of panic. "Where's John?" was her first question. She looked behind him to see if John was there, but he was nowhere in sight. "Theo! Where's John?"

"He's not home?"

"Of course he's not home. He should be with you! Where is he?"

Because of Elizabeth's state of hysterics, Theo had great trouble explaining to her why he had thought John would be at home. He told her it had been getting dark, and the game coming to an end, when one of the Council members had approached him, wanting to discuss something he considered urgent. He had been obliged to listen, so told John to go home. The conversation had lasted more than twenty minutes, by which time it was dark, and the crowds had dispersed, leaving the streets almost empty. He had then come straight home, expecting to find John already returned.

Theo's explanation was no consolation to Elizabeth, and now not to himself either, so he told the housekeeper to keep his wife company, then left the house again in search of his son. The first place he went was to the Blue Boar Inn, where he found Stephen George and his wife in a similar state of anxiety, because their son was not home either. The only option was to gather some burgesses together, and go out to search for them.

Within a half hour they had gathered about thirty men, who divided up into groups, each group setting off in a different direction. Stephen George knew his son liked to go down to the river to see the ships, so his group, including Theo, went down to the quay area. Here they asked everyone they saw if they had seen two ten-year-old boys together. All they received in response were shakes of the head. They searched the river banks, and as the tide was in, but well on the ebb, making it treacherous, they went quite a way downriver, just in case the boys had fallen in and had been washed away.

By eight o'clock, they were hoarse with shouting, but had still not found them. However, as the boys would have heard the curfew bell of St. Mary's church ringing no matter where they were in town, the worried fathers hoped they would have heeded it and gone home. In full expectation of this being the case, they returned to their houses, but this yielded nothing; the boys were still missing.

Normally, the constant barking, baying and howling of foxhounds everywhere did not bother Theo, but tonight, as he searched the town for John, and his anxiety for his son's safety heightened, the noise just added to his distress. When he had first arrived in Haverfordwest, he had not even been able to sleep because of the noise of foxhounds. The problem was that, in Pembrokeshire, it was the custom of the gentry to expect their tenants -- such as innkeepers and other tradesmen in town -- to look after and feed their hounds for them. These people were afraid to refuse for fear of losing their tenancy -- take the hounds, or you're out, was the attitude of their landlords -- and the gentry's arrogance annoyed Theo more than usual tonight, surrounded as he was by the constant baying.

Not finding their sons at home, the men set off again, and were still searching at eleven o'clock, when James caught up with Theo, and let him know the boys had been found, and were now safe. Both fathers stormed home, ready to bring down their full wrath on their wayward sons. Theo arrived to find mother and son weeping in each other's arms.

Elizabeth put a hand up to try to stem her husband's anger before it erupted, but Theo, apart from having suffered his own anxiety, was also exhausted after running all over town for the last eleven hours, first after a football, then after his son. He was ready to drop, and the combination of this and his immense relief at seeing his son unharmed, was too much. He seized John by the collar and swung him round. "Where have you been?" he stormed -- Elizabeth's attempts at calming the situation going unnoticed.

Before giving John a chance to answer, he shouted at him again, "Where have you been? Look at your mother! How do you think she's been feeling all these hours? How do you think I feel? I told you to go home! Why didn't you do as you were told?" Theo ran out of breath, let go his son's collar, and sank down into the nearest chair. He put his face in his hands. "All right. What happened? I want to know before I decide how to punish you."

"I... I didn't hear you tell me to go home, and..."

"Didn't hear me! How could you not have heard me?"

"It was all the noise of everyone milling around with the football and everything..."

"Well, if you didn't hear me, you shouldn't have gone off without me. Didn't you think?"

"You were talking for so long, and I didn't like to interrupt you... You both looked so serious, and I didn't know the other man."

"So you didn't want to interrupt... Then what happened?"

"I met up with John George and some other boys, and we decided to go up to Portfield Common and pretend we were the militia."

Elizabeth, who had listened in silence to this exchange, put her hand to her mouth. "Portfield Common! At night! Oh John! It's dangerous there! You could have disappeared, and we'd never have found you!"

"There were six of us, so we thought it would be all right."

"That still doesn't answer the question as to why you didn't come home by eight o'clock," said Theo. "You know all

279

boys must be home by that time, and you *must* have heard St. Mary's curfew bell."

John nodded, and started to cry again. "We didn't know how late it was. Then when we heard the bell, we knew it was too late to go home."

"What do you mean?" said Theo. "'It was too late to go home'. How could it be too late?"

John was sobbing. "We were afraid we'd be caught and transported to New South Wales."

Both Theo and Elizabeth looked at their son in amazement. "Transported to New South Wales!" they both cried in unison. "Whatever made you think you'd be transported anywhere, let alone to New South Wales?" Theo added.

"John Evans said if we didn't get home by eight o'clock, and we were caught, we'd be transported to New South Wales, and we were so frightened we hid in a culvert, and were going to wait till morning."

Theo rolled his eyes. "That's ridiculous. You might get a lashing from the old whip-dog, but you'd have to do something really bad to be transported."

He stood up, towering over his young son, and looked at his wife. "Hmm. What do you think? Perhaps he's had punishment enough?" He looked down at John, standing there with his wavy black hair and fair skin covered with mud and scratches from gorse bushes, his brown eyes full of tears. To Theo, it was like looking at himself at that age. He put his hand on John's shoulder, but Elizabeth had not finished with her catalogue of what might have been. "You could have frozen to death on the common all night... and you know the common is a dangerous place to be... and you could have been attacked by some of those cattle wandering around... There are dangerous people who wander over the common too... and, and... what about all the drunks leaving The Whale?"

Theo let his wife vent all her pent-up anxiety, while young Joseph, who had been watching the proceedings from a safe distance, gave his brother a holier-than-thou smirk from behind his parents' backs.

John lunged at him. "You wait till I get hold of you," he shouted at his brother.

Theo put up his hand. "That's it! Off to bed with both of you! It's well past midnight anyway, and if I hear another sound out of either of you, you'll both be in trouble, and I mean it."

That was something both boys knew, and without another word, they left the room, shutting the door behind them.

"*Don't* say a word," said Theo to Elizabeth.

CHAPTER 30

It was nearing the end of his term as sheriff, and Theo was relieved that, although it had been an exhausting year in that so much of his time had been expended in carrying out his duties, it had been more rewarding and less onerous than he had envisaged. He had enjoyed playing football all around the town, even though it had ended in such an alarming way, and he had enjoyed Whit Monday, during which nothing untoward had happened, unless he could count the large hole it had left in his finances.

Whit Monday was Haverfordwest's big parade day, when all the local dignitaries dressed up in their finery, and did the town the honour of -- or were supposed to do the town the honour of -- surveying its boundaries to ensure all was as it should be. Its origins were lost in history, and over the years it had become instead a day on which the town dignitaries could expect to be treated to a sumptuous and magnificent breakfast, provided at the expense of the reigning sheriff, after which, those still left standing would ride around the town, not only themselves dressed in their finery, but their horses also. Any other gentlemen or even townsfolk who wanted to take part in the parade were also welcome, all watched by an appreciative audience that lined the streets and provided applause at their passing by.

Elizabeth had wondered at their ability to entertain the Mayor, twenty-five councillors, a number of aldermen, mace bearers and other council employees in their dining room, but was soon relieved of this responsibility by Theo who, as he had suggested earlier, engaged the Blue Boar to take care of everything, at his expense, of course. Elizabeth, who did enjoy entertaining, was nevertheless delighted at the change in venue, as their own dining room, spacious as it was, was certainly not adequate for such an event.

'Breakfast' it may have been called, but the meal matched any fine dinner one might expect to eat, and Stephen George did everything demanded of him by way of provisions. So excellent was the repast, indeed, that by the time the parade began its way through the town, it was almost two o'clock in the afternoon, and there was a significant risk that some of the participants might have difficulty in staying on their horses.

Lord Kensington, being Haverfordwest's representative in Parliament, led the parade. He was followed by Mr. Robert Bateman Prust, the Mayor and member of a well-known Haverfordwest family. Third in line was Theo, dressed in his sheriff's regalia and, as in the case of all those in the parade, his horse, Hercules, was caparisoned like a medieval charger. To Theo's delight, Hercules had entered into the spirit of the parade as happy as any warhorse. Theo held the reins in his right hand, and with his left saluted the cheering crowd, while Hercules tucked in his chin and pranced sideways all the length of the parade, lifting his feet high off the ground, his fine body as well collected as any. As a proud Elizabeth remarked later, they were the handsomest pair in the parade.

Then there had been the assizes, during which balls had been held at the Town Hall three nights in succession, Lord Kensington being responsible for the first, Lord Milford for the second, and the mayor for the third, and Theo, as sheriff, had felt obliged to attend all three. Happy as they normally were to dance and socialize until the early hours of the morning, three nights in a row had proven tiring for even them, especially as it was summer, and hot in the ballroom.

Other than the enjoyment of the various celebrations held during the assizes, there was, for Theo, the much less pleasurable task of having to stand on the left-hand side of the judge throughout the actual court procedures, while the County Sheriff stood on his right, and most detested of all, the necessity for presiding over the Hundred Courts, held twice during his year of office, and covered petty crime and misdemeanours. As all discovered who were near him for at least a week before and a week after these courts, he was not good company.

Despite the negative aspects of his term of office, Theo had been able to achieve at least one improvement in the running of the town. The year after he became a burgess, he had taken the opportunity to meet Mr. John Howard, the philanthropist and prison reformer who visited Haverfordwest while on a tour, the main purpose of which had been to inspect prisons across the country. On a visit to Haverfordwest six years earlier, he had inspected the new prison that had been built within the walls of the castle just three years before his visit, and at that time had found it clean and quiet. However, on this occasion he told Theo he had found a great change, finding it filthy.

As a result of his conversation with Mr. Howard, Theo determined that one thing he would do as sheriff would be to inspect the prison regularly for cleanliness, and make sure the inmates were not suffering unwarranted hardships. He appointed as gaoler a man he knew to be of good character and honest, and posted in the gaol the proper notices Mr. Howard had told him should be there, but were not. The one notice was that of the Act concerning the preservation of the health of the prisoners. The other consisted of the three clauses from the act concerning the prohibition of liquor in the gaol.

Thus, by the end of his own term of office as sheriff, one thing he would have achieved was the ability to commit to the stewardship of his friend Stephen George, landlord of The Blue Boar Inn, and the next sheriff, a prison as fit for human habitation as possible, and in which prisoners were being treated fairly. How long things would remain this way he could not tell; it all depended on the attitude of the sheriff in charge, and the man he selected to run the prison.

So it was that Theo thought he would be able to say that, while he was sheriff, nothing of undue moment had taken place, nor had he been put in a position in which he felt out of his depth.

It was all the more surprising, therefore, when, just a few days before he was to relinquish his post, he was woken in the middle of the night by someone banging on the front door. He rushed downstairs, getting there even before James who, getting on in years, was not as nimble as he used to be.

The man at the door was a messenger from the farmer who owned land overlooking Nolton Harbour. The farmer, one of the county sheriff's constables, after hearing his sheep bleating just after midnight, decided to check on them to make sure they were all right, that none had fallen over the cliff edge, or were being harassed by stray dogs. On reaching the edge of the cliff, however, he had seen the silhouette of a ship moored offshore. Then, as he looked down into the harbour, he had noticed lantern lights and a number of smugglers transporting sacks and crates up the narrow cove to above the high water mark.

The county sheriff was too far away to notify, and the Lord Lieutenant, Lord Milford, was known to be indisposed, suffering from a protracted flare-up of gout, so the next highest law enforcement officer in the area was Theo who, although so near the end of his term in office, was still sheriff of Haverfordwest.

Theo sent the boy to wake up Stephen George at the Blue Boar, as well as John Jones, who had been sheriff the previous year. Over the next hour they assembled a group of about twenty-five burgesses and a few servants, including James, and they all met at the edge of town.

By the time they reached the farm at Nolton, the farmer had rounded up three more constables, including the bailiff at Haroldston Hall, and after a brief conference, they decided that all the horses should remain at the farm, and they would proceed on foot to a place where they could survey the activity on the beach, while remaining hidden by the clumps of gorse growing above the sides of the valley. This they did, keeping their bodies low to the ground lest their shapes be visible against the night sky, which by this time was already beginning to lighten behind them.

There were about a dozen smugglers, nine of whom seemed to be doing all the work, while three others, armed with blunderbusses, acted as lookouts.

Theo and his men lay there on their stomachs, watching them make repeated trips back to the mother ship, then rowing their cargo to shore, and Theo knew it was up to him to decide how to proceed.

He signalled his men to retreat further away from the valley, where they were just about to discuss their strategy, when Stephen George noticed a large ship appear round the headland several hundred yards out to sea. Although Theo did not know it at the time, it was Mr. Daniels, the excise man, with his armed cutter, Esmeralda -- similar to the ship Theo had seen up close on his trip from Ireland to Haverfordwest twelve years before. The smugglers had seen it also, and smugglers and sheriff's men alike watched as the gunship turned its broadside towards the shore, and fired off a warning salvo. It also let down two large rowboats, which were speeding towards the shore, firing at the smugglers as they advanced.

Straight ahead of the smugglers was the impenetrable marsh surrounding the stream delta, so they began to scramble up the steep cliff side, and Theo and his men heard the screams of one of them as he tumbled back down towards the beach.

With the rest of the smugglers approaching the place where he and his men were hiding, Theo needed to act quickly, so waited until they were within about fifty yards, then shouted, "You're well outnumbered, surrender now or face our guns." The untimely question flashed through his mind as to where these stilted words had come from, until he remembered they were lines he had once spoken in a play. Regardless of the source, they had, in part, the desired effect, as all nine of the unarmed men gave themselves up and stood still with their hands in a position of surrender, unable to tell where the voice had come from. This was not the case, however, with the three armed men, who fell flat on their stomachs, and began firing at will into the bushes. As far as they knew, the opposition might consist only of the one man who had shouted. It was a fatal mistake: not only had they miscalculated the number of armed men they were facing, but at that moment the rising sun appeared from behind a bank of cloud, and sent its rays directly into their faces, blinding them, and making them perfect targets. Within seconds, all three were dead, shot where they lay on the ground.

Theo sent one of the constables to gather up the guns lying beside the bodies, and by the time they had roped together all nine remaining smugglers, Mr. Daniels himself had climbed up the cliff to join them. Being now the most senior man in charge, he instructed Theo to take all the prisoners back to Haverfordwest, but to leave the dead, as his own men would take care of them. He congratulated Theo and his men, and explained how he came to be in the vicinity at such an opportune moment.

It seemed that, on the preceding afternoon, he had seen the smugglers' ship, but it had been carrying a Royal Navy pennant in an attempt to disguise itself. "I've been in the business too long to be fooled," he told Theo. "But rather than tackle them out at sea, and risk losing both ship and cargo, I let them think we hadn't recognized them, and kept on the same heading, towards Cardigan. Once round the headland we hove to, and waited. I had a good idea as to where they were planning to unload, so we gave them plenty of time to do this, and it seems we arrived at the right moment." He looked around. "Well, I suggest you start on your trip back to town. I'll take charge of everything here now. You can leave it all to me."

The horses were brought from the farm, and as Theo and his men mounted and turned away, leading the prisoners in a long file, Mr. Daniels called after them. "Good day to you, and thank you for all your help."

Theo acknowledged the thanks with a wave, and they set off on their way back to Haverfordwest, Theo bringing up the rear, so as to make sure no one would try to escape. Beside him, as usual, was James. They had scarcely gone a hundred yards when a shot sounded behind them. Theo swung Hercules around, and saw smoke coming from a gun in the hand of one of the supposedly dead gunmen. He looked to see if Mr. Daniels was still standing, but he was running to where the gunman lay, and Theo looked around to make sure everyone else was safe. At the same moment James's horse flew past him, riderless, and then he saw James lying face down on the soft turf. He was not moving. Theo leaped off Hercules, and ran to his servant's side, where, turning him over with great care, he shouted his name. James's eyes were open, but they had no depth to them, and stared through him, no more animate than flat disks of coloured glass. Theo knelt on the ground looking at his beloved servant, then jumped as James's chest gave a sudden, heaving sigh as his last breath left his body. He was gone. James, who had watched over him for over thirty years, was dead.

The other men came back to see, but Theo waved them away, indicating they should return home without him. He then picked James up, holding him like a baby. While he stood there, Mr. Daniels came up, unaware of the emotional state of the sheriff, who stood gazing down at the dead man in his arms. He peered at James. "You know this man?"

Theo nodded, but did not look up.

"A bad thing... a bad thing to lose a man," he commiserated. "I suppose we're fortunate there were no more killed. All in all, we were lucky I have to say..." He peered again at James, and shook his head. "It's too bad though." He pushed a flintlock pistol under Theo's nose. "This is what did it... Had it hidden in his belt, and was lying on it, so your constable wouldn't have seen it. Anyway, we all thought he was done for, didn't we?... He is now," he added. "I made sure of that." He looked at James again. "Do you know who he was?"

Again Theo nodded.

"Right. So you'll be able to return him to his family then... A nasty duty that, having to tell the family." He turned to leave. "Well, I must be off. Other than losing one man, I must say the whole operation was a success, and we have the ship and its cargo as well." He walked away. "A great success," Theo heard him repeat as he disappeared back down the hill.

Theo continued to stand, holding James in his arms. The blaze of sunshine that had appeared too early in the day for it to last, had disappeared, leaving instead a pewter sky from which a fine drizzle began to fall. Soon it had soaked him, and its accumulated wetness dripped from his bent head down onto James's upturned face. What was it that Elizabeth had said to him that time at Stackpole Court? "Some things I do expect, but while the things I expect to happen, don't, the things I least expect -- things I've not thought of even -- do."

Theo pulled out his kerchief and wiped away the water, and closed his friend's eyes. Mr. Daniels and his crew had long since departed, and Theo stood alone in a silence broken only by the sound of dripping rain. Unable to control his emotion, he threw back his head, and made a sound unlike any he had ever made before; it was a primeval howl of despair.

It was fortunate for all that Theo was not called upon again before the end of his term, as he was so thoroughly shocked by James's death, he thought of little else, and felt incapable of achieving anything if asked. Time and again he went over in his mind the lifelong relationship they had had: first when he was just a child and James a young man, then as he grew up, and all through his adult years James was always there. The status of servant he may have had, but there was far more to it than that. Though Mr. Daniels could not have known it, he, Theo, *was* James's family. James had known him better than anyone else in his life, and that included Elizabeth, who had not witnessed his transformation from child into man the way James had, or been there to help him through the worst moments of his existence. He had been able talk to James in a way he could talk to no other man; he had been trusted friend and confidant -- like a father to him. But now he was gone, suddenly, needlessly, and Theo felt utterly bereft. No loss in his whole life had ever touched him like this.

CHAPTER 31

As time went on Theo's family grew, and by 1796 Elizabeth had borne him ten children. When little Edward had died nine years before, she had been inconsolable for many months, and it had been another two years before she was willing to try again. Another four healthy children had then arrived, and taken their place in the family.

Then, once again, a baby boy had been born, and they had named him after Elizabeth's uncle, Thomas Morris. Three years after that she gave birth to another boy, whom they named in honour of Sir John Campbell's first son, Frederick.

While he loved his children as a father, and wanted only the best for them, Theo's attitude towards them was more detached. He had not seen them and been with them in the way Elizabeth had, and although he liked to play with them for short periods, his own enjoyment of such entertainment wore off long before the children were ready to find something else to do, leaving him bored and with his mind wandering into more pleasurable pursuits. If only he could have had intelligent conversations with them, and been able to teach them about ideas in which he was interested, that would have made all the difference, but how did one converse with a baby who just gurgled, or a three-year-old, whose vocabulary and attention span were so limited?

Jumping them up and down on his knee, or giving them piggy-back rides while crawling on the floor, while of endless amusement to the children, had, for their father, lost all its appeal after the first few minutes, and it was ever a wonder to him how Elizabeth could tolerate, let alone revel in hours of being surrounded by squealing, laughing, rowdy, and often quarrelsome children -- a situation from which he would find any excuse to extricate himself as soon as possible.

By now though, his two older sons had assumed definite personalities, and Theo had, for several years, watched the development of their characters with interest. What amazed him was the difference in the two of them: it seemed that it would be impossible for two children, brought up in exactly the same house and in the same way, to be so unlike each other -- yet different they were, not only in looks, but in temperament.

John, now nearly sixteen, was the one Theo had expected to be most like him. After all, he looked like his father, so like him, that people would remark on it, saying, "Well! There's no mistaking whose son *you* are!" But John was not like his father in any other way, nor was he like his mother either, and it puzzled them both as to whom he took after.

That his son was intelligent, there was no doubt, because once he had learnt something, he remembered it, so Theo was not sure if his son was indolent, slow to understand when a point was being made, or just off in his own world of dreams when being talked to. Theo had told his wife he was sure it was the latter, because he had been telling John something one day and, convinced the boy was not paying attention, said in the middle of a sentence, "... and then his leg fell off, and he had to stop walking," words that had elicited no surprise at all, proving his son was not listening to what his father was saying.

John's inattention and seeming lack of interest in anything other than wandering around town with his best friend, John George, was more than irritating to Theo; he found it exasperating that someone, gifted with intelligence, should show so little enthusiasm for learning, that he was unwilling to ever exert himself more than was necessary. Theo had tried hard to encourage his son any time he showed even the slightest sign of enthusiasm for something, but these moments were at best transitory, leaving his father frustrated and annoyed.

There was also some indication that John resented it that his father, while well able to afford to buy an estate of his own, had not done so. If he had, then John, as the eldest son, would have expected to inherit it on the death of his father, leaving him at liberty to live the life of a gentleman, a life to which he, again unlike his father, gave every sign of being well-suited.

It was apparent too that, although John's reign as only child had lasted no more than three years -- he discounted his sister Elizabeth as she was, as he said, only a girl -- he was jealous of his brother Joseph, and found every opportunity to tease him and make his life miserable, thus incurring even more irritation from his father.

John's best friend since childhood was still John George, but John, the same age as John Potter, had already made up his mind that he wanted to join the Royal Marines as soon as he was old enough, and could not wait until he could ask the Reverend Cleaveland to help him get a commission -- something Mr. Cleaveland had already offered to do for him by writing a letter of reference to the appropriate authorities. John George was strongly encouraging his friend to do likewise, but although he expressed an interest, and declared that he thought it might be something he would like to do, John Potter had so far not had sufficient enthusiasm to ask Mr. Cleaveland's help, even though the latter had told Theo it was something he would be only too delighted to do for his son.

It was in young Joseph that Theo saw himself, not so

much in looks, for Joseph, while tall like his father, looked more like his mother. To Theo's delight, even as young as six years old, Joseph had shown a brightness, a good-natured humour, and best of all in Theo's estimation, a love of acting! He was never happier than when he could dress up, and try to organize his less-than-enthusiastic siblings into presenting little dramas for his parents, dramas that would be staged behind the huge curtains of the library, and in which Joseph would spend most of his time telling his reluctant cast what they should say and do next. They were dramas his parents found to be entertaining and amusing, whether or not their son intended them to be comedies or not -- the tragedies often being the more amusing -- although they were careful not show such a reaction to their solemn-faced little boy on these occasions.

As Joseph grew, Theo began to take him to the best of the various theatrical entertainments constantly arriving in town, and even thought that when Joseph was ready, he would produce a few performances himself, something he had not done since *The Taming of the Shrew*. This would give Joseph the best opportunity to develop his talent. In the meantime he devoted whatever time Joseph wanted to training him and passing on to him all his theatrical knowledge.

Although Theo had given up going to most of the theatrical performances that came to Haverfordwest, he nevertheless had continued to go to those that were managed by his friend, Henry Masterman, who came to perform in Haverfordwest every winter, and on occasion would have in his troupe actors who had been with The Smock Alley Theatre -- occasions on which Theo entertained them at his home, and used the opportunity to reminisce about his old theatre, now long-since closed.

He had the additional enjoyment now of taking Joseph to performances with him, performances which, for lack of a proper theatre in Haverfordwest, were still usually held in the largest room of inns like The Blue Boar, or sometimes in the Town Hall.

It was with Mr. Masterman's troupe that the twenty-two-year-old actor and composer, Thomas Dibdin, came to Haverfordwest when Joseph was just ten years old, and Theo remembered it was exactly twenty-five years before that, that he himself had seen the premier of *The Padlock*, at Drury Lane, for which Thomas Dibdin's father, Charles Dibdin, had composed the music and had played the part of Mungo, the black servant.

It was now, in Theo's lending library in Haverfordwest, that the young Thomas Dibdin spent an afternoon composing a song, which he later that evening sang for his Haverfordwest audience at a special benefit performance. It was while Thomas was still in the lending library that Theo introduced Joseph to him, and Mr. Dibdin said, "Would you like me to read my new verses to you, Joseph?"

Joseph nodded. "Yes please, Mr. Dibdin." It was a song Joseph would always remember:

"Oh, Haverfordwest is a mighty fine place,
Where Welsh hospitality shines in each face;
Only walk thro' the streets you'll find it's true,
For each countenance seems to say 'How do you do?'

If the truth of my ditty casts any doubt,
Only step to the door and then take a peep out,
You'll see the church steeple with head all askew,
As if it was nodding a 'How do you do?'

If you're sick, and in medicine seek for a cure,
See the doctor approaches with visage demure,
Perhaps did he not call 'twould be better for you,
But he pockets his fee with a 'How do you do?'

And the lawyer so wise, how he opens his brief,
And prattles and chatters beyond all belief;
The oyster he swallows, the shell he gives you,
And then, Mr. Client, pray 'How do you do?'

The actor, for whom this is benefit night,
Just peeps thro' the curtain to see 'tis all right;
If he finds a good house, he's so pleased with the view,
That he welcomes you all with a 'How do you do?'"

After reading his verses out loud to Joseph, Mr. Dibdin asked him what he thought of them, and after some hesitation, Joseph replied, "What does the church steeple with its head all askew mean?"

"Haven't you noticed, young man, that the steeple of St. Mary's church leans to one side?"

"No." Joseph shook his head. "But why does it lean to one side?"

Mr. Dibdin sat forward in his chair. "Do you know something, Joseph? I don't know why it leans to one side." He looked at Theo standing nearby. "Do you know why it leans, Mr. Potter?"

"Yes, it just so happens I do. It was struck by lightning a number of years ago, and it's been that way ever since."

Mr. Dibdin stood up. "There you are, young man. Now you know."

And Joseph had run out of the library to take a good look at the leaning steeple of St. Mary's church.

CHAPTER 32

Although Theo enjoyed immensely, and took part in the lively discussions that took place at his reading room, unlike a number of the men present, he had not been to Oxford, or to any university, and except where light-hearted banter and the exchange of witticisms were concerned, had tended at first to be diffident about expressing his opinion about more serious subjects, for fear of revealing his ignorance.

He had been given the best possible education that private tutors could give, but finding himself in a position in which he had no idea what the others were talking about, was a situation abhorrent to him. It was with his innate desire to learn as an additional driving force, therefore, he had from the start used their discussions as a starting point for learning whatever he could about a topic, so that he too would be able to offer his own observations and thoughts from the standpoint of knowledge. Thus it was that, like many self-taught people, he had been so anxious to be as thorough as possible in teaching himself, he often succeeded in learning more about a subject than those who had been taught formally. In doing so, the more knowledge he acquired, the more he realized how little he knew, teaching him also to recognize when it was wise to remain silent. It irked him as well, that so many men in a position to make life-changing decisions for others, were ignorant, and the more ignorant they were, the more pompous, self-satisfied, declamatory and officious they tended to be. In Theo's opinion such people could do a great disservice to those they professed to serve, because they did not know they were ignorant, or what they were ignorant of -- and making decisions from such a position could have disastrous effects.

Such was his opinion of some of those who frequented his reading room, but although the discussions could sometimes become heated, there was one subject Theo made a point of barring, and that was religion. Religious faith, forming as it did for almost everyone the cornerstone of their lives, rarely if ever allowed room for doubt, or for the way in which each believed faith in the Almighty should be demonstrated. Rarely did it allow unemotional, rational discussion, but instead, could be the cause of heated and vitriolic arguments -- and the last thing Theo wanted was for his reading room to be the source of such animosity, or even duels as a result of it.

He himself, having been raised by an Anglo-Irish family, had been brought up in the Anglican Church, as had most of his friends, but several well-known families in the county had converted to Methodism as a result of the various visits to Haverfordwest made by Mr. John Wesley; and although they would have had to be married in an Anglican church, as the law required, when it came to Sunday, it would be one of the town's many non-conformist chapels that they would attend.

Most of those who came to his reading room had connections to either the political arena or to the armed forces, or both, so their discussions usually centred around these areas. It had not taken Theo long to adjust to the numerous political discussions, but when it came to weaponry, army or navy manoeuvres and battle strategies, he found himself at a loss, remembering only too well young Foley's description of the moonlight battle off the coast of Portugal, and how he, Theo, had not known the difference between a frigate, a cutter, or any other ship, other than the sloop on which he had made that first trip to Wales.

To remedy this he had begun to make a mental note of the outlines and rigging of the many different vessels he saw sailing past while on his trips to Druid's Town beach, drawing them from memory when he arrived home, then using his drawings to ask his naval friends to tell him what they were. After a while it became a real hobby, and he would note any divergence in form or rigging, then ask his naval friends about it, until at last he could recognize any vessel as well as any old sea-captain.

It was on one of his trips to Druid's Town one day that he noticed a ship he had not seen before, so at the next opportunity, asked Foley, who was home on leave, what it could have been. Foley looked at Theo's detailed drawing. "Oh that would be a French warship captured by us at some time, and commissioned into the British navy." He laughed. "Let's hope you'll be seeing more of them in future... although not all at once of course, and not filled with French invaders! That's something we certainly don't need!"

Everyone had laughed at that.

"Let's not joke," warned Lord Milford. "There's plenty of talk in London of the possibility, and Parliament is nervous as to the reception they might receive, especially in Wales. Remember last year when the Hook colliers came to Haverfordwest to protest about their lot in life, and there was all that trouble they stirred up on Quay Street with their chanting 'One and all! One and all!'? I tell you the authorities are extremely nervous that such people could well join the French were they to invade. Why do you think we clamped down on their demonstration at once, by reading them the Riot Act?... Even so," he added after a minute, "I imagine the French would select a more appropriate place to land than

Pembrokeshire."

Some laughed again at what still seemed such a ludicrous prospect, but Sir John Campbell, recently made Lord Cawdor, remarked, "You never know. As Milford just pointed out, there are plenty of Welsh supporters for the French Revolution. Look at Dr. John Price, for example. And what about David Williams? He even went over to France, and became a French citizen! Then there's that Iolo Morganwg, who's over there all the time, giving the French the impression the Welsh are all ready for their own revolution here in Wales... They probably think the Welsh can't wait for the French army to come and rescue them from the English! Who knows what ideas they've given the French about the Welsh and the reception they would get if they did choose to come and *liberate* them!"

"Still unlikely, though, that they'd come to our county. Surely even the French can't be that foolish!" added Lord Milford.

Everyone decided it was all indeed unlikely, and on the discussion coming to an end, Cawdor announced it was time for him to go. There were mutterings of agreement, and before long Theo was left alone in his library, sitting with his legs stretched out before a fine fire, gazing into the ever-changing shapes of the white-hot embers, and wondering how he himself would react if the French did invade Pembrokeshire.

CHAPTER 33

Another hunt ball was due to take place, it being November. Elizabeth, who had declared she loved to have a baby in her arms, and looked forward with pleasure to each new arrival, had given birth to her fourth little girl the previous July, and they had named her after Lord Cawdor's wife, Isabella.

She had always remembered the little miniature of fourteen-year-old Lady Isabella Caroline Howard that her mother, the Countess of Carlisle, had shown her during their stay at Stackpole Court, and had been delighted when, four years later, in 1789, Campbell had married the young heiress, even though he was fifteen years her senior.

Elizabeth was not at this moment expecting another child. She looked and felt well, and was happy to be able to choose a fashionable gown to wear to the ball, even though her waistline, now that she had turned forty and had borne so many children, could no longer be called slim. Theo, she knew, did not mind; he had always loved her, and always would.

While Mary-Anne combed and styled her hair in readiness for the coming evening, she sat, hands folded in her lap, thinking. She and Theo had been married seventeen years already. She herself felt fulfilled, surrounded as she had always wanted to be, by her many children, with whom she spent most of her days, but she frowned slightly as she thought about Theo, knowing his sense of fulfilment had not equalled her own. She looked back at the energetic, high-spirited twenty-six-year-old Irishman she had first met, and knew he had borne disappointments that had dampened those spirits, and most of those disappointments she felt had been of her making. Perhaps he had spoiled her by giving in each time to her refusals to go away with him, thinking more of her children than she did of him. His needs as a man had been fulfilled, but those requiring the outlet of his artistic and creative talents had not, and looking back, she wondered at her own unwillingness to make those sacrifices that would have meant that perhaps, by now, he would be a famous actor like Mr. David Garrick before him. She shook her head, causing her maid to drop the comb. "I'm sorry, Mary-Anne. My mind was somewhere else, and I thought of something I didn't want to contemplate."

Mary-Anne picked up the comb and went back to work. "Yes, Ma'am."

No, it would not have done. She could never have left Pembrokeshire. Theo had known that, and he had chosen her rather than his career. She could, though, have relented perhaps, and at least been willing to go where he could have had the opportunity to see great plays being performed in a real theatre, to listen to opera, go to concerts and to revive his energies and spirits by immersing himself for short periods in the culture and vibrant life of a big city, a life that the humdrum and sleepy little Haverfordwest could in no way offer. It was a side of life he had been obliged to watch their best friends enjoy for many years, a side of life the nearest to which he could approach was to listen to their tales of where they had been, and what entertainments they had attended. He himself had had to content himself with releasing his built-up frustrations by galloping his horse at full speed along a wild and lonely Pembrokeshire beach.

At one time he had suggested they buy their own house in London. This way the whole family could go there for weeks at a time, as their friends did, but to this too she had been opposed. "What about the business?" she had reminded him.

"Mr. Sutton and William are well capable of looking after it."

But then their older children, who had never left Pembrokeshire, and not having been exposed to any other life, could not imagine having to leave their own friends and interests for weeks at a time, so had been equally disapproving of the idea. With so much opposition, Theo had simply given up.

At the time it had all seemed so impossible to her. She had, of course, spent much of her seventeen years producing those children she had wanted him to give her -- not that he had complained at that -- and travelling around was often, but certainly not always, an impossibility, and this is where he had been understanding and had given in to her refusals. She sighed. The time had gone so quickly, and now Theo at forty-four, even had some grey hair, and she felt sad that he rarely laughed with his eyes anymore. He had not even suggested their making a trip to London or Dublin for a long time now, and Lord Kensington's invitation to his home in the big city had gone unaccepted for nearly seven years.

With all these unwelcome thoughts filling her mind, her eyes began to well up with tears; it was so sad to see the Theo with whom she had fallen in love, bent over in a gloomy shop, putting bindings on books.

There was a tap on the door of her room, and belying all her thoughts, Theo, tall and handsome as ever and, she noticed, eyes smiling, came in.

She could not help it. She jumped up, sending the comb flying across the room, and rushed to him, flung her arms around him, and reached up to kiss him. "Oh Theo! My very dearest Theo, I do love you so."

He laughed. "Indeed? Then I'm glad to hear of it... although it sounds as though you've been thinking that perhaps you didn't, and have now changed your mind." He hugged her. "Never mind, my dear Bess," he assured her with a smile. "I love you too."

Mary-Anne retrieved the comb, curtsied and left the room. She used to be embarrassed at the demonstrations of affection in front of her between her mistress and the master of the house, especially when they called each other by their Christian names. It was something that would normally never take place in the presence of the servants. Some couples never called their spouses by their Christian names even in private, but Mary-Anne had become used to, and had forgiven what she considered this deviation from decorum, and was able to appreciate that she had the good fortune to be employed by such an understanding and generous family.

For a few minutes Elizabeth and Theo stood with their arms around each other, saying nothing. "I'm having a happiness," Theo announced.

"I too." It was an expression familiar to both of them, and to them alone, and indicated that sudden flow of intense euphoria, a uniting of spirits in great happiness that only those who truly love each other can experience. It had nothing to do with sexual arousal; it was a pure and beautiful emotion that simply welled up out of nowhere -- a true acknowledgment of mutual adoration.

The ritual of going to the Hunt Ball was, after all these years, nothing to Elizabeth and Theo. Their children were not yet old enough to attend, so it was still only "Mr. and Mrs. John Theophilus Potter" for the announcer to proclaim at their entrance. They still loved to dance, however, and still caused comments of admiration when they did so.

Tonight, still surrounded in the warm glow of their special happiness, they presented to the world a truly handsome couple, and there were many others of their age who envied that special something that Theo and Elizabeth seemed to have that made them stand out from the rest.

After many dances, and when both the orchestra as well as the dancers were ready for some respite and refreshment, Elizabeth sought out her lady friends with whom to sit and chat, and Theo went off, as was customary, to stand and talk with their husbands.

It was not many minutes after Elizabeth and her friends had found one another, and had seated themselves, that Mrs. Carswell was seen to be advancing upon them like a ship in full sail. For once, her daughter was not with her. With an imperious wave of her fan she indicated to a passing servant to fetch her a chair, and once seated within the group, interrupted their conversation without further ado, and with an air of superiority that surpassed even her own normal level of self-importance, greeted them.

"Ladies! Good evening!"

She received a response of polite nods and some mutterings of "Good evening", followed by silence.

"Well!" Mrs. Carswell began with her familiar and strident tones. "Are you not going to ask me where Miss Carswell is this evening?"

Mrs. Carswell's own presence was so overwhelming of itself, the absence of her daughter had gone unnoticed. She did not wait for an answer, but continued, " Miss Carswell is in London!" She leaned forward. "And I'm delighted to announce her engagement!"

Given that Miss Carswell was now nearly forty, this announcement did raise some eyebrows, but was still incapable of arousing anything more than a few polite smiles and murmurs of, "Indeed? How felicitous!"

Mrs. Carswell then delivered her pièce de résistance. She waved her fan with affected grandeur. "Yes, I'm pleased to announce Miss Carwsell's engagement to Lord Thompkinson of Hove."

This did arouse slightly more curiosity, and Mrs. Carswell's sense of superiority over the other ladies was elevated higher than ever before. "Yes," she continued. "My husband and Miss Carswell and I were spending some time in Town, and had the pleasure of being introduced to his Lordship at a function being held in the most elegant part of town, you know… A charming gentleman he is, and we could see at once how taken he was with our lovely daughter. He proceeded to pay her every attention, and at the end of the evening invited us to his magnificent London townhouse for dinner the following evening. Naturally we were only too delighted to attend, and so charmed was he with our elegant daughter, that by the end of the week he'd asked Mr. Carswell for her hand in marriage!" Having started slowly, her monologue had increased in tempo, and now out of breath, she was obliged to pause. It was but a temporary pause. "She will of course be Lady Thompkinson of Hove, and when not at their London townhouse, they will be residing at their large estate in the country. You may well be asking yourselves," she continued, "why we're here, back at home on our estate in Pembrokeshire at the moment, rather than in London where, as you may know, the season is at its height."

It appeared no-one was wondering, but Mrs. Carswell continued anyway. "Well, Mr. Carswell and I have decided that in view of our daughter's elevated status in society, and the strong likelihood that she and her husband won't be appearing here in Haverfordwest in future, it only makes sense for us to lease out our estate here, and remove ourselves to London. We have already bought ourselves a townhouse there… in the most fashionable quarter, naturally, something that Mr. Carswell is well able to afford, of course, and we're here now only in order to finalise the lease of our estate, before removing to London permanently, where we'll be moving in the best circles, as you can imagine." She paused to catch her breath again, and misinterpreting the expressions of delight from the rest of the ladies, she continued. "Yes," she told them, "yes, I do declare! Mr. Carswell and I are privileged indeed to have so deserving a daughter as our dear Miss Carswell." She stood up. "Well, I must leave you ladies to carry on with your chat. As we'll be moving in different circles in future, I doubt our paths will cross, unless you ever happen to be in Town and leave your calling card at Lady Thompkinson of Hove's London home and, if not otherwise engaged, I'm sure she'd see fit to return your call at some time."

She began her departure, but Lady Sinclair forestalled her move.

"Whatever happened to your daughter's acting career then? I've not seen her on the playlists at Drury Lane," she said without a hint of a smile.

"What! Acting! A lady in her position! Nothing happened to it! She decided it was way beneath her dignity to pursue such a career!" And Mrs. Carswell swept on her way to the next group of seated ladies, leaving the first reduced to silence.

There was a long pause. "I've met Lord Thompkinson… of Hove," said Lady Sinclair.

"You have?"

"Yes, Sir Thomas and I met him in London last season. His second wife had just died in childbirth, leaving him a widower at seventy-two."

"Seventy-two!"

"Yes, and gossip had it that, while he has the title, his estate is greatly in debt and in dire need of an infusion of money."

"At least tell us he's tall and handsome…"

"Alas no. He's a portly man of florid complexion and ordinary demeanour. He also has seven young children still at home."

CHAPTER 34

It was Wednesday, 22 February, 1797, and Theo needed to take one of his therapeutic rides out to Druid's Town beach. He had not slept at all the previous night for various reasons he no longer wished to dwell upon, so it meant that by seven o'clock in the morning, with the sun not yet risen, and without breakfast, he had already set out on Hercules.

The horse was now over twenty years old, and although he was always ready to make the almost seven-mile trip to Druid's Town, Theo no longer galloped him flat out along the beach, and they took longer getting there and back -- and at forty-five himself, Theo no longer tried vaulting onto his horse's back. By the time they reached their destination, the sun was coming over the horizon, and the day was so warm for February that Theo took off his coat, and tied it to his saddle.

As they arrived at the top of the cliff, he stopped Hercules, and sat there, looking out at the wide expanse of ocean, this morning as flat as glass. In the distance, gannets were diving for their breakfasts, and Theo watched in fascination as, from a great height, they would suddenly fold their wings and hurtle like spent arrows deep into the water below.

He gazed further out to sea, his attention caught by the sun flashing on something in the distance, and was just in time to see the outlines of four ships sailing towards Ramsey Island. Because of his interest in spotting and identifying the different ships sailing past, he always carried his spyglass, so he took it out of his saddle bag, and trained it on the ships.

There was no mistaking them. They were French warships, one of them just like the one he had seen some years before. This was a corvette, and he could see it had twenty-four guns. Then there were two identical large frigates, again, unmistakably French. These were fairly bristling with guns, and knowing that what he saw on the one side would be mirrored on the other, he counted in all forty guns on each one. There was also a small lugger, also armed with another fourteen guns. He sat there looking at them through his spyglass, and remembered Foley's words, "Let's hope you'll be seeing more of them in future... although not full of French invaders! A invasion is something we certainly don't need."

He continued to sit there, disbelieving, but a second look confirmed to him that, although he could not see what flags they were flying, there would be no likelihood at all that four French warships, captured by the British, would be sailing in formation close into the Pembrokeshire coast -- or into any British coast, unless they were manned by the enemy and planning to land. He did a quick mental calculation and estimated they could be carrying among them over a thousand men, and a third look confirmed that the decks were indeed crowded with people, presumably soldiers.

He turned Hercules around, and pushed the old horse to return to Haverfordwest as quickly as possible, all the way trying to decide what to do about his discovery. Should he take any action at all? What if he were wrong? What a laughing stock he would become if his claims were believed, then found to be a false alarm! His need to make a decision troubled him as he rode back towards Haverfordwest. On the other hand, what if he were right, and did nothing? How could he live with himself if, because of his fear of being wrong, he failed to act, and the result was disaster? And if he *were* to act, whom would he tell?

Haverfordwest had no army presence of its own, at least, not at that moment, and to relate the information to the sheriff or mayor would only lead to a great deal of pondering, followed by a roundup of the Council, which would then decide on the need to form a committee to discuss such an outlandish claim. To go to the Lord Lieutenant, Lord Milford, at his home in Picton Castle would be the easiest option, but Theo did not know his Lordship that well, and for reasons he could not explain, did not feel that comfortable in his presence.

Theo knew this was an emergency; he knew they were French warships, and their actions in sailing so close inshore revealed that their intentions were far from friendly. He had no doubt at all they were looking for a place to make a landing on Welsh soil, be it Pembrokeshire, or further north on the Cardiganshire coast.

By the time he arrived back at the livery stable in Haverfordwest, he had made his decision. He would go straight to the man he knew best, and whom he himself considered the most capable in the county, and the most clever and intelligent -- his friend Campbell -- and prayed he was about to do the right thing. Cawdor may be his friend, but would any friendship survive his persuading someone in Campbell's position to raise forces against a non-existent foe? Campbell, he knew was at his home in Stackpole Court, and it was there he needed to go if he were to act at all.

He handed Hercules over to the care of the groom at the livery stable, and deciding that to act, whatever the cost, was preferable to doing nothing, asked to hire their fastest horse, and while the horse was being saddled up and got ready for him, he rushed home, and told Elizabeth he needed to go off for the day, and not to worry if he did not return until the morrow. Before Elizabeth had time to question him he was gone again.

The groom held the horse while Theo mounted, then patted it on its rump. "She might be a bit lively," he commented. "She wasn't taken out yesterday."

Theo nodded without listening, and set out for Stackpole. She was a young filly, excited at the prospect of a good day's romp, and she sidled and pranced along the road, tossing her head and mouthing the bit. It was nothing he had not handled in the past, and thought nothing of it.

Once off the dangerous cobbles of the town, and out on the road leading to Johnston, Theo gave her a nudge in the ribs with his heels, just as he would have done with Hercules.

The effect took him surprise, as she put her head down and gave an enormous buck, dislodging his feet from the stirrups and almost throwing him off, and before he could collect himself, she bolted, and she was, as he had been told, fast. Although she did not have the bit between her teeth, Theo guessed that whoever had broken her had not done it well, as the bars between her teeth, where the bit lay, had been ruined and rendered insensitive, and no amount of pulling on the reins had the slightest effect. At first Theo thought to let her run herself out, but that was too dangerous, and she could founder, injuring them both, so his only option was to let the one rein go slack, and using both hands he hauled on the other, pulling her head around so far she could not see where she was going. This had the desired effect, although they both nearly landed in a gorse bush in the doing, and soon the two of them were standing in the middle of the road, Theo greatly relieved, and the horse with her nostrils flaring and flanks heaving.

After a few minutes in which he allowed her to regain her breath and himself his composure, they set out again, this time at a controlled gallop. Because of her earlier over-exertion, by the time he had reached the ferry at Neyland, the horse was beginning to flag, but there being no livery stable in the area, he knew he would have to keep her until he reached Pembroke.

When he arrived at the ferry, he could see the boat was about half way across the river, on its way to the other side, and he did not have the time to wait for its return. He looked around for a suitable craft to transport him across, and noticed a small boat towing a raft just offshore. He hailed the man in charge of it, and in return for the promise of a handsome financial reward, was able to persuade him to take them across. More time was wasted in getting the filly onto the raft, and many anxious moments keeping her on it while making the crossing. There was a time Theo was even beginning to think it would have been quicker to have made the twenty-mile longer trip via Canaston Woods, but despite the delays, by the time he reached Pembroke he knew he had made the right decision in coming the shorter route, having made excellent time overall.

In Pembroke, he left the horse at the livery stable with instructions to be sure to walk her around for the next half hour, and not to give her too much water lest, in her heated condition, she get colic, and letting the groom know he would be picking her up sometime the following day. He then hired another horse, and finally arrived at Stackpole Court in the evening.

As he arrived on the estate, he encountered a number of yeomen and gentlemen and their horses gathered in readiness for a large funeral to be held the following morning for one of their illustrious members, who had died just a few days previously. It seemed a grand parade was planned in his honour, and the funeral cortege was to march to the Church in Pembroke, where the man was to be interred. In preparation, they were all spending the night on the Stackpole estate in the vicinity of the mansion.

Theo rode up to the entrance, handed his horse to a servant, and asked to be taken to Lord Cawdor at once. His lordship, who, despite the solemnity of the forthcoming funeral, was entertaining some of the higher ranks of his men to a grand dinner, accompanied by plenty of excellent port, much of which had already been consumed.

His surprise at seeing Theo was immense. "Potter!" he exclaimed. "What on earth are you doing here?" He waved his glass at him. "Come on in. Come on in." He pointed to an empty chair, and signalled a servant to bring his new guest a glass of wine, but Theo shook his head, and did not even take the proffered seat. Instead he walked up to his friend and whispered to him.

"I need to speak to you in private, Campbell. Now."

The urgency of his request produced the required response. Campbell stood up and took Theo by the arm. "Yes, yes, of course." He offered his excuses to his other guests. and the two men left the room and went into the library where Campbell shut the door.

Theo then told his friend what he had seen, and Campbell, knowing Theo to be a intelligent man unlikely to make wild claims or let his imagination get the better of him, believed him. He did, however, ask Theo many questions, at the end of which he sat back in his chair, and tapped his fingers on the desk in front of him.

"And you told no one in Haverfordwest of this?"

"No."

"And you didn't go to Milford?

"No."

"Why didn't you go to Milford? He's the Lord Lieutenant of the county, and theoretically in charge of the county's defences."

"You know why I didn't go to Milford. I…"

"Yes, yes. You don't have to explain. I understand." He paused. "Let me think a minute." He put his head back, and shut his eyes. Theo himself stood there, still fearing he might have been wrong in coming here at all, but one thing he was sure of: it was too late now to change his mind.

Cawdor, still young at forty-three, was a brilliant man, capable of summing up a situation in an instant, and knowledgeable in military matters although still only a captain, but Theo's news had come as a surprise, and he needed to gather his thoughts and decide on what he must do next. If Theo were right, which he assumed he was, he was faced with a formidable task.

Finally he stood up. "The Pembrokeshire Militia are in Felixstowe at the other end of Britain at the moment, but the Cardigan Militia happens to be stationed in Pembroke, which is fortunate. But we have no idea yet where the French intend to land, or worse yet, where they may have already landed." He looked at his friend. "You should really have reported your sighting to authorities in Haverfordwest, or at least to Milford. However, I do understand why you came straight to me and, for myself, I have to say I'm glad you did, as time here is of the essence, and ..." His voice trailed off, and he looked at the large long-case clock ticking off the seconds in the corner of the library.

It was now dark and approaching seven o'clock. He turned back to Theo. "Whatever happens tonight, I want you to stay here until the morning. I myself, along with my men, will need to wait here until I hear news of exactly where they have landed, as I can't just march off without knowing where I'm heading, but until then, your prior warning will give me time to think -- time that is essential, and for which I thank you, my friend..." He hesitated before adding, "The reason I want you to stay here is because it may not be wise for you to be seen arriving with me in Haverfordwest, or wherever we go. There would most surely be some feathers ruffled by your failure to inform others first, and to save you from their displeasure, we'll say nothing of your visit... and I doubt there is anyone here tonight who would have recognized you."

Theo nodded in agreement, and Campbell rang the bell for a servant, who was instructed to take Mr. Potter to a guest room, to provide him with all necessary comforts and food, and to make sure he was taken care of. The servant held the library door open for Theo to leave with him, and Theo, all his physical and emotional energy spent, and faint with hunger -- not having eaten all day -- was grateful that, should Campbell leave during the night, he did not have to accompany him.

Campbell waved him off. "You've done your share, Theo, so go. Have a good meal and a good night's rest. Depending on what happens next, I'll be happy to have you join my men wherever we happen to find ourselves tomorrow or the day after. If anyone asks me anything, I'll say a personal friend from Haverfordwest came to visit me. Good night!" He watched Theo leave the room. "And thank you. You're a good friend," he called after him as the servant shut the door behind them.

Theo went to bed still asking himself, "What have I done?" but sleep overtook him before he could consider the implications any further.

When he awoke the next morning, the sun was already high, and he recognized the room he was in as being the same one he and Elizabeth had occupied nearly twelve years ago. Then, James had been here with them, and if he were still alive, James would be with him now, but it was already almost seven years since he had been killed.

A sigh of sadness escaped him. He had never replaced James by getting another manservant. It would have seemed an insult to his memory to think he could be replaced, and although he regularly missed the attentions a manservant would provide, he had preferred to deprive himself of them, rather than keep reminding himself of his old friend and confidant.

He climbed out of bed and stretched, sore from the many

hours spent in the saddle the previous day. He rang the bell for a servant, and while waiting for him to arrive, looked out of the window. The lily ponds, so much talked about on his last visit, were still in the process of construction, but were taking shape. Other than that, the place seemed to be deserted; there was not a soul in sight. Men and horses had left, and even the house was silent. If the servant had not knocked on his door minutes later, he would have imagined himself to be the only person left on the Stackpole estate, and it was just as the servant arrived, the thought came back to him that he might have made a terrible mistake in coming here at all. Cawdor and all his men had left. Had they gone to a funeral, or to war? And if they had gone to war, was it a real one, or one of his own imagination? From his personal point of view it was hard to decide which was preferable.

"What time is it?"

"Coming on for noon, Sir."

"Noon!"

The servant nodded.

Part of Theo wanted to ask, "Was I right?" It was not a question he could ask a servant, so he said instead, "Would you please bring me a tub and hot water please. A bath would be good."

The servant nodded, "Yes, Sir. And shall I bring you some breakfast in your chamber, Sir?"

"That would be most acceptable." Theo smiled, and the servant left, returning a few minutes later with the tub and the water which was carried by three separate maidservants.

"I thought you would like to take your bath first, Sir, before breakfast," he added by way of explanation.

"A good idea." Theo waited for the maids to leave the room, then undressed and climbed into the tub.

Down in the kitchen, the word was passed around that a handsome gentleman was right now taking a bath in the guest

317

chamber, and was expecting breakfast. A slight altercation followed in which each maid expressed her opinion that she had the right to deliver the breakfast. In the end it was the cook who had to delegate the responsibility.

"Would you like help, Sir, or would you like to be left alone to carry out your ablutions?"

"A back scrub would be good."

"Right you are, Sir."

"What's your name? You sound as though you come from Scotland."

"Green, Sir. And yes, Sir. I am from Scotland. The former Sir John Campbell, God rest his soul, brought a number of servants with him when he came down from Scotland to Stackpole. My family name really isn't Green either, Sir."

"No?"

"No. It's MacArthur, but his Lordship didn't want to keep calling out "MacArthur", so he called me by the colour of my kilt.

Theo thought it a shame that a man should lose his true identity in such a way, but felt he could not criticize the former Sir John. "That was innovative of him," he said.

"Yes Sir."

Theo changed the subject. He was anxious to know what had happened, but wanted to avoid sounding over-concerned. "When did everyone set out from here, and do you know where they went?"

"I was in bed myself, Sir, but cook told me this morning she thought someone had arrived here at about eleven o'clock last night to say the enemy had landed in Fishguard at two o'clock in the afternoon."

"Fishguard, eh? So that's where they were headed!" Theo wanted to let out a whoop of joy that indicated, "I was right!" but under the circumstances, such an expression could be misinterpreted. Besides, he realized his own relief at having been proven right, should at least be tempered by the knowledge that Wales had indeed been invaded by the French, a sobering thought when considered on its own.

"Yes, Sir. It seems the news arrived in Haverfordwest at about six o'clock. Then someone else arrived from Lord Milford's at about midnight to confirm it."

"So they set off right after that, did they?"

"Yes, his Lordship expressed his intention of going straight to Picton Castle to confer with Lord Milford, and then they all left."

His bath finished, Theo dressed, then ate his breakfast. As he ate, he was at last able to relax, knowing he no longer faced being ridiculed for coming to Cawdor with false reports, and with that fear out of the way, he attempted to work out the logistics of all that had happened so far. In doing so, he wondered exactly how, if it had taken four hours for the news to travel the sixteen miles from Fishguard to Haverfordwest over the turnpike road in broad daylight, how had someone managed to cover the same amount of miles in the pitch darkness of a February night, including crossing a river, and in some cases finding his way along small country lanes, in just one hour more -- and that was assuming the person had left Haverfordwest the minute the news had arrived there. He shrugged and put on his coat. Maybe Green had got it wrong. Anyway it did not matter. Here he was, all alone in Stackpole, and he needed to return home.

By the time he had exchanged horses in Pembroke, crossed the river -- by ferry this time -- and ridden back to Haverfordwest, it was dark again, and as there was nothing he could do, or wanted to do that night, he went home, and went to bed, where he told Elizabeth about his adventures before falling into a deep sleep.

When he woke the next morning, he learned that Cawdor

and his cavalry, along with the Cardigan Militia and the Pembroke volunteers who had joined him in Pembroke, had arrived in Haverfordwest and then assembled outside the Castle Inn in the square at just about the same time as he was waking up in Stackpole the day before.

Having been preparing to make their way to Fishguard, they were by now almost twenty-four hours ahead of him. Still, as a burgess of the town of Haverfordwest, it was his duty to catch up with them regardless of anything Cawdor had said about joining him. This being the case, Theo expressed his intention of setting off to find them.

Elizabeth knew she should not try to stop him, but was so ill with fear for his safety, she was overtaken by one of her panic attacks, and had to take to her bed.

"I'm sorry, my dear," he told her, "but this is something I'm honour bound to do." He unclasped her arms from around his neck, and took his leave.

"I know... I know you do Theo..."

He left to the sound of his wife's sobs.

It was now 24th February, and having secured at the livery stable a good, solid horse much like Hercules, he went to the Castle Inn, from whence the assembled army had left the previous morning. There he learned that about six hundred men had been gathered in front of the inn, all on foot except for Cawdor's cavalry, other officers and those burgesses wealthy enough to own their own horses. All the militia had swords and pistols, but only some of the volunteers had muskets, these having been provided by the government, but there had not been enough to go round, so many had armed themselves with whatever could be used as a weapon in an emergency.

Bread and cheese had been handed around to those who had already made the march from Pembroke during the night, and Theo imagined the plight of all those volunteers who had made that march, and who had then -- with but a few hours' rest -- to set off again for Fishguard. Aware that although many people thought nothing of walking up to thirty miles a day, others would not be used to walking such long distances, and he wondered how many painful blisters were already causing distress -- and who knew what was yet to come?

Theo had armed himself with a musket he found in the cupboard under the stairs. It had been there for more years than he could remember, and he did not even know where it came from. It had taken him an hour or more to clean it, then to find the wherewithal with which to fire it, all the time hating the sight of the weapon, and hoping he would never have to use it as he was not sure he could bring himself to pull the trigger, even to save his own life.

All the information he had to go on as he set off from the square was that the whole force was now twenty-four hours ahead of him, presumably somewhere in the vicinity of Fishguard, so he set off on his own, reminding himself of Don Quixote, and hoping that before being required to tilt at any windmills with his musket, he would catch up with Cawdor and not the French invaders.

He arrived in Fishguard just after two o'clock in the afternoon, just in time to learn from the jubilant locals that it was all over. The French had surrendered, and were at this moment coming down Goodwick hill onto Goodwick sands, where they were to gather together and surrender all their arms, supervised by the Fishguard Fencibles.

Theo then continued down West Street, and down the hill onto Goodwick bridge to witness the event, where he met up with a few of Cawdor's men, standing guard. He joined them and waited, as did the whole population of Fishguard and the surrounding area, while the laborious process went ahead, the French prisoners playing their pipes and drums as they trundled down the steep hill from the Llanwnda heights.

While he and the cavalry men stood on the bridge, Theo

was able to learn about the surrender, and how the outcome might have been quite different if Cawdor had not made a wise decision the previous night. His forces had arrived in Fishguard just before dark, and after a scouting foray into what had become enemy territory up in the crags between Llanwnda and Manorowen, Cawdor decided to advance on their positions by night. However, it being a dark night in which it was almost impossible to see where they were going, Cawdor called off the attack, which was just as well, as the French commander's only remaining forces he could trust to follow orders, had been lying in wait to ambush them, and Cawdor could have suffered serious losses.

It was four o'clock in the afternoon before the whole legion was assembled on the beach, after which they started their slow trek, under guard, to Haverfordwest. It was all over, and there was nothing for Theo to do but to return home to Haverfordwest along with everyone else, which he did, arriving back in town just before midnight.

Only later did he learn how the French had really lost their invasion for themselves. Fourteen hundred of them, mostly undisciplined convicts, had plundered farms, drunk themselves silly on the large supply of port the locals had recently retrieved from a wreck, and had made themselves ill by eating chickens they were too hungry to cook properly. Their commander, the Irish-American Tate, had himself been disillusioned when he discovered, not only that the Welsh in no way welcomed his presence on their soil, but the so-called army supposedly under his control, was not. That the total British forces had amounted to at most six hundred and fifty men against his fourteen hundred had further added to his humiliation. The whole affair had been a shambles, a shambles that no doubt would provide its heroes and its traitors, not to mention all the spectators, with a source of conversation and tall tales for many years thereafter.

CHAPTER 35

For some time Theo had been concerned about his eldest son, John, who was now nineteen years old, and had received an excellent education at Haverfordwest Grammar School under the tutelage of the Reverend T. Phillips. Like all the other pupils before him, he had carved his name in the long mahogany desk, but despite everything, seemed disinclined to fix himself into any way of achieving anything in life that would provide him with a living.

Like his father he was sociable and amiable, but unlike his father, these positive attributes were not supported by any drive or energy. John himself had not dwelt on the reasons why he was as he was, but an outsider might have noticed it was Theo himself who may unwittingly be to blame.

To other eyes it might seem as though the boy was in some way diminished whenever he was anywhere where his father was also present. When he entered a room, Theo was a man whom everyone noticed; he had a presence, an aura that somehow eclipsed others, and however unintentionally, drew attention to himself. Maybe it was just his magnetic personality alone, but whatever it was, it had seemed to have had a profound effect on his son who sank into insignificance when his father was around, even though he looked exactly like him.

His father had another effect on his son: industrious himself, he failed to understand why John should not be likewise. He did not understand John's way of approaching his world, and his response to this, instead of encouraging his son, had the opposite effect. Even Elizabeth, who on occasion had been present during altercations between father and son, had felt it necessary to admonish her husband. "Not everyone has the will, or even the stamina, to live their lives with the same zeal and intensity as you, my dear Theo. Indeed, were I a man, I know I should not."

Theo had nodded his head and agreed that perhaps he sometimes did expect too much of others.

Since he had waved goodbye to his lifetime friend, John George, several months ago in January, down by the kilns, John appeared to have become even less energetic. He missed his friend, and regretted he had allowed him to leave Haverfordwest to pick up his commission in the Royal Marines without giving him a positive answer as to whether he would join him. He confided in his sister, Elizabeth, just one year younger than he.

Elizabeth had grown into a smart young woman. Like her younger sisters, she had been taught by her mother everything considered necessary for a young lady: she could sew, do embroidery, play the family spinet, and draw likenesses, but did not possess a voice that would encourage her to sing at gatherings where people outside the family would have to listen to her. Like her father and mother, she enjoyed reading, and was what might be considered a serious and studious young lady, and unlike other young ladies of her age, was not interested in visiting Haverfordwest's various haberdashery and drapery establishments to view or purchase the latest fashions. She had been only nine years old when she had been lifted onto her father's shoulders to see the great Mr. John

Wesley standing on the horse block outside The Blue Boar Inn, preaching and using Mr. John Green's shoulders as his lectern.

The force of Mr. Wesley's words had had a profound effect on the young girl's mind, leading her to respect the powers of the Lord, and to fear the retributions he was capable of inflicting on sinners; and as she grew into adulthood, she had developed a tendency to lecture everyone -- including her parents -- on anything she considered to be transgressions of His word. This included their attendance at the many balls held during the season, which she herself considered a frivolity showing disrespect towards the Almighty. Her advice to her older brother, therefore, was to put his fate in the hands of God, who would guide him down the right path, but, she warned him, as it appeared he was being led into temptation far too often, he must rectify this, or face eternal damnation in Hell's fires.

Finding no satisfaction in his sister's advice, John went to see Mary, John George's sister, who was most anxious for him to join her brother in the Royal Marines. She set down the young Potter in a chair in the family's private apartments of the Blue Boar, and made him listen while she read from her brother's latest letter, hoping to convince John to join him. She had run her finger down the page, looking for the spot where her brother mentions his friend. "Ah! Here it is. He wants to know if you've decided to enter the Marines, or not." Then she moved her finger further down the page. "And, here again he says to give his love to all his friends, and names you especially. See!" she said to him. " He thinks of you, and truly misses you. Can't you promise me to join him in the Marines, so I can relay your message to him in my next letter?"

"Tell him I'll make up my mind really soon."

"Oh please do, John!" She pulled out another letter from a box where she was keeping all her brother's mail. "Look! Here! See what he says, John." She held out her brother's letter. "You read it," she demanded.

"He says he's lonely…" He left the rest of the sentence unread, and handed back the letter. "Poor old John. It must be hard for him so far away from home."

"Yes," said Mary, "and all the more reason why he needs his best friend."

"There's no guarantee we'd ever be posted to the same places, or be on the same ships though, Mary."

"I know, but just knowing you're in the Royal Marines together must surely be a great comfort to both of you."

John stood up. "Tell him I'll let him know soon," he said again, and took his leave, but Mary called out to him just as he was leaving, "By the way, John, how is your mother? Have they named the new baby yet?"

"Mother's doing well, thank you Mary, and my new brother's name is Thomas."

While John was being urged to go to sea by his ten-year-old brother Edward (named after the first little Edward), who had already determined he himself was going to join the Royal Navy, he found talking to his brother Joseph to be just as difficult as trying to confide in his father.

Joseph was in every way too much like Theo, and if it were not for the difference in appearance and age, John would often feel he might as well *be* talking to his father. That he continued to hold a certain jealousy towards his brother for that special relationship Joseph and his father enjoyed, was yet another reason not to discuss his problems with him.

Joseph was always full of energy, and had inherited his father's constant urge to achieve something. He had grown into a man of whom his parents could be proud, well known as he was about town for his humour, friendliness and elegant manners, just as his father was. Unlike his brother John, he never balked when asked to perform tasks, and again like his father, was always willing to learn something new. His love of acting had become a constant pleasure for Theo, who watched as his son had not only grown into a competent player, but showed signs he would also make an excellent theatre manager. Of all his sons, it was with Joseph that Theo felt the greatest bond.

In the meantime Theo, unaware of any adverse effect he himself might have on his eldest son's lack of direction or ambition, was determined that John should not spend all his days playing cricket, or generally wasting his time wandering around town with others of his age, and had therefore secured a position for him helping John George's father at the Blue Boar.

Mr. Stephen George needed the extra help, not only because his own son was no longer there, but because he was suffering from an attack of gout, making it difficult for him to carry out his job as landlord on his own. However, Theo, who along with many others of the town's elite, also frequented the inn -- often calling in for a pint of Welsh ale -- had noticed of late, that his son seemed to be spending more time in front of the bar with the patrons, than behind it.

"It won't do, John," he reprimanded him. "You're there to help Mr. George with lifting and carrying heavy objects that he's unable to handle himself right now, not to stand around chatting with whomever comes into the inn -- welcoming as that may be. Mr. George and I being old friends, he'll refrain from chastising you as he ought, out of respect for me, but I won't have you take advantage of the situation. He has every right to remove you from his employment, and I've indicated to him that that's what he must do if you continue to idle away your time there and expect to be paid for your inactivity."

John ignored his father's chastisement. "I've decided to go into the Royal Marines," he announced.

"Indeed! And what brought about this decision all of a sudden after you've been playing around with the idea for so many months?"

John stood in front of his father and explained. "I've decided there's no future for me here; there's nothing I want to do in Haverfordwest... and I've no wish at all to go into the business of setting type, fiddling around trying to bind books, or printing brochures and books like you. So I've decided this is what I want to do, but I need your help, Father."

Theo showed his surprise at his son's outburst. "Oh? Well, I must say you've chosen to express yourself bluntly. So you wouldn't want to join Bill and Mr. Sutton in the printing business? I suppose I'll have to accept that, although with Mr. Sutton about to retire, I had hoped..." Theo shrugged his shoulders.

John ignored his father's expressed thoughts. "Yes. I regret now I didn't ask Mr. Cleaveland for his help by asking him to write to the Admiralty on my behalf, so now the only option is to ask Lord Kensington, and I can't do that myself. Would you do that for me, Father? Please."

"You realize Lord Kensington, like Mr. Cleaveland, isn't in good health either now, and that in all likelihood I'll have to go through Lady Kensington, and she can be..." He spread his fingers out on his knees. "Besides, Lord Kensington may not be as generous as Mr. Cleaveland, and I think you may have to expect that. You may be disappointed."

"It's my only hope Father. There's no-one else with that amount of influence, and Lord Cawdor is off travelling in Italy again."

Theo ignored the reference to Lord Cawdor, knowing others had been known to complain about the amount of time that gentleman spent away from his constituency. "You're sure you do want to do this John? It's a hard life; the pay is poor indeed for a young lieutenant, and you know the only way you'll make an acceptable living will be if the ship you're on is fortunate enough to capture enemy vessels as prizes. Whether you become rich or not is a matter of pure luck, and you could get killed in the process. You know that, don't you?"

"Yes, I know Father."

"Very well. I'll see what I can do, but I can't guarantee at all that Lady Kensington will be willing to bother her husband with this assignment, but before I do as you ask, I suggest you go to talk to Captain Allen, and ask his advice first."

Theo stood up and shook his head. "Alas, your poor mother is going to spend her life in the constant misery of worrying about you, but that's something I myself will have to be the one to live with, I fear." He sighed at the prospect.

John went to see Captain Allen, and returned even more determined to follow his plan, then went to see Mary George and told her of his decision, giving her a letter to send to her brother along with her own, a letter to which John George soon replied, expressing his delight, and assuming correctly that it would be Lord Kensington who would be sending in his friend's application.

Theo went to Lady Kensington as promised, and she, after some hesitation, agreed to get her husband to send the requested letter of application for a commission to the Admiralty. However, a month passed and it was now late September, and John had still not received news regarding it. The time passed slowly as he continued to wait, but then, in the first week of October, it came; he had been refused. Even Theo felt let down, and wondered what Lord Kensington had said, or not said, that had caused the Admiralty to refuse his son, but although no reasons were given, Theo thought there was the possibility also, that his son had been refused because of his eyesight, which did bother him at times.

As a father he felt sorry for his son, understanding as he did the disappointment of not being able to follow one's chosen career. For his own sake, and that of Elizabeth, however, he had to admit his sorrow was tempered by relief, and he set about finding an alternative occupation for John. On discovering that another inn in town was in need of a landlord, and knowing John had enjoyed working at The Blue Boar, he asked him if he would like to consider taking on the position.

It was only two weeks since he had received his refusal from the Admiralty, and, feeling depressed as a result, John could say only that he supposed this would do. Thus, far removed from a career in the marines and from his friend, John George, he became instead the landlord of an inn, and his sister, Elizabeth, felt the necessity to say extra prayers to ensure his salvation.

CHAPTER 36

Joseph, "Theo incarnate," as Elizabeth liked to call him, was nineteen years old, and still as full of enthusiasm for life, lust for learning, dynamic energy and love of acting as his father had been; and his father now nearly fifty, but as youthful in his outlook and in physical energy as ever, wanted to give his son everything to allow him to achieve his dreams in a way he had been unable to do. And so, on one day in the spring of 1802, when all the children old enough to attend family dinner were gathered around the table, Theo announced his intention to form a little theatre company that would allow Joseph to display his talents in public.

"I'm not envisaging a large professional company at all," he told them, "but some little show we can take around the county during the summer season for the amusement of people in general." The joy for Theo in his idea was that he and Joseph worked together in perfect harmony, something he had never been able to achieve with John.

As far as young Edward was concerned, he was still determined to go into the navy, and the three younger boys, Frederick, Edwin and Thomas were still too young to know what they wanted from life, little Thomas being not yet two years old.

His daughter Elizabeth, now twenty, had continued to develop into a young woman somewhat severe in both outlook and countenance, who showed no interest in finding a beau, spent much of her time in worshipping the Almighty, and seemed quite content to go to the printing business on High Street to offer her services by greeting and seeing to customers' needs. She had proved most useful in this respect, and while his eldest daughter was an enigma to him, Theo appreciated her willingness to be of help, unless, of course, that help required her to act against what she considered to be God's wishes. Thus, where the plans for a theatre were concerned, she would refuse -- she had informed them in advance -- to help even in the making of the necessary costumes.

As for Joseph and his father, if there was any difference between them at all, it would be in that the former tended to favour the more dramatic than the comedic, although both were adept at either, and it was with this in mind they got together, and decided on a play to satisfy them both.

At their first serious discussion of the new project it was decided that Theo, of course, would be manager, and would look after all the finances and bookings. Next came a discussion as to what play was to be chosen for their first performance. After Theo's difficulty in finding suitably talented actors to perform in his production of *The Taming of the Shrew* all that time ago, it was considered necessary to find a play requiring a small cast, at least as far as the main characters were concerned, and after much discussion, they decided upon Mr. Henry Fielding's comedy, *The Mock Doctor*, which had been successful with audiences for nearly seventy years, and so seemed a safe choice.

Based on M. Molière's farce, *Le Médecin malgré lui*, the plot concerned a simple woodcutter, Gregory, whose wife, Dorcas, seeks revenge for his beating her, by tricking him into having to pretend he's a physician. As Dr. Ragou, therefore, he's called upon to treat Charlotte, the daughter of Sir Jasper. Charlotte pretends to have become mute because she doesn't want to marry the man her father has chosen for her. Instead, she wants to marry her young lover, Leander. In the end, of course, as the result of Dr. Ragou's 'cure', she has her way, and all ends happily.

Having decided on their play, they then agreed the part of Gregory was perfectly suited to Theo, who was as excellent a comedic actor as he was tragedian, and although it was by no means as large a part, or even as humorous a part as he would have liked, Joseph should play the young lover, Leander, because, as his father pointed out, he was just a fledgling actor, after all.

The task then was to find creditable actors to fill the other three important roles, namely Gregory's wife, Dorcas, that of Sir Jasper, and of his daughter, Charlotte. Theo's other children were much too young for any of the roles, even if they had wanted to play a part, and his daughter, Elizabeth, although the right age for Charlotte, was out of the question.

As Joseph himself said to his father, "She thinks you and I have sold our souls to the Devil already. The only role she'd ever play would be that of Joan of Arc, and in order to feel redeemed as a result, she would have, at the end of it, to be literally burned at the stake."

"Now Joseph," his father had half-heartedly rebuked him.

As it was, they were able to find a young woman who was quite adequate for the part of Charlotte, and when it came to finding actors for the other two roles, they were more than fortunate.

The previous year Theo and Joseph had attended a performance given in the town by two excellent travelling actors, a husband and wife team, and on contacting them, Theo had managed to persuade them to join them in this production. That they had been promised all performances minus expenses would be to their exclusive benefit, was a significant inducement, and it was arranged that rehearsals would start in the near future. This was necessary as they needed to perform their play at the height of the summer season when the most visitors would be in the county to see them.

Elizabeth had long-since given up questioning her husband's idiosyncratic ways. Although she never knew, and never had known, what method he would devise next in which to expend whatever energy it was that drove him, as everyone else seemed happy to accept him just as he was, she no longer found the need to apologise for what she herself sometimes considered as his antics, so far was his behaviour from the decorous manner in which she herself had been raised.

With Joseph seemingly to have been cast in the same mould as his father, she now had the two to contend with. Moreover, ever since Joseph had been of an age to be treated by his father as an equal, the two of them together had been enough -- so Elizabeth often told them -- to drive her to distraction in that, given that her character was such that she was the type of person so easy to tease, this is what they found great amusement in doing.

Not that they would have ever dreamt of being unkind to her, or of dispiriting her in any way. Their teasing was purely of a gentle nature, just enough for her to scold them by saying, "Oh! What am I to do with the two of you? You're as bad as each other! And you! Theo! You're worse than the children!" And then they would always make her laugh.

Now that all was set to proceed with the production, the actors and the venues secured, the dates set, and the costumes designed, there was nothing left to do until the actors were all in place so that rehearsals could begin. With nothing to do but wait, Theo and Joseph decided to perform a small, improvised drama on their own, and this would involve Elizabeth.

Elizabeth was alone in her own private sitting room at the

time. The younger children were having their afternoon naps, the older boys were at school, and Ann, Eleanor and Isabella had finished their lessons for the day, so she was using this quiet time to learn to knit. It was her first attempt, so the resulting article was to be a simple, long scarf for Theo. She had completed half a dozen rows, but had just dropped a stitch, which she was in the act of recovering when there was a knock on the door and her husband and son entered, looking extremely downcast.

Elizabeth put down her knitting, losing her stitch in the process, but, concerned about the ill-fortune that appeared to have stricken the two of them, she watched as, dejected and in silence, they trailed across the room, and slumped themselves down in the two remaining chairs, Theo shaking his head.

"What is it? Is everyone safe? Nobody has been hurt have they? Theo! Joseph!" she cried, when they still said nothing. She was already getting to her feet, her knitting falling to the floor as a result, when Theo finally spoke.

"It's a disaster," he moaned, shaking his head. "A complete disaster."

Joseph nodded in sympathy.

"What's a disaster? Please! Tell me!" Elizabeth sat down again, her knitting lying unnoticed at her feet.

"The play," said Joseph, seeming to hesitate.

"Yes," said Theo. "Dorcas... The woman who was to play Dorcas has fallen ill, and is unable to take the part... and it's impossible to do it without her... such an important role," he lamented.

"And there's no time now to get a replacement... such a waste... venues all booked and paid for..." Joseph added to the misery of the situation.

"There's nothing to be done except cancel the whole project," Theo added.

Elizabeth, thankful no one in the family was sick or had

died, was relieved, although sorry for them to have had their plans thus spoiled. "That's certainly a great shame, I agree. You've worked so hard too." She bent down to retrieve her knitting, only to find all the stitches had come off the needles. "Oh dear! Now look what's happened!"

There was another silence, accompanied by much head shaking. At last Theo perked up. "I know!" He looked at Elizabeth, his expression having changed from one of utter disappointment to one of great enthusiasm. "Bess! Of course!"

"What?"

"*You* must play the part of Dorcas!" He slapped his hand on his knee and looked across at Joseph, who was so near to laughing that, head down, he pretended to be busy plucking from his breeches some imaginary specks of fluff.

"Yes! Why of course!" his father continued. "Why didn't we think of it sooner, Joseph? There's no other way! *You* must play Dorcas, Bess! Yes, of course you must!"

Joseph looked up, his face reflecting his father's enthusiasm. "Why yes, Mother, you'd be *perfect* for the part... Father, I heartily agree with you. An excellent idea! Perfect! We can perform our play after all! It would have been terrible to have had to cancel it after all the work we've put into it! Mother! Thank you! Thank you! You're exactly the right age for the part too, and...!"

"Yes!" Theo enthused. "And you would get to box me on the ears, and say terrible things to me! And..."

Elizabeth, having listened in horror to what her husband and son were suggesting, at last managed to get a word in. "Theo! Joseph! How could you? Don't be so ridiculous! I? Act in one of your plays? Impossible!"

Theo held up his hand. "No! Wait Bess! I know when you hear more about the part, you can't possibly refuse." He took the script of the play from his pocket. "Here! Now just listen! Here's an example of what you'd say to me: '*Touch me if you dare, you insolent, impudent, dirty, lazy, rascally... '"*

"But..."

"No! No! Wait a minute, I insist." Theo found another line for his wife to say in her role as Dorcas. Joseph meanwhile had his head bent down once more, his shoulders shaking with silent laughter.

"Ah! Here! Now let me see. Yes. I get to beat you, then you call me a *'poor beggarly insolent fellow'*." Theo's eyes shone with enthusiasm. "I know you'd thoroughly enjoy it, were you just to attempt it... And to have my own wife playing the..."

Elizabeth stood up, indignant. "Have you lost your senses, Theo? I must tell you this minute... Sorry as I am that you'll have to abandon your enterprise, I'll never, ever stand on a stage and call you anything at all! Such indignity! You should know I'd never... I've never approved..." She could find no more words with which to describe her distaste.

Theo looked at her in shocked disbelief. "My dearest Bess! But why not? Surely you wouldn't stand by and force us to cancel everything! And I know you'd be perfect for the part!" Theo's look was one of extreme disappointment at his wife's unreasonable attitude.

"Mother! I can't believe you'd do such a thing to us! It's so little to ask of you! You surely can't mean what you say... I simply can't believe that my own mother..." Joseph shook his head.

"But you know I can't act! I've never acted! Even if I were to agree to it -- which I assure you I most certainly won't -- I'd ruin your play, and you'd wish you'd never asked me." She looked at her two loved ones, whose countenances were so forlorn at her refusal, she was next to tears at being forced to deny them. She shook her head. "I just can't," she said, and looked down at Theo's ruined scarf, all six rows of it. "I just can't."

When complete silence greeted her words, she looked up, tears beginning to well up. It saddened her to disappoint them so, but... What greeted her were two wide grins.

"What?" she began. "What! You two! What are you up to? What's all this?" Theo and Joseph continued to grin. "Oh! Oh! You...You...You've been teasing me again... I've a good mind to..."

She stood up, not having the least idea what she had a good mind to do. With her two tall, strong and handsome men standing before her laughing, what *could* she do other than laugh as well, and while she continued to give them both a sound scolding for their antics, they put their arms around her, enveloping her in big hugs, kissing her, and laughing good naturedly at her some more.

The day finally came in late July, when Theo, Joseph and their troupe of actors set off for their first destination, which was to be Tenby. The evening before, Theo had walked over to Dunstable Hall to see Hercules. Hercules, now twenty-six years old, had been out at pasture at the Edwardes's estate for about eighteen months. Theo remembered perfectly the day he had taken the horse out there to spend the rest of his life frolicking in the meadows with the other horses; it was the day on which he had read the announcement proclaiming the Union Jack as the flag of Great Britain.

As he walked, he thought about something else he had read only this day, this being that his old friend, Thomas Foley, had just married the twenty-one-year-old daughter of the Dowager Duchess of Leinster. This certainly brought back memories, as he remembered so well being invited by the Duchess and her husband to a Christmas ball at the Rotunda, in Dublin, in 1777, and dancing with another of her daughters, the Lady Emily Mary Fitzgerald, who was his own age, being also born in 1752. He looked around him at the rolling

Pembrokeshire countryside; that life all seemed such a long time ago now.

Theo usually walked out to the Dunstable estate every few days to see his old friend, and could be seen from the house, talking to him for as much as an hour sometimes, every now and then giving Hercules a carrot to munch on. On this night Theo told him he would be away for a week, so he spent some extra time with him, and fed him some extra carrots. On leaving, he patted him on his neck. "I'll see you in a week," he told the horse, and Hercules snickered, and nuzzled his neck.

The trip to Tenby was uneventful, and the troupe arrived there on Saturday evening in readiness for giving the first performance on the Monday evening.

The theatre in which they were to perform was quite small, but adequate, and when Monday evening arrived, they were delighted to perform to a full house. The Wednesday night performance produced equal results, and word of their success meant that, after the Friday night's performance Theo and his cast of players found themselves being introduced to none other than Lord Horatio Nelson and his paramour, Lady Emma Hamilton, who had graced them with their presence -- Lady Hamilton's husband, Sir William, bringing up the rear, as usual.

The illustrious couple, it appeared, had been to Ridgeway to dine with Nelson's -- and indeed Theo's -- friend Thomas Foley and his elder brother, John Herbert Foley, and being on their way back to one of Sir William's seats at Colby after a visit to Pembroke Dock, had decided to visit Tenby en route.

After their introductions, and Theo and Joseph had returned to their room at the inn where they were staying, they felt free to offer their impressions of the lovers. "I'd never have believed Lady Hamilton to be so incredibly, yes, extraordinarily, fat!" exclaimed a disillusioned Joseph, who had heard so much about the lady's legendary beauty. "Her face is quite ugly too! And she's only one-and-forty years old!"

His father agreed. "To think she's five years younger than you mother as well, and has had only *two* children! I can't imagine your dear mother ever looking like that, and she's had eleven children…What about Lord Nelson too? He's six years younger than I am, yet looks like an old man -- all skin and bone. And did you notice he kept coughing all the time? He must be a sick man, Joseph."

The following morning they all made their way back to Haverfordwest, and as they arrived home while the sun was still well above the horizon, Theo decided a walk out to Dunstable Hall to see Hercules would be just what he needed after a week of so much excitement and success, so after dinner he set off.

It was a warm summer evening, with a haze that promised another day of sunshine for the morrow. In another three days the troupe would be leaving again, this time to perform in Carmarthen, so he was looking forward to the respite. His mind at ease, he arrived at the Hall, with the intention of first paying his respects to his cousins, Mr. Edwards and Mrs. Edwardes, now in their early seventies.

The footman greeted him at the door, and Theo was led as usual into the drawing room. Greetings over, Mr. Edwardes invited Theo to follow him to the library, where he offered him a chair. He went to the tantalus, and poured them both some Irish whiskey. Theo accepted his and raised his glass in salute.

"Theo. I'm so sorry, but I have some bad news for you."

"Oh!" Theo put down his glass.

"The morning after you left for Tenby, one of the stable boys went out to the meadow to check on the horses, and…" He looked at Theo's horror-stricken face. "Yes, I'm so sorry, Theo, but he found Hercules had died in the night. I'm sorry too that we had of course to bury him. Nothing could wait until your return."

Theo had risen unceremoniously. "Please excuse me." he said, and fled from the room. He raced down to the meadow and leaned on the gate. The other horses were grazing peacefully, but, as he already knew, there was no Hercules to come and greet him. He had known the horse was getting old, but had hoped to be able to come to talk to him for several years yet. But it was not to be, and he walked home, fighting the tears that kept welling up.

As he walked he thought about life and how it seemed to move on in definite and finite phases. When he had left the home of his godparents at the age of twenty-one, it had been the end of a phase. When he had married, another, and when James had died, that too had been the end of a phase. Now Hercules was gone as well. In what way would the next phase end itself, he wondered.

CHAPTER 37

The winter of 1803 brought considerable snow to Haverfordwest, much to the delight of the younger children, but adding to the hardship of those who found traversing the steep and uneven surfaces of the town's streets difficult at the best of times. To add to the inconvenience, some of the town's sedan-chair carriers had sustained accidents in which both they and the occupants of their chairs had been involved in upsets of such a serious nature, the remaining carriers had balked at carrying out their duties for fear of meeting with the same misfortune.

For the Potter family, who lived at the top of the town, and had no need to negotiate either High Street or Market Street at this time, the inconvenience of the weather was not so great, although the ice formed overnight from the day's melted snow could be a hazard for anyone.

Elizabeth could not be persuaded to leave the house, and blamed the inclement weather for her unusual tiredness in recent weeks, but as St. Mary's Church was within easy reach, she did agree to join the family for the annual Christmas Eve service there.

A fine-looking family at any time, it was now a pleasure to see them all dressed in their best clothes, making their way to church to take part in the celebrations -- Theo, Elizabeth and their children, from three-and-twenty-year-old John to five-year old Thomas.

"I wish they'd do something about replacing our church steeple," Theo remarked as they approached.

"Yes, my dear, so you keep saying."

Theo knew he complained about it constantly, but continued anyway. "And why not? Every time I walk up High Street now, I can't help but be reminded of it." He pointed to the empty sky, formerly pierced by St. Mary's "not-so-crowning glory," as he liked to call it. "How can *anyone* help but be reminded of it? Anyway, I miss it, and I don't care if it *was* crooked."

He doffed his hat to a passing couple. "Merry Christmas, Mr. James, Mrs. James. Another fine day."

"Indeed it is, Mr. Potter, Mrs. Potter; and a Merry Christmas to you too." And the couple went on their way.

"They're on their way to the non-conformist chapel. So many people are converting, you know, Theo," said Elizabeth.

Theo nodded, his mind still on the missing steeple. "The Council shouldn't have bowed to Lady Kensington's fussing. What on earth made her suddenly decide the steeple was going to fall on her house, I can't imagine... If it had been going to topple, it would have done so a long time ago."

"You don't even know for sure it *was* Lady Kensington who insisted on it being pulled down, my dear."

"Maybe, but that still doesn't alter the fact that now the whole church looks out of proportion -- makes the whole of High Street look out of proportion too, if you ask me."

"My dear Theo. All I can suggest is that, whenever you go up High Street in future, you keep your head down, and not look at it... at least when you're with me. It makes you so terribly grumpy." Elizabeth patted his arm, and looked up at him.

Theo laughed, and squeezed his wife's hand. "For you, my dearest Elizabeth, I'll do anything. In future, therefore, I shall make a point of scurrying up High Street, head down, looking to neither right nor left, like old Mrs. Parsons." He bent down, and began scuttling up the street, Elizabeth being forced to trot alongside him. "There! How's that?" He peered up at her from beneath the brim of his hat, grinning.

"Oh Theo... Stop it! Everybody's looking at us!"

"My dear! Is there no pleasing you?" And muffled laughter came from Joseph, bringing up the rear.

The discussion over the loss of the steeple brought to a close on their arrival at the church, the family joined the rest of the worshippers already filling it in happy expectation of enjoying their favourite carols.

During the service, Theo's attention was continually drawn to his wife who, instead of sitting quietly in the pew, her hands folded in her lap, seemed to be feeling the need to rub one gloved hand with the other, as though she had an irritation that simply could not be left unattended. He looked at her, and realizing she was drawing attention to herself, Elizabeth made an effort to keep her hands still, although at times she just could not help scratching them, so great was the itching that had developed, but it was not until they were on the way home that Theo mentioned it.

"My dear Bess, if I'd not known better, I could have well imagined you to be suffering from the attentions of a flea, you were scratching so."

"I'm sorry, but I don't know what it is, but lately my hands have been itching so badly, I can't help but constantly scratch them." And when they arrived home, and she removed her gloves, Theo was horrified to see that, in places, his wife had even drawn blood.

"Maybe I ate something that didn't agree," Elizabeth

explained. "My stomach has been out of sorts lately as well, and I've been more tired than usual."

"I'd noticed you seemed not to be eating as well as you usually do... you're usually such a hearty eater... but as we all go through short periods of being out of sorts, and as you said nothing to alarm me, I assumed it would soon pass." He looked at her hands again. "But this is different. I think we must ask the physician to take a look at you... Maybe he can suggest some liver pills to set you to rights."

Elizabeth agreed, and young Mr. Nash was sent for, his father having been retired for several years now. It was young Mr. Nash's opinion, on examining the patient, that yes indeed, she appeared to be suffering from some ailment involving her liver, and gave her some pills to take, and some balm to apply to her hands.

New Year came, and over the following weeks it became apparent that not only were the pills and the balm proving to have no effect, but Elizabeth's condition was deteriorating. Now, in addition to the itching on her hands, her whole body was overcome with intense irritation, her skin had turned from its usual healthy rosy tones to a sickly greyish-yellow, and she was covered from head to foot with unsightly, and in some cases septic scabs from where she had scratched her poor body raw. Food caused intense pain in her stomach, and what she could not digest, she threw up, so that by the end of April she had become so thin, tired and listless, it became obvious to all that Elizabeth was not going to recover as the cancer -- a parasite intent only on satisfying its own insatiable appetite -- drew unto itself all her strength, nourishment, blood and flesh until nothing remained; and on the night of May 15 in the year 1804, on her daughter Elizabeth's twenty-third birthday, and herself just seven-and-forty years old, Elizabeth died, notice of her death appearing in *The Cambrian* newspaper. On the 18th, she was buried. Theo was fifty one.

PART III

CHAPTER 38

Theo's response to the death of his beloved wife of five-and-twenty years was of such shock that some wondered if he too would succumb. It was not that he grieved in hidden silence, locked away in his library, nor -- except for once -- did he venture out into the countryside, idling away his time gazing sadly at the ever-changing scenery and mourning his loss, or even over-indulging in good Welsh ale as some did under similar circumstances.

Instead, he tried to behave in a similar manner to that in which he had behaved so many years ago, when he had faced his sorrows by immersing himself in acting at Dublin's Royal Theatre, and by which he had been able to lock his despair in his little Pandora's Box.

Now faced with an even greater tragedy, he engaged himself with an almost ferocious intensity into whatever he considered needed to be done for his life to continue. This time, however, there was no acting career in which to immerse himself, to drain off his anguish, or in which to hide it, nor was there anything he had done in the last twenty-five years that had successfully replaced it, and would now be of help to him.

Nothing.

His old naval friend, Thomas Foley, who had seen him charging about the streets, bent on some seemingly important mission, had described him as a magnificent square-rigger in full sail before the wind, and moving so fast he threatened to sink himself beneath his own bow wave; and in the months following his loss, despite all his endeavours, Theo found himself achieving nothing, succeeding only in exacerbating his problems.

Mr. Sutton having retired, the business was almost in disarray, but prevented from collapsing by Joseph to whom Theo finally abrogated all responsibilities. He insisted on continuing to perform in their plays, but the comedies suffered in the process, and by the following year he could no longer go on.

His children too suffered, especially the younger ones, who had lost not only their doting mother, but their governess and disciplinarian as well. As father, Theo had been more of an indulgent figurehead, and without Elizabeth to curb their behaviour, and to continue with their education, they became unruly to the extent that both Joseph and his sister Elizabeth felt it necessary to take control. Little Thomas, who had celebrated his sixth birthday just two days before his mother died, and who, as the youngest, had received more of Elizabeth's loving attentions than she had ever had time to offer to his older siblings, was the most adversely affected, and was reaching a point where he was almost impossible to handle.

While all these outward manifestations of Theo's loss were there for all to see, inwardly Theo knew his life was out of control, but try as he would, he could not bring back any order to it. There were too many problems to be faced, and every time he tried to focus on the one, attempts to resolve it merely raised another hindrance somewhere else. He could not concentrate, and he had no-one with whom he felt comfortable discussing his dilemma. The vicar had called on him several times, but although Theo listened to him politely, the intercourse was one-sided as Theo felt a barrier preventing him from pouring out his sorrows to him. It was not that Theo was not a religious man, but he did not believe in blind faith either.

Many years ago he had subscribed to *A Treasury of Theological Knowledge: wherein Christianity, And the Divine Authority of the Holy Scriptures are proved: And the most plausible Objections considered,* by Mr. Morgan Williams, and it was now that the *plausible objections* came to mind whenever the Reverend called upon him to trust in the Lord.

He found also that many people were so at a loss as to what to say to him about his bereavement, they avoided him altogether, while others were unable to carry on a normal conversation with him, so nervous were they about being discreet about his wife's death that, other than briefly offering their condolences, they would chatter in artificially cheerful tones about anything *but* his bereavement.

It was Elizabeth to whom he needed to talk. It was Elizabeth to whom he had, for the last quarter century, brought all his problems, and with whom he could think aloud and know that, unlike anyone else he might try to talk to -- even the vicar -- Elizabeth was actually listening, and not merely thinking about what she herself wanted to say the minute he stopped talking. But Elizabeth was gone, and all the problems churning around in his mind needing to be expressed, resolved and thus put to rest, left no room for rational thought, and like a windmill in a gale, they continued to whirl, giving him no peace.

One day, he went to the hostelry and rented a horse. Alone he rode out one last time to the headland overlooking Druid's Town Beach, where he reined in the horse, and looked out across the Irish sea towards the land of his birth, where he had spent the first twenty-six years of his life. He sat there, thinking about all the people who had impinged upon, and affected that life: people of wit and understanding, mirth and high intellect, people who had helped shape his life and had led and encouraged him to become the person he was. Tears wet his cheeks as the thought that all those who had possessed that great wisdom, enthusiasm for life, accumulated knowledge and wit were all gone. They had had opinions, concerns, loves, hates and passions, but as with all life it was dust to dust, and after a while, in which he sobbed at the memories, he became once more an actor as, to the wild west wind he recited from Macbeth what the wise Shakespeare had understood, and what few ever realize until they face their own mortality:

> *"Tomorrow and tomorrow and tomorrow,*
> *Creeps in this petty pace from day to today*
> *To the last syllable of recorded time;*
> *And all our deaths have lighted fools*
> *The way to dusty death. Out! Out, brief candle!*
> *Life's but a walking shadow, a poor player*
> *That struts and frets his hour upon the stage,*
> *And then is heard no more.*
> *It is a tale, told by an idiot, full of sound and fury,*
> *Signifying nothing!"*

Other than James, the people Theo was thinking of, were people his beloved Elizabeth would have never heard of, let alone know about. Only James had shared his early life, and Theo, looking out over Skomer, faced his own mortality. He turned the horse around, rode home, and never returned.

CHAPTER 39

Friends of many years' standing watched in dismay as the once happy and well-governed family was breaking apart under the strain, and by the time Elizabeth had been gone for over two years, determined that something needed to be done, and soon.

It was Sir Thomas and Lady Sinclair who came up with a plan; the problem was to get Theo to agree to it. Floundering as he had been without Elizabeth's steadying influence and loving presence, yet a man always used to being otherwise in control of his life and his independence, he still did not see the extent to which he and his children were suffering from his inability to get his life in order, and it took all the persuasion of his loving friends as well as the insistence of his three eldest children to get him to understand what they were trying to tell him.

Theo's presence being more of a hindrance than a help, Sir Thomas, along with John and Joseph, suggested he accept an invitation of the Sinclairs to be their guest in Bath for the upcoming season. At first Theo was adamant his children could not survive without his being there, but as Joseph pointed out, even if John were unable to help out, he himself had just turned twenty-six, the same age his father had been when he had first come to Haverfordwest, and Elizabeth was twenty-seven. They were perfectly capable -- now even more so than their father -- of taking care of the children.

At last they were able to get Theo to agree they were in all likelihood correct, and so a few weeks later he ventured further from home than he had been since he and Elizabeth had made their trip to Ireland over a quarter of a century before.

There could not have been a better choice of chaperones for the still handsome though melancholic fifty-three-year-old who spent the next five months with them at their stately townhouse in Bath. Solicitous, but not overly so, their judgment and timing in calculating what would be acceptable to Theo in his current state of mind were perfect. Suggestions and invitations could be accepted or declined; his presence at their soirées was welcomed with subdued calmness, and if he chose not to be present, that too was accepted with equal equanimity.

They were likewise careful in their choice of guests to any dinner or soirée to which Theo had agreed to come, and at one dinner they hosted, they sat him next to a young, recently bereaved widow of just thirty-five years old. Her name was Mrs. Susanna Harman, and their hosts watched as the two engaged in conversation, although by the end of the evening were disappointed that no apparent plans had been made for them to meet again.

At first, Theo could not even be persuaded to attend any performances at Bath's splendid new Theatre Royal, which had opened for its first season just the previous year, and was now well into its second, successful season. He finally agreed to go, however, when he was told the performance for which the Sinclairs had obtained tickets was to be *The Rivals*, written by his fellow countryman, Richard Brinsley Sheridan, whose father, Thomas Sheridan, had once headed Theo's old company, The Smock Alley Theatre in Dublin, and had been his own mentor. Nor did he demur when told Mrs. Harman, whom he had met the previous month, would be joining the party.

This time the Sinclairs did not seat the couple together in their box, deciding instead to let matters take their course. They were more than pleased, therefore, when Theo sought out the young widow during the interval, and even more so when they discovered he had asked her if she would like to accompany him on an excursion into the Somerset countryside the following day. She had answered that she would be delighted.

That night Theo did not sleep. "What was I thinking?" he asked himself. "What fool would ask a lady out for an excursion into the countryside in the middle of winter, when there is even snow on the ground?" When he had made the invitation his mind was so addled, he had imagined them out in an open curricle, enjoying the scenery. Now it seemed he would have to hire an enclosed carriage, and the idea of that did not please him at all; it would be much too intimate, and what scenery were they going to enjoy anyway in an enclosed carriage? He would have to hire a driver, as there would not be much point in him being outside, driving, while the lady he was supposed to be accompanying, was sitting on her own on the inside. He groaned at the thought of what he was committed to doing. As if he did not have enough clutter in his brain without adding this embarrassment to it! At least she had not looked askance at him at his suggestion that they take a turn around the countryside in the middle of winter; she had, he remembered, seemed to be truly agreeable to the idea.

By the time he arose in the morning he was pleased with himself to discover that, for the first time since Elizabeth's death he had made a decision, and small though it was, he felt better for it. The decision was that, regardless of the weather -- which he noticed was a dry, clear and crisp day with plenty of sunshine and a bright blue sky -- he would still hire a curricle and pair, and before that, he would go out and buy the best rug that money could buy, and a sable bonnet and muff for his passenger to keep her warm. It was the least he could do.

His hosts smiled at each other when they perceived the marked change in their guest at breakfast. He did not say much, but they could tell by his expression that something had occurred to raise his spirits; his eyes, so long dull and lifeless, showed the hint of a sparkle, and there was even an upward turn to his lips. Sir Thomas and Lady Sinclair wisely said nothing, and when Theo departed, merely expressed their hope he would have an enjoyable outing.

Mrs. Harman was ready and waiting when Theo arrived outside her fashionable apartments. As she emerged, two impressions came to him: the first was that she looked perfectly at ease with the idea of going out in an open carriage on such a frosty day, and the second was that she had been sensible enough to have dressed appropriately -- and pretty she looked too!

It was so long since Theo had paid any attention to another woman, he felt almost awkward as he helped her up into the curricle, then sat down beside her. He was embarrassed too about the large and be-ribboned bandbox that occupied the space between them, and which contained things he now realized she did not need.

Mrs. Harman smiled at him, and unlike him, was obviously at her ease. She pointed to the bandbox, and smiled. "What have we here?"

The footman had released his hold on the horses, and Theo began to guide them through the crowded thoroughfares of Bath. "Ah, well," he said, looking straight ahead so as to make sure they did not run into anything, or anyone. "It occurred to me that there wouldn't be much point in going out into the country in a closed carriage, and I didn't want you to be frozen in an open one, so I bought you a couple of things to keep you warm." He turned his head briefly to look at her. Her blonde, curly hair was peeping out from under a warm bonnet. "However, I see you're already well equipped," he commented.

"Not at all! I think it was so very thoughtful of you, Mr. Potter… May I take a look?"

"Why yes! Of course!" Theo kept on driving as Mrs. Harman opened the bandbox. She carefully laid the lid down on the seat, and set the box on top of it to stop it from being blown away, then very gently removed the layers of protective tissue.

"Oh my! Oh my!" Mrs. Harman's delight was genuine. "Oh Mr. Potter! A sable bonnet and muff!" She turned to him, eyes shining and holding the soft fur to her cheeks which, Theo noticed, were rosy from the cold air.

"Well…" She laid the bonnet and the muff gently on her lap, put back her shoulders, raised her head and said in a determined voice, "I see nothing wrong with this. I am, after all, an old widowed woman, and I'm going to give you a hug!" And she did.

And for the first time since Elizabeth's death Theo felt another sensation, and it surged through his body. He wanted to close his eyes, and let it continue to flow, but this was not the time, and certainly not the place, so he just turned to her and smiled -- it was another first. Mrs. Harman then put on her new bonnet and muff, and put her others in the bandbox. She did, Theo decided, look most attractive.

From that day on their relationship grew, and for Theo it was made easy because there was no way in which he could compare Susanna with his beloved Elizabeth; they were entirely different in every way, and this of itself was an excellent recommendation, because where there could be no comparisons made, there were no expectations that were not forthcoming.

Susanna, Theo discovered, was of a lively and quite idiosyncratic disposition, somewhat similar to his own. She was also spontaneous, often taking him by surprise. She was happy to go here, there and everywhere, to try anything and everything, and sometimes he even feared for her safety, when she thought nothing of climbing a steep, rocky hill, simply to find out what could be seen from its top. She was also a good horsewoman, and delighted in racing him over open fields and meadows.

They even went to the theatre and danced at the Assembly Rooms, and the time came when the Sinclairs had to admit they now saw little of their guest, but from what little they did see, he appeared to be a changed man, and the old Theo was gradually emerging, like a handsome moth long imprisoned in its cocoon.

Theo discovered in Susanna someone to whom he could talk at last, and this ability was one shared equally by Susanna, who found in Theo a willing and sympathetic audience for her own sad loss; and after the initial explosion of their long pent-up emotions and sorrows, like two huge breakers colliding, the result was a calm that neither had experienced for a long time.

By the time the season had ended, Theo had asked Susanna to marry him, but she suggested instead that she go home to Haverfordwest with him; she knew only one aspect of his life, and that was the one she had experienced in Bath, and although she loved him well enough now to be happy at the thought of spending the rest of her life with him, she was well aware that back home there were nine children, and that was something she wanted to experience before committing herself.

Theo could not deny her reasoning, and so it was agreed she should return with him to Haverfordwest in the guise of governess, where she would take up residence in the Potter household. This she did, and they arrived back in

Haverfordwest in the March of 1807. By the end of May, Susanna was able to give Theo the happy news that she could think of nothing more she would like than to marry him, and on July 12th, 1807, just over three years after the death of Elizabeth, and witnessed by his son Joseph, John Theophilus Potter and Susanna Harman were married in St. Mary's church, Haverfordwest, and signed their names in the church register.

EPILOGUE

It was no easy matter for the young widow to be accepted into a family where she was just a few years older than the eldest child, and where a most beloved mother was still so desperately missed by the youngest children. For them -- and in particular young Thomas, who was only eight -- that their father had accepted their governess as a replacement for their dear mother, was a situation they found intolerable. It was in this regard, therefore, that Susannah was grateful for the support of Joseph and Elizabeth, who were old enough to recognize the wisdom of her being there, and willingly gave her their assistance when the younger children showed signs of getting out of control. They also did their best to explain to them that it was only right and fair that their father's enjoyment of life did not end with their mother's death, and as they themselves could see, he had found in the young widow someone so attuned to his character, that he had become his old self again, and they were happy for him.

Susanna enlivened Theo's life in another way too, for not long after their marriage she prevailed upon him to reintroduce into it an aspect denied him for so many years. Like Theo she craved the cultural stimulation and excitement of city life, and soon recognizing that Haverfordwest was a backwater in this respect, suggested they buy a townhouse in London.

At first Theo was hesitant. He had spent thirty years in Haverfordwest, and had many friends there. He had a thriving business there too, and was well respected. It was also where his beloved Elizabeth was buried, and he could not abandon her any more than he could abandon his children if they did not want to leave their home town.

"I'm not suggesting we *leave* Haverfordwest and *move* to London, never to return," Susanna explained to him. "What I'm suggesting, my dearest Theo, is that we do as so many of your gentry friends here do. We could go to London for the season, and return here to Pembrokeshire for the summer, just as they do. Besides," she added, "we both know that many of your old theatrical friends from Dublin are still in London. Take John O'Keeffe, for example. He spends all his time there now, and from what you tell me, you were great friends; Richard Sheridan too." She reached up and kissed him. "So it's not as though you don't *know* anyone there," she reminded him. "You would have a ready-made coterie of friends already waiting for you... and any of the children who want to spend time with us in London," she added, aware of what might be holding him back, "will be most welcome of course, but at the same time, if they don't want to leave their friends, they could stay here in Haverfordwest with their older brothers and sisters... Joseph and Elizabeth have already told me they will

358

be only too happy to look after them," she encouraged him.

It had been years now since Theo had even considered the possibility of going to London. A long while back he had made a point of stopping himself even thinking about it, because the longing had caused too much anguish for him. Not thinking about it had also meant making a conscious effort to not think either about all his old writer and actor friends who were always travelling back and forth from Ireland to London. As a result of barring them from his thoughts, he had led himself to consider them, like Elizabeth, gone forever.

Now though, he was being asked to consider the possibility, nay being requested even, to bring them all back into his life again, and as he permitted the idea to take hold in his mind once more, the more enthusiastic he became. Was it truly possible? After all these years? He was still only fifty-five years old, so there was still the chance, God willing, he could spend as many years in their company again as he had now spent without them.

It did not take long for him to make up his mind. "Yes! Yes! Yes, my dear Susanna!" He had picked her up and swung her around. "Yes! Yes! Yes! We'll do it! Oh yes, indeed!"

And like Elizabeth before her, so Susanna was made aware of the sparkle in his eyes, noticing too that he suddenly seemed ten years younger.

Thus it was, therefore, that soon after their first son, Theophilus John Potter, was born in Haverfordwest in 1808, they secured a house for themselves at 12, Warwick Place, in the little village of Hackney, already a centre of culture, having long had an association with the theatre, Shakespeare and actors, and home to many writers, artists and political activists. It was within easy reach of London too, with its own theatres and concert halls -- all that he could ever want, and had so-long yearned for. And so Theo began yet another phase of his life.

And God *was* willing, for He gave him another thirty-two years in which to enjoy this new life, his new wife, a new business, and six more children.

THE END